RED SKY,

BLUE MOON

Bruce Golden

Cover art by David Perez

ISBN-13: **978-1484133224**
ISBN-10: **1484133226**

Shaman Press

http://goldentales.tripod.com/

<u>Also by Bruce Golden</u>

Mortals All
Better Than Chocolate
Evergreen
Dancing with the Velvet Lizard

For Troy

RED SKY,

BLUE MOON

PROLOGUE

D*uring the Age of Exploration, at a time when our forbearers were predominantly corporeal in nature, they launched a great ship to survey the galaxy. No other sentient species were discovered during this trek, which led them to dead worlds, worlds on the verge of life, and worlds where life had advanced by various stages. Some of the primordial oceans on these newly developing planetoids were seeded with the protoplasmic material found on other worlds. The reasons for, and exact nature of, these experiments have been lost, due to the impermanent and fragmentary records of the time.*

However, the experiment was not forgotten, and eons later, during the Age of Science, the great ship returned to see what the experiment had wrought. What it discovered was one particular world teeming with life, and one specific genus of creatures living in pockets of crude civilizations. These attracted the attention of the surveyors, and it was decided, by the ship's command, to not only observe, but to conduct a variety of investigative studies. The basis for that decision was not preserved in any known records. We have no knowledge whether the morality of such invasive research was ever debated or even questioned. Records do indicate the field tests that were conducted resulted in the contamination of many locales. Though the records, even from that time, are incomplete, what is known of each socio/industrial experiment can be accessed through files referenced by native designations including, but not limited to, Akhet Aten, Yax Mutal, Puh, Nasca, Mn Nefer, Puma Punku, Aymaraes, and Chi Cheen Litsha.

There is no question these studies had, at the very least, a minimal effect on localized divisions of the planet's native populations. However, it was the undertaking of the great speciation experiment which has had repercussions not only on the alien world, but on our own, continuing even now, into the Age of Reason.

It began when a single sampling of native animal life and their immediate environs were transplanted to a similar clime in a region of the homeworld (which had been deemed an appropriate planetary body to accommodate the creatures). It is recorded that this initial sampling was undertaken immediately before the dominate species, a form of biped, would have been destroyed by seismic activity. While the act may have seemed humanitarian, it was not. Nor were those that followed.

Sometime later (more than a thousand of the subject planet's revolutions around its star), the ship returned and culled another, though dissimilar culture of bipeds from the

1

planet and transported them to the homeworld. Then again, some 700 revolutions later, shortly before the beginning of the Great Debates, a third cluster of the subject species, along with a sampling of other nearby less intelligent species, was obtained.

How or if the disappearance of such large numbers of beings was ever explained by the native populations, or the subsequent effect on the planet's development is not recorded—concern for such reactions obviously of little importance to the surveyors.

The Great Debates, however, led to a new philosophy that marked an end to the Age of Science and the beginning of society's more introspective phase.

Though study of the subject species was discontinued at that time, it was soon discovered that the creatures' emotional emanations could be absorbed using specific meditative trances. The effects of those emanations are as varied as the emotions themselves, and continue to be a subject of concern and debate.

—A Societal History as Compiled by Osst
"Speciation"

1

When you were born you cried and the world rejoiced.
Live your life in such a manner that when you die,
the world cries and you rejoice.
—The Wisdom of Fire In His Eyes

He woke with a start, sweat on his brow, damp bedraggled hair, his heart a stampede. He realized at once he'd been dreaming—that same dream. Not a fanciful vision, but a dark one full of chaos, death, and *maza* beasts that spewed thunder and fire. He tried to fight the monsters, as he had each time the grim dream swallowed him, but he couldn't. He was powerless, as he'd been when the *wasichu* had taken him prisoner. But this time, there was something new, something different in the dream. A white wolf had stood over him snarling, as if it were about to rip him to pieces and devour him. Instead, it leaped over him and fell upon his enemies.

The dream had no conclusion. He woke without seeing the fate of the white wolf. He opened his eyes only to the degradation of his imprisonment, and the memories of that treacherous day.

Others in his hunting party had been captured as well, and some had been killed, including his sister's husband. He'd not seen his fellow captives in many days. Their unknown fate only added to his shame.

He was shamed because the *wasichu* had caught his party unaware, and because he was the one who had initially welcomed the hairy ones as traders. He'd even spoken in front of the Naca Om to convince the council they should be greeted as friends. At the time he thought his words were wise. He spoke of the peculiar ways of the *wasichu* and their unique devices, and what his people might learn from them. Now he felt only foolish. He was a fool who had lost face, and now thought of nothing but vengeance. Yet even as such thoughts gathered like a storm cloud in his mind, he understood vengeance was a fool's game. Acceptance of such wisdom, however, did not come easy in his current circumstance.

Though their ways were indeed strange, he didn't understand why, after a season of peaceful trading, the *wasichu* had suddenly attacked. He only wished he'd died in battle instead of living in shame. He worried about his people, about his wife and his children, but he couldn't help them. He couldn't help himself. He didn't even know how long he'd been held prisoner.

He and his fellow hunters had been bound with *maza* ropes, taken to the sea where the *wasichu's* enormous *wahte* was harbored, and thrown into a dark hole for many days. How many, he couldn't be certain, for he couldn't see the sun. At least as many days as the fingers on his hands. By the movements of his prison he knew they'd passed that time traveling across the sea. When they arrived in the land of the *wasichu* he'd been separated from the other captives, and placed in the stone cave where he now sat. At least here was a hole through which he could see the sun, and the sea as well. He'd counted 16 sunrises from his prison, and was certain New Birth Moon must have passed by now. How many moons would he be trapped here in the land of *wasichu*? Would he still be here when the time came for his people to prepare for the *wiwanyag wachipi*? Would he see his daughter dance the sun dance? Would he be there when his son completed the rites of manhood? Would he even still live when they began the joyous celebration, the feasting, and the purification?

Though his opportunities were few, he contemplated escape. He'd already fashioned a knife of sorts from a loose stone, and, despite the *maza* ropes that bound his legs and arms so he could only hobble about, he was certain he could escape if he tried. But where would he go? He knew he was far from his home, but in which direction did it lie? Certainly towards the rising sun, but where exactly? He knew he must learn more before he attempted to escape.

He'd already developed a meager understanding of the *wasichu* language from the time he spent trading with them. Now he listened closely to his guards, and to the shouts he heard from outside his prison. Every day he was learning more. But he hadn't yet learned what he needed to know. How could he return home?

He tried not to dwell on thoughts of home and family, but the memories of his wife and children were all he had to sustain him. Even now he fought with himself to push their images from his mind, feeling disloyal all the while. At times the dank, dark walls of his prison seemed to close in on him, and he became so desperate he prayed to the spirit of Wan Blee to fly down from the sky and carry him home. But prayers of desperation only added to his dishonor.

A distant sound disrupted his inner struggle—a solitary drum that beat slow and steady. He went to the hole in his cage, pulled himself up to it, and pushed his head as far through the barred opening as he could.

4

His nose had been broken when he was taken captive, and had healed like a twisted branch, but it hadn't dulled his sense of smell. As always, the air had a foul stench, tainted by something unnatural. It smelled of sickness, of *wicocuye*, as did everything in this *wasichu* world. Only the sporadic sea breezes gave him respite.

Though he couldn't see the setting sun, the hollow sky had taken on the hue for which he was named. As often was the case, his view of the distant horizon was tarnished by the sight of many *wasichu* sea vessels, like the one that had carried him to this cursed land. He saw them coming and going, and couldn't prevent himself from wondering if more of his people were being abducted — whether or not his own family might be inside one.

The drum he heard was beating much closer to his confined space than the distant vessels. Though his view was obstructed, he could see a ceremony of some kind had commenced far below his prison perch. The gathering of people, the drum beat, the parade of women in like costumes told him this was a rite of sorts. A somber one by the spaced cadence of the drum beats.

The women lifted a pallet upon which was the body of a man, dressed, no doubt, in his *wasichu* finery. It was a funeral, as indeed the doleful drum beat intoned. The women marched slow and steady through the gathering, down a path made of timber that pushed out across the top of the sea. There, floating in the restless waters was a small *wahte*, fitted with a hide the color of snow. At one end, carved like a totem, was the head of fierce beast like a giant snake or lizard.

The women lowered the pallet and the body onto the *wahte*, which had been filled with tinder, and retreated back the way they'd come. Several men released the vessel and, using poles large enough to brace a *thipi*, pushed it out to sea. It started away slowly, almost turning back, then the wind filled its hide.

A lone archer with a torch in his hand walked to the end of the timber path. He set the torch into a place in the wood and drew an arrow. He held it in the fire, pulled back on the bow and aimed. The arrow flew high, traveling in a flaming arc, but it flew true. It landed aboard the *wahte* and its flames spread.

What a barbarous ritual he thought, lowering himself from his perch. The mourners sang no death song, the body was burned instead of letting it lay in peace so its spirit could be carried away by the winds of Tahte. Still, the pomp of the ceremony and the size of the gathering were impressive. The dead one must have been a great warrior.

2

Never regret the cost of doing business.
—Words of Chairman Wulfstan

"**H**e was a great financier...in his time," said Vikar, a glint of the distant flames reflecting off the ornate silver headband that held his long, dark-blond hair in place.

"A fitting funeral for an executive of his caliber, and a fitting death," said the thane next to him. "Certainly better than wasting away with the blight. He's reallocating capital and closing deals in Niflhel now."

Vikar nodded. "No doubt trying to fleece Hel of her due even as we speak."

Decorum demanded the executive stifle the chuckle that rose to his lips, but he smiled and nodded in response, resting a hand on the ostentatious dagger in his belt.

"Fortunate for you, Cousin, he had no sons to pass his corporation on to," said Vikar as the burning sail collapsed in on itself and the boat's momentum slowed. "Bjorco will be in better hands now regardless."

"I thank you for your confidence, Cousin, but I've not been selected jarl yet."

Vikar flicked his hand dismissively. "It will happen." His stoic expression could have been chiseled from marble. "I have sway with the right people. You'll have the votes."

"Your support is greatly appreciated. Once I assume the position, I can promise the tribunal's levy for our departed colleague's liquidation will be minimal."

"Unimportant," replied Vikar. "The cost of doing business."

The parade of priestesses in their white gowns passed by, their heads held high, their long blond tresses unencumbered, a simple silver brooch in the shape of a hammer their only ornamentation. Vikar waited until the women had passed.

"What do you think will come of Bjorco's negotiations to finance Trondtel's green oil?" asked Vikar, though he already knew the answer.

"Why I can tell you with certainty that such negotiations will go nowhere. The idea of producing fuel from green slime is obviously preposterous. Bjorco will not be a part of such a high-risk investment."

"A wise decision, I'm sure," said Vikar. "The idea that somehow algae can replace jor oil *is* rather preposterous. Since Bjorco won't be moving forward with that, I assume you're amenable to the merger we discussed?"

"Most assuredly, Cousin. With such a merger we would virtually control the price of iron. It would be the first corner of such a vital commodity since the Corporate Wars. We would be foolish *not* to agree to such a venture. It's unfortunate my predecessor didn't have the foresight to understand the advantages of allying himself with the Trellestar Corporation."

"Yes," said Vikar, "unfortunate."

A lady who'd been conversing nearby took leave of her group and approached the two men. She was a magnificent looking woman of ample charms, despite having surrendered her youth years ago. Her long blond hair was tied back in traditional Aesir fashion, though her gown was a bit garish and revealing for the occasion. Her imperious green eyes and haughty perfume declared she cared little for the conventions of others.

"Thane Njalsson, I believe you've met my wife, Estrid," said Vikar, taking her proffered hand.

"Certainly," responded the executive, his gaze drawn momentarily to her exposed cleavage. "Mistress Magnusson, your Valkyrie sisters have honored the departed with an admirable funeral befitting his station."

"Yes, yes," she responded indifferently. "Though I think it was unnecessary to adorn the proceedings with the Vanir riffraff." She glanced at the gallows on the periphery of the gathering where the bodies of nine men dangled in the gentle sea breeze.

"You know Wotan must be honored," said Vikar. "Those captured B'serkers make a fine offering."

"I just hope they're taken down before they begin to stink." Estrid turned to the executive and flashed a faux smile. "If you don't mind, I've familial business I must discuss with my husband."

"Certainly, mistress. I'll take my leave then," said the executive with a slight bow. "Jarl Magnusson, we'll talk further at the board meeting."

Vikar nodded, absentmindedly adjusting one of his rings. As the executive departed, he said to his wife, "Are our children in attendance?"

"Rikissa is yonder with her friends," said Estrid, motioning to a cluster of young women. "I sent Furyk on an errand, but I don't know where Gudrik is. He was here a moment ago, but..." She shrugged.

"He should be here," said Vikar. "So should Furyk."

"I've spoken with family Tryguasson," she said, changing the subject to match her whim as she was accustomed to doing—a habit she knew irritated her husband. "The marriage, in concept, has been approved. It is to you now to finalize negotiations."

"It will be done." Vikar responded stoically.

He scanned the gathering, spying Oleg Gripsholm of Trondtel. His rival happened to notice him at the same moment, and they acknowledged each other with perfunctory nods.

Vikar couldn't locate either of his sons in the crowd, so he turned his attention to the funeral craft. It had burned nearly to the waterline, and drifted near the rocky shoals of the jetty. The ceremonial aspects of the services complete, those gathered began departing, or cluster in smaller groups where, no doubt, both business and innuendo had their place.

A younger man with close-set green eyes and straight blond hair that marked him as his mother's son scuttled through the dispersing crowd and was breathing heavily when he approached much too quickly for his father's liking.

"Mind yourself, Furyk," commanded Vikar. "This is a solemn occasion."

Furyk caught his breath and composed himself, though it didn't disguise the scowl he wore. He looked around, to be certain no one but his parents could hear his words.

"Rikissa is pregnant," he blurted.

Vikar's glare was oppressive.

"How do you know this?"

"A blade to the throat of her maidservant extracted the truth." The leer on Furyk's revealed he'd relished the inquisition.

"Then it's true," said Estrid. "I suspected as much. That foolhardy girl. How could she be so careless?"

Vikar looked to where his daughter had been conversing with friends, but she was no longer there. He couldn't find her in the crowd.

"Who's the father?" asked Vikar.

"One of the housecarles—Tordan."

"Yes, I know the one," replied Vikar, stroking his trim beard thoughtfully. "He's been the subject of several disciplinary actions."

"Shall I have him arrested, Father?"

"No. We mustn't," replied Estrid. "Any public reprimand would create a scandal that would ruin our plans for Rikissa's betrothal."

"Your mother's right."

"Then let me eliminate him," said Furyk, his anger all too public. "We can't allow this Vanir scum to despoil my sister and not be punished."

Vikar sighed. Furyk had always tested his patience—hotheaded and rash. Not at all like his older brother Gudrik. But Gudrik had his failings as well.

"Killing this housecarle wouldn't be a very frugal use of resources, would it?"

A snarl grew on Furyk's thin lips, but he stayed silent.

Vikar looked out across the sea, then high above it where a black form was taking shape. An airship was returning from its deep-ocean operations, where it had no doubt spotted dozens of jormun for Trellestar's fishing fleet. He turned back to his son.

"If you're to supplant me someday, Furyk..." At this mother and son exchanged almost imperceptible looks. ". . . you'll have to learn not to let anger make your decisions for you. Especially when it comes to business. Don't worry, I have plans for our lusty warrior. The housecarle will pay for his transgression."

"What about the baby?" wondered Furyk.

Estrid stared into the eyes of her son, making certain he understood her words. "There will be no baby. There *is* no baby. It never happened."

At that moment the chairman of the board and his entourage swept by, halting when Chairman Halfdan Tryguasson spotted Vikar and his kin.

"Jarl Magnusson, Mistress Magnusson, Vikarsson...Wotan will be pleased by today's rite, don't you agree?" The chairman's long hair and full beard had long-since gone white and his eyes were shot with scarlet, but he still projected an air of vitality, despite the rumors—or maybe because of them.

"Aye, Chairman. All the gods must surely be smiling down upon us."

"You know, of course, there will likely be a hearing regarding our colleague's death to determine if familial compensation is in order."

"Of course," replied Vikar.

"But I wouldn't worry," added Halfdan casually. "These things have a way of working themselves out.

"On a more pleasant note, I understand our bloodlines may soon be crossed. I look forward to the negotiations."

"As do I, Cousin."

Halfdan sidled closer to Vikar and said with more than a hint of intrigue, "I'm very curious about those Serkland savages you purchased from us. The sale occurred before I got to examine them. Perhaps you wouldn't mind

9

showing me one when I come to visit."

"Certainly," replied Vikar, "though I'd say the specimens are particularly unimpressive."

"Ghastly creatures, or so I've been told," spoke up Estrid. "They should all be exterminated."

"Possibly, mistress, quite possibly. Well, I'll leave you to yourselves now — Mistress Magnusson, Vikarsson."

They exchanged casual bows and the chairman strolled off with his entourage in tow.

When they were out of earshot, Furyk said, "I've heard talk the chairman has the blight."

Vikar had heard the talk too, and from likely more reliable sources than his son had. But he responded, "Don't believe everything you hear. Rumors are like backroom negotiations—easy to start, but much harder to legitimize."

"You know what they say," added Estrid. "Anyone who gets the blight has to have at least a little Vanir blood in them."

Vikar noticed his son sneered at the thought, and wondered what Furyk would think if he knew the truth of it.

3

One man's tale is but half a tale.

—Book of Runes

Tordan pulled his sword belt around him and fastened the buckle. He looked back at Rikissa. She still lay on the bed, naked but for her silver arm rings and the disarray of her long blond hair. How beautiful she was, he thought, how childlike.

"I'm leaving Trondheim for a couple of days to visit my family," he said, throwing his cloak over his shoulders and tying it.

Rikissa sat up.

"No," she said, and sprang out of her bed, grabbing a robe to cover herself. "Why do you want to go to that awful place?" She hurried to Tordan and threw her arms around him, as if she wouldn't let him go. "Every time you leave me I'm afraid I'll never see you again. Without you...without you I fear I'll become my mother."

Tordan laughed, thinking how unlike mother and daughter were. Gently he pried her slender arms from him and took her face in his hands, lifting it to gaze into her blue-green eyes.

"Worry gives a small thing such a big shadow." He kissed her. "I'll see you upon my return."

Tordan opened the door, looked down the corridor in each direction, and slipped outside before she could cling to him again.

No sooner had the door closed behind him than someone rounded the corner in front of him. He continued forward, the two men approaching each other with a steady stride. They wore identical grey cloaks and engraved headbands, but otherwise were quite different. The other fellow was noticeably shorter, stocky of build, his face rounder, his hair darker than Tordan's thick, reddish blond mane. Tordan sported a neatly-trimmed mustache under his high-bridged nose, while the other man's broad jaw was embellished with an imperial goatee, and his nose gave the impression of having been broken more than once. Which Tordan knew it had.

When it seemed the two men would collide, they raised their right arms and struck forearm against forearm.

"Greetings, brother Tordan," said the dark-haired one.

"Greetings, brother Magnir."

The fellow looked back at the door Tordan had exited.

"The Lady Rikissa? You're playing a dangerous game, Brother."

Tordan chuckled. "There's no denying that. But it's my game."

His friend took the meaning—that it was none of his business—and shrugged. "Had I been invited to milady's chambers, I'd likely be as foolish. I pray Lofn looks upon you fondly.

"Where are you off to?"

"I'm traveling to Oseberg to visit family. Would you care to accompany me?"

"By Thor's hammer, you know we're not welcome in Oseberg. One look at your circlet and sword, and they'll mark you as a skaldor for certain."

It was Tordan's turn to shrug. "I was born in Oseberg. It's where my brother and his family live."

"Aye," replied Magnir, "I was born there too, but that won't mean anything to our Vanir cousins. They won't look kindly upon you no matter where you sprouted."

"I know. But it's been some time since I've visited. I can take care of myself."

"I know you can. But watch your back," warned Magnir, scratching his fleshy nose. He shook his head thoughtfully. "I'm thankful I've no family to worry me."

"There are times I wonder if it wouldn't be better that way," said Tordan.

"I must go. I have the duty," said Magnir, already moving off. "I'll see you on your return."

Tordan smiled and called out in a boisterous manner, "When I return we'll raise a tankard to Thor, and then one to each of the other gods."

Magnir laughed as he hurried off. Tordan broke into a trot himself, not wanting to miss the departure of the rail.

Estrid Magnusson dared not speak her mind until she was safely back in the family keep. Even then she stifled herself until they'd passed the pair of low-ranking housecarles guarding the entrance. Her pace was so brisk Furyk had to rush to keep up with her.

A servant girl stepped out of a room into the corridor as they were passing, and stutter-stepped seeing the lady of the manor. Because of her surprise, her respectful bow was a bit awkward.

"What are you doing?" Estrid demanded.

"Nothing, mistress."

"Nothing? Why are you doing nothing, you lazy, misbegotten—"

"I was on my way to the kitchen, mistress. My duties require me there."

"Then on with you. Get to the kitchen."

"Yes, mistress."

The girl skittered off like a terrified animal, and Estrid continued down the corridor, Furyk in her wake. His mother didn't stop until they came to the alcove where the familial flame burned. High above the flame, on a huge wooden crossbeam set in the arched ceiling, sat an owl, eyeing the humans who'd disturbed it. Owls were a household's good luck charm—the favored of Wotan—and they kept the manor free of rodents.

On either side of the eternal flame was a magnificent tapestry. Though they differed stylistically, each was woven as a representation of a tree—a family tree—framed by an interlacing of roots. She looked up to the one that traced her own pure bloodlines, going back 14 generations and ending with her— she'd had no brothers to carry on the line. The other, which she ignored, depicted her husband's line, and contained the names of her own children. In one corner was the signet of the Trellestar Corporation, a baying white wolf set over a sapphire moon.

Estrid turned from the tapestry and glared at Furyk. His normally defiant carriage folded under the weight of her gaze.

"You should have come to me first. I might have been able to council you on how you could have used the information about your sister's condition to your own advantage. You'll never be an executive if you don't start thinking like one."

"I was outraged," barked Furyk. "I wanted to cut that Vanir scum's throat myself, except..."

"Except the housecarle would have spilt your entrails in the blink of an eye. You're a business man, not a ruffian—remember that." Estrid reached to straighten the hair protruding from Furyk's silver and brass headband, and softened her voice. "Your father's right. If you don't learn to control your emotions, you'll never succeed. Besides, your sister's dalliance is not as troubling as her negligence—letting her bloodline be contaminated. Don't worry, she'll be dealt with. Let your father take care of the housecarle. You stay out of it."

"What did Father mean about me supplanting him someday? Why would he say that? Gudrik is the eldest. By the Law of Odal he will inherit the family business. I'll get almost nothing."

She put her hand on his chest and stroked it as if to calm him. "Your father is no fool, Furyk. He knows Gudrik has no interest in business. He has no ambition."

Furyk turned away from her attentions and stared up at the owl.

"Maybe. Or maybe he'll become ambitious after Father is gone."

"Gudrik is weak and indolent, corrupted by vice," said Estrid, the timbre of her voice rising angrily. "He'll never succeed your father. You must see to that." She clamped her hand on her son's shoulder and he turned to look at her. "It's your familial duty, Furyk."

The countryside between Trondheim and Oseberg was serenely pastoral and golden with sunshine. Cattle grazed, farmers worked their fields, and, in the distance, a grove of apple trees ran up a mountain slope. Tordan found it odd he took so much pleasure in the vista. However, it wasn't a long journey to the town of his birth, so his respite from the twisted intrigues of Trondheim was brief. Upon his arrival in the slums of Oseberg the streaming sunlight disappeared, as though a veil of dark clouds hung over the city in perpetuity.

He knew that wasn't true, but it seemed so. Especially now, looking out at the dilapidated buildings and refuse-strewn streets. It wasn't the city he remembered from his boyhood, as short as that had been. Or maybe nostalgia colored his memories.

Something else was different. In the distant skies above Oseberg he saw a pair of airships looming ominously over various sectors of the city. The dark ships hung in the air, seemingly motionless, no doubt tasked with surveillance, given the unrest he'd heard of.

Sitting across from him, down a ways in the railcar, were three young Vanir. They were pure redheads, all of them, and they were starring daggers at him. No doubt they carried the real thing under their cloaks. Tordan knew by looking at them they were ruffians, itching for a fight. Their hair was cut short, a new fashion he'd heard had taken hold in parts of Oseberg that was more a matter of dissent than style. They'd most certainly taken him for an Aesir, and couldn't believe their luck in finding one alone. How wrong they were. He was no Aesir, though his apparel might give that impression, and they were in no way fortunate—not if they were planning what he thought.

They were probably wondering if he was carrying a firearm, but Tordan wouldn't carry

such a weapon into his brother's house. He had his sword — that was more than enough. It wasn't an ornamental blade like the Aesir nobles wore. His was forged by the finest skaldoran craftsmen. He'd trained for years after being conscripted, and served as a dragnir for even longer before attaining the rank of skaldor, and the sword that went with it. Once a skaldor earned his sword, he never went anywhere without it.

The railway slowed for its first stop. Tordan watched the trio of Vanir who, in-turn, observed him. They made no move to leave. As the railcar nudged forward, Tordan got up from his seat and disembarked. Normally he would have waited until the next stop, closer to his brother's home, but he wanted to see if the Vanir thugs would follow him.

They did, and made no attempt to conceal the fact they were after him. They either weren't smart enough, or observant enough to recognize the hammer and lightning bolt insignia stamped into his headband. It should have been enough to warn them off.

Tordan paid no attention to them. He never turned to look back, never altered his gait. His steady pace and long strides made it difficult for them to keep up. Soon they broke into a trot, then a full-run, coming up behind him with unbridled recklessness.

Just when it seemed as if he wouldn't react, Tordan wheeled and, in a single motion, threw back his cloak, drew his sword, and relieved the closest attacker of his right hand. The knife held by the severed hand clattered to the street. The man howled in pain.

Instead of fleeing, the other two came at him from opposite sides. He didn't know if they were bravely defending their comrade, or simply fools on an errand of hatred. No matter, the result would be the same. With movements so quick his attackers would have been dazed, were they not already dead, he decapitated one and impaled the other.

Tordan knelt to wipe his sword on one dead man's cloak and looked up at the fellow with the bleeding stump. The gleam in his blue eyes was all that was needed. The would-be assassin was running down the cobblestone street before Tordan had finished cleaning his blade.

4

*Long ago, at the dawn of the Age of Reason, we
abandoned the homeworld, finding its satellite more
attuned to our newly evolved discorporeal essences.
Though the necessity of such journeys are still debated,
pilgrimages to the ancient habitats are common, both for
rejuvenation and as a type of spiritual retreat.
Unfortunately, these visits were what, initially, brought
us within closer proximity to the emanations of the
subject species, and exposed us to the onslaught of its
emotional turbulence.*

—A Societal History/Proem

Tordan arrived while his brother was still at work in the steel mill that had employed him nearly all his life. He was greeted by Jorvik's wife, Marta, and their two children. Time had taken its toll on Marta. He read it in her face.

Canute was only nine, still enough of a boy to be impressed with Tordan's sword. But his niece Kristina was now 13, and a budding beauty, beginning to take the form of a woman. She greeted him formally—a marked difference from the enthusiasm she'd demonstrated at his last visit. Tordan guessed the radical rants of her father had made an impression. Her uncle was "tainted" by the Aesir.

"Can I get you something to drink?" asked Marta.

"Some water, if you please."

"Can I hold it?" asked Canute, still looking at his sword.

"Canute!" scolded his sister.

Tordan looked at Marta. "It's okay, if your mother says so."

"Alright, Canute," replied Marta, unwilling to douse her son's excitement. "But you'd better not tell your father."

Tordan unstrapped the sheathed blade and handed it to Canute. "Be careful now."

The boy unsheathed the sword. Even with two hands he found its weight almost too much to lift. He laid it on the table.

Tordan took a drink of the water Marta handed him, and found the metallic taste of it so bad he wanted to spit. Of course he didn't.

"Is it true, Uncle, that a skaldor's blade is forged on Thor's anvil—that it's magic?"

"I don't know about magic, but aye, I'm told it was forged on the anvil of Thor."

Canute ran his fingers down the blade, caressing it as if it were a beloved animal, careful not to touch its two keen edges. "It's stronger than anything then—right? It can't bend or break."

"It hasn't broken on me yet."

"Did you use it to fight in the Corporate Wars?"

"Aye, I did."

Canute traced a path over the metal guard with his tiny fingers, and onto the ivory hilt where runic inscriptions were carved wraparound fashion below the smooth, round pommel.

"Is this really the fang of a jormun?" asked Canute.

"It is," assured Tordan. "The hilt of every skaldor's sword is carved from the tooth of that sea monster, and every sword has its own name."

"What's your sword's name?" The boy asked, full of wonder.

"It's a secret," said Tordan, "but I guess it's alright if I tell you. You won't tell anyone will you?"

The boy shook his head vigorously.

Tordan leaned down and whispered in Canute's ear, "I call mine Thor's Razor."

"Alright, Canute, that's enough," said his mother. "Go with Kristina and wash up for supper. Your father will be home soon."

Kristina escorted her brother from the room. Tordan sheathed his sword and set it aside.

"They've grown—both of them."

"It's been a long time since you've visited," replied Marta. "Sit, sit," she said as she went about preparing their meal.

Tordan pulled out a chair. "I would visit more often, but..."

"But you and your brother don't see eye to eye."

"No, we don't."

Tordan watched her go about her work in silence, and wondered what it would be like to have a wife and children to come home to every day. It was a far different life than the one he led. Not that he was one to complain about his

17

station. He was proud of being a skaldor—it was the only life he knew. But on this one account, he envied his brother.

"Kristina seemed subdued," said Tordan. "Is it just that she's no longer a child, or has she been influenced by her father's opinion of me and my brethren?"

"A little of both I imagine," said Marta. "But I worry for her, Tordan. She will soon be of age, and either have to marry or go work in some factory. She's too young. She's not ready for marriage, and I shudder to think of her in one of the factories."

"As I recall, you were about her age when Jorvik took you for his bride."

Marta paused wistfully a moment, then went back to work.

"Yes. As I said, she's too young."

"I can arrange for her to work in Trondheim as maidservant in the house of Jarl Magnusson."

He was certain Rikissa would take on his niece if he asked.

"You could?" said Marta hopefully. Her tone changed. "Jorvik wouldn't like that."

"No, he wouldn't," agreed Tordan. "But it would certainly be much better for her than working in a factory. I could see she was well-placed, and I could watch over her."

"Yes, yes, it would be better," said Marta. "But Jorvik..."

"You'll have to convince him, won't you?"

Marta looked at Tordan, smiled, but said nothing.

Before her smile faded, Jorvik walked in, started to greet her, and saw Tordan sitting there. It wasn't a smile that welcomed Tordan, but a frown.

"Well, Brother, what brings you to the slums of Oseberg?"

Tordan didn't care for the tone in which Jorvik said "Brother," but he rose from his chair and grasped his sibling's forearm in greeting. "I came to see my brother and his family, to see that all is well."

"Oh yes," replied Jorvik, sarcasm evident in his voice, "all is well."

They released their grip on each other and sat. Tordan realized by the way Jorvik slumped in his chair he was exhausted. Work in the factories of Oseberg wasn't easy, and watching her husband day after day was why Marta was so afraid for her daughter.

Jorvik leaned back and stared at Tordan, as if taking his measure and less than impressed.

"I'm surprised you were willing to take leave of your rich wines and lavish saunas and perfumed women to—"

"Jorvik! I won't have such talk," Marta admonished, adding a stern look. "Now dinner is ready. Clean yourself up. I'll get the children."

Jorvik's scowl showed he didn't care to be upbraided by his wife, but as he stood the scowl became a smile and he said, "She also makes a mean stew."

When dinner was over, Marta escorted the children into a back room, purposely leaving the brothers alone. Once they'd gone, Jorvik said, "Join me in an ale, Brother? Or is skyr too lowly for you?"

"Hardly. I'd love a tankard of skyr. My skaldoran brothers and I drink it all the time."

While Jorvik filled a pair of mugs, Tordan studied his older brother.

Jorvik was shorter and stouter of build than he, but with the same pale blue eyes. He still had the bright ruddy hair Tordan had been jealous of as a boy. Yet he wore it more closely cropped than Tordan remembered—much like the trio of rogues he'd dealt with earlier.

"Truly, Brother, how are you? Marta and the children seem fine."

Jorvik handed Tordan his mug. "Marta is not fine," he said, resuming his seat. "She has the blight."

"No." Tordan leaned forward, his fist slamming the table. "She doesn't seem ill."

Jorvik didn't respond.

"What kind of treatment is she getting?"

"There's no cure for the blight," Jorvik said angrily. "None the Aesir have shared with us anyway."

"It's true," said Tordan, "even the high-born of the Aesir die of the blight. They have no cure, but doctors are sometimes able to slow the spread of the disease with certain treatments."

"Surely you know we have no doctors among the Vanir," replied Jorvik. "Only menders of broken bones and severed limbs. Healers whose remedies are scant better than wishful thinking."

"I'll have a doctor dispatched to see Marta. I can pay him, and he can—"

"No, Brother, no. The consequences of your own visit will already be tough to deal with—neighbors seeing what looks to them like an Aesir coming into our home. No, a doctor can't delay the inevitable. Marta will die of the blight as did our mother and father, and nothing can change that. It's a battle not even you, a vaunted skaldoran warrior can win. The only thing we can change is how we're treated by the Aesir. That's the only battle worth fighting. Not for ourselves, but for our children."

"Now you talk like a B'serker," said Tordan. He tasted his drink for the first time.

"What of it? I won't let my children grow to become slaves of the Aesir masters."

"You're not a slave."

"No," responded Jorvik, "I'm a karlar, a free man, a craftsman of my trade, like our father was of his. He was a great shipbuilder. But he was treated as a slave, as I am—a drudge fit only to serve the *noble* race."

Jorvik drank deeply.

"This is what you teach your children—to hate the Aesir—to hate me?"

Jorvik wiped the skyr foam from his lips. "I don't teach them to hate you, Brother, but you do live with the Aesir. You bow to them, fetch for them."

Tordan stood abruptly. "I bow to no man. I simply observe courtly courtesies, as does every civilized person."

"So we're uncivilized now are we?"

"I didn't mean that," said Tordan, returning to his seat. "You forget I am also Vanir."

"No, I don't forget—I never forget. But you must agree, in most things, you're more Aesir than Vanir."

Tordan couldn't disagree. His brother was right about that.

They both drank deeply.

"What you say is true, Brother," said Tordan. "I'm not Vanir and I'm not Aesir, I'm..." Tordan didn't finish. He took another sip. "I often wonder why I was taken. Why me? Why not you? You were the older brother."

"Don't you know?" said Jorvik. "It was the color of your hair. Yes, I was a bit old to begin their skaldor training, but it was your hair that was the difference. Yours was lighter, more akin to the blond of the Aesir than mine."

Tordan had never thought about it—never realized why he'd been taken. But, knowing the Aesir as he did now, it made sense.

"They said you would be educated, taught skills. They told our parents it was an honor. Father and Mother had no choice but to treat it as such."

"The guilt of it infects my soul," admitted Tordan, surprising himself with his candor. "That I live how I do, while you and yours are forced to reside in the squalor our city has become. I'm not blind to it. I'm shamed there's nothing I can do to remedy it."

Jorvik reached across the table and placed a meaty hand on Tordan's shoulder. "It's not your fault you were taken, Brother. You were just a boy, with no say in the matter. It's never been your fault."

Jorvik released his grip and grabbed his mug for another drink. He swallowed and wiped his mouth with the back of his hand.

"Take heart, Brother. The Vanir will not suffer the tyranny of the Aesir forever. Change is afoot."

"What do you mean?"

"Only that we will not buckle under the yoke forever."

Tordan was certain his brother knew more—meant more—than he was saying. He'd heard rumors of angry rallies among the Vanir workers, of sabotage, of secret B'serker groups planning a revolt. But he'd never imagined his brother could be involved. Now he felt certain he must be, in some manner or another.

"You don't say the words, Brother, but your tone is one of insurrection. I know better than to try and sway you, but be cautious. Remember what Father used to say. Don't sail out farther than you can row back."

Jorvik laughed. "Wasn't that a song he used to sing?"

"Yes it was. Do you still have your gittern?"

"I do," he said, fetching it. "But you know I'm not very good with it."

"Well hand it here," said Tordan. "I play for my fellow skaldors quite a bit. Now, let me see if I can remember Father's song."

He strummed the four strings of the instrument, testing it, then began.

"My friend is the sea
The sea is my friend
I sail with Njord's grace
Until Ragnarok's end
The warmth of my hearth
Burns for me at home
My wife's much warmer
She's fertile as loam
I sail the Skagerak
Like the karlar I am
I watch for the jormun
Til I get back to land
I teach all my sons
Gauge the wind, then tack

And sail no further
Than you can row back
Sail no further
Than you can row back."

5

Only the purest of metals can be forged into the crown of a king.

—Ancient Aesir Proverb

The room was filled with corpses, and the inevitable stench that accompanies medical research. Vikar did his best to ignore the smell, but he couldn't avoid the eviscerated bodies. He didn't mind the blood, that was everywhere, but the open body cavities were a bit grisly, and there were various organs lying about like so much defective merchandise. They were savages of course, and that made the gruesome scene tolerable.

"Jarl Magnusson, I wasn't told you'd be visiting today," said the man who approached him.

He wore gloves, a bloodied apron, and goggles, all of which he hurried to remove. The others in the room were similarly attired. They paid notice to Vikar's entrance, but then went busily back to work.

"I wanted to see how your work was progressing, Doctor," Vikar said, peering into an open chest looking for the heart. It was missing. "Quite some time has passed since I provided you with these specimens. What has my chief medical researcher learned?"

"I'll have my associate put together the research documents we've compiled and—"

"I don't have hours to spend deciphering your scribblings, Dr. Thorgrim. Provide me with an overview."

His discomfiture apparent, Thorgrim cleared his throat. "Well, I can tell you that each of the skraelings we examined was exceptionally healthy. Heart, lungs, all the organs we studied were without defect. There were no signs of the blight in any of the subjects."

Vikar turned from his own visual examination of the nearest body to look at the doctor. "You're certain of this?"

"Absolutely. We also believe, in accordance with our morphological studies of various sternal ribs and the auricular surfaces of the ilium, that the skraelings have unusually long life spans."

"What exactly do you mean by 'long life spans'?"

Dr. Thorgrim gestured at a nearby corpse. "Take this fellow here for example. From outward appearances, he would seem to be a man of only 25 to 30 years. However, we're fairly certain he's at least 50 years old."

Vikar was astounded. "How can that be? What do you mean 'fairly certain'?"

"Our representative sample is somewhat small," said the doctor motioning to the room's contents. "We would need a much larger sampling and further study to be positive to a scientific certainty. As for what would lead to such a long life, it could be genetic, environmental, dietary..." Thorgrim shrugged. "We were surprised by another finding as well. The blood chemistry and anatomy of these savages is remarkably similar to our own."

"Don't be obscene, Doctor," admonished Vikar.

"Of course there are genetic differences," Thorgrim added quickly.

"Of course there are," said Vikar. "They're skrael. Even the Vanir are more human than such savages."

"Yes, yes of course," agreed the doctor. "In light of what we've learned, we'd like to conduct some new tests on a live subject, to confirm our theories. We understand you still have one such captive."

"I've other uses for that one, Doctor. However, I'll supply you with as many live subjects as you need, as soon as I can. In the meantime, continue your work here, and provide me with regular updates. I also want you to run complete tests on my three children. I know their blood was examined thoroughly at birth, but I want those tests run again."

Rikissa absentmindedly counted the strokes as she brushed her hair. Unfettered, the straight blond tresses fell past her shoulders, almost to her waist. She studied herself in the mirror, chagrined by her own reflection. She was pretty enough, she guessed, in a plain sort of way, though not nearly the beauty her mother was. Still, there was a distinct family likeness she couldn't deny. It was those similarities she loathed. Only her eyes stood out. Their blue-green tint was much more like her father's.

A noise outside her door disrupted her thoughts. Was it Tordan? Had he returned early? Rikissa hurried to the door, flung it open and peered into the corridor.

At first she saw no one. Then from under a guard stand marched Prince Dax. The old cat had captured a mouse, holding it firmly in his jaws. He sat on his haunches, his black tail whipping back and forth. Rikissa saw a drop of the rodent's blood on the cat's snow white chest. Though it didn't struggle, Rikissa

24

realized the mouse was still alive.

"Good boy, Dax. Go on now, take it away."

Prince Dax had been her playmate when she was little, but now he spent most of his time roaming the halls of the family keep, engaged in a never-ending territorial dispute with the owls. There used to be quite a few cats in the manor—her mother had said they were portents of fertility—but Prince Dax was the only one left. He sat looking at her, as if waiting for more words of praise, the green glint of his eyes showing through a black mask.

Rikissa didn't want to see what he did next with the mouse, so she stepped back inside and shut her door so the cat would not attempt to present his catch to her as some kind of offering.

She hadn't even considered the possibility before, but now her disappointment that it hadn't been Tordan at her door consumed her. Why did he have to go visit his family now, when she had something important to tell him? Especially when his family lived in such a horrid place. Of course she knew he was Vanir by birth—a thought that filled her with unrepentant satisfaction. She wished she'd said something to him before he left, but she hadn't had the courage.

As she resumed brushing her hair, there was a perfunctory knock on her door. Before she could give her permission, the door opened and her mother glided in, her movements graceful as always, though her face spoke of matters more weighty.

"What is it, Mother?" asked Rikissa, tying her hair back. "I was preparing to go for a walk."

Estrid stopped just behind Rikissa, who still faced the mirror. The reflection of mother and daughter together only served to remind Rikissa of the resemblance she so detested.

"You won't be going anywhere," said her mother in a tone of command.

Rikissa turned round to face her. "What do you mean?"

"I mean your comings and goings are to be severely restricted."

"I don't understand. What are you talking about?"

"Your father and I know about your illicit liaison with the housecarle," said Estrid, keeping her hands calmly folded over the ruffles of her fur-lined dress. "We also know you're pregnant."

"How could you...?"

Rikissa's inner world crashed in upon her. How could they know? Only her maidservant knew about the pregnancy. That little bitch would pay. How could she have been so stupid as to trust her? Of course that's the way she was, and she despised herself for it. Always impulsive—never thinking things through.

"Don't bother trying to deny it," said Estrid, walking away, casually fingering the silver and opal brooch that held her robe, looking over her daughter's room as if for some evidence of her sordid affair. "What upsets me most is your carelessness. After all the instruction I've given you, to let yourself be impregnated by this...this..." Estrid threw her free hand up in a gesture of contempt, unable to even say the words.

While part of her was mortified her mother and father knew of her affair with Tordan, another part was glad they did. It must rankle them to know she'd found love in the arms of a low-born Vanir.

"Alright, I admit it. And I'm in love with him too."

"Oh, I'm sure you are," replied her mother with such nonchalance Rikissa was suddenly afraid. "The important thing now is that we deal with it, and deal with it swiftly."

"What do you mean?"

"I mean, Daughter, the pregnancy will be terminated—immediately."

"No, you can't!"

"I certainly can. It's already been decided." Estrid turned and her gaze was severe. "Come, Rikissa, what did you expect? Did you think we'd let you keep the Vanir brat? Make it a Magnusson? Pollute the bloodline? You know better, so don't act as if you're shocked. You've had your little dalliance, now we must keep it from becoming a family embarrassment."

That's all it was to them, thought Rikissa, an embarrassment to be dealt with, to be kept quiet so as not to interfere with the family business. However, amidst the clash of her emotions, she admitted to herself that she knew what her mother said was true. As much as she dreamed of herself and Tordan being together, she knew it would never happen. She knew they'd never let her keep the baby. It had been a self-indulgent fantasy.

"Nothing to say? Good. I'm glad you have at least some sense about you." Estrid walked to the door. She turned back to her daughter. "And another thing. Your father has come to terms on what he expects to be a very profitable merger. I'm sure you'll be pleased to know he's arranged for your marriage. The details still have to be worked out, but an oral contract has been confirmed. You're to marry the chairman's son. I believe his name is Edvard. I'm certain you'll be quite happy together."

Rikissa couldn't even pretend to be surprised—not deep down. She knew this day would come, though she never admitted it to herself. It was the way things were done.

"Don't worry, my dear," said Estrid. "Being young is a fault which diminishes daily."

Rikissa looked up, wanting to say something, anything, but her mother was already gone, leaving only the enduring strawberry fragrance of her too familiar perfume.

The walk from the laboratory to the detention center was a short one. Even though the pair of housecarles who escorted him had remained outside, Vikar saw the relief on their faces to leave the lab behind them. He would never say so, but he had to agree. It was a messy bit of business, but one he strongly believed could lead to enormous profit.

"Open it," he commanded when they reached the cell door.

The housecarles each grabbed a spear from the guard rack and unbolted the door. Vikar followed them in.

His escort held their spears at ready, but the savage made no move toward them.

His skin was sun-bronzed and his tousled hair as black as night. He stood as they entered, chains binding both his wrists and ankles, and stared at Vikar. He'd been stripped of all but a loincloth, but by his posture you'd have thought he was adorned with the finest embroidered robe, and that his chains were prestigious silver bracelets. Vikar almost admired his haughty stance.

The savage looked in good health. He'd ordered the creature be relatively well-fed. Looking at him now, after what Thorgrim had told him, Vikar couldn't help but wonder how old this skraeling was.

"They tell me you refuse to talk. That you won't utter a sound—not even in pain. Maybe I should have one of my men poke you with his spear to see if it's true."

The savage only stared, making no attempt to conceal the hatred burning in his almond eyes.

"Of course, you probably don't understand a word I'm saying, do you? You're an ignorant savage, barely more than an animal, so one can't expect intelligent discourse. That's alright. For what I have in mind, you needn't say a word."

Before Vikar had even finished his last sentence, the savage folded his arms across his chest, turned from his captors, and faced the stone wall. Vikar reigned in his anger at this blatant show of disdain, and the urge to strike the insolent creature. Instead he wheeled, red-faced, and stalked out of the cell, his fur-lined robe flying behind him, like the wings of his rage.

6

Everything in this world has a purpose—every animal,
every plant, every rock. So, too, does every person,
even if, for a time, it eludes them.

—**Sicangu Adage**

"So, Doctor, how is my blight progressing?"
Truvor didn't respond, but continued to listen to the burgrave's lungs. Despite his often cavalier demeanor, Guttorm Andersson was a good fellow, an honorable man compelled to assume an ignoble position. Truvor had grown to like him, and had even come to appreciate his droll sense of humor.

"How long do I have, Doctor? At least tell me that."

Truvor stood.

"I'll be able to tell you more once I get your samples back to my lab. You won't be dying anytime soon, Guttorm. You can get dressed now."

"That's a shame," said Guttorm, pulling the tunic back over his rotund form. "I was looking forward to having a cavalcade of Valkyries whisk me away to Valholl."

"Why, Burgrave Andersson," said Truvor, trying to match his jovial tone, "if I didn't know better, I'd think you wanted to die just so you could relinquish your post here in Serkland."

"You know me too well, Doctor. It's a sad commentary on life when death seems bright with seduction." The burgrave fastened his cloak and straightened his clothing, assuming a new posture. "Well, I must fulfill my obligation to the chairman. I guess someone must oversee this barbaric outpost."

"It's not all that terrible, Guttorm."

The burgrave grunted in disagreement. "Tell me, Doctor, how are you doing...your blight I mean?"

"I'm still in the early stages. I've no physical effects yet. You needn't worry about me, you have enough on your plate."

"Yes. Speaking of which, it must be time for lunch, don't you think?"

Truvor smiled. "It's good you're not letting your illness affect your appetite. You know they may not serve *tatanka* steaks in Valholl."

29

"So true, Doctor. This savage land does have its beneficent quirks. Which reminds me—what of the horse men you requested permission to trade with? Are they amenable?"

"Yes, indeed, some seem to be. My assumption was correct. There are many different tribes. They live apart, follow different leaders, even war with each other on occasion. However, thankfully, their tribal languages, are similar—at least from what I've been able to learn so far. But..."

"But what, Doctor? Come now, I see it in your eyes."

"We've discussed this before. The more I learn about these people, the more I question whether or not we're intruding in a place where we don't belong. These horse men aren't the simple savages they appear at first glance. It's a matter of ethics."

"Ethics, Doctor? Since when did the corporatocracy care about ethics? It's about commerce, Doctor, about profit. You know that as well as I. This outpost is only the beginning. This equatorial region is rich with agricultural potential, not to mention what minerals we may discover. Each of the nine major corporations covets this land. Believe me when I tell you the machinations involved in who will control what would dizzy you. Don't fool yourself with peaceful ideals. We can look forward to aggressive expansion sooner rather than later. And there's nothing either you or I can do about it."

"Yes, you're right of course. But the infamy of what I foresee is almost too much to bear." An edge of bitterness sharpened his voice. It had become more telling with each passing day, though he'd promised himself not to let it consume him. "I'd better get these samples back to my lab. I'll leave you to your lunch."

"You know why we were both stationed here, don't you, Doctor?"

Truvor looked up and saw the spite in the burgrave's deep-set, sunken eyes. It was in his eyes, and in his rapidly graying hair, that the blight revealed itself.

"They sent us here so they wouldn't be reminded of the fate that may await them. Out of sight, out of mind, as it were. They prefer not to acknowledge the idea that an Aesir of the blood can develop the blight."

Truvor didn't bother to disagree. Guttorm was given to platitudes, but there was some truth to what he said.

However, he had his own theory on why *he'd* been sent from Trondheim. It was because he'd had the audacity to suggest the blight was not wholly genetic. His theory it could be the result of environmental factors such as industrial toxins or even solar radiation was not well received.

"Burgrave Andersson, and Dr. Svein—excellent."

As Truvor was about to leave, Storman Ragnarsson appeared, accompanied by the sounds of clashing metal and stomping boots. He swept into the room—a one-man assault force. All that was missing from the entrance was the blare of trumpets.

"I need to speak with you both."

Truvor thought of Ragnarsson as the definitive soldier. His uniform always clean and wrinkle-free, the sea snake signet of Roskildcorp proudly adorning his sleeve, his sword slung ready at his side. The man was nothing if not a model of consistency and obedience to form. Today he was in full battle armor, as if he'd just returned from the front lines. His silver shoulder plates glistened and his chain mail shimmered against his black tunic. Under his arm he carried his horned helm.

"What is it, Storman?" asked Guttorm, not bothering to disguise his dislike of the outpost's military commander.

"I've received new orders from Chairman Tryguasson. I'm to capture more savages as soon as possible, and transport them to Trondheim."

"Is that really necessary, Storman? We have enough problems with these horse men now."

"Those are my orders, Burgrave. I've been sent additional troops, Heimdalls, airships, and artillery to carry out my orders."

"If you must," replied the burgrave, moving behind his desk. "But do try to limit the carnage, would you?"

"If it were up to me," said the storman, "I'd exterminate them all, down to the last dirty, bawling brat."

Truvor barely restrained himself. He wanted to speak up, to argue against such cruelty, but he had no say. His first impulse was to appeal to Storman Ragnarsson's better nature, but, as far as he knew, the commander didn't have one. His impression of the man was that he was a cool, calculating sadist. The perfect choice for his role here. Truvor could only hope to play on his self-interest.

"Storman Ragnarsson, I would suggest you refrain from taking any captives from the peaceful tribe I've been dealing with. Their goodwill and alliance may prove useful in the future. There are many other tribes you can cull from."

The storman looked at him with intense cerulean eyes. "Peaceful? Are you referring to the savages whose language you've been trying to learn?"

"Yes."

31

The storman mulled the idea over before responding. "Understanding their language *would* allow us to interrogate them. We know almost nothing about them, and I don't like facing an enemy I don't know. Alright, Doctor, you designate which band of these mongrels you give sanction to, and we'll leave them untouched. But I'll need regular reports from you on everything you learn about them, including their language. I want you to step up your efforts in this regard. With the burgrave's permission of course."

Guttorm waved his hand as if the issue were of no concern to him.

"Certainly, Storman."

"Very well then." Ragnarsson delivered a curt bow before exiting.

Burgrave Andersson sat behind his desk and shook his head. "That man will be the death of me...if the blight doesn't get me first."

"Burgrave, you must try to reason with the chairman. We should continue our attempts to communicate with these people—continue to trade with them. It's wrong of us to make war on them."

"War? My dear, Doctor, there will be no war. If I know Storman Ragnarsson, it will be a slaughter."

7

You might as well expect rivers to run backward as that any man who was born free should be contented to be penned up and denied liberty to go where he pleases.

—Sicangu Adage

In order to ignore the shame of his position, he tried to concentrate on the language—on the words he heard all around him. He'd been forced into a smaller cage—an animal cage by the stink of it—and the cage had been loaded onto what his captors called a "wain." But that wasn't the only new word he'd learned. He'd been listening and learning for many days now. Some of it was still nonsensical chattering, but much of what was being said he could understand.

His pulse quickened when he saw the wain attached to a pair of horses. For a moment he thought if he could get free, he could escape on horseback. But the idea faded as quickly as it sprung forth. What horse could take him across the great sea?

When the *wasichu* guards were ready, one climbed aboard the wain and started the horses. The others walked alongside. He'd seen such wains before, when he'd traded with the *wasichu*, but he was still amazed at how they rolled along. He saw many strange things as they traveled, including something else he both saw and heard before it moved quickly out of sight. It looked much like the wain he was carried in. It rested on similar wheels but moved along without the aid of any animals, and made a ghastly noise as it went. He was certain Iktomi must be tricking his eyes.

But when he saw the white wolf, he knew it was no trick of the eyes. Upon the clothing of each of his guards was a symbol. A sacred circle like the medicine wheel, but inside the circle was a howling wolf—a white wolf. Behind the wolf was the moon. Was this the white wolf of his dream? What did the symbol represent? He thought on it a while, to no good, then turned his attention to his surroundings.

The structures they traveled past were enormous. He was certain the highest among them must touch Father Sky. Many seemed as wide and long as they were high. How they were constructed, he had no idea. It was certain the *wasichu* had knowledge of many things that surpassed that of his own people. The idea worried him more than any other, even though he knew knowledge was not the same as wisdom. That, however, was little solace.

He didn't know where they were taking him, but it felt good to be outside and feel the warmth of the sun on his skin again. He took a deep breath, but the air still reeked of poison. He was no longer surprised by the stench. Everything he saw of this *wasichu* world was foul and unclean. The people who stood and stared at him were largely unwashed, the grounds of their immense village strewn with rodent-infested refuse. Even the children were unruly. They threw stones at him while their parents pointed and laughed. Despite their laughter, he saw they feared him. Why they did so, he couldn't understand. Because he was strange to them? He certainly was no threat to them, bound as he was in this cage.

He could only listen, learn, and bide his time. When he was ready, he'd give the *wasichu* a reason to fear him.

The rodent sprinted down the dusky corridor in short bursts, unaware it was being watched. It kept close to the wall, stopping at intervals to sniff and look for danger. But the threat was too far away, too high for it to see. Only the barest wisp of wings upon the air gave it warning, though too late. The gray owl swooped down from its perch, clutched the mouse in its talons, and flew back. As it landed, a door opened.

Estrid hurried down the corridor toward the Valkyrie birthing room. She'd been informed Lady Dagre was giving birth, and the portents had not been kind. Though it was her duty to be present, along with the other the high mistresses, such an event always stoked the fires of her memories. The recollection of her own blemish was never far away.

It had been a quick labor. The infant's cord was being cut as she entered. Lady Dagre tried to get a look as they carried the newborn into another room, but she was too weak to push past those ministering to her.

As soon as Estrid was able to get a good look at the child, she knew extensive testing would not be required. For a moment she was overcome by a haunting sadness. But she didn't allow the feeling to linger. She took a last look at the infant. It was almost perfect.

When the high mistresses reentered the room, Lady Dagre strained to see if they were carrying her baby. When she saw they were empty-handed, she screamed and began sobbing hysterically. The midwives restrained her, but couldn't console her no matter how they tried.

Estrid grabbed the distraught woman's clammy hand and leaned next to her. Speaking softly, she said, "I'm sorry, the child is deformed. It's missing a finger."

"A finger? Only a finger?" said Lady Dagre between sobs. "That's not too bad. It's not is it?"

"You know such a child is likely to have the blight," said Estrid. "You know that."

"But...but—"

"Shush now, milady," said Estrid, putting her fingers to Lady Dagre's pale lips. "I know it's hard, but you know the conventions as well as any of us. We must eliminate contamination. Only the purest of metals can be forged into the crown of a king."

"But I don't understand," said the boy, confusion evident in his eyes, "if the Aesir are so evil, why does Uncle Tordan live with them?"

Kristina and her brother had been listening to another long-winded rant against the Aesir by their father. She'd heard enough over the years to know about the weight of the Aesir yoke. Father would never let them forget. But now he turned his back and remained silent, as though he didn't want to answer her brother's question.

Finally her mother spoke up. "Your uncle Tordan was taken from his home here among the Vanir when he was a boy—just like you Canute. He had no choice. The Aesir took him and trained him to work for them."

"Why doesn't he leave them?" asked Kristina. After all, Uncle Tordan wasn't a boy anymore.

"It's not that simple," replied her mother.

Her father turned back to face his children. "Tordan is a skaldor. A skaldor can't live with the Vanir."

Kristina knew all about the skaldors, how they were the greatest of warriors, supposedly warrior-poets. Though she didn't know if she believed a warrior could be a poet.

"Are they going to come and take me?"

Kristina thought Canute's question was an obvious one, and was surprised by the look of horror on her mother's face, and her father's outrage.

"They will never take you, Canute," said Jorvik, grabbing the boy by the

35

shoulders. "I won't let them take you. Don't you worry."

"What if I want to be a skaldor like Uncle Tordan?"

Kristina knew that question wouldn't sit well with her father, so did her mother.

"It's time for bed, children," said Marta, moving her arms to herd them out of the room before Jorvik could explode in another rant. "Come on. Your father's tired and must work another long day tomorrow to feed us."

Kristina took over and guided her brother to their bedroom, but moments later crept back to where she could hear her parents talking.

"Did you hear that? Did you hear the boy?" Her father was angry. "He wants to be a skaldor."

"Now that's not what he said," responded her mother in her best soothing voice.

"No, I understand. Why wouldn't he want to? Why wouldn't he want to leave this place and live the luxurious, glamorous life of a skaldor among the Aesir?"

"Jorvik, he's just a child. A boy with adventurous dreams, dazzled by his uncle's sword. Don't let it upset you."

"I know—I know. And I know it's not Tordan's fault. He's a good man."

"I'm surprised to hear you say that," replied Marta. "You don't usually have anything pleasant to say about your brother."

"You want surprise? I almost thought of asking Tordan to join the Modi. That surprised even me."

Kristina knew the Modi were a group of Vanir who defied the Aesir, but she'd had no idea her father was one of them.

"Why *didn't* you ask him?"

"It's no longer his fight. And, the truth is, I'm not positive I could trust him. He's a servant of the Aesir. He might think it his duty to spy on us."

"I don't believe that," said Marta, "and I don't think you really do either."

Her father mumble something, but Kristina couldn't make out the words. Then he said, "It doesn't matter. We're close now. The Aesir and all their housecarles and skaldors and armies won't be able to stop us. It's going to happen sooner than you think."

"I hope to live to see it."

"You will, Marta, you will."

Kristina couldn't see them, but she heard her father take hold of her mother and kiss her. She knew why. Even though they hadn't told her and Canute,

Kristina had overheard enough to know her mother had the blight. It was another reason her father hated the Aesir so much—a reason she understood.

"I want to talk to you about Kristina," her mother said.

"What about her?"

"You know she will be of age soon."

"Yes, I know."

"She's too young to marry, and I won't have her working in some factory."

"You know the law, Marta. What would you suggest? Shall we hide her in the vegetable cellar? I don't want to see her working in a factory either. Maybe marriage is the better alternative."

Marriage? Who would she marry? Kristina couldn't think of a single boy she wanted to marry, let alone some old man.

"I tell you she's too young. I don't want to force her into a marriage of convenience."

"What do you want?" scoffed Jorvik. "Do you want her to fall in love? There's not much love left in the Vanir."

"Because you're all too full of hate." Her mother sounded angry.

"Kristina will learn to love—just like we did."

"Maybe, maybe not. She's a smart girl, proud and stubborn. I don't think she'd do well in that kind of marriage—and I don't want it for her. There's another possibility."

Kristina didn't want to marry *or* work in a factory, so she waited to hear what her mother was going to suggest.

"Tordan has offered to find her a place in the Magnusson household where he would be able to watch over her."

"You want our daughter to work for the Aesir?" Her father was angry again. "How can you suggest such a thing?"

"I say it because it would be the best thing for her," replied her mother. "If she worked in a factory would she not be working for the Aesir as well? How many people are injured every day working in those factories—how many are sickened? At least working in an Aesir household she'd be safe."

"I don't want to discuss it."

Kristina heard her father walk off.

She considered the idea. She didn't want to leave her family, and she certainly didn't want to go work for some Aesir. But, from everything she'd heard, she didn't want to work in a factory either—and she didn't want to marry some man that was picked out for her. She wouldn't admit it to herself, but a small part of her was intrigued by the idea of going to Trondheim and seeing how the Aesir lived. It was a very lavish life according to the tales she'd heard. Maybe living there wouldn't be so bad.

8

*The ethics of the great speciation experiment
conducted by our ancestors continues to be debated.
It has increasingly come to be viewed as an
embarrassment. Many depict it as an immoral act.
Some go as far as to say a criminal one. No
resolution as yet been reached.*
—A Societal History/The Great Debates

Rikissa hurried to the dining hall, though she didn't want to go at all. That was why she was late—she kept creating new excuses for not getting ready. There was no avoiding it though, and now her mother and father would both be angry with her. Though no formal announcement had been made, this was to be her betrothal dinner. Chairman Tryguasson, his wife and son would all be there, along with her own family. She'd met Edvard Halfdansson only casually once, though she'd seen him at various public functions. He seemed pleasant enough, a scholarly sort as she recalled, and though they were close in age, she thought of him as a boy. There was certainly no comparison between him and Tordan. The thought carried her wistfully back to her last encounter with the skaldor. She longed to be in Tordan's arms again, but knew the risk of such a liaison was now greater than ever.

"Daughter, there you are," said Vikar as she stepped into the great hall. "Our guests have just arrived."

Indeed, everyone was there. The chairman and his family, as well as her two brothers and her mother.

"You're late, Daughter," scolded her mother, using her restrained public voice. "I was about to send the housecarles after you. What have you to say?"

Rikissa offered a crisp curtsy and said, "Please excuse my tardiness, Chairman."

Chairman Tryguasson waved his hand. "Think nothing of it my girl. We're all family here—or soon will be."

Rikissa tried not to react to the inference, but glanced at Edvard. He was staring at her.

"Shall we sit?" suggested her mother. "Beatrix, you and your husband and

39

son may sit on that side. Rikissa, across from Edvard if you please. Gudrik and Furyk on either side of your sister."

Rikissa noticed the large dining table had been replaced for this occasion with the more intimate, smaller one, though the distance between her father at one end and her mother at the other was still spacious. The table was inlaid with bands of silver, as were the heavy wooden chairs. The great hall had been adorned with the family's finest tapestries, the decorative jor oil lamps were all lit, and her mother had selected the family's best silver dinnerware. Somewhere, in a nearby room, a musician played a light, whimsical melody on his gittern.

Tankards of the traditional skyr, as well as glasses of wine were already laid out. After they sat, servants moved in and out, bringing with them several varieties of bread, fruits, and vegetables. Her mother, as expected, was sparing no expense to impress. Yet even though it was a significant occasion, Rikissa noticed how immodestly her mother had dressed. It seemed to her the older her mother became, the more she deemed it necessary to reveal her cleavage. It was becoming an embarrassment.

"Look at all these colors," said the chairman's wife. "Yellow, green, red, orange...Estrid I don't recognize some of these foods. What are they?"

"We've imported some Serkland delicacies for the occasion, Beatrix. The assortment of produce coming from that savage land is truly amazing."

"Halfdan, why haven't you told me about this?" Beatrix queried her husband. "You haven't informed me of this abundance."

"Milady, I've been dealing with many things that have priority over agricultural concerns."

"Of course. But you must arrange a sampling for me as soon as possible."

"Certainly," replied the chairman.

"I've never tasted many of these myself," said Gudrik, as if to smooth over any slight Lady Tryguasson might have felt. "I believe this is the first time we've been served such exotic fare, isn't it, Mother?"

"Quite so," admitted Estrid. "In honor of our guests."

"I was under the impression Roskildcorp presided over the Serkland colony," said Gudrik. "How is it, Father, that you've acquired this bounty?"

"A business arrangement," said Vikar. "I've negotiated certain research entitlements with the chairman's corporation, in exchange for full disclosure."

"Speaking of which," said Chairman Tryguasson, "after dinner I want to see this savage prisoner you have hidden away, this horse man. I understand he's an interesting one."

"I've already arranged it, Cousin, though I don't know how interesting he'll prove to be," replied Vikar. "He's just another savage as far as I can tell."

"What do you mean *horse* man, Chairman?" asked Rikissa. "Are these savages part man, part horse?"

"No, no, my dear, though they live like animals."

"The term 'horse men' came about because they're predominantly nomadic, and journey everywhere by horse," explained Edvard. "I've heard from our skaldors who've seen them, that these skraelings are incredible horsemen. They travel, they hunt, they make war, they even sleep on horseback. I'm told, at times, they will even eat their horses."

Rikissa, Gudrik, and the chairman's wife all made faces. "They eat horses? Disgusting."

"They're savages," said Furyk, "what do you expect? They probably fornicate with their horses as well."

"None of that kind of talk at this table, Furyk," scolded Estrid rather mildly.

One of the servants placed a basket of bread on the table and turned to go, Estrid grabbed her arm.

"What is that?" she inquired, pointing at an empty bowl on the table.

"What, milady?" asked the confused girl.

"That empty bowl. What's it doing there? What's its purpose?"

"I...I don't know, milady."

"There are no empty bowls at my table. Take it away and bring it back full."

Estrid released the girl's arm.

"Yes, milady."

The girl grabbed the bowl and scurried off. Rikissa saw everyone at the table ignored the exchange, though her father managed a frown—a rare display from his typically chiseled expression. Her mother's disdain for servants was certainly no secret in her own family, though she wondered what the Tryguassons might think.

Other servants began bringing platters of steaming hot meat. It had a texture unfamiliar to her. Furyk was the first to stick his table knife into it and cut off a bite. "What is this?" he asked, still chewing. "It's not horse is it?"

"Of course not!" snapped Estrid.

The chairman tasted it. "It's very robust. Is this meat from the Serkland colony as well?"

"Yes, it is," responded Estrid. "It's from some kind animal we haven't seen before, but I'm told it's common there."

Rikissa had no desire to taste it. Meat from some strange animal? Even if it wasn't horse, the thought made her gag. But she wasn't interested in eating much. She was so full of conflicting emotions she had no room for food.

"I believe it's from a beast much like our cattle," said Edvard. "The skraelings call it *'dah-tank,'* or something like that."

"How do you know this?" asked Vikar.

"I've been reading the reports Father's officials in the field have been sending him," responded Edvard, the enthusiasm obvious in his voice. "It's all very fascinating. Not only the new kinds of plants and animals we've discovered there, but the people themselves."

"The savages?" muttered Furyk between bites.

"Yes. We haven't learned much yet, but the native inhabitants seem to be completely unlike us. The way they look, their language, their dress, their culture. We're just beginning to learn about them."

"Their culture?" said Estrid with scorn. "Certainly you don't suggest these savages have culture?"

"Not as we know it of course," said Edvard. "But likely some primitive form of society, religion, and such."

"And likely as much variety in their beliefs as their produce," said the chairman. "My understanding is there are many different tribes of these horse men, scattered over a wide area. They have no single ruler, no chairman as it were."

"A weakness to be exploited," added Vikar. "I'm impressed, Edvard, that you've taken it upon yourself to stay informed about our colony in Serkland. I'm sure your interest in business is a matter of pride for your father."

As he spoke, Vikar glanced at his own two sons. Furyk was busy eating, oblivious to his father's comment. Gudrik caught the reference, but only smiled. Rikissa knew the subject was a long-standing sore point between her father and his sons.

"I'm interested in many things, Jarl Magnusson, not only matters of business," replied Edvard.

"Edvard even named the colony for me," said the chairman.

"Oh? Pray tell, what did you name it?" asked Estrid, dishing a helping of vegetables onto her plate.

"Hestvoll," replied Edvard. "It means *valley of the horse* in the dialect of our ancestors."

"I didn't even know there *was* an ancient dialect," said Gudrik. "Where did you learn that?"

"Just some historical research I did on my own. I've learned many fascinating things."

Rikissa saw her mother was bored, and her brother, Furyk, was about to burst with some sarcastic comment about Edvard's intellect. However, he restrained himself.

"For example," continued Edvard, "did you ever wonder why we have no gold mines? We have a few gold heirlooms passed down through the generations—gold-hilted daggers, some jewelry, cups, trinkets, but no gold has been discovered anywhere during our lifetimes. It's a mystery, don't you think?"

"Not so mysterious, I'd say," offered Vikar. "The answer is the metal is so rare the last of it on this continent was mined hundreds of years ago. It's likely we'll find more in Serkland, once mining operations begin."

"Possibly," replied Edvard as if that wasn't *his* theory. "I've other thoughts on the matter I won't go into now."

"It seems you're quite the thinker," said Estrid.

Her mother tried to disguise her condescension, but Rikissa heard it in the way she said *thinker*.

"I'm also intrigued with the idea of exploration," said Edvard. "Someday I plan on traveling either by sea or airship, to explore our world further. There is much we don't know—much still to be discovered."

"Ah yes, exploration is a young man's game," said Chairman Tryguasson. "But business concerns must take precedence. The young don't always understand they have responsibilities." He turned to look at his son. "We elder folks may have seen our better days come and go, but we understand responsibility."

Rikissa saw her mother grit her teeth, and knew the comment had struck a nerve there.

"Speak for yourself, Chairman Tryguasson. Some of us are not so old."

"Forgive me, Lady Magnusson. I was not speaking of you, nor my own wife, but only of myself. My weary muscles and creaking bones no longer let me deny the onslaught of age. Yet we're not here to talk of endings, but beginnings. The beginning of new lives and the extension of our families." The chairman glanced at both Rikissa and Edvard. "If I may be so bold as to ask, has the Valkyrie High Council given its blessing to the pairing?"

43

Though she'd likely already informed her husband of the decision, Beatrix looked to Estrid and nodded.

"The genetic match has been approved," announced Estrid. "Only the business formalities remain."

"Then I proclaim a toast," said the chairman, grabbing his tankard of skyr and standing. Everyone at the table did likewise, though Rikissa was noticeably slow to rise. "To the impending nuptials, and the joining of our families. May we be blessed with many grandchildren."

Everyone joined the chairman in drinking, though Rikissa peered over the rim of her tankard at Edvard. Behind his neatly trimmed, youthfully sparse beard he looked as embarrassed as she felt. But when he saw her eyeing him he smiled. She looked away, trying not to think of her husband-to-be. Instead she thought of Tordan, wishing he was the one she could marry, knowing it could never be.

9

The wise man believes profoundly in silence — the
sign of perfect equilibrium. Silence is the absolute
poise or balance of body, mind, and spirit.
Silence is the cornerstone of character.
>   **—Sicangu Adage**

They'd left him tied to the stone wall with those *maza* ropes they called "chains" fastened to both wrists and ankles. He thought if he tried he might be able to rip the chains from their hold on the wall, but he wasn't ready—not yet. His prison was otherwise barren, with no view of the outside. Even if he hadn't been restrained, sturdy *maza* bars formed the remaining walls of his enclosure. There were other cages on either side of him, but through the shadows of his confines he saw they were empty.

Captivity had withered him. He knew if he was going to escape, he'd have to do it soon. His captors weren't feeding him much, and what they were feeding made him sick as often as not. His strength was ebbing day by day, and still he did not know how he would get home, once free of his bonds.

A noise sounded from outside his cage. Someone was coming.

Four men appeared, the cage door swung open, and two of them stepped inside to stare at him. One of the men he'd seen before. The one with the blue-green eyes and hair the color of grain. He had hair all over his face, as did most of *wasichu,* and he held himself as would a *wicasa,* a man of influence and power. The other man was much older, not frail but weak of health or heart. His hair had turned white and his eyes were streaked with red.

"My, look at how little body hair he has—like a woman. You say he hasn't spoken a word since his capture? Not even in his own language?"

"He refuses to utter a sound."

"And you're certain none of the savages show any sign of the blight?"

"We've only examined a dozen of the brutes, but so far our doctors haven't found any trace of the blight or any other malady for that matter. In fact, and forgive me for saying so, but our autopsies have shown there's no real physiological difference between the skrael and the Aesir, and no genetic reason the doctors have been able to determine for their long lives or lack of the blight."

He knew "skrael" was what the *wasichu* called his people, and they referred to themselves as "Aesir," though the words "autopsies" and "genetic" were new to him. But it wasn't the first time he'd heard the word "blight." He'd deduced it was a kind of sickness that must infect their clan. He'd also heard his captors talking about long lives, and he knew they'd been examining other captives, as well as himself. He was beginning to think the *wasichu* were sickly, and that they wanted to steal the very *ni* from his own people, to suck the breath of life from them.

"Amazing," said the white-haired man. "Just how long do you think these horse men live?"

"Without further study, we can't be certain. However, the current estimate is that their lives are twice ours."

"Twice? That's incredible. How can this be?"

"We're still trying to determine that. My top scientists are working on it. Because they've found no physiological differences, their theory is that there must be some deeper genetic disparity we haven't discovered yet, or an environmental cause. Maybe something in their diet."

"You mean they may be eating a cure for the blight?"

"It's quite possible. For all we know, one of the foods we ate tonight could be the cure, though even if that were true, we have no idea of the quantity or duration necessary for such a treatment to work. Which is why I've requested you order more savages be captured for further study, along with any native foodstuffs we can acquire."

Hearing this, he tensed and pulled at his chains. They were going to take more of his people. He couldn't wait any longer. He must return home to warn them, to defend his family.

The older man turned and said to the men outside the cage, "Leave us a moment." They walked away and he turned to the other fellow.

"Vikar, ordinarily I would not reveal this, but since we are about to undergo a familial merger, I will tell you...I suffer from the blight."

So the older *wasichu* was indeed ill. The other man's expression told him the news was not a surprise.

"I'm sorry to hear that, Cousin. All the more reason we need to invest more of our resources to study these horse men."

"Perhaps we need to launch a full-scale of invasion of Serkland to find this cure."

"I'm not sure that's the best strategy at the moment. I've another, less expensive idea I hope will yield more exact results."

"Tell me."

"I rather not, not now, not in front our guest."

"But you said he doesn't speak. Do you think he can understand what we say?"

His captor moved closer to him. His stare was probing.

"I don't know. There's something about this fellow's eyes, something that speaks of some savage intelligence." He turned, walked to the old man and put his arm around him. "Before I detail my plans for Serkland, shall we set a date for the negotiations of the mundr? I think it might be better if the wedding were sooner rather than later. Don't you agree?"

"Certainly. I can think of no reason why not."

"I was thinking of adding your medical research division to my own. It's not really that profitable, so the cost to you is minimal. But by combing our research efforts, we should be able to find the cure even quicker."

"If that's all you want, I think we can complete negotiations on the mundr today, Cousin." Both men continued talking as they walked out. "With one proviso. I'll give you my medical research division as your bridal price with the condition I receive the first blight treatment."

"That goes without saying, Cousin. But we will incorporate it into the agreement. May Freyr guide our endeavors and reward our families with prosperity."

The other men returned, closed and locked his cage. They stared at him briefly, then departed.

He took a deep breath and tried to relax within his chains as he considered his situation. He had to escape. He could no longer bide his time. Even if he had to swim across the great sea, he had to warn his people. He'd let his guard down in order to pursue the knowledge of the *wasichu*, and in doing so had betrayed his brethren. What he knew now about these barbarians made his heart even heavier with guilt. He would break free at the first opportunity.

10

Wealth is transitory — reputation is eternal.
—Words of Chairman Wulfstan

"He's holding one of the savages in his family keep?"

"Yes, and he's made no secret of it."

Oleg Gripsholm got up from his chair, threw his hands behind his back, and slowly paced the floor. The expanse of his office gave him plenty of room, and the open beamed ceiling that was twice the height of a man made it seem even larger.

Despite its size, it was an austere place. A massive utilitarian desk, a few chairs, one large rug on the floor and a couple of simple tapestries on the walls. One wall was covered with books, shelved in tiers. Nothing else of note could be seen, other than the familial flame that burned in a niche above his desk.

"What is Vikar's interest in Serkland?" he said, thinking out loud. "I don't see the profit in it, not at this juncture. Eventually, of course, but not now. It seems folly to me."

As much as it appeared foolish on the surface, Oleg knew Vikar Magnusson was no fool. Something was going on, and he had to find out.

He stopped pacing and looked at his executive manager, who waited patiently, along with his mid-managers, to go on to the next item on the agenda.

"Do you think he's scheming to make a secret agreement with the skrael? Maybe mineral rights?"

"It's possible, sir, but from what we know of the skrael, they have no business sense and speak only their savage language. Besides, the chairman's corporation controls all rights to Serkland at the moment. I doubt Jarl Magnusson would violate that without obtaining a legally binding easement."

"We know he's recently met with the chairman. Could they be forming some kind of alliance regarding the territory?"

Oleg looked up. Neither the manager nor any of the mid-managers had a response. He sat back at his desk and stroked his circle beard.

"What else is Trellestar up to?"

The manager looked at his notes.

"The research and development section of his manufacturing division has been working on something they're trying to keep secret. We believe it's a new kind of weapon—some improved firearm."

"Hmmph," grunted Oleg as if uninterested. "What about the negotiations with Bjorco, concerning our green oil project?"

"As you know, when Jarl Ulfberht was killed, negotiations came to a halt. Now we're hearing from the provisional jarl that Bjorco is unwilling to consider such an investment."

"The whole thing smells of Magnusson. He doesn't want any competition to his jor oil production. He'd have us running our factories by candlepower if it meant more profits. We'll have to find financing elsewhere."

The manager cleared and his throat and said, "At our last meeting we discussed pursuing assassination as a possible course of action. Have you given that any further consideration, sir?"

"It's too risky now," said Oleg. "I want to know what Vikar's up to before I commit to such a course."

Though assassination was a time-honored business practice, it carried potential risks that often outweighed the gains. As much as he would have loved to give the go-ahead to eliminate his rival, Oleg knew now wasn't the time. Besides, such attempts were not always successful. It would take only a single blunder to weaken his position on the board.

"Speaking of assassinations, how goes the investigation into the death of Jarl Ulfberht?"

One of the mid-managers spoke up for the first time.

"We're certain the death was an assassination, and we have evidence that points at Trellestar. We should be able to prove a connection by the gathering of the Althing. I can foresee no instance in which the court could justify the death."

"Good, good. I want it on record at least. How many secure votes do we have on the board at this moment?"

"Only a dozen, sir," said the manager. "But Trellestar lacks a majority as well."

Both he and Vikar Magnusson were positioning themselves as contenders to become the next chairman of the board. So far, neither had the advantage. But it would take only one mistake to turn the tide for or against either of them.

"Sir, I wanted to alert you to the mounting difficulties we've been having with our Vanir workers. It seems one fellow went so far as to throw himself into the machinery to protest working conditions."

Oleg slammed a fist on his desk.

"These damn B'serkers. What do they want? Where would they be without the corporations to employ them? The ungrateful mongrels."

"What would you have me do, sir?"

"Do? We do nothing. We give them nothing. They can work or they can starve."

The manager responded to a knock on the door.

"Enter."

A messenger, apparently out of breath, hurried to the manager and whispered in his ear. The manager's expression said the news was notable. He waved off the messenger and approached Oleg's desk.

"Good news, sir. Our geologists report the discovery of a huge iron ore deposit in the northernmost region of the Miming Forest. The initial report estimates a large enough deposit for us to counter Trellestar's stranglehold on the iron supply."

Oleg stood. "That *is* good news. Well, well, Vikar, it seems the scales of Freyr have tipped back in favor of Trondtel." Oleg moved around the table to reinforce his next point. "We must do everything possible to keep this a secret for now. It'll take many weeks to get mining production up to full speed, and we don't want our competitors to be able to prepare for our emergence into the marketplace."

"Yes, sir. Our people are aware of the need for secrecy. However, I will stress the necessity."

"Yes, be sure you see to it."

"Shall I be about that, sir? Or will there be anything else?"

"Yes, one more thing." Oleg motioned to one of the mid-managers. "Have my motorcar brought around." Oleg turned and looked at the familial flame above his desk. The jarl was dressed casually, in a simple old tunic lined with seal fur, and a small ornamental dagger in his belt. The dagger had been in his family for centuries. "How is Glyfe," he asked his manager. "Any word?"

"I checked with the family a few days ago, sir. He's doing well. Everything is fine. You needn't worry about him."

Oleg lost himself in thought for a moment, then said, "Alright, you can go."

He stared through the flames of the ancestral fire. Even the thought of his son left Oleg poisoned with shame. Both shame that he was not a proper father and that his loins were impure. He lived with that ignominy every day, and the

50

fact his darkest secret was more important to conceal than even this new mineral discovery. It was a secret that could destroy him.

11

The fruit of tomorrow lies within the seeds of today.
— Ancient Aesir Proverb

"**...a**nd what of the situation we discussed previously concerning my son Furyk?"

"My man is in place, Jarl Magnusson."

"Good, good," said Vikar, moving around his office as he spoke. "One more item, Captain. Could one of our thunderboats carry enough fuel to reach Serkland?"

"Why, I'm not certain, sir. No one has ever tried. It's possible if extra fuel was stored onboard."

"Has your man Tordan been trained in the use of the thunderboat?"

"He's a skaldor, sir. Their training is comprehensive."

"I want you to equip one of the boats with as much fuel as it can carry, enough food and water for two, and keep it at ready."

"Sir, if you have a special assignment in mind, may I suggest you choose someone other than Tordan. He's a bit of discipline problem. He, occasionally, flaunts the rules."

"And yet you retain him among your housecarles."

"Well, sir, he's good man to have with you in fight, a superb skaldor warrior, a true hero of the Corporate Wars. He's skilled, smart, but..."

"But a troublemaker?"

"Yes, sir."

"I'll keep that in mind. I'll explain the complete details of my plan later. That will be all, Captain. Send in Tordan."

Dressed in his best livery, replete with the Trellestar signet, Tordan waited outside Jarl Magnusson's office, as ordered, while Captain Griffenfeld went in. The only reason he could think of that he'd been called in front of the jarl was his liaisons with Magnusson's daughter had been exposed. He knew such a discovery was inevitable. Despite that, he'd given his passion free rein. Now it was time for the reckoning. He had no idea what his punishment would be. He was somewhat surprised he still had his head, and that Jarl Magnusson wanted to see him.

The affair had been foolishness, no doubt about that. It was risky from the beginning, but deep down he knew the danger was what made it so alluring. Not that he didn't care for Rikissa. She was a nice enough girl, if a might immature. He hoped Jarl Magnusson hadn't been too hard on her.

Tordan stood straight as Captain Griffenfeld came out of Magnusson's office and glared at him. "Jarl Magnusson wants to speak with you, Skaldor. Mind your respect now. Report to me when the jarl is finished with you."

He'd had more than a few run-ins with the captain, and knew he wasn't favored among the housecarles. The man's tone spoke of extra duty shifts, but he doubted he be getting off so lightly.

Thinking he might as well get it over with, Tordan stepped smartly into Jarl Magnusson's office and waited to be noticed.

"Skaldor Tordan," said Jarl Magnusson, walking behind Tordan, looking him over, "Yes, I remember you. Captain Griffenfeld tells me you're somewhat of a troublemaker."

Tordan continued to face forward.

"Don't you know how lucky you are to be a member of this household? Not many Vanir have achieved so lofty a status."

A witty reply came to mind, but Tordan held his tongue.

"We could dismiss you from our service completely, but I've spoken with Captain Griffenfeld, and we've decided to give you a chance to redeem yourself." Magnusson stepped around Tordan and faced him. "I've a special assignment for you, Skaldor. One requiring more brain than brawn. I'm told you're capable in this regard."

Tordan felt a sudden wave of relief. This wasn't about Rikissa. Their encounters hadn't been discovered.

"This is a clandestine assignment. Only myself and Captain Griffenfeld will know of it. You're not to tell anyone. Is that understood?"

"Yes, sir."

"I'm holding one of the skraelings prisoner, and I'm going to imprison you in an adjoining cell. I want you to befriend the savage, bond with him as best you can, and then help him escape and return to Serkland."

"Sir?" Tordan was both relieved and baffled. "How do I bond with a savage? And why?"

"The how is up to you, Skaldor. As for why...we believe the skrael have some secret to long-life and a cure for the blight. Something they eat or drink, something in their environment. Your assignment is to find out what this miracle substance is, and return to me with a sample."

"But, Jarl Magnusson," responded Tordan, trying to see the logic of what he was being asked to do, "if it's a secret, the savages are not likely to reveal it to me, that's if they don't cut out my eyes first."

"The assignment is not without danger," said Magnusson. "Do you refuse it?"

It was plain to Tordan. The jarl was almost daring him to refuse. What then? Was he to be thrown out? A pariah to both Aesir and Vanir?

"No, sir. I'll do my best."

"I'm sure you will," said Magnusson, moving behind and desk and sitting. "You'll be given some maps to study, as well as a quick lesson in the skrael language. Admittedly, we know only a few words, and I would suggest you not reveal any knowledge of these words to your fellow prisoner—at least not at first. It might be...suspicious. A thunderboat will be ready upon your escape—Captain Griffenfeld will tell you its location. You have until tomorrow to familiarize yourself with what we know of Serkland and its people. That's all. You're dismissed."

Tordan left the jarl's office wondering if maybe it would have been better had his affair with Rikissa been discovered. Take a thunderboat across the sea? Was that even possible? The task Jarl Magnusson had given him wasn't only dangerous, but unlikely to succeed as far as he could see. It was a stab in the dark, and he was the one most likely to be left bleeding. However he had little choice but to obey. If there were a cure for the blight, he could bring it home for Marta and all the others who were afflicted.

By Thor's hammer, at least it was an adventure—one likely worthy of an epic ode.

12

Friendship you must pay for isn't worth anything.
—Book of Runes

T he wind was slight but brisk when they removed the miniature hoods and released the tethers. Furyk held out his leather-clad arm and thrust it forward like he might the blade of a sword. His hunting falcon spread its impressive wings and soared upward. Furyk watched the bird fly off over the snow patched hills, and observed as his companion sent his own bird off on the hunt.

"They're fine birds, master Furyk. Very fine."

Furyk smiled at the housecarle—the smile evolving into a smirk.

"There are many fine things for those loyal to the Magnusson Corporation."

He'd selected Hrolf for this hunting trip for several reasons. Furyk thought he had an ambitious look about him—always like a man looking for an opportunity—and though he'd been a Magnusson housecarle for years, Hrolf was no skaldor. Furyk didn't trust a skaldor to do what he needed done. Also, Furyk had made it a point to be friendly with this particular housecarle for several weeks. He'd even been generous. On more than one occasion he'd invited the fellow to share wine, women, and song with him. Now, like the predator he'd just released, he was ready to swoop in for the kill.

Furyk walked to the precipice of the cliff they stood on. Hrolf followed him. Below them they could see almost all of Trondheim, with its majestic citadels and expansive keeps marked by lush, green gardens. Several airships dotted the skies, and he spotted the tower of the Valkyrie, where his mother spent most of her time, and the massive bastion of the Ve where the board of directors met and the Althing court was convened. Looming over Trondheim, in the distance, was Mount Helgafell. The serpentine smoke wafting from its mouth attested to the fire that burned below, the inferno of the gods, ever-threatening to spew its fury.

Further to the south he saw the ocean and the sails of several sea schooners. To the west he could barely make out the town of Oseberg, recognizable only because of the smoky mantle of factory dross that hung over the wretched place like a portentous pall.

"Someday, Hrolf—and that day is coming soon—Trellestar will control all the major industries of the Aesir. It's already the most powerful corporation, thanks to my father." Furyk stroked the hair on his chin and looked into the man's eyes, trying to read him as he spoke. "But I'm the future of that corporation. Someday I may even be chairman."

Hrolf smiled slyly, to show he meant no disrespect, and replied, "But what of your elder brother? Is he not destined to succeed your father?"

"My brother Gudrik has no head for business, nor any inclination towards power," said Furyk, still studying the housecarle. "Besides, he will only succeed my father if he's still alive when the time comes."

"Ah, yes, that's true," said Hrolf, his smile revealing a small mouth crowded with teeth.

"Then we understand each other?"

"Yes, I believe we do."

Furyk turned back to look over the vista. "Good, good. When I'm jarl, I'll need a new storman. Someone whose loyalty and obedience I can trust."

"I've always been loyal to House Magnusson, master Furyk."

Furyk nodded in acknowledgement, and pulled an ivory whistle from the pouch sewed into his forearm glove. The shrill sound it made carried across the hills and canyons that were otherwise silent.

Furyk was content he'd laid the foundation of his scheme. But there was much more to do. Soon there would be no more talk about how smart Gudrik was—how clever he could be when he wanted. He'd show his father his own cunning. By the time he was finished, it wouldn't be just the falcon that responded to his whistle.

His bird approached at incredible speed and Furyk held out his arm. Even though he braced himself, the force of its landing and the grip of its talons reminded him of the falcon's power. He quickly tethered the bird and replaced its hood to calm it.

The other falcon dove from the sky and landed on Hrolf's outstretched arm, a small rabbit clutched in one of its talons.

"Ah, Freyr smiles on me today," said Hrolf. "Yes, it's an excellent bird, master Furyk."

Furyk masked the disappointment of his own bird's empty talons and replied, "Then the bird is yours—a gift from me. A gift from House Magnusson."

"You're most generous, master Furyk."

56

"A trifle compared to the generosity of a chairman, Hrolf, a mere trifle."

Tordan was resolved to carry out Jarl Magnusson's scheme to the best of his ability. He was prepared to face whatever he encountered. It wasn't until the cell door clanged shut and the guard turned the lock that he was having second thoughts.

The skraeling eyed him at first, when the guard gave him an unnecessary shove into the cell, but then ignored his presence.

Tordan had never seen a savage before. The fellow was lean, probably near-starving, with sun-darkened skin and a wiry musculature. He had brown eyes, prominent cheekbones, and though he wasn't as tall as Tordan, his defiant bearing added stature to his frame. His shaggy, straight black hair fell past his shoulders, but he had no facial hair. In fact Tordan was surprised at how little hair grew on the near-naked savage's body. Compared to the skraeling, Tordan would seem a shaggy animal.

It was apparent by the bruises and sores on the fellow's wrists and ankles that he'd been held in chains for some time. Sitting on a pile of straw where he could still see the skraeling through the bars, he continued to study the man without being obvious. Though he was disregarded for the most part, he did catch the occasional glance from his fellow prisoner. After some time, he decided to break the silence.

"So, what's your name? What do they call you?" The savage didn't respond, or even look at Tordan, but he didn't expect the fellow to understand him. "I'm Tordan...Tordan Thordsson." When the skraeling continued to ignore him, Tordan pounded his fist sharply against his chest. "Me, Tordan."

The savage casually glanced his way, but their moment of eye contact was short-lived. The fellow seemed almost contemptuous of Tordan's presence

"Alright. I understand. You don't want to talk. I get it. We'll just sit here and rot together in silence." He got no reaction, but a spark in the fellow's eyes hinted he might comprehend more than he let on. "Mind if I sing? Singing helps me take my mind off my troubles. You don't mind do you? It's too bad I don't have my gittern. I could play you something real pretty. Well, I'll have to make do with a poor skaldor's voice."

Tordan stood and stuck his face through the bars of his cell.

"Ohhhhh
Sail, sail, across the high seas
Pray to the wind, storms do heed

Sail, sail, may Njord be pleased
All you do Wotan sees
Ohhhhh
Fight, fight, for blood and honor
Swing sword and ax, know not fear
Fight, fight, for the pleasure of Tyr
Die to the sound of Wotan's cheer
Ohhhhh
Drink, drink, to victory
Your cup be filled with history
Drink, drink, to patron Bragi
At Wotan's table all is free
Ohhhhh
Love, love, a maiden that's fair
Ruby lips and golden hair
Love, love, is Freyja's lair
Wotan prefers a maid that's bare."

Still no reaction from the savage. He hadn't even glanced at Tordan, who was about to continue his song when he heard someone coming.

"What's all that caterwauling?" called out a familiar voice. "Who dares use the name of Tyr, god of war?"

"Magnir, you son of a walrus. It didn't take you long."

"Where else would you be?" His round face broke out in a smile, then grew serious. "Though I couldn't get a straight answer on why they've locked you up this time. It wouldn't have anything to do with the Lady Rikissa would it?"

Tordan couldn't tell his friend why he was really here, but preferred not to lie, so he just shrugged.

"I told you such intrigue would end badly. You're up to your arse in Hel's brimstone cauldron now." Magnir noticed his fellow prisoner. "What's this?" He studied the savage a moment, stroking the patch of hair on his chin. "One of them horse men, huh? I can't believe they've got you in here next to this savage."

"He's alright. Doesn't say much."

"Still the jester eh, Tordan? I hope you're still laughing when the crows are plucking out your eyes. Speaking of which, I know how little they feed you in here, and I couldn't let a brother skaldor starve." He pulled the sack from over his shoulder and handed it to Tordan through the bars. "Some bread, cheese, and a shank of lamb. Sorry there's no flagon of skyr."

"Thanks, Brother. I was already getting hungry."

"Well, eat while you can. Who knows what Magnusson has planned for you. But it's your mess, so I'll leave you to clean it up."

"Until we raise our tankards again," Tordan called out to his departing friend.

Magnir didn't look back. Tordan didn't expect him to.

He reached into the bag and pulled out a loaf of bread. He took a bite and considered what his fellow skaldors would think when he ran off with the skraeling. They'd think him a traitor or a coward or worse. No one would know he was acting under orders, and if he didn't make it back, they'd probably never know. The Skaldoran Brotherhood was the only place he really belonged. To lose that kinship would be to lose everything.

He looked at the savage, tore off a chunk of the bread and offered it through the bars. The skraeling just sat there, jaw resting on his fist as if in thought, his expression unchanged. The look in his eyes wasn't that of a mindless barbarian, thought Tordan. It was more angry intelligence. And why not? The fellow had been ripped from his people—his family. Taken to a strange place and imprisoned.

Tordan knew what that was like. Now he was supposed to pretend to befriend the man, spy on him and his people, and provide information that would likely lead to their extermination.

13

*There has been much discussion concerning the idea
that the emotions of the subject species are causing
disruptions within our own society. The theory has
been dismissed by the most respected intellects, some
of whom have hypothesized such "stimulants" are
good for society. My own opinion falls to neither camp.
I lack enough data to theorize one way or the other.
I have, though, observed larger numbers of the populace
spending more time absorbing these raw emotions,
which seem to have an endless variety.*

—Osst Personal Journal

Truvor had established what he thought of as his classroom, and was
regularly visited by a handful of elder tribesmen. Sometimes they were
accompanied by children, who were both curious and hoped to get a treat
of some sort. Truvor always tried to oblige. Today only four old men, his prime
students, were in attendance. They were the ones most interested in learning
his language—in sharing their own. They'd proven extremely adept at learning,
and teaching as well. By no means were they the "savages" his own people
thought of them as. In fact, Truvor was somewhat chagrined his students
learned his language quicker than he was able to decipher theirs.

They sat cross-legged on ground before him, refusing chairs the first time
he'd tried to get them to be seated. There was one other "student" today, though
she sat way back, away from the men. Truvor thought he'd seen her once
before, with a group that came to trade. She was a comely woman, attractive in
a way he found few of the native females. He was curious how she'd managed
to arrange her visit to his class. It was his understanding tribal women had too
much work to do, to attend his classes.

He started with what he'd learned in the last session. He pointed at himself
and said, "*Wasichu*." He pointed at his students and said, "*Wichasa*."

Lame Bear, his number-one student, pounded his fist against his chest and
said, "Ikche Wichasa."

Truvor repeated, "*Ik-che Wichasa*."

Lame Bear nodded.

Truvor held up a glass of water, remembering how his students had marveled at the glass the first time he'd shown it to them. He took a drink and said, "*Mini*," forgetting which syllable to stress.

"*Mini*," corrected one of the men.

"*Mini*," replied the doctor.

He handed the glass to the man who'd corrected him. The old man took a sip and said, "Water." He passed the glass and each man in-turn took a drink and pronounced it "water." They'd done this many times before, but Truvor believed repetition was the best teacher.

When the fourth man handed it back to him, Truvor walked to the rear of the tent, approached the woman, and offered her the glass, saying, "*Mini*, water."

She hesitated and one of his students called out something he didn't understand. The woman took the glass, pressed her fingers against it in wonderment, and sipped the water. She handed it back.

"Water," said Truvor, motioning with his hand to get her to repeat it. "Water."

She understood and replied, "Water."

"Very good." He turned to move back to the front of his class.

"*Pilamaya*," she said.

Truvor recalled this meant "thank you very much," but he'd forgotten the proper response. "You are welcome," he replied.

He turned this into another lesson.

"*Pilamaya*, thank you very much."

He motioned and his four students echoed his words. He saw the woman trying as well. He pointed at Lame Bear. "Thank you very much."

Lame Bear replied in-kind.

"You are welcome," said Truvor.

"You are wel-come," responded Lame Bear.

Truvor made it a point to always speak slowly and clearly, and tried to remember to use no contractions that might confuse his students. He was about to move on to his new words for the day, when his lesson was interrupted by a messenger. It seemed Burgrave Andersson wasn't feeling well, and needed the doctor to see to him forthwith. Knowing the burgrave as he did, Truvor was certain it was no more than a case of indigestion. He wasn't about to rush to the man's side. He told the messenger he would see to the

61

burgrave shortly. As he spoke with the man, he saw one of his students move to the back of the tent and begin to harass the woman. He didn't understand what was being said, but it was evident from the gestures he was telling her to leave.

"Blind Dog, please sit," he said to the upset elder tribesman.

The woman had stood, but stubbornly refused to leave.

"What is going on here, Lame Bear? What is wrong?"

"*Witkowin*—crazy woman," he told the doctor. "Boy, son, *wicocuye*, sick. Want *pejuta wichasa*—medicine man, doctor."

"Her son is sick?"

Lame Bear nodded.

Truvor frowned, wrinkles framing his green eyes. "That is not crazy. Not *witkowin*. What is her name?"

Lame Bear thought a moment, translating in his head.

"Walks Apart."

Truvor was certain many natives must need medical assistance, but he couldn't help them all. However, this could be an opportunity to visit one of their villages, learn more about these people. Perhaps he could convince the burgrave—no, no, better he not ask for permission he was unlikely to get. He would simply steal away without asking, without an escort. It could be dangerous, but the blight already eating away at him diluted his fear.

"Tell Walks Apart I will try to help her son. But tell her I have no magic, only science. I cannot promise anything."

Lame Bear translated, and the face of Walks Apart lit up.

"*Pilamaya*," she said, "*pilamaya*."

Her mind was elsewhere as she studied the wrinkles in her face. The longer she looked, the more her thoughts grew detached, dispassionate, as if she declined to acknowledge it was her own face she was examining. She wasn't old, she was certain of that. Therefore no age lines crossed her visage—no crow's feet bedecked her eyes.

As she stared blankly into the mirror, she saw something else. Something that couldn't be there. The very substance of it was unreal—wraithlike. It coalesced as a hairless head and two eyes. It was there, directly in front of her, then it was gone.

Did she only imagine it? Had it really been there? Was it...was it his ghost? She'd been thinking more and more about him lately, thanks to Rikissa's dalliance. She'd even had a dream. Maybe that's all it was—a waking dream. Surely that was more likely than him returning now to haunt her.

Her door opened without any request to enter, so she didn't need to turn to know who it was.

"By the gods, woman, staring into that glass won't make you any younger."

Vikar came up behind her and glanced at his own reflection. Estrid stood and her husband wrapped his arms around her, finding a breast for each hand to hold.

"You're still a beauty, my dear. You still inflame my love for you."

She wasn't certain Vikar was capable of actually loving anything, but she felt his lust rise up and press against her back. She let him fondle her for a moment, then pulled away.

"What woman would not want the great Vikar Magnusson, Jarl of Trellestar," she said, even as she walked away. "What tears you from the bosom of the corporatocracy this fine day?"

Vikar approached her again. "The thought of my lovely wife, alone in her chamber. Is that not enough?" He took her by the shoulders and kissed her. Not a passionate kiss—more of a testing of the waters.

The waters proved to be lukewarm at best.

"Let us not play this game to absurdity, dear husband. You have your servant girls—"

"And you have your Valkyrie orgies," he said brusquely. "That doesn't mean I can't have my wife should I choose."

"Of course not, my dear." Estrid moved to her bed and laid down. "Alright, dear husband," she said with a spurious smile. "I'm ready."

Vikar's stone face didn't crack, but his eyes flashed with anger. He started to speak, but a knock on the door disrupted the moment.

"Enter."

One of his bodyguards entered and said something so softly Estrid couldn't hear.

"Yes, permit it," responded Vikar.

The housecarle exited, closing the door behind him.

Estrid's curiosity got the better of her.

"Permit what?"

"It seems our daughter wants to visit her lover in his prison."

"And you're letting her? The scandal..."

"There'll be no scandal, woman. I believe her visit might be a convincing little scene for our resident savage."

"What are you talking about?"

"I want the Serklander to be convinced Rikissa's favored housecarle is indeed a prisoner. I've ordered this Tordan fellow to befriend the savage and help him escape back to Serkland."

Estrid was astounded. "Whatever for?"

"Because, my dear, my scientists tell me the savages have something that not only combats the blight, but keeps them young, extends their life."

Estrid's eyes widened.

"Yes, I thought that might get your attention. Tordan has been ordered to discover this secret and return to me with the answer."

Estrid's enthusiasm waned as she considered the housecarle's prospects.

"The savages will likely kill him out of hand."

Vikar shrugged. "That's entirely possible. If so, I'm sure our daughter will mourn for a day or so, and then forget the man. But I'm not entrusting the entire enterprise to this skaldor. I'm also sending a team of biochemists, pharmacologists, and other specialists separately. One way or another, I intend to make the secret mine, and take control of what will become the market's most valuable commodity."

14

Every man has some friend, even among his enemies.
—Lakhota Saying

He'd only been in the detention cell beneath House Magnusson for a day, but Tordan was more certain than ever the skrael was no ignorant savage. It didn't matter the man still made no attempt to communicate. He could see the intelligence in his fellow prisoner's eyes. He watched, he listened—Tordan knew he was just waiting for the right moment to make his move. Tordan was supposed to provide that moment. He wouldn't be surprised if the wild man understood every word he heard.

The fellow was proud, willful, but he wasn't stupid. The bread and part of the lamb shank Tordan had given him sat untouched until Tordan had fallen asleep. When he woke this morning the bread was gone and the bone was picked clean. He was hungry alright.

Tordan heard someone coming down the corridor. Would this be his opportunity to escape?

"Tordan?"

It was Rikissa. *By the beard of Brage, what was she doing here?*

"Tordan, where are you?"

"Here, milady."

He rose to greet her, taking hold of his prison bars.

"Oh, Tordan, what have they done to you? This is my fault."

She kissed his hand, placed hers over it, and cried.

She thinks I'm here because of our affair, thought Tordan. But I can't tell her why her father put me here. The savage is listening.

"It's not anyone's fault, milady. It's Wotan's will."

Rikissa glanced at the skrael in the next cell, but only had eyes for Tordan.

"Mother and Father know, and it *is* my fault. I knew this would happen when they found out about us. I knew you'd be in danger."

So Jarl Magnusson knew about the affair. Tordan thought he must. This precarious assignment he'd been given was just another way of separating him from his head. Magnusson didn't really expect him to succeed.

"Come now, dear Rikissa, we both knew our romance could never go anywhere. True, once it began to flourish we were caught up in its fervor, but neither of us were blind to our prospects."

"But I love you, Tordan."

"And I you, but you're young. You will love others before your time comes to an end."

"I won't," she said with childlike stubbornness.

The truth was, Tordan didn't really love her—not truly. He knew his encounters with her were, in part, a snub at Aesir nobility. He'd grown to like the girl, to enjoy their trysts, but he knew the jarl would marry her off someday.

"My parents also discovered I'm with child—your child. They're going to make me abort it and have arranged a marriage. And you..." She wept so hard she couldn't go on.

A child? He hadn't anticipated that, fool that he'd been. Now the child, *his* child, would be aborted, and there was nothing he could do about it. The thought nagged at him, evoking his ire as well as his guilt.

Tordan reached through the bars and rested his large hands on her shoulders. "I want you to forget me, Rikissa. I want you to forget me and learn to love your husband-to-be."

"I can't," she said between her tears. "I won't."

"Yes you will, in time. Better for you that time was now."

She looked through teary eyes at him, wanting to say something, but standing mute.

"I want you to do something for me. I want you to take my niece, Kristina, daughter of Jorvik Thordsson, into your household, if her parents will allow. Give her comfortable employ. Watch out for her as I would. Promise me you will."

"I will, Tordan. I promise. I'll treat her as my own."

The woman had the look of most *wasichu* females he'd seen. Hair the color of straw, piled on top of her head somehow. Decorative ornaments around her arms and neck. Clothing that covered almost her entire body and trailed on the ground behind her. He wondered how the *wasichu* men found their way in.

She was very young, and crying, he surmised, because her man had been imprisoned. He wondered what his fellow prisoner's crime had been, to be caged here like an animal. This *wasichu* had the bearing and scars of a warrior. Perhaps he was an enemy from another clan who'd been captured in battle. But if so, how came his woman to this place? Why did his clothing bear the same wolf symbol as those who guarded him? Was he an outcast of the wolf clan?

When the woman, still crying, was finally escorted away by the guard, he decided to take a chance.

"Your woman?"

The *wasichu* did not hide his surprise. "Well, you *can* talk."

"Your woman?" he repeated, trying to get the *wasichu* to speak so he could learn even more.

"Not anymore."

"Why you here?" He found trying to speak the *wasichu* language much more difficult than listening and understanding it.

The *wasichu* sat with his back against the wall, facing him.

"Her father does not approve of my interest in his daughter. He's a powerful man whom one does not trifle with."

"I understand. Father chooses another."

"You probably have the same thing where you come from."

"No, not same. My people not put man in cage."

"Well I guess your people are more enlightened."

The *wasichu's* tone of voice was different than others he'd heard. There was an air of jest about it. As if the man were *heyoka* instead of warrior.

"They call me Tordan. What's your name?"

He wasn't about to reveal the power of his true name to this *wasichu* while being held prisoner.

"Santee," he said, placing his fist against his chest.

"Santee? Does that mean something in your language?"

"*Santee* is..." He hesitated, thinking of the proper *wasichu* word. "...knife."

"It's a good name," said Tordan. "I'm familiar with the ways of the blade myself."

"What is 'abort'?"

"What?"

The man was surprised by his question.

"Your woman say child would abort. What is abort?"

The *wasichu's* face darkened like an approaching storm. His jutting jaw hardened and his blue eyes narrowed. The question clearly made him uncomfortable. He took quiet pleasure from the man's discomfort. It was the first time since his capture he'd been able to strike back at his captors in any way, though he didn't understand what it was he'd said.

"It means they're not going to let the child be born. They will kill it in the womb long before it takes its first breath."

He cringed at the thought. It sickened him. *What savages! To prevent the birth of a child? To take its life while it was still inside of its mother?* These *wasichu* were more than brutal foes. They were evil.

He must escape. He must return to his people to warn them, tell them what kind of enemy they faced.

15

Man does not weave this web of life. He is merely
a strand of it. Whatever he does to the web, he
does to himself.
        —Wisdom of Fire In His Eyes

Truvor kept wanting to stop and look as he walked through the village, but Walks Apart and Lame Bear urged him on. Though primitive by the standards of the Aesir, he was fascinated by the way these people lived. He already knew they were a nomadic folk, who moved with the seasons, often following the great herds of *tatanka*. Their homes were nothing more than cone-shaped tents made, he guessed, from the skins of the *tatanka*. He estimated the wooden poles that met and crossed at the top of the tents must be about 14 feet high with a diameter at the base almost the same size. Each of these was painted with a variety of colorful depictions, and, oddly enough, he noticed each entry flap faced in the same direction. He wondered if the reason for it was spiritual or meteorological.

He'd already learned his students were from the Lakhota clan, which Lame Bear had proclaimed the largest of the clans. The people themselves, like his students, were similar in appearance—at least to him. Each had straight black hair, brown eyes, sun-darkened skin, and pronounced cheekbones.

The women wore two-piece dresses, as did Walks Apart. Their hair was often adorned with feathers, seashells, and even bones. Young girls wore their hair in braids.

Though it was only spring, most of the men wore little more than breechclouts, some with short buckskin leggings. Unlike the Aesir, they had little body hair, though many were resplendent with body piercings and tattoos. A few sported quilled armlets. Some went barefoot, but most wore a variety of heelless shoe made of stitched animal hide.

He saw two women had stretched out an animal skin tightly between an array of wooden pegs. They were scraping the remnants of meat and fat from the hide with a flat bone. The skin looked much like the hides that served as the coverings for their tents. Truvor was shocked to see another woman nursing a boy who must have been three or four years old—long past the age when Aesir children were weaned.

Walks Apart finally stopped at one of these tents, but her way inside was blocked by an elderly fellow dressed in full ceremonial regalia. The man was a medley of feathers, bones, and rawhide strips. Unlike the other men Truvor had seen, he was clothed from the neck down, and his attire was splashed with black, white, red, and yellow designs. A circle was painted on his shirt, using all four colors. He held a gourd rattle in his hand and was uttering some kind of prayer....or curse.

"Wakan Tanka unsimala ye. Kuje kin le asniwayin kte. Pejuta kin le wak'u kte. Ho hece omakiya yo."

"Pejuta wichasa," Lame Bear told him, "medicine man."

Truvor had already guessed, by the fellow's outfit, this was the local shaman or some other fellow of high standing. It was obvious he was none too happy with Truvor's arrival. The exchange between Walks Apart and the shaman quickly grew heated. They spoke much too rapidly for Truvor to make sense of anything. He noticed Lame Bear said nothing, and seemed content he wasn't part of the conversation.

Finally the old shaman stepped aside, folding his arms across his chest. Walks Apart motioned for Truvor to follow her inside the tent. He complied, noticing the indignant look the tribal medicine man gave him as he passed.

Inside, lying under a blanket Truvor recognized as one he'd traded to the horse men, was a young boy of about seven years. He was conscious but feverish, and obviously having trouble breathing. Truvor bent to his side and checked his pulse. He recognized the symptoms right away. It was likely a mutant strain of a common virus, known as pig's bane because it usually originated with pig farmers.

Because it was common among his own people, he had the proper medication with him. He reached into his bag, filled a hypodermic, and swabbed a spot on the boy's arm. As he was about to inject the boy, Walks Apart grabbed his arm, looking alarmed. Truvor placed his hand on hers and patted it, trying to reassure her.

"It's alright. I'm going to help him. This should cure him. *Pejuta.*"

Lame Bear said something else to her, and repeated the word for medicine. Walks Apart was unsure. She studied Truvor's eyes, as if trying to determine his intentions. Then she let go and he proceeded with the injection.

"He should eat," said Truvor, making a spooning motioning to his own lips and then pointing at the boy. "Maybe some soup." He continued the spooning motioning and made a slurping sound. Lame Bear and Walks Apart stared at him, not understanding at first. "You know, hot water with..." He didn't know the word for soup. The best he could come up with were the words for fire water. "*Peta mini.*" He thought quickly and added, "*Tatanka peta mini.*"

Lame Bear and Walks Apart looked perplexed again, then Lame Bear said, "*Wojapi, tatanka wojapi.*"

Walks Apart nodded and hurried out of the tent.

Lame Bear looked down at the boy. "He run again?"

"He should be fine in a few days," replied Truvor. "Yes, he will run again. He looks worse than he really is. His is a common ailment. My people recover from it all the time."

Lame Bear grunted. Truvor had heard him make that sound before. It wasn't a happy sound.

"Before *wasichu* come, people no *wicocuye*—no sick much. Now many sick, many die. *Wicocuye* everywhere."

"You think the *wasichu* bring sickness to the *wichasa*?"

Lame Bear nodded and looked back at the boy.

An overwhelming sense of chagrin flooded Truvor. It was possible Lame Bear was right. He'd never even considered the likelihood. Viruses his own people had developed tolerances to, could prove to be a deadly plague among these natives. Their immune systems might well be defenseless against them. He hadn't seen any pigs in the village. It was possible they had none. If so, the virus had almost certainly come from the colonists.

He glanced at Lame Bear, but couldn't look him in the eye. Truvor had been so concerned, so outraged by the militaristic tactics of men like Storman Ragnarsson, he hadn't thought he himself might be a carrier of an even more fatal invasion.

Vikar knew he'd be spending most of the day at his desk. There were mining reports to read, financial figures to double-check, and documents to sign. Much of the work he should have assigned to his executive manager, Sitric, or one of his managerial assistants, but there wasn't a single one he trusted entirely. There were certain aspects of the corporation he wasn't comfortable delegating. They required his attention—his personal touch.

He wished he could delegate some of it to his sons. He wanted to be able to discuss his long-range plans with them—either of them. But Furyk was headstrong and not too bright. As the younger son, it wasn't really his duty to take over the corporation, but Vikar knew how that could change in the wink of Wotan's eye.

Gudrik, on the other hand, was not only his eldest, but the smarter of the two. He'd be the perfect partner except he was a fop, a beardless, ambitionless waste of a man. He didn't have the stomach to make the hard decisions that must be made. At least Furyk was tough, ruthless almost to a fault.

The fact was, he didn't completely trust either of them. Not that trust was something he easily bestowed on anyone.

A knock on his door diverted his thoughts.

"Yes?"

Sitric entered.

"Dr. Thorgrim is here to see you, Jarl Magnusson."

"Send him in."

Dr. Thorgrim, wearing his usual white lab coat, entered, along with one of his fellow researchers.

"I have the results of the familial blood tests, Jarl Magnusson."

"Doctor," said Vikar, looking at the other man, "I told you I wanted those test results kept private."

"Jarl Magnusson, I have every confidence in—"

"Please wait outside," interrupted Vikar.

The other doctor glanced at Thorgrim who nodded.

When he was gone, Thorgrim said, "That was unnecessary, sir. All of my doctors are sworn to protect the privacy of—"

"Enough!" demanded Vikar, cutting him off again. "Tell me what you've found."

Dr. Thorgrim composed himself and replied, "We've found absolutely no abnormalities among your offspring, Jarl Magnusson. However, each of them does carry the same gene as yourself—which is to be expected. However, while there is a genetic disposition to the blight, there are no signs of the disease in any of your children, nor in yourself."

"This gene," asked Vikar, "could it be due to my great grandmother's Vanir blood?"

"Vanir?"

Thorgrim was taken aback by this disclosure, and Vikar realized he hadn't meant to reveal that fact. It was a slip of the tongue. Thorgrim realized it as well, and continued in a professional tone as if he'd heard nothing.

"Sir, it has never been proven the Vanir are genetically more predisposed to get the blight than the Aesir. That's what we call a myth of supposition."

"No? Isn't it true far more Vanir are stricken with the blight than Aesir?"

"That's true, sir, but there is no scientific evidence discovered as yet that the cause lies within their genetic makeup."

"What you're saying is that you don't know why. It seems to me, Doctor, you and your staff need to work harder to uncover the answer."

Thorgrim understood the implication. "Yes, Jarl Magnusson."

Impatiently Furyk paced the halls of the familial crypt—what he called the chamber that housed the tapestries of the family trees. Above him the familial flame flickered this way and that, as if his own unrest created a draft upon the flame, and left the shadows dancing and darting about him.

He'd sent away his personal bodyguards, certain they were spies for his father. He didn't want anyone to know what he was about to do, even his mother. Though he was determined to keep it a secret, he thought his father would approve of his motives. After all, it was a matter of business. He wasn't only about to strengthen his personal ties, but those of House Magnusson as well.

"Master Furyk?" His bodyguards reappeared, followed by three other men. "Edvard Halfdansson has arrived."

Furyk masked his impatience with a smile and moved quickly to greet his guest.

"Edvard, I'm pleased you accepted my invitation." He made a dismissive gesture. "You men may wait outside."

Edvard nodded to his own bodyguards, and the four housecarles left together.

"I was happy to accept your invitation, Furyk, though surprised by it. Your message was so esoteric, it...well it intrigued me."

Furyk didn't know what "esoteric" meant, but he stroked the hair on his chin thoughtfully.

"Yes, well, I wanted to keep this meeting, or at least the reason for it, a secret. As much as one can keep a secret these days."

They both laughed, exchanging knowing glances.

"I thought, since you're betrothed to my sister and we are about to become family, you might honor me by partaking in the fostbrooir."

Furyk took pleasure in the look of astonishment that paled Edvard's face.

"The blood-brotherhood?" muttered Edvard as if it were the one possibility he'd never considered. "Why...why it's you who honor me, Furyk. I...I accept."

Furyk knew the chairman's son could do nothing else. To refuse would have been a great insult. Joining in the fostbrooir ceremony would give him an unbreakable bond with a potentially powerful ally. That potential to be realized the day Chairman Tryguasson drew his last breath.

"I'm honored by your acceptance. In anticipation of your willingness, I've invited you here, beneath the light of my familial flame, and have had a basin of Trondheim's richest loam brought hence."

Furyk pulled out his silver dagger and watched for Edvard's reaction. As he expected, the weakling cringed at the sight and almost took a step back.

"Join me," said Furyk, stepping to the soil-filled bowl.

Hesitantly, Edvard moved next to him.

"Wotan, I beseech you to bear witness to my oath." Furyk drew the dagger across his left palm. Blood pooled in his hand like a rose in bloom. He turned his hand over so the blood dripped into the soil. "I swear to avenge any wrong done to my sworn brother, Edvard Halfdansson. Let no man nor god come between this bond."

He handed the dagger to Edvard, whose reluctance and uncertainly was obvious. At this point, however, he had no choice. He drew the blade across his own palm, wincing as he did.

"Wotan, I beseech you to bear witness to my oath. I swear to avenge any wrong done to my sworn brother, Furyk Vikarsson. Let no man nor god come between this bond."

Edvard held his hand out and let his blood mingle in the dirt with Furyk's.

Furyk wasted no time sealing the bond. He grasped Edvard's wounded hand in his own and gripped it with all of his strength. It was his way of letting the fellow know who was the dominate member of this blood-brotherhood.

He released his hold and offered Edvard a scarf to squelch the flow of blood.

"Come, Brother," declared Furyk jovially, "let us celebrate."

16

The poor live on hope, the rich live on fear.
—Declaration of the Modi

Sedition, Jorvik was discovering, was hard work. The rants had waged back and forth, becoming louder and less coherent. Nothing was being accomplished. He tried to separate his thoughts from the chaos. He ran the fingers of both hands through his close-cropped hair, closed his pale blue eyes, and rested his head in his hands. When the squabble reached a momentary lull, he spoke up—shouting to be certain he was heard.

"Brothers, arguing amongst ourselves is doing no good. We all agree the Modi must take the next step toward freedom, but what is that next step? All out rebellion? Shall we wage war against all the Aesir? What would the outcome of such a conflict be?"

"We'd pulverize 'em!" called out Gunnar, who proudly supported just such action. Shouts of agreement sounded.

"Maybe," continued Jorvik, "but at what cost? You know me, Brothers. I'm not afraid to die. But how many of our families would be left fatherless if we were to attack now? The Aesir are not all weak. They have a trained military force, they have weapons. I would not vote for such action now—not yet. We're not ready. We don't have enough support. The time will come, I'm certain. But until then, I say we refuse to work. There is much support for such action. I say we mobilize the factory workers, the farmers, the fishing fleets, and we all lay down our tools until our demands are met."

"You think the Aesir will bow to our demands because of a strike?"

"No, Gunnar, no I don't. In fact I think there will be violence and bloodshed, and they will not give us so much as a mug of skyr. But when the Aesir use force against the workers, more Vanir will rally to the cause of the Modi, and we will become stronger."

A healthy murmur of ascent spread among the 30 or so members who'd gathered. A few shouted, "Strike, strike, strike..." Soon the entire room was united in chorus. "Strike, strike, strike, strike..."

Estrid watched as Gudrik's playmate tied his left wrist to the bedpost. She had secret surveillance points in each of her children's chambers. It was necessary precaution in order for her to perform all her maternal duties. That she hadn't discovered Rikissa's dalliance with the skaldor only made her more vigilant now.

The fellow inside the chamber with her son took his time, glancing back at Gudrik, enjoying the look of delicious anticipation on his face.

"Is that too tight?"

"Tighter," ordered Gudrik.

He pulled the bonds even tighter, then positioned himself to do the other wrist.

Estrid slipped from her covert spot and made her way to the chamber's front door. She knocked. There was no reply. She knocked again.

"Gudrik, it's your mother. Open the door."

"Mother," she heard Gudrik hiss. "Quickly, untie me."

Fumbling sounds of panic came from inside the room.

"Faster, slut, if you want to keep your head." That was Gudrik's voice again.

"Get out, through the servant's door, go."

Estrid became impatient.

"Gudrik!"

"Coming, Mother."

Gudrik unbarred the door and opened it. Estrid stood there, hands impatiently slapped to her hips.

"Why was your door barred, Gudrik?"

Gudrik yawned and turned back into his room. "For privacy, Mother, why else?"

Estrid tramped in, pretending to search the room as she did.

"You've interrupted my nap, Mother. What is it you want?"

"I want to talk to you. It's time you lived up to your responsibilities to House Magnusson."

Gudrik ran his hands down his cheeks and rested them on his smooth, hairless chin.

"Responsibilities?" He sighed. "What is it you'd have me do, Mother?"

"I'd have you act like a man for one," she berated. "Make your father happy and grow some hair on your face."

Gudrik only smiled that amused smile his expression so often took.

"But that's not why I'm here." Estrid turned and her tone softened. "I think it would be an excellent idea for you to take a wife and sire some grandchildren for me."

"*Really*, Mother," replied Gudrik as if affronted by the distaste of such a suggestion. "I would have thought you found the idea of becoming a grandmother repugnant."

"What I think, and what you want, is unimportant. You're the eldest. It's time. Were you to consummate a politically-wise, business-wise marriage, it would greatly please your father. Your standing with him would soar to new heights."

"Yes, I'm sure it would," responded Gudrik, stroking his long hair. Like his mother's, it had been bleached an even lighter blond than its normal color. "Who would you suggest become my betrothed?"

"I have a couple of young ladies in mind. I'll make inquiries."

Estrid knew Gudrik was smart enough to know she was right. If he married, and it didn't really matter who was chosen, his father would cease troubling him about that and other matters.

"Alright, Mother, make your inquiries."

Rikissa had been summoned to the Hall of the Valkyries early in the morning, and she knew why. Today was the day they would take her child from her—her perfectly healthy child, as far as she knew—Tordan's child. The thought was too much to bear. So as the Valkyrie midwives disrobed her, put her on a table and covered her with a sheet, she shut her eyes and closed off her mind. Instead she thought of Tordan, of his teasing eyes and dimpled chin, of what it had been like in his arms. She thought of the pleasure that had led her down an errant path to this pain.

She did not regret what she'd done. Though others would laugh at her childish naivety, it had been done for love. Her love of Tordan was real—she knew that. The loss of this child would not wean her of that. What worried at her, what gnawed at her soul, was what would become of him, imprisoned by her father. What would his fate be?

What of her own fate? To be married to Edvard Halfdansson? She guessed it could have been worse. At least he wasn't some ugly old burgemeester. He was young and not unhandsome, though hardly the man Tordan was. What would she feel when he touched her? Would it be pleasure, or would it simply inflame her memories of Tordan?

"We're done," said one of the midwives. "You can get dressed now."

Done? It was over already?

Rikissa looked around. Her mother was nowhere to be seen.

"Can you tell me...what was it?"

"It was a boy."

17

In calm waters every ship has a good captain.
—Book of Runes

Vikar strode down the passageway with his entourage in tow. The usually quiet, empty corridors of the Ve were crowded this late spring morning with chief executives, ambitious thanes, earnest bankers, minor functionaries, bodyguards, administrators, secretaries, assistants, political strategists, financiers, and jarls of major and minor corporations alike. He did his best to ignore the rabble, though protocol required he acknowledge his fellow jarls with at least a nod.

He made his way inside the enormous gathering hall, under the towering ebony legs of Wotan. The obsidian colossus of their chief god stood at one end of the great hall, while a similar figure of Thor stood sentry over the other. The imposing sculptures were there to remind all men they were only mortal, and that the gods were watching their actions. Vikar didn't have much use for gods, but he understood their place in the corporatocracy.

Great tapestries adorned the walls of the colossal chamber, each telling the story of a particular family, a bit of cultural history, or an honored myth. They depicted battles of sword and axe, the quests of long ships, and the conflicts of gods. The image of Thor held sway in more than one portrayal, as did one-eyed Wotan. There was a scene of Valkyries carrying slain warriors to Valholl, and another recounting the legend of the Volkerwandering, rendered as a titanic ship, a great longboat, sailing off the edge of the world, through the sky and beyond as it passed into a galaxy of stars.

Between these magnificent tapestries were ornate recesses where torches burned, and below each torch was a corporate signet. Beneath the alcoves were the designating seating areas for each corporation's representatives. Even the 23 minor corporations were represented by their familial flames and corporate icons.

The largest, grandest embroidery of all adorned the wall above the dais reserved for the chairman of the board. It featured the tree of life, Yssdrigril, whose roots intertwined up and around the borders of the tapestry, creating a frame of sorts. Within the branches of Yssdrigril were the nine worlds, representing the nine major corporations. It was commonly referred to within these walls as "the Tree of Commerce."

By the time Vikar reached the Trellestar domain, the Ve had filled almost to capacity. The low rumble of voices had grown to a din that threatened to deafen those in attendance. Vikar, however, held his own counsel, engaging no one in conversation. He and his retinue took their seats in orderly silence.

The gathering of the Board of Directors was traditionally an exhibition of pomp and extravagance. Only men were allowed in the great hall, and each wore his finest seal fur-lined cloak, his most ostentatious silver arm rings and headband, and his most-prized heirloom dagger. Firearms were forbidden anywhere in the neutral territory of the VE, as they traditionally were within household domains—though rumors had spread of houses that violated this convention. Even the housecarles with their swords and other weaponry were not allowed within the meeting chamber. It had been that way long before the Corporate Wars, and was neutral ground even during the conflict. Each jarl commanded his bodyguards to remain outside with the motorcar drivers, where they were known to engage in games of chance and other more physical contests, mostly of the good-natured sort.

A herald circulated through the outer corridors announcing the imminent beginning of the proceedings, and warning the door to the great chamber was about to be sealed. The language he used was ceremonial in nature, a phrasing of tradition that never varied. Hearing his call, the last of the executives scurried into the hall. Vikar made note of both his allies and his rivals, seeing that all were in attendance. There would likely be no surprises on this day—except maybe one he and the chairman had in store.

With the resounding slam of the door, the clamor of voices dwindled. When the chairman of the board stood and began pounding his staff against the dais on which he stood, all the voices silenced.

"I, Halfdan Tryguasson, Chairman of the Board of Trondheim and all it holdings, call this meeting of the Board of Directors to order. Is there any challenge to my authority to do so?" Not even a clearing of the throat could be heard within the chamber. "Having heard no objections, I authorize a commencement of the proceedings."

"Jarl Atterdag of Vikenex, if it please the board."

A lean, elderly man with a tiny chin beard and a pencil-thin mustache stood. Vikar counted Atterdag among his allies.

"I wish to broach an issue that affects us all. Because it does, I feel we must all be in concordance in deciding how to deal with our Vanir workers."

Another man stood. He was a rotund fellow, whose bulk clashed with his corporate symbol—a swooping falcon.

"Jarl Volsung of Sveabordcorp. What is there to decide? An iron fist is always best when dealing with the Vanir."

"And what of the violence that will likely ensue when we move to quell the rumored strikes?" The Vikenex CEO asked of the room in general. "Where on our ledgers do we account for the associated costs?"

"Jarl Gripsholm of Trondtel, may it please the board."

Oleg Gripsholm had been a member of the board of directors longer than even the current chairman. Like Vikar, he was known to covet the chairmanship. But neither of them had enough backing—at least not yet.

"Jarl Atterdag is right. The problems associated with the Vanir are becoming more costly. It seems, among many other demands, they believe they are entitled to free medical care. However, I agree with Jarl Volsung. We cannot capitulate to even the most inconsequential demand. To do so would be to open the floodgates of dissension and economic upheaval."

Fists hammered seating platforms in the traditional manner of assent. It was clear most everyone present agreed with Gripsholm's view on the matter.

"Though keep in mind this scintilla of wisdom I gleamed from my own father," continued Gripsholm. "Volatility results only when a leader emerges to convince the worker there is hope for freedom from bondage. An iron fist slammed at the wrong target can do more harm than good. We simply must control the leaders, coerce them, crush them if we must, but never allow such hope to fester."

Another boisterous round of assent echoed through the chamber, signaling an end to any further discussion of the topic.

"Jarl Eriksson of Vineland Enterprises. If it please the board and the chairman, I would like to call for a referendum."

Eriksson was admired by many in the room for his forthrightness, but Vikar thought the man's naivety was the reason his company never advanced to major corporation status.

"I propose the territories of Serkland be opened to widespread exploration and all other ventures, to include mineral excavation and agriculture. For too long the economic possibilities of the territories have been restricted. I say it's time to open up this new land to free enterprise."

Jarl Volsung stood again. "I second the motion for a referendum with the

81

addendum we begin the eradication of the savages who inhabit the territories. Their belligerence will only impede any investments we choose to make."

This was the last thing Vikar wanted. Not now, not yet. He hadn't planned to speak at all. But now he must. He stood directly beneath the wolf/moon corporate signet of Trellestar.

"Jarl Magnusson of Trellestar. If it please the board, I would speak against such a referendum at this time." Vikar's gaze swept the room, his blue-green eyes issuing a silent challenge. "It's true there will come a time when we must open the Serkland territories to all enterprises. But this is not that time. Chairman Tryguasson's own foray into those faraway lands proves we need more time to study both the savages and the territory's potential. A single misstep at this juncture could lead to expenditures we could never imagine. These ongoing studies will not only inform us as to the potential wealth of Serkland's natural resources, but as to the disposition and strength of the savages. I'm sure you'll all agree when the time comes to exterminate them, we want to minimize the cost."

A murmur of assent spread through at least a small majority of the those gathered.

Gripsholm stood. "I'm surprised at your passivity on this matter, Jarl Magnusson. I would have thought a CEO of your pugnacious reputation would vote for immediate eradication." This elicited a few chuckles from the gathering. "This hesitancy on your part wouldn't have anything to do with the savage you hold in your dungeon would it? You're not negotiating a secret exclusive mineral rights deal with the horse men are you?"

The intimation was insulting, but in such a sly, subtle way as to prevent Vikar from returning the insult in-kind.

"I would consider such a covenant, Jarl Gripsholm, except for the fact the skrael not only have no legal rights, resources, or assets as recognized by this board, but that they have no concept of money."

This provoked a raucous range of laughter throughout the hall, deflating Gripsholm's modest witticism.

"I must agree with Jarl Magnusson's general assertion," said Chairman Tryguasson. "The reports from my agricultural colony confirm we haven't enough information as yet. I have, however, at my own expense, sent several teams of researchers and surveyors to gather more information. I'll share that information when it becomes available. So, at this time, I decline the request for a referendum. Is there a dissent to call the matter to a vote?"

Several jarls spoke with their advisors, looked at each other, but no one stood to dissent. It was obvious they didn't have the votes to overcome the ruling of the chairman.

"A call for a referendum." It was Jarl Volsung again. "If it please the board, I would like to re-open the subject of price controls."

A smattering of boos greeted this.

Volsung held up his hands in a vain attempt to silence his critics.

"We all know Trellestar controls a virtual monopoly on both iron and oil, and continually raises its prices. Sveabordcorp is not the only company whose profit margin has been thinned to near extinction by this. There must be limits."

The ensuing discussions and catcalls created a roar as loud as anything Vikar had ever heard within the chamber. It was a contentious issue, but one that cropped up every now and again when some corporation or another was in the midst of financial instability. He would say nothing on the issue, as he always did. Let his allies speak for him.

However, it wasn't one of his corporate allies, but his rival for power, Oleg Gripsholm, who stood, waiting for the clamor to die down.

"It's true. Often it's a bitter fruit to taste when certain resources are priced beyond our means. But, by Wotan's missing eye, telling someone how much they can charge for their goods or services would be the death knell of the corporatocracy."

This was greeted by more fist slamming and shouts of agreement. Vikar was puzzled. Why was Gripsholm supporting his control over the price of iron? What did he know that Vikar didn't? It was a matter to be investigated.

"While I have the floor, if it pleases the board and the chairman, I regrettably must call for an Althing court to sit in judgment over the matter of Jarl Ulfberht's death. Trondtel is in possession of evidence the death of our fellow CEO was an incident of assassination—evidence it must now, by law, turn over to the board of directors. Trondtel further requests that, should the evidence be sustained, all customary fines be levied, and appropriated reparations be made to the family of Jarl Ulfberht."

Vikar had expected this, but had already set aside the funds necessary to pay any remuneration the Althing required.

"I hereby decree the Althing will be convened at a date to be determined, and that all customary penalties and compensation be made should the death be found unjustified," said the chairman. "Thank you for upholding your duty, Jarl Gripsholm.

"Is there any other business to be brought before this board? If not, I have one declaration of a personal note to make. I would like to announce the betrothal of my son, Edvard, to Rikissa, daughter of Jarl Magnusson. May their union be a profitable one."

The announcement set off another murmur through the delegates, and a look of consternation, Vikar noticed, on the face of Gripsholm. Apparently he hadn't expected such a union—though he should have.

"I, Halfdan Tryguasson, Chairman of the Board of Trondheim and all it holdings, now call this meeting of the Board of Directors to a close. Is there a challenge?"

Hearing no challenge, Chairman Tryguasson rapped his staff three times against the dais. Isolated pockets of conversation commenced as the crowd of representatives dispersed.

There would be much more business conducted on this day, but the formal meeting had come to an end. As always, Vikar set about engaging his allies and those whose alliances were tenuous, in order to strengthen his position and allay concerns that might affect his own plans. It was the politics of good business.

18

Freedom begins with sacrifice — wisdom begins with compromise.

—**Declaration of the Modi**

Kristina was in the room she shared with her brother, listening to her parents. It wasn't hard to hear every word. They were arguing, as they often did. Only this time it was about her.

"Is it an invitation or a summons?" snarled her father.

"I don't know," responded her mother calmly. "It simply says the Lady Rikissa of house Magnusson presents a notice of service for Kristina Thordsson, and that an escort will be sent on the morrow to see her safely to Trondheim."

"This is Tordan's doing."

"Yes, it is. But with my blessing. Jorvik, I think this is the best choice for Kristina now. I ask you to open your judgment to it. Open your heart for your daughter."

She heard nothing but silence for a moment. Kristina held her breath, waiting for a clear declaration of her fate. The anticipation was almost too much for her. She wanted to speak up and say the decision should be hers. But her father would never allow that. Besides, she was still unsure what she wanted.

"If you don't agree to this," said her mother, "then resign yourself to sending her off to work in a factory, or choose a husband for her and have her resent your choice for the rest of her life."

"I know what choices we have, Wife. I simply can't abide by any of them. To send our daughter to live with the Aesir, to work for a jarl? It's unthinkable. Though you're right about the alternatives."

"Kristina," called her mother. "Kristina."

She opened the door and made her way to the front of the house.

"You were listening?"

"Yes, Mother."

"You know what must be decided then. What do you want, Kristina?"

She looked first at her mother, then her father. He turned from her gaze, as if too shamed to look her in the eye.

85

"I don't want to leave you both," said Kristina. "I don't want to leave my home, but...I don't want to marry. I *won't* marry anyone not of my choosing. I could stay, work in a factory. You did before I was born, Mother."

"It's hard, often dangerous work, Kristina. You see what it does to your father."

Jorvik still wouldn't look at her. He stared out their lone window.

"Forgive me, Father," Kristina said softly, "but part of me finds the idea of traveling to Trondheim exciting. I do wonder what the world of jarls and ladies is like. Maybe it would be best if I go where Uncle Tordan has gone—at least for now."

Without a glance at her father, her mother put her arm around her and said, "I'll help you gather some things to take with you."

When a quartet of soldiers showed up at his door the next day, Jorvik's anger returned. Even though he'd come to accept the idea of his daughter leaving, he was loathed to let her go with these men who represented everything he hated.

"Jorvik Thordsson?" inquired their leader.

"Yes, I am Jorvik Thordsson."

"I am Magnir, skaldor of House Magnusson. I've come to escort your daughter, Kristina, to Trondheim, where she will be employed in the service of Lady Rikissa."

"And if I refuse to let her go?"

The skaldor looked bewildered at his response, but the men with him reached for the hilts of their swords.

Marta appeared and gently took hold of Jorvik's arm. Her touch calmed him.

"I could take the girl by force if need be," responded Magnir. "But I'm not going to do that. It's my understanding this request comes as a personal favor to my brother Tordan."

"He's my brother, not yours," growled Jorvik.

Marta spoke up. "You're correct, sir. We are thankful, and beg you protect our daughter on her journey."

"I vow to you I will protect her with my life," said Magnir, ignoring Jorvik. "But we must be off."

"Kristina."

Kristina appeared at the door, satchel of belongings in hand.

"Miss," said the skaldor, "I'm to take you to Lady Rikissa. Are you ready to leave?"

Kristina nodded.

Marta took her daughter in her arms and kissed her, fighting back tears. Jorvik was still staring defiantly at the soldiers when Kristina reached up and kissed him on the cheek.

"I'll be alright, Father. You take care of Mother and Canute."

With that she bounded off the stoop and walked off with the soldiers.

Marta took hold of his hand, but said nothing as they watched their daughter grow smaller in the distance.

Now that he'd formed a blood alliance with the son of the chairman, Furyk was feeling good about himself. Of course that was only the first part of his overall plan. He knew the prevailing opinions of his business acumen were less than flattering, but he'd show them. He'd show them he could scheme just as well as the next Aesir—maybe even better.

Right now he felt like having some fun, while at the same time poking his father in the ribs.

He knew his father had imprisoned the housecarle Tordan for his brazen affront to House Magnusson. The impudence of the man, daring to lay hands upon his sister. No doubt his father planned a public execution. Furyk could think of no other reason why he'd waited.

The man *should* be separated from his head, thought Furyk. But before that, while his father was away at the Ve, he was going to give the order to separate Tordan from the appendage he'd used to violate his sister. That would send a message to any other low-born contemplating a similar breach of decorum, as well as annoy his father for giving such an order without consulting him.

Estrid had taken her seat among the Valkyries' inner council, and listened as they discussed, approved, and disapproved several impending marriages and requests for procreation. But she was distracted. Her acknowledgment of various reports on bloodlines and genetic imperfections was superficial. What dominated her thoughts was the apparition. She'd seen it again, just before leaving her chambers to attend the session of the inner council. She was certain now who it was, and why it had returned at this time to torment her.

"Do you agree, Sister Estrid?"

"Agree? I'm sorry, I was thinking of something else. Agree with what?"

"That Dakonsson's petition for procreation should be denied due to the grandsire's diagnosis of the blight."

"Yes...certainly—of course."

"Very well," said the sister who had organized the day's agenda. "Let's review the next petition."

"I'm so glad we don't have to deal with the Vanir," said another council member. "It's tedious enough just keeping the Aesir bloodlines pure."

"Yes, I'm certain we all want to complete our work here so we can retire to more pleasurable pastimes. However, we have one final petition. The impending marriage of Edvard Halfdansson to Rikissa, daughter of House Magnusson. I believe, in this instance, we can forego the preliminaries and move to vote. Is there a dissent?"

Estrid knew they were discussing her daughter's betrothal, but she couldn't get the ghost out of her mind. If her sisters knew, would they approve the marriage? Would they approve of her?

"I hear no dissent. The marriage is approved. Congratulations, Sister, you've made an excellent match."

"Oh, yes," muttered Estrid. "Thank you. Thank you all for your blessing."

19

The eagle flies higher than any mountain.
—Lakhota Saying

Many days had passed since his capture, surely more than it took for Hanwi to travel across the dominion of Father Sky. He longed to see her blue face once again, and to feel the warmth of her husband on his skin. But the uncounted days *had* been good for one thing. He now believed, but a for a few words here or there, he understood the *wasichu* language. Since he'd began communicating with his fellow prisoner—who called himself Tordan—he'd learned that speaking like a *wasichu* was much more difficult than understanding it. Trying to remember the correct words to give his thoughts tongue was not as easy as simply listening.

Despite his comprehension, he was frustrated. He still hadn't learned how he could return home. This lack of knowledge, lack of direction, prevented him from attempting escape. But each day it became harder to stay in this cage. He yearned more and more to kill the *wasichu* who kept him prisoner. Even this Tordan, who seemed friendly, was, in truth, his enemy. Outside this cage they were as likely as not to find themselves locked in combat.

Now that he had established at least a tenuous bond with his fellow prisoner, he planned to question him, subtly of course, to see if he would reveal to him the way home. He was contemplating how he might do so when he heard the sounds of someone approaching.

It was more than one person—a trio as it turned out. Two guards he'd seen before, and a third man in a white garment like a woman's clothes. They weren't coming for him. They opened Tordan's cage, and, for a moment, he was afraid he'd lose his chance to further question the man. The guards used their chains to bind the *wasichu* warrior's hands behind his back.

"What's this all about?" asked Tordan. "Are we going somewhere?"

"By order of the Trellestar Corporation," said the man in white, "you, Tordan Thordsson, are to be castrated."

"Castrated? This is a prank, right? Magnir put you up to this, didn't he?"

Castrated was another new word. He didn't know its meaning, but he sensed the alarm in Tordan's voice, despite his words. He saw the man's muscles tensing, preparing for action. He prepared himself as well.

The guards held Tordan by his arms as the man in white knelt down and began removing his breeks.

"Wait, this is a mistake," said Tordan, beginning to struggle. "You've got it wrong. Check with Jarl Magnusson—this isn't what's supposed to..."

As quickly as a snake strikes, Tordan kicked the fellow dressed like a woman in the head. In the same motion he butted his head against the face of one of his guards, sending the man reeling against the bars.

Acting instinctively at the opportunity, though his feet were still chained, he hopped forward, stuck his chained wrists through the bars, and pulled the chain back around the throat of the *wasichu* guard. By the time he released his limp body and let it fall to the floor, Tordan had knocked both the other guard and the man in white unconscious, using only his feet. This *wasichu* warrior was indeed impressive.

"Can you reach his keys? There, hanging from his belt." Tordan stuck his foot toward the guard he'd killed.

He managed to reach through the bars and grab the keys.

"Alright, unlock these chains," said Tordan, backing up to the bars that separated them.

Though Tordan was taller than him, he could have reached out and strangled the man at that moment. But if he did, he'd be right back where he was. He might be able to escape, but then what?

"You have to find the right key, put in the notch there, and turn it." Tordan waited. "Come on, man, hurry. This is our chance to get out of here."

He fumbled with the keys, tried two wrongly before finding the proper one. It turned and one of Tordan's wrists pulled free.

"Okay, give me the keys."

He hesitated, but only for a moment. He passed the keys over to Tordan, who unlocked his other wrist, then hurried around to open the cage that held him.

The *wasichu* bent down and unfastened the chains binding his ankles.

"Alright, I'm going to take these off your wrists and then we're going to get out of here. You're not going to attack me, right? We'll have a better chance of making our way together. Do you understand?"

"Yes." He understood. He would follow the *wasichu* warrior, at least until he knew how to reach his home on his own.

Tordan unlocked the savage's wrists, noticing how raw with sores they were.

"When we get out of here, we'll have to find something to help heal that."

The fellow didn't reply, but looked anxious for them to be on their way. Tordan was as well. He took the short-sword one of the guards was wearing, but didn't think to offer his fellow prisoner the other one.

Their way was clear until they reached the outer chamber. He surprised the lone guard sitting there, bashing the pommel of the sword on top the man's head, knocking him unconscious. He didn't want to kill anyone he didn't have to. These were his fellow housecarles. Many of them he knew by name. It was possible during their escape he might even encounter some he called friends. But if kill he must to get away, he would.

He searched the weapons rack, not daring to hope, but his search wasn't in vain. It was still there. He guessed Captain Griffenfeld must have ordered them to keep his sword there so he could retrieve it upon his escape. He tossed away the guard's weapon and strapped Thor's Razor to his side. He felt much better with the skaldoran blade on his hip—not invincible, but close to it.

He turned to his companion. Santee had armed himself as well. He'd passed on any of the larger weapons and taken possession of a sturdy dagger. He was obviously more comfortable with the familiarity of the smaller blade.

For a moment their eyes met and locked. Tordan saw the hate, the ferocity in the savage's gaze, the gathering tension in his muscles, ready to uncoil in an instant. He knew the man's instincts told him to kill, and Tordan wouldn't have blamed him if he tried. Who knows how long he'd been locked away, and what atrocities had been committed against him and his.

Tordan smiled.

"Alright, my friend, we're going to be quick and quiet. At least as quiet as we can. Are you ready?"

The savage nodded.

"Let's go."

Tordan led them at a swift jog down a dimly lit corridor. He knew the keep well, and where the housecarles were stationed, having manned those posts himself. As he moved, he couldn't help but wonder about his supposed mission. Was the order to castrate him part of the strategy to spark his escape? Or had the whole thing been a lie? Would the thunderboat be where it was supposed to be? Deception made no sense. Why would Magnusson bother with such a ruse when he could have had him imprisoned or killed outright?

91

In a matter of minutes, Tordan found the exit he was looking for. It was nearly dusk outside. If they found a place to hide and wait, it would be dark soon. But he knew they didn't have long before their escape would be discovered, and every housecarle in the keep would join the search. They needed to keep moving. If they were careful they wouldn't be seen.

Just as he thought they might slip away, a trio of guards spotted them. "Halt!"

His first thought was to bluff his way through.

"Put your hands behind your back as if you're bound," he told the savage quietly. Then, louder, he called out. "Hail there, Brother. It's I, Tordan. How goes it? It's a beautiful evening for the duty, eh?"

"Tordan? Who's that with you?"

"It's a just one of the savages. I've been ordered to take him to the jarl."

"Hold there," said another guard. "I heard Tordan had been locked up."

"You must be thinking about that time I drank too much skyr and roamed the streets naked. That was a fine night, I tell you. Of course Captain Griffenfeld didn't think so."

"No, no, I was there yesterday when the captain himself said you were ordered imprisoned by Jarl Magnusson," said the third housecarle. "How did you get—"

Tordan slammed his fist into the man's jaw before he could finish. He dropped like a stone in the ocean. The other two came at them.

Tordan parried a clumsy slash of the man's sword and shoved him backwards.

"I don't want to hurt you, Brother. Why don't you just let us be on our way?"

"You're no brother of mine, Skaldor," he snarled.

It was true this housecarle was no skaldor, but Tordan still didn't want to kill the fellow if he didn't have to. Off to his side he saw the other guard, armed with a pike, trying to stick his savage friend.

"I don't think I like the way you say skaldor, my friend. You should be more polite to your betters."

Tordan pressed him with a collection of moves designed to set the fellow on his heels. The housecarle almost tripped and fell as he executed several desperate parries. He was no match for Tordan, and he quickly realized it.

"To arms! To arms!" he cried out, hoping for reinforcements.

Meanwhile, Tordan saw Santee was nimble enough to avoid the awkward thrusts of the other guard's pike. He saw the savage measuring his opponent, getting ready to move in for the kill. He'd no doubt the man *would* kill. He'd demonstrated that back in the prison. However, as Santee was about to lunge, his foot caught in a crevice between the stones of the walkway and he slipped.

Tordan parried a weak lunge by his opponent, countering with a riposte that plunged his blade into the man's ribs. He pulled his sword free and spun as the savage was about to be skewered. Thor's Razor flashed downward and cut the pike in two. He crashed shoulder-first into the guard and knocked him against the wall. The fellow dropped and didn't get back up.

"Let's move!" he growled, seeing Santee back on his feet.

They ran now, with no thought of whether they'd be seen. Shouts of alarm echoed through the keep, and Tordan realized they had only seconds to make their escape.

Fortunately he knew exactly where he was going. They were outside and away from House Magnusson much quicker than the housecarles could organize a proper search. As the sun set and the streets darkened, he led the way to the docks, hugging the shadows as much as possible.

He was free now, but he wasn't. He had no choice but to continue following Tordan. This *wasichu* village was a vast maze, lined with endless numbers of stone-paved trails. He knew his homeland lay across the great sea in the direction the sun rose, but that was all he knew. He'd have to trust this *wasichu* a little longer. He reminded himself the fellow *had* possibly just saved his life— though he felt certain he would have been quick enough to avoid the *wasichu* guard's spear had not Tordan intervened.

They were getting closer to the sea. He could smell it, even through the stink of the *wasichu* village—which was much worse here than in the stronghold where he'd been kept prisoner.

His guide froze and motioned for silence. They stayed in the shadows a moment as a group of men passed, then continued their flight. Once they were over the next rise, he saw the water himself. Its vastness spread beyond the horizon, and he knew his home, his family, was still many days journey away.

Tordan led him down to where the *wasichu wahte* were kept—boats they were called. Here the smell of fish was strong, and he could actually hear the lapping of the water against the land. Tordan bypassed several larger vessels, finally stopping when he came to a much smaller one. He followed him and felt the sway of the boat as they moved onto it. Tordan searched through a number items stored within the boat.

"Well, good to his word. Looks like we've got enough fuel, food, and water—for a few days anyway."

"What is fuel?"

"It's what makes this boat go."

Tordan began untying the ropes holding it steady, then pushed so the boat drifted away from its tethers.

Tordan did something he couldn't see, and suddenly there was such a clamor he reached to cover his ears. The boat jolted forward and he lost his balance, falling roughly backwards.

Tordan, holding onto something resembling a medicine wheel, looked over his shoulder. "Sorry, friend. I should have warned you about the take-off. It should be smooth sailing from here, Njord willing. Hold on. I'm going to get us out of here quick enough so no one can follow."

The boat's roar was louder than the stampede of a thousand *tatanka*. He covered his ears once more and marveled at how swiftly the craft moved, using a power beyond his understanding.

Slowly he uncovered his ears and looked behind them. Now in the distance, the immensity of the *wasichu* village struck him. It ascended in an enormous mountain of stone, its night lights stretching beyond the limits of his vision. His heart sang to see it recede in the distance and he called out in a joyous voice.

"*Hoo-hoo-hoo-hooooooooo-yah! Washtay, washtay!*"

Tordan glanced at him, then faced seaward again.

"Aye, I like a good sea breeze myself."

20

*The initial session of the council on the possible crimes
of our forebears was held to discuss what many are
calling the wrongful abduction of the subject species,
and what should be done about it. The majority, for
now, appear to favor self-determination—leaving the
bipeds to their own fate. Some, however, spoke for
offering aid to the "poor creatures." This faction is of
the opinion the species consists merely of dull-witted
brutes. If they had studied my reports on the breed,
they would know this idea is in opposition to the facts.
There is still another faction, consisting primarily of
elders who still refuse to think of the ancient experiment
as a transgression of any degree, and believe we should
continue to manipulate the "beasts" for study.*

—Osst Personal Journal

Her breasts were larger than they'd been, and she didn't like it at all. Not as large as her mother's, thank Freyja, but a reminder of how she might look someday. Rikissa was certain the increase in size was due to her recently terminated pregnancy, and hoped they'd return to normal soon.

She dressed, making sure to select something modest that would conceal them. A knock on her door came as she finished.

"Enter."

It was one of the housecarles.

"Milady, your new maidservant from Oseberg is here."

"Let her in."

The housecarle directed the young girl inside and closed the door behind her. She was a tiny thing, slender like Rikissa, maybe 13 or 14 years old—on the cusp of womanhood. There was some resemblance in her face to Tordan, but she had the typical reddish hair of the Vanir. It was long, tied in the back, peasant-like. Her clothes were...well they were so dreary and worn that Rikissa would have to find her something else to wear. Maybe she some of her older clothes, packed away, would fit.

"What's your name?"

The girl curtsied a bit awkwardly and said, "Kristina, milady."

The girl was obviously terrified, and why not? She'd been taken from her home, her family, to a place she knew nothing of. Rikissa thought to say something to put her at ease.

"Kristina is a beautiful name—a noble name. My grandmother was named Kristina."

The girl looked up and smiled.

"You are Tordan's niece?"

"Yes, milady."

"You should know it's out of the respect I hold for your uncle that you are here."

"I know, milady."

Rikissa wondered if the girl knew about her and Tordan.

"What do you know?"

"I know Uncle Tordan arranged for me to come here to Trondheim to work."

Rikissa saw no sign she knew anything else, and had no reason to think Tordan would have told her—not that it mattered. It was no longer a secret.

"As my handmaiden your duties will include, among other things, helping me dress, bathe, washing my clothes, cleaning my chamber," she said sternly, then smiled. "But we will have fun too."

Kristina returned her smile.

"Right now I'm to meet with my betrothed. You can come with me. But we can't have you looking like that."

Kristina looked down at herself, not sure what her new mistress meant.

"Here, take this robe and put it around you."

Kristina did as she was told, marveling at the feel of the fabric.

"Good. Alright, let's get this over with."

When she reached the receiving hall, she whispered to Kristina to remain at the door and keep quiet. Edvard Halfdansson was waiting for her. He stood promptly upon seeing her.

"Good day, milady."

"Good day...may I call you Edvard?"

He smiled. "Certainly."

"Then you must call me Rikissa. There's no reason for us to be so formal when we're in private."

"I agree," he said. "I'm not one for formalities anyway. I believe many of them to be antiquated and in need of modification, if not outright expungement."

"Shall we sit?" she asked, doing so without waiting for him.

"Indeed."

He joined her, a respectful arm's-length away, but an awkward moment of silence ensued.

"I understand preparations for the wedding are proceeding smoothly," he finally said.

"Yes, I'm certain our mothers have everything well in hand. I'm sure we can look forward to many more formalities than either of us care for."

He laughed at her sarcasm, and she let slip a petite laugh of her own. Again she reminded herself she was fortunate. Edvard wasn't a bad fellow, even if he did sometimes use words she didn't understand. Her fate from an arranged marriage could have been much worse. However she couldn't help but compare him to Tordan, and there he fell far short.

"Speaking of formalities, your brother Furyk requested I join him in the fostbrooir."

"Did you agree?"

"Of course. I...I could hardly decline. It was a noble gesture of friendship."

Knowing her brother, Rikissa doubted it had anything to do with friendship...or nobility. She didn't believe Furyk had any friends. What schemes he was up to, she had no idea. But making friends was certainly not on his agenda.

"I'd advise you to tread carefully when dealing with Furyk," said Rikissa. "As a matter of fact, be cautious with my entire family."

Edvard smiled, almost laughed, then saw she was completely serious.

"Yes. I guess that's the essence of our social order. I've never understood the cutthroat nature of politics and business. It seems we would thrive more as a society if we refined our moral ideals." His comments were the slightest bit seditious, and he looked to gauge her reaction. "Do you agree?"

"To be honest, Edvard, I've no interest in either politics or business. However, I do agree change of some kind would benefit our society."

"Don't tell my father," he said conspiratorially, "but I've little interest in business myself. I try, for his sake, but what I'm really interested in is science and history. Did you know our people once lived on another world?"

She looked at him as if he were daft.

"Oh, you mean the story of the Volkerwandering?"

"Yes, but I believe it's more than just a story," he said, the enthusiasm apparent in his tone. "My studies have convinced me the mythic journey was a real one. There are records going back a thousand years—records of our ancestors talking about the sky changing—about the stars being different. I believe that's why we have relics made of gold, but no record of any gold mines. Because the gold we have did not come from this world.

"Of course I've no substantial proof yet." The passion in his voice subsided noticeably. "So I haven't really told anyone else about this. But I plan to continue my research."

He looked into her eyes for some kind of affirmation or even a sign she might be interested in his research.

"I hope you don't think I'm completely mad or anything."

Rikissa laughed. "I don't think you're mad, Edvard. A bit peculiar maybe." She laughed again to show she was having fun at his expense.

He blushed.

"You know, my brother Gudrik will be performing in the Trondheim Theater's upcoming production of the Volkerwandering legend."

"Is that so? Then I hope you'll allow me to accompany you to the theater, and that you'll grace my family's alcove with your presence."

"Certainly," replied Rikissa.

She was about to explain more about the part Gudrik was playing when a pair of housecarles wearing House Tryguasson colors strode into the room.

"Excuse us, sir. Chairman Tryguasson needs to see you at once."

Edvard stood and took Rikissa's hand.

"If you'll forgive me, milady. It's been more than pleasant speaking with you. I look forward to our...next encounter."

He kissed her hand and was off with his men. As soon as they'd gone, Kristina hurried over to Rikissa.

"He is to be your husband?"

"Yes. A marriage arranged by my mother."

"He seems...nice," said Kristina.

"Yes, I guess so. But he does not appeal to me, not like..." Rikissa caught herself. She had to stop thinking about Tordan. He was imprisoned, and likely headed for the executioner's block or the hangman's noose. It would do her no good to dwell on him. She couldn't compare every man she met with a skaldor like Tordan. She would have to make the best of it with Edvard Halfdansson. She had to admit to herself Kristina was right. He was nice, if a bit peculiar.

21

What people wish for, they soon believe.
—Book of Runes

Estrid stroked her son's long blond hair, reveling in its downy suppleness. "I've news for you, Furyk. It's a secret you're to share with no one, do you understand? *No one.*"

Furyk's persistent scowl wavered. His green eyes ignited with interest. "Of course, Mother."

"I've learned your father has the blight."

She wasn't worried about how she told the lie. She knew Furyk would believe anything she said.

"No—not in our family." Furyk was dumbfounded. "How can this be?"

"My dear son, it's a badly worn myth that the high-born can't suffer from the blight. It occurs much more often than you know."

She could see Furyk's rather limited brain working hard, digesting the news and wondering how it would affect him. She decided to make it easy for him.

"Of course, that could mean your brother will inherit even sooner."

"How long does Father have?"

Estrid wrapped her arms around her son, hugging him from behind. "The doctors don't know. It could be a many weeks, or it could be years. But what if it's only weeks?"

"Yes, yes," said Furyk, and she could hear the rattle of thoughts behind his words. "That means Gudrik will have to be...convinced to step down very soon. Sooner than I planned."

"I agree. But there's something else. Your brother has asked me to arrange a marriage for him. A politically-strong marriage."

"What?" Furyk pulled away from her. "Why would he do that? We both know he has no interest in women, *or* in the politics of business."

Estrid shrugged. "Maybe he's changed. Maybe he's decided to take an interest after all."

"A marriage is a complication I hadn't planned for," groused Furyk. "A wife may goad his interest in business."

"That's always a possibility." Estrid moved closer and took his hands in hers.

"It'll be alright. I'm sure it'll all work out for the best." She pulled him to her, kissed his cheek, and whispered in his ear. "I'll delay Gudrik's marriage as long as possible. You needn't worry about that. But time is short."

Estrid backed away, holding Furyk at arm's-length.

"Remember, don't mention your father's blight to anyone—especially not your father. Am I understood?"

"Of course, Mother."

"That's a good boy. You'll make a fine jarl. It will be a glorious day when House Magnusson becomes House Vikarsson."

Eight days after he'd treated the native boy, Walks Apart returned to his classroom, bringing her son with her. He'd fully recovered from his illness, and Lame Bear helped to translate his mother's gratitude. Along with some native foodstuffs, she'd brought a gift for the doctor—a pair of the heelless shoes the men of her clan wore.

Truvor thanked her for the gift, and replaced his own shoes with the softer footwear, much to her delight. He found them very comfortable.

That day she and her son stayed for the language lesson. They would return for his next two lessons, and when Walks Apart mentioned many others of the Lakhota had the same sickness as her son, Truvor returned with them to the village, fully stocked with more medicine, as well as an experimental vaccine he'd created, hoping to prevent future outbreaks of the virus.

Thanks to the praise of Walks Apart, who guided him, most of the people were welcoming and appreciative. Some, of course, were apprehensive. But Truvor was followed from *thipi* to *thipi* by the village shaman, whose name he learned was Howling Dog. His presence, likely unwittingly, seemed to lend a certain credence to Truvor's work.

Howling Dog watched Truvor's every move with both interest and suspicion. Whether he was looking for an excuse to banish the doctor or trying to learn, Truvor wasn't certain. However, he made no attempt to interfere with Truvor's ministrations. Walks Apart did her best to translate any questions the shaman had about what Truvor was doing, but he could see the frustration in both of them.

Most of the people suffered from the same viral infection of pig's bane that had stricken Walks Apart's son. Though easily treated, it could prove fatal if left untreated, especially if these people had developed no resistance to it, as Truvor believed. Before they'd left the colony, he showed Walks Apart and

Lame Bear one of the compound's pigs. They'd never seen such an animal. Apparently they didn't even have wild boars.

He was now certain the virus had been conveyed to the Lakhota by his own people—maybe even by himself. He worried if the Lakhota clan had been infected, other clans might be too. But he'd no way to treat them all, scattered as they were across the region. He could see this visit alone would deplete his supply of the medicine, and it would be many, many days before more could arrive from Trondheim.

Other than the virus, the Lakhota were the picture of health. Even the older men who attended his classes seemed fine physical specimens for their ages, though Truvor wasn't certain what their ages were. He once tried to get Lame Bear to tell him how old he was, but the Lakhota had no measurements for time. They knew the seasons and the phases of the moon, but they kept no records of the passing of years. They had no calendar. After he'd taught his students to count with basic numbers, he asked Lame Bear again. However, it appeared the concept was still unclear, because the count the old fellow gave him was preposterous. Lame Bear had flashed the fingers on both of his hands eleven times, and Truvor was sure the man wasn't 110 years old.

It was late by the time Truvor finished his work, so he agreed to spend the night in the village, but not before he was served a sumptuous and exotic meal. He delighted in the various dishes so much that Walks Apart gave him more food to take with him when he left the next day. That night he stayed with Lame Bear, who lived alone in his *thipi*. He wanted to ask his host about this family—if he had a wife or children—but refrained from doing so. The old man never brought up the subject, so Truvor left it alone.

22

Two wooden stakes stood in the field. On them I hung
my hat and cloak. The stakes had character in their
fine clothes. Naked I was nothing.
>   **—Words of Chairman Wulfstan**

Furyk had intended to tighten his bond with the chairman's son, maybe plot strategy for the future when, if everything went according to plan, they'd both be jarls. Instead, all the fool wanted to do was ask about his sister.

"What does she like? How does she spend her time?"

Furyk had no idea what his little sister did with her time, and didn't care. This Edvard was a weakling, with no business sense Furyk could see. All the more reason he might be receptive to Furyk's guidance on such matters.

"Rikissa likes powerful men who—"

"Our sister likes music and dancing."

Furyk looked up to see who dared interrupt him. It was Gudrik, leaning against the arched entrance, smiling the way he did when he was trying to goad his younger brother.

"What kind of music does she like?" asked Edvard.

Gudrik walked into the room. "Oh, she likes different kinds. Why don't you come with me. I was going to library. I'll tell you all about Rikissa." Gudrik looked at Furyk. "You don't mind, do you, Brother?"

Furyk glared at Gudrik, but waved them away. "Go on then. I'm sure my brother has more insight into the ways of women than I," he said with contempt. "We'll talk later, Edvard."

The pair walked out, chattering as they did. Furyk wasn't sure which was the greater buffoon. But that would just make it easier to influence Edvard, and to eliminate his brother when the time came—which it would very soon.

With that thought in mind, he decided to locate Hrolf and continue his recruitment of the housecarle with further enticements. Maybe a trip to his favorite brothel would be just the thing. Furyk would enjoy it as well. There he could be himself, drop the facade of civility and deference in which he cloaked himself daily. He longed for the day when it would no longer be necessary, when submission to his father would...*by Wotan's eye! As* he thought of his

102

father, the old man stalked into the room, looking as angry as a taunted dragon.

"You dare disobey me?"

Vikar slapped the back of his hand across Furyk's face before he could react. Furyk recoiled from the blow, stunned. His shock quickly turned to rage, but he contained his anger.

"You reckless dolt! Your order to castrate the skaldor could have disrupted the entirety of my plans. You have no idea what you were meddling with."

"If you'd share your plans with me, Father, then I would know," said Furyk, reaching for his pained cheek.

Vikar looked as if he were going to strike Furyk again.

"Remember your place! You're not jarl yet, though your longing for the position is as obvious as the rising sun. I'll inform you of my stratagem when it suits me—when it is necessary. Until then, you'll do as you're told. You're fortunate your interference did no damage. The skaldor and the savage made their escape as planned."

"You planned the Vanir scum's escape?" Furyk was dumbfounded.

"See how little you know," Vikar berated him. "The skaldor Tordan is to be my spy among the savages. That's why I spared his life."

"But what possible—"

"Are you questioning me again? I'd advise you to busy yourself with your falcons and your whores. The next time you disobey me or interfere with the business of House Magnusson, I won't be so lenient."

As quickly as he'd entered, Vikar strode out the room, leaving Furyk fuming.

It wasn't the first time his father had struck him, but he'd been only a lad, unable to defend himself, the last time it had happened. He remembered it well. His memory burned with each instance his father had hit him, had berated him over the years. He wanted so badly to pull his dagger and bury it in the old windbag's heart. But that would only serve to make Gudrik jarl. So he'd restrained himself, using every fiber of his willpower to do so. The time would come though—the time would come.

"See this?"

He examined the object Tordan showed him. It was an arrow with four heads floating in a container of water, each a different color, each pointing in a different direction.

"This is how we find our way. See how one end is blue? The blue arrow always points north. To reach your homeland we want to travel east, where the red arrow is pointing. Then, once we reach land, we'll go south a ways."

They'd been traveling all night, and he'd asked Tordan how he would guide them across the water. He wondered if he would use the stars and the sun to find his way, but he had a *wasichu* device.

"The journey, how many days?"

Tordan scratched his head.

"Well, I'm not certain. Three, I think, if we're lucky...and we don't run out of fuel. As far as I know, this is the first time a thunderboat has attempted the crossing, so it's uh...hard to know for sure."

He grunted. Only three days—faster than it took the big boat that used the wind to carry him to the *wasichu* land.

"The storm will slow us."

Tordan checked the horizon. "What storm?"

"A storm is coming."

"If you say so, but I don't see it. Let's pray to Njord you're wrong. This little boat won't carry us through a big storm."

"Njord is Wakan Tanka—your Great Spirit?"

"You mean my god? He's one of them. We've got a lot of gods. Too many if you ask me."

"We also, many gods. Wakan Tanka is Great Spirit. Not just god. He is all, everything, everywhere. All gods part of him."

"Wotan is our chief god, but they're all different. Njord is the god of the sea. He's a sailor's friend, unless he quarrels with Ran, the goddess of storms. She likes to drown men and take them back to her realm."

"*Unktehi*—water demon."

"Aye, like that. Speaking of which, I'm dry as jarl's wife. You pilot and I'll get us some water. Just keep both hands on the wheel, keep it straight, make certain we're headed in the direction of the red arrow."

He took hold of the wheel, clutching it at first as he would if he were riding a great *tatanka*. He expected the noisy beast to fight him, but its pull was more gentle than he imagined. It was a strange feeling, guiding this boat across the water.

"There's food too, thank Thor. Old bread and dried fruit. No feast, but it'll do. I'll have a bite and then you can eat. Just keep her steady."

"Into the storm?"

Tordan took a bite of bread and stood. "I don't think..." He stared at the distant horizon where the undulations of the sea were ribboned with foam and a swell of dark clouds had begun to gather. "You must have better eyes than I do, or did you just sense a storm coming?"

The fellow didn't respond.

"Well, we can't go around it. We could go back."

The look on his face was the only reply Tordan needed.

"You're right. We're not going back."

23

However long the night, the dawn will break.
— Ancient Aesir Proverb

R ikissa wanted to see Tordan. She told herself it was because she wanted to tell him about Kristina, about how she was taking care of his niece. It was a good reason, but the truth was she yearned to see him, even if he was locked up.

She doubted the guards would let her in again without permission — certainly they'd been chastised after her first visit — so she went straight to Captain Griffenfeld. He'd always been kind to her, even when she was a little girl. He wasn't the captain of the guard then. She'd called him Griff, and he'd called her Riki. It had been years since she'd spoken to him so informally, but she felt they still had a bond. She was certain he'd let her see Tordan.

"Good day, Captain Griffenfeld."

He stood when she entered his office. "Good day, milady. What may I do for you?"

"The housecarle Tordan, your prisoner — I'd like to speak with him."

"I'm afraid that's impossible, milady."

"Please, Captain. I've taken in his niece, and I want him to know she's being cared for."

Griffenfeld moved from behind his desk and rested his hand on her shoulder. It was a breach of decorum that recalled their less formal relationship of years gone by.

"I'm certain Tordan would be glad to hear you're caring for his niece, but you can't speak with him."

"Why not?" she asked, sounding much like the little girl who used to wheedle him to get her way.

"Because the prisoner Tordan has escaped."

"Escaped?" Tordan was gone? It took Rikissa several moments to accept the notion. Where would he have gone? Why hadn't she heard from him? "But I don't understand...how could he have...?"

"He's a skaldor, milady. He's as skilled a warrior as there is in Trondheim. Escape would not have been hard for the likes of him."

"Is a search being conducted?"

Griffenfeld moved back around his desk, his head bowed in thought.

When he didn't reply right away, Rikissa pressed him. "Have you found him? Is he alright?"

"Milady, Tordan escaped along with a savage we were holding prisoner. They took one of our thunderboats, and likely made for Serkland. I'm afraid he's gone, milady."

She couldn't believe it. Why would Tordan go to Serkland with a savage? She understood why he'd be afraid to come to her, but why wouldn't he go to Oseberg and hide with his family among the Vanir? It didn't make any sense.

She was glad he'd escaped and was no longer subject to whatever punishment her father had planned, but to leave Trondheim...to leave her...

"There's nothing you can do for him, milady, except continue to look out for his niece. I'm sure that's what he would have wanted."

"You speak of him as if he were dead."

Captain Griffenfeld looked at her, but didn't reply.

"I thank you for your time, Captain," she said, turning to go.

"You should forget about him, Riki. Look to your betrothed for comfort."

She'd already been on the verge, and his use of her pet name was all it took to send her over the edge. She started crying. Captain Griffenfeld took hold of her, afraid she might faint and fall. She wrapped her arms around him, continuing to cry.

"Oh, Griff."

The wind was fierce and the ocean swells titanic next to the small boat. No longer worried whether their heading was true, Tordan struggled to see through the rain and navigate up and down the swells so as not to capsize. He had Santee lash the remaining fuel and provisions securely to the bulwarks, and told him to hold tight.

Silently he cursed Ran and petitioned Njord for relief, all the while believing neither would do any good. He could only hope to pilot the boat through the tempest before it upended them.

Santee called out to him, but he couldn't hear over the wind.

"What?"

"Land!" shouted the savage again. "Land!"

Tordan looked across the port side to where Santee was pointing. Through the rain-darkened sky and over the rolling ocean, he thought he saw something. It *was* land. But how could that be? They couldn't have reached the mainland yet, and there was nothing out here—at least according to the map he'd studied. How far off course were they?

He turned the boat north and made for what he hoped would be a safe harbor. If not, the waves would shatter this boat into splinters against those shores. That's if something was really out there, and it wasn't just Ran luring them into her maelstrom.

Fortunately Tordan found a partially sheltered cove he could pilot into. He navigated past a few rocky outcroppings, hoping there weren't too many he couldn't see beneath the surface. They reached the shore and both he and Santee jumped into the surf, grabbing lines and pulling the boat far enough up the shore to beach it.

By the time they tied the lines to a nearby tree, the storm had begun to dissipate. Though already soaked, they took shelter beneath an overhanging cliff and waited for the rain and wind to cease. The storm blew off almost as suddenly as it had swept upon them, and the sun appeared between scattering clouds.

They emerged from their shelter and began to scale the modest cliff face.

"I don't guess this looks familiar to you," said Tordan.

"No," replied Santee, "these are not my people's lands."

"I didn't think we could have traveled that far. This has to be some small island that wasn't on the maps I've seen. There won't be any fuel, but we should take a look and see if we can find some food or water before we head back out."

"Why no fuel?"

"You don't find jor oil just lying around. It's made from the jormun."

"What is jormun?"

"It's a sea serpent—a giant snake that lives in the ocean."

"I have not seen this beast."

"Believe me, you don't want to."

After making sure the boat was secure, Tordan took two empty water jugs and put them in a large sack. Together they started out, making their way through the thick, green brush. Neither of them had ever seen a jungle, or even had a word for it. Santee tried leading them through the areas of least resistance, but the going was rough. When they stopped to catch their breath, Tordan realized the savage heard something.

"What is it?"

"Water...nearby."

"Let's go."

It wasn't long before Tordan heard the rushing water himself. It was a narrow, quick moving stream, but the water was clear. He bent to fill the jugs, but when he finished he couldn't locate Santee. He scrambled further up the hill until finally he saw the savage motioning for him to climb higher.

Breathing heavily by the time he reached the summit, Tordan asked, "Did you...find any food?"

Santee just stuck his arm out and pointed.

Tordan looked and was astonished by what he saw. In the midst of the tropical wilderness was a massive structure, looking as if it were carved from white rock. It wasn't tall, but it spread out over a wide area. The strangest thing about it was its shape. It had no squared edges like the edifices Tordan was familiar with. Though much of it was covered in greenery where the local vegetation had taken back the land, what he could see of thing's roof—if you could call it that—was an endless set of soft rolling hills. Vines had begun to crawl over its knobby, oblong surface, but it's contours were unmistakable.

Santee started towards the structure, but Tordan held him back.

"We don't know who lives there. We should go carefully, quietly."

The savage nodded and continued.

They heard nothing but the sounds of a few birds as they approached the unusual configuration. When they were within sight of what looked like an entrance, they stopped and waited. There was no sign of life. The white rock-like walls were cracked in places where tree roots had taken purchase, and emerald vines grew helter-skelter, creating bizarre patterns against the weathered ramparts.

Santee gestured he was going inside. Tordan followed.

Stepping through the entryway, Tordan ran his hand across the wall. It wasn't rock or any other material he recognized. It was smooth, but solid, dense.

They passed under an archway and found themselves in a courtyard of sorts, open to the sky. Several openings led away from the courtyard, but they, too, were strange. They weren't doorways or any kind of portal Tordan was familiar with. They were smallish, perfectly round holes, as low to the ground as his knees. The openings were too small for him to climb inside—not that he had any desire to—but he stuck his head in to see what he could see.

The structure was honeycombed endlessly by tiny tunnels and alcoves that stretched beyond his range of vision. It reminded him of a bee hive he'd once seen broken open. Inside the tunnels was a strange dim light whose source he couldn't determine. It was almost as if the walls of the complex were glowing like smoldering coals.

He pulled his head out and examined the walls more closely. Where the vines hadn't completely covered the walls, strange runes were carved into the white material. He couldn't tell if the symbols were supposed to be a writing of sorts, or some strange artwork.

"People did not live here," said Santee, his arms folded across his chest.

"I agree. But if not people, then who...or what?"

The savage had no answer.

"I see no tools, no weapons, no remains, no sign of the inhabitants at all. It's like they vanished."

"Maybe enemies drive them out, kill them."

"Maybe," said Tordan as if he wasn't so sure. "But if invaders destroyed them, there'd be some evidence, some remnants. One thing's for sure. This place is ripe with ghosts. Let's get out of here."

Santee nodded. "I own the ghosts of many warriors slain in battle, but this place also troubles me."

"We're agreed then," said Tordan. "Let's get back to the boat and leave this island in our wake."

24

*I compelled my essence closer to the creature, until I
was positioned directly between it and its reflection.
As I tried to fathom the emanations I considered the
possibility the emotions emitted from this breed may
be having a deleterious effect upon my populace. It
had become a common pastime to absorb the
emanations produced by the subject species. The
distances involved meant the emotions were more
diluted than I was experiencing now—relatively
tame and, as of yet, harmless. But I wondered about
the cumulative effect of such diversions. No studies I
was aware of were being conducted to ascertain this.*
—Osst Field Notes/010269390

"It took quite a bit of testing, adapting the size and weight of the
ammunition, barrel length and pressure points, judging accuracy,
distance, penetration, and—"

"How does it work?" inquired Vikar, wanting to dispense with the more
technical aspects of the weapon's development.

"See how the cylinder revolves, sir? Each time the hammer is drawn back, it
rotates to reload, immediately prepared for the next shot."

"Must the hammer be cocked each time?" asked Captain Griffenfeld.

"No, sir. The hammer need not be cocked if the trigger is engaged."

Griffenfeld picked up the weapon, felt the balance in his hand, and aimed it
at an invisible enemy. "How many projectiles does it hold?" he asked.

"There are nine chambers in the cylinder, holding nine cartridges."

"Cartridges?" asked Vikar.

"Yes, sir. Unlike the old hakens, that required ball, powder, and paper to be
loaded into the muzzle separately, we've developed a self-contained cartridge.
Loading is much simpler and much faster than with the hakens. We've been
using the cartridges in our long barrel rifles for some time with success, though
they are still single-shot. We're in the process of developing a rifle that can hold
several cartridges at once."

"We've had some problems with misfires using those cartridges," said Griffenfeld.

"We believe we've corrected those problems, Captain. "

"Where can I fire this?"

"Right over there, Captain. We have a target set up."

Griffenfeld walked over and took aim at the target.

"When can we begin mass production?" asked Vikar.

"Testing is complete. We're ready to streamline the process as soon as you give the order, sir."

Captain Griffenfeld fired the weapon and the explosive sound echoed throughout the factory's back room. Quickly he fired off three more shots in succession.

"Well, Captain?" inquired Vikar.

"It's a fine weapon, sir. Only accurate for short range, but it'll give us a distinct advantage over any opponent."

"Good. Begin production immediately and continue development of the new rifles. I want all my housecarles armed with these revolvers as soon as possible."

They floated aimlessly as Tordan poured the last of the jor oil into the boat's fuel tank. He hoped it would be enough to get them where they were going. There had been no sight of land since they'd left the island, and he had no idea how far off course the storm had blown them. More than that, he sensed a palpable tension growing in the savage. It could be he was anticipating reaching his home soon, or maybe he had other plans, like cutting Tordan's throat while he slept. Not that he'd slept much since they'd raced out of Trondheim. But he'd have to soon, and for more than a few minutes.

"Well that's it. That's the last of our fuel."

He tossed the empty container overboard and started the engine.

If they ran out of fuel before they reached their destination, they'd be adrift. It wouldn't be long after that before they ran out of food and water. He wondered if his savage companion was a cannibal.

If he was going to sleep, he might as well do it now, before they reached land. Once there, once the skrael reached his homeland, Tordan would be at his mercy.

"Here, you take the wheel for a while. I'm going to try and sleep."

Santee came forward and took hold of the wheel.

"Just keep us headed in the direction of the red arrow."

"Red is good," replied Santee with the barest hint of a grin.

It was the closest thing to a smile he'd seen yet on the savage's face. If there was something funny about what he'd said, he was too tired to figure it out. He laid down in the stern, curled up, and fell asleep.

While Tordan slept he piloted the boat, constantly straining to see beyond the horizon, hoping to catch the first glimpse of land—his land. But even after days aboard this noisy *wasichu* machine there was nothing to see. The longer they traveled the more he thought of his family. Fearing him dead, Snow Deer would be in mourning. She will have cut off her beautiful hair, cut her arms and legs. She will have sung his death song for many nights. He wondered if she would still be singing it after all this time, or would she already be considering the many suitors who would call her name?

Will his daughter have undergone the *Isnati Awiealowan*? Will his son have earned his name of manhood? Each thing was nearing its time.

He considered all these things—things that may have come to pass in his absence, and his heart was weighted with anguish. He couldn't allow himself to think such things. What would happen would happen. He could only guide his own hand.

He turned his eyes away from the horizon and looked behind at the expanse of ocean they'd crossed. The sun was creeping ever closer to the water. Soon it would be night again. Before he turned forward, something caught his eye. It was only a flicker, a brief shadow. His first thought was that it wasn't possible. Then he looked up.

He slowed the boat as he'd seen Tordan do, and stepped over to rouse him.

"Wake," he said, nudging the *wasichu* warrior with his foot.

"What?" Tordan woke immediately, but was still groggy. "How long have I been sleeping?"

He ignored the question and said, "We are close."

Tordan pulled himself up, shaking off the last vestiges of sleep. "Close? Close to what?"

"Land."

"Land? I don't see anything. What makes you think so?"

"Look."

He pointed up at the sky. High above them flew a bird.

"A bird, so what?" An expression of comprehension flickered across

Tordan's features. "A bird has to have a nest somewhere—a place to land."

"Yes. We cannot see it, but it must be close."

"By Thor's hammer, we just might make it."

Tordan slapped his back in what was obviously a friendly gesture, but the touch made him think. What would he do with this *wasichu* when he reached his home? How would the people react? He was certain they, like he, now hated the white-skinned invaders. Would he speak for Tordan, or would his own hatred quiet him?

"I think we've got enough food left for one good meal, so we might as well eat it now."

While Tordan dug through the sack containing their provisions, he kept the boat on course. Then he spied something else. It was in the water, moving at great speed, and it was enormous. He turned the wheel slightly to get a better look. Something broke the surface briefly, then disappeared again. What he saw had no head, it was only a slick hump, rounded like a tree trunk, but many times larger.

"What is that?"

Tordan stood. "What is what?"

"There." He pointed as another portion of the creature rose from the sea. "Is it *Unktehi*—the water demon?"

"It's not Ran, but it's one of her pets," said Tordan. "It's a jormun."

"The sea snake? The one whose oil fuels the boat?"

"That's right. It's probably none too happy we're burning one of its cousins. We can't outrun it. We've got to cut the engine and hope it ignores us."

Tordan turned the engine off.

The immediate silence was layered with tension. The sea serpent surfaced, and this time he saw its head before it dove again. It was massive. The skull alone was larger than the biggest *tatanka* he'd ever seen. Its jaws could consume a pair of horses in a single bite.

"It's circling us," said Tordan. "It knows we're here. It's too late to play dead. We've got to try and run for it." He started the engine once more. "Hold on."

He grabbed hold of boat's railing as it stuttered and took off. The ocean waters were fairly calm, but he saw the swells were still large enough to make maneuvering at high speed impractical.

Tordan did what he could, trying to avoid traveling in a straight line. But flight was useless. The jormun followed them—seemingly it was all around them. He wondered if more than one of the creatures pursued them.

114

The forefront of its great body burst through the water only feet away, spraying them with sea water. The boat swayed as if to upend. But it flopped back down and Tordan regained control.

The monster had the appearance of a snake, but with ridges and insect-like antennae protruding from its scaly head, and a single fin running down its back. But his view of it was brief. It quickly submerged again.

They both scanned the water for its reappearance. Nothing. Their boat continued with no sign of the jormun.

"Has it gone?"

Tordan shook his head. "I don't know. It might have just been playing with—"

The collision was instantaneous and violent—a crack of thunder. The upheaval sent them both flying through the air. He caught only a glimpse of the creature's titanic form crashing down on the boat before he hit the water.

25

Freedom means choosing your burden.
—Ancient Aesir Proverb

When he returned to visit the Lakhota many days later, his patients had all recovered. That wasn't the only thing that had changed. Most of the people knew him now. He was a welcome guest. Welcomed by everyone but the clan shaman, Howling Dog, who did not interfere with his work, but kept his distance, always watching with suspicion.

He was greeted almost everywhere he went, but understood only a fraction of what was being said. Though it wasn't directed to him, he kept hearing one phrase over and over. It was being spoken in low tones among the people when he was first spotted. He thought he recognized one of the words, but asked Walks Apart what it meant.

"You heal sick. They call you *Wichasa Wakan Okinihan*—Great Holy Man."

Walks Apart had come a long way since her first language lesson. She'd attended every class since then, and now spoke almost as well as Lame Bear. Still, Truvor was certain her translation must be incorrect.

"I'm no holy man, just a doctor. I use science, not magic."

She only shrugged.

He found no new outbreaks of the viral infection, which he attributed to his vaccine, even though not everyone had agreed to be inoculated. After checking on his patients he told Walks Apart and Lame Bear he was ready to leave. They urged him, with much insistence, to conduct one of his language classes while he was here. He agreed and, when word spread, his outdoor class was so large he had to raise his voice to be heard. It seemed many were curious, though only his regular students actually participated. Walks Apart's son, who had been attending classes with his mother, sat with some of the other children, proudly translating what he knew.

When he ended the class he was invited by Walks Apart to join her and her son for dinner. She also invited Lame Bear, as he still helped them communicate at times. It began modestly, but other villagers kept stopping by with this and that, until they had a feast that would feed a troop of doctors.

Truvor was delighted with his acceptance by the Lakhota. He'd fostered the relationship needed to develop trade and an exchange of ideas. Yet he knew such optimism was doomed. In a way he felt guilty for the regard these people showed him. A nagging voice inside him said he should warn them — warn them against his own people. For surely what the corporatocracy had planned would not be beneficial to them. Their way of life, their very lives, were likely to suffer from the intrusion — no *invasion* — that was coming. And here he was, a model guest, belying the cruelty to come.

"Want more?" asked Walks Apart, offering him some of the delicious berry mash he'd already sampled.

"No thank you," he said, putting his hands on his already packed stomach. "I can't eat anything else. It was all good, but I'm too full of food already."

"Me full too," said Lame Bear, grabbing his belly.

Walks Apart nodded and said something to her son. He ran off.

Truvor learned during dinner her son did not have a name, as the naming of children took place when they were older, and had undergone a number of trials. Until then, he was simply referred to as the son of Running Elk.

"I never asked you about your husband, Walks Apart. Where is he?"

"Husband dead. He hunt, fall from horse. *Tatanka* kill."

"I'm sorry to hear that."

"Running Elk a respected warrior," said Lame Bear. "Before she marry, many Lakhota not like Walks Apart. She different. But husband give respect. Now, Dr. Svein give respect. Wichasa Wakan Okinihan give respect."

"I'm a doctor, not a cleric. Why do the people call me Wichasa Wakan Okinihan?"

"Because you heal sick," replied Lame Bear. "But also..." He searched for the right words. "There is a story, a very old story, about how Wichasa Wakan Okinihan will come to the people, heal the sick, and unite all the clans against a great enemy. Some say you may be the one."

"That's absurd of course," said Truvor with a laugh. However, he noticed Lame Bear and Walks Apart were not laughing. "You don't believe this, do you?"

Lame Bear shrugged. "It is an old old story."

It was cold, and something kept slapping against his face. He didn't want to leave the dream. It was warm, and Rikissa was there. But consciousness returned regardless of his desire to crawl back into the vision. He was slapped again. He was wet. Someone was throwing water on him.

Tordan opened one eye, then the other. He was lying on wet sand, a beach of some kind. He saw the water, the tide rushing toward his face. He sat up, remembering as he did.

He remembered the jormun, how it had crushed the boat with a single blow, how he'd sunk and then struggled to the surface, all the while expecting the giant sea snake to swallow him. He remembered swimming, swimming until exhaustion left him barely able to float, letting the current take him where it would. He didn't remember reaching the shore. It was either blind luck or the will of Njord that he survived.

Tordan surveyed his surroundings. Nothing anywhere—an empty beach. Then he spotted something on an outcropping of rocks. It looked like shards of his boat. The current had carried them here as well. But where was Santee? He saw no indication anyone else had been on this beach, and he had no recollection of seeing the savage once the boat had been sunk. Poor fellow must have drowned...or been consumed by the jormun.

He stood, wobbling a bit, and was amazed to discover Thor's Razor was still in its scabbard at his side. He looked around for any signs of life. There were large rock formations leading into the sea in both directions down the beach, creating a small cove. Landward were stony ochre cliffs as high as any manor house in Trondheim. But there were rough paths carved into the cliffs, and natural footholds here and there. It wouldn't be easy, but Tordan was certain he could climb to the top. There he'd be able to get a better view of where he was.

He found the climb harder than it looked—especially since his muscles still ached from his exhausting swim. Once he thought he had a firm hold and the soil gave way. Desperately he grabbed a dry vine. It held his weight long enough for him to regain his footing.

He had to stop and gather his strength several times before he reached the summit. The last stretched proved the hardest, but he wasn't about to retreat after coming so far. He used his sword to carve his own hand and footholds into the cliff wall, and with his last scrap of energy, hauled himself over the top.

He lay on his back for some time, resting and looking up at the sky. A scattering of small clouds moved lazily with the wind. He closed his eyes and felt like he could sleep away the rest of the day. He fought the desire to do just that. Though he had no idea where he was or what he'd do next, he knew he couldn't sleep—not yet.

He stood and looked around. Stretched out before him were rolling prairies as far as he could see. The land wasn't flat, but the slope of the grassy hills was so gentle as to remind him of ocean swells. Indeed, it was a vast sea of grass. There wasn't a tree or rock formation in sight. It was unlike anything he'd ever seen. His own lands were mountainous, rough and rocky. Plots for farming were small and scattered over wide areas. The size of this plain from horizon to horizon was startling.

Tordan saw nothing that would help him decide which way he should travel, so he randomly chose a direction and started off. He decided to follow the coastline instead of aimlessly wandering across the interminable grasslands, guessing he was more likely to encounter settlements near the shore.

He'd been walking only a short time when he heard a distant rumble. It sounded almost like rolling thunder, but he saw no sign of a storm anywhere in the sky. He turned inland towards the sound, and began climbing one of the grassy hillocks. The rumble swelled and the ground beneath his feet began vibrating. He'd felt quakes before, but he'd never heard one.

Moving faster now, he topped the hill and looked down into the sloping valley below. There was nothing there but more grass, yet the sound became tumultuous.

It came within view so suddenly he flinched and backpedaled, even though it was quite a distance away. He saw it as clear as the day—a black wave cresting the hill on the other side of the valley—a massive throng of strange beasts surging down into the gorge like an angry swarm of demons.

The creatures were dark, shaggy, four-legged brutes with giant horned heads, humped backs and stick-thin legs. They most resembled bulls, but the resemblance was slight. There were hundreds of them, and they pounded down the vale like an enormous pack of disturbed rats he'd once seen. The ground shook and the noise became deafening. Tordan thanked Thor they weren't headed in his direction. He couldn't imagine what had riled them so, and what they were running to...or from.

The passing of the herd stirred up such a cloud of dust it became difficult to see exactly how many of the creatures there were. They kept coming and coming, and he began wondering if there were thousands instead of only hundreds. Then he saw something else. Because of the dust he couldn't be sure, but it looked as if men on horseback rode amongst the beasts. Were they trying to escape the onslaught? Were they guiding it? He couldn't see well enough to tell.

119

From the corner of his eye, he spotted movement off to his left. It was a young boy who seemed to pop up out of nowhere. A skraeling by his dark skin and black hair. As soon as the boy realized he'd been seen he ran. Tordan gave chase, but the boy was just as fast. Neither of them could gain ground on the other. Tordan stopped to catch his breath. When the boy saw this, he did likewise. They stared at each other. In between breaths, Tordan called out one of the few skrael words he'd learned before he'd been imprisoned, "*Kola!*"

It was supposed to mean "friend," but the boy's wary expression didn't change.

Tordan thought of something else. "*Kola!* Santee *Kola!*"

Still the boy didn't react—but at least he didn't run away. Maybe he wasn't saying it properly. He tried something else. He pulled his sword from its scabbard and laid it on the ground in front of him. He stood, hit his chest with his fists, held out his empty hands and called out, "Kola."

The boy was intrigued, as much by the sword as anything. The fear on his face faded, but he didn't move or say anything. He still looked ready to run at the slightest provocation.

Tordan was trying to think what else he could try, when he heard something coming rapidly up behind him. He turned, expecting to see the herd of monstrosities had turned his way, but instead saw several savages on horseback. Before he could retrieve his sword, or even react, one of the savages howled animal-like and threw something. It came at him sounding like Thor whistling, wrapped around his neck, and smacked against the side of his head. The blow was enough to dizzy him and make his ears ring. Before his head could clear, his legs were pulled out from under him, and he slammed against the ground. His attempts to struggle were met by several blows, and he lost consciousness before even getting a good look at his attackers.

26

It did not occur all at once. It was a gradual process,
which witnessed the onset and termination of many
generations of the subject species. It crept upon us
like a silent predator. By the time any formal
revelation was declared, it was too late.
—A Societal History/Proem

It was the first time Rikissa would appear in public with her betrothed, and she was determined to look her best, despite her disinterest in the performance. She'd seen the same play when she was a little girl. At the time, it was all very glamorous, very exciting, dressing up and going with her mother and father to the theater, along with the rest of the Aesir high-born. Now the idea of a theatrical production bored her. She didn't know why. Maybe it was because Edvard was so excited about it. She didn't know if he just wanted everyone to see her on his arm, or if it had something to do with his own theory involving the Volkerwandering.

This adaptation of the old legend was simply titled "The Journey." The only thing that piqued her interest even mildly, was that her brother Gudrik was one of the players. She'd laughed out loud when he told her he was playing the part of Thor.

"What are you laughing about?" he'd asked.

"I'm sorry, Gudrik, but it's hard to imagine you as the powerful god of thunder," she'd said when she'd stopped laughing.

Gudrik had feigned an expression of chagrin, then laughed himself.

"Yes, yes, I know. I said the same thing when they first suggested it. But that's why they call it *acting*."

He'd thrown his arms into the air with a flourish, and she'd laughed again.

Now, as their motorcar approached the theater, and she saw all the people dressed in their finest attire, her enthusiasm to be among them grew. The motorcar stopped. The driver opened the door. Edvard stepped out first, then helped her. Her voluminous dress squeezed through and she immediately fluffed it back to its former shape and pulled her cloak around her.

The women in attendance sported a wide variety of garments and jewelry.

Necklaces, silver arm rings and headbands, rare golden heirlooms, jewel-encrusted brooches, fur-trimmed capes—it was a feast for the eyes and, Rikissa knew, a competition of sorts. She couldn't wait to see what her mother had chosen.

She didn't have as much time as she would have liked to observe the theatergoers. They'd arrived late, due to her last-minute primping, so Edvard hurried her upstairs to the chairman's alcove where they would sit. Chairman Tryguasson and his wife were already there, as were her own father and mother. As she suspected, her mother was adorned in a silvery, ermine-lined dress, her finest jewelry, and a large emerald pin in her swept-up hair.

Her mother was busy chattering with Beatrix Tryguasson. Her father looked bored.

Not long after they sat, the lights dimmed and the curtain went up. The narrator walked on stage and began his soliloquy.

Rikissa knew the tale—every child did. There was no mystery as to how the story would unfold, nor how it would end. Her only interest was in watching Gudrik's performance.

It began with the rattling of swords and talk of a war between the gods. The evil Loki had used his magic to stir up trouble with the frost giants, and formed an alliance with Holler, the god of disease and destruction. Now Asgard teetered on the brink of Ragnarok.

War was bad business said Wotan, but sometimes it couldn't be avoided. His son, Thor, worried about the mortals he protected. He wanted to save at least some of them from the end the gods feared would soon be upon them. Mortals were innovative, hard-working beings, and deserved the chance to survive, to thrive, he told his father. The rest of the story was about the malevolent intrigues of Loki, and about Thor's quest to protect mankind.

Rikissa surveyed the audience below her. Though the lighting was faint, it seemed most everyone was rapt by the performance. She thought the quality of the production was middling, and had to stifle a laugh every time Gudrik walked on stage carrying his prop hammer. His big scene came after Wotan and Thor defeated Ymir, the greatest of the frost giants.

"We have defeated Ymir, my son," said the actor playing Wotan, "but the war is not over. I fear Ragnarok may still be upon us."

Gudrik walked to center stage and bent down on one knee. "Father, I beseech you to allow me to use the great longboat and carry away a lone tribe of mortals to a safer place."

"What safer place is there?" asked Wotan.

"You can use your power, Father, and hurl the body of Ymir into the stars. Freyr and Gerd will fertilize his remains, and upon them a new world will grow. We'll call it Midgard. It will be a place where humanity can start anew."

Wotan seemed to think on this before he replied.

"You believe these mortals to be worthy of such a feat?"

Gudrik rose to his feet. "I do, Father. I believe they are capable of great enterprise, given time and materials. The fruits of their labor shall someday be the source of great wealth and prosperity."

"Then, by the sacred fires, go," said Wotan. "Have Hermod inform the Valkyries. Gather your worthy mortals. I will cast Ymir's body into the heavens, and you may use my horse Sleipnir to guide the humans to their new world. May the Norns be with you."

Gudrik raised his hammer into the air. "Thank you, Father. Mortal man will praise your name forever."

The story continued. There was more godspeak and some minor trouble when, at first, the mortals didn't want to leave their homes. But Thor convinced them it was necessary, and they began loading their belongings, their animals, even some of their seeds and minerals onto the great longboat.

After one final speech, Gudrik/Thor left the stage with a flourish. As the mere mortals portrayed by bit players continued to work in the background, the narrator reappeared onstage.

"And so this select group of mortal men would board the great longboat, travel across the sea of Skagerak and off the edge of the world. They transversed the heavens, traveled through the stars, the great sea serpent Jormungard pulling the longboat, Sleipnir, the eight-legged steed of Wotan guiding the way to the world known as Midgard. And that is where my story ends. But it is only my story, and one man's tale is but half a tale."

The narrator bowed, the stage lights winked out, and the audience erupted in applause.

Rikissa joined in with mild enthusiasm. She saw her mother and Edvard applauding madly, though her father's clapping was merely perfunctory. On the whole, the audience seemed to enjoy the production, and the applause continued as the players came back on stage, in order of importance. The ovation for Gudrik was resounding. Her mother could hardly contain herself, and continued clapping long after Gudrik left the stage. She had to be quelled by her husband once the house lights came back on.

As they made to leave, Edvard whispered to her, "A fine dramatic composition, well-produced, don't you think? Even though that's not what really happened."

"Oh? You know what really happened?"

Edvard shrugged. "No, I don't. But I think the gods had little to do with it."

27

Above the clouds, the moon is always blue.
—Sicangu Adage

His first feeling when he saw his wife was joy—overriding abundant joy. She hadn't cut her raven hair nor marked herself in anyway. She hadn't given him up for dead. He imagined the pressure exerted by the other women to mourn for her husband, but she'd resisted. He wasn't surprised. Snow Deer had always been a strong, willful woman.

He took her in his arms and held her tight. She didn't say a word, but responded in-kind. When he finally let go of her he stroked her hair and she looked at him. She reached up and traced her fingers over his broken nose. It reminded him that, while he was home, he was not unscarred.

However, it wasn't his nose that concerned him as much as his standing within the clan. He'd been a *blota hunka*, a *wicasa*. But he'd failed his people, and now many of them were dead. Snow Deer must have seen the guilt on his face.

"I am glad you are home, Husband. All the people are glad. You have fought the *wasichu* and returned to us. The warriors are anxious to hear your tales."

"I have no tales of victory to tell, Wife. I was captured by the *wasichu* and held prisoner in their land far away."

"But you escaped, and now the people want to know how. They want to know everything you learned about the *wasichu*. It is your knowledge that will protect us all from the white-skinned demons."

Her words did not temper his feelings of guilt, but they were wise. Yet wisdom was not always enough.

"What of Willow Tree? Does she...?"

"She is your sister. She is Sicangu. She accepts what has happened. She does not blame."

He nodded, even as he was sure his sister must hold some resentment for the loss of her husband.

"Now, your children are outside. They wish to see you."

He nodded and she pulled back the flap of their lodge. He straightened his shoulders and tried to stand proud. When his son and daughter entered, they showed no customary restraint. Each grabbed hold of him as he had taken hold of his wife. His daughter, not usually given to tears, cried. Both held their tongues, but he felt their love with each grasp. Though her body was beginning to show signs of womanhood, it made him glad to see Two Rivers' hair was still in braids. That meant he hadn't missed her *ishnata awicalowan*. She was still his little girl—not a woman yet.

After a few moments, Snow Deer spoke. "Come, Daughter, we must prepare something for your father to eat. He is as lean as a ghost."

When they departed, he looked his son up and down.

"I am told you returned from your vision quest only today. Tell me what you witnessed."

The boy excitedly revealed the details of his quest. He spoke of the animals he saw, the stars he watched, the great *tatanka* hunt he'd witnessed, and about the strange man he'd encountered.

He already knew of the prisoner the hunting party had captured. While he hadn't seen the fellow for himself, he was certain the captive must be Tordan, the man he'd escaped with. Somehow they'd both survived the encounter with the giant sea snake.

"Is the stranger one of the *wasichu*, Father?"

"I do not know. I will see him when the sun rises. But now you must take a name, so you may undergo the other rites. You spoke of watching the stars, and seeing one plunge to the ground. From this, you shall be known as Falling Star. May it be the first of many honored names you shall bear."

His son beamed with pride and reached to hug his father once more. But his father stopped him.

"You are almost a man now. You must begin to act as one."

The boy stood as straight as he could. "Yes, Father."

"Go now. Go tell your mother and sister your name."

He rushed out of the *thipi* and his elation was his father's elation.

He was home and his family was safe. Snow Deer was right. Now he must use his knowledge to keep them safe, no matter what guilt he felt. He would call for a council. But what of the *wasichu* Tordan? The man had helped him escape, but he was the enemy. What would he advise the council to do with him?

He would have to think on that. But now he wanted to go see Fetawachi. It had been much too long, yet he had no doubt his horse would remember him.

Tordan awoke to a crimson sky. Though he was still dizzy, he saw the sun

126

had set. His more immediate surroundings were less clear. He saw numerous fires, several strange structures, and a number people, but everything was a blur. He tried to move but couldn't. He was in a sitting position, arms behind him, bound tightly to a wooden stake thrust securely into the ground. His legs stretched out before him, but his ankles were tied. He was covered in mud. His body ached from head to toe. His breeches were ripped to shreds in places and through the rents he saw his legs scraped raw. Apparently he'd been dragged for some distance.

Despite the lack of clarity in his vision, he realized he was being held prisoner by the skrael. Without his companion Santee, he had no doubt of his fate. Why he was still alive was a mystery. Was he to be the subject of some savage ritual?

As the dizziness faded he saw more clearly. It seemed he was being held in a large settlement of skrael, though few people were about. Those that passed mostly ignored him, though a few children threw stones at him until an old woman shooed them away. Their throws were accurate enough to sting his bruised body.

The structures he saw were indeed strange. They were conical in shape, not large, tapering at the top, more than twice the height of a man. Most were decorated with various odd symbols, and many were lit by fires from within. He saw horses tied together and a few dogs wandering the encampment, but no other animals.

The village was situated on an enormous plain that ran parallel to a line of sawtooth mountains. They weren't particularly tall, as mountains went, but erosion had left them looking like the wrinkled face of the world's oldest man. There was no sign of the sea, so he guessed they were located farther inland from where he'd been captured.

Two women worked together over a fire. One held a large bag that looked like an animal skin. The other filled it with water and then dropped in several bumpy yellow things shaped like the pommel of a sword. Food he guessed.

Using an arrangement of sticks, several hot stones were taken from the fire and dropped into the bag. The bag was tied and left to hang. An curious way to cook, thought Tordan. But he saw no pots or pans of any kind, nor evidence of any metal objects. These savages were indeed primitive.

As he continued to watch the women go about their work, one of the village dogs approached him tentatively. It was gray in color, wolf-like, but much scrawnier. Its demeanor was more fearful than fearsome. It had a bedraggled,

127

uncared for appearance.

"You're a scruffy-looking fellow, aren't you?"

The dog hesitated, then moved close enough to sniff him.

"You look as hungry as I feel. I just hope you don't have any plans to chew on me."

Despite his own hunger, the sight of the emaciated dog was so pathetic Tordan wished he had something to feed it. The dog advanced another two steps, almost close enough to touch Tordan with its nose.

"*Tokhel iyaya!*" A woman, carrying a jug in one hand waved the other at the dog. "*Shuka iyaya! Tokhel iyaya!*"

The dog got the message and scurried off into the dark of the evening.

The woman approached Tordan, stopped and stared down at him until he looked up at her. She quickly averted her eyes, as if his own contained some sort of malevolence.

Her expression was solemn, almost so plain as to be expressionless. She wore a two-piece dress made of some kind of soft animal hide, and shoes of the same material. Her hair had been cut short recently, and not in a particularly careful manner. Tordan noticed she had fresh scars on her arms, and not the kind she might have gotten in a struggle. The wounds were more methodical.

"*Mini,*" she said, bending down and lowering the jug to his lips.

Tordan opened his mouth and she poured him a drink of water, spilling only a little down his mud-caked tunic. She let him swallow, then poured again. She stood and turned to go.

"Santee," said Tordan. "Santee *kola.*"

She looked at him as if he were demented.

"Santee?" he did his best to make it sound like a question.

The woman showed no sign of recognition. She only shook her head and walked away. For all he knew, these were not even Santee's people. He had no idea how many skrael settlements like this there were, or how many tribes.

"*Pilamaya,*" he called out, hoping he remembered correctly. According to what he'd been told, it meant *thank you*.

Whether he'd said it correctly or not, it had some effect. The woman stopped and looked at him again, more curiously than before. She didn't look long, but quickly moved on. As she walked off, Tordan wished he knew the word for food. His stomach had started to growl.

28

The branches are rarely better than the trunk.
—Book of Runes

The steam was so thick he could taste it on his tongue. Rivulets of perspiration ran down his chest and back, soaking the towel that wrapped his loins. He liked the heat, the steam, the sweat. He liked it as much as the pleasure that would follow. But he wasn't so concerned with his own gratification at the moment. He was more concerned that his co-conspirator was content.

"Is the heat to your liking?" asked Furyk.

"It's just right," replied Hrolf. "I enjoy a good, hot sauna."

"I've a feeling you'll enjoy what comes later even more."

"I'm intrigued." Hrolf took a drink of skyr from the mug beside him and wiped his lips.

The housecarle was thickly muscled, and sported a number of battle scars. He certainly had the strength and skill to do what needed to be done. More than that, Furyk was certain he was a man who could keep his mouth shut afterwards. That, after all, was as important as the deed itself.

"As I'm sure you're aware, since most of the house guard is, my brother Gudrik prefers the company of men to that of women."

Though it wasn't spoken of amongst his family, Furyk was certain his brother's sexual dalliances were common knowledge.

Hrolf nodded and said, "He's ragr. Everyone knows that."

"What you might not know, is that he likes to be tied up."

Hrolf grinned. "He does, does he?"

"I was thinking that bit of information might prove useful."

"It could," said Hrolf, "it could. *When* do you suppose it might prove useful?"

"Soon, my friend. Very soon. I'll keep you informed. When the timing is right, you must be ready."

"I'm ready now."

"Good, good."

Furyk clapped his hands together twice. A pair of women, naked and carrying cedar boughs, appeared out of the steam. Gently they began brushing the boughs against backs of the two men. Gradually the stroking became harder, more fierce, until they were actually beating the men's backs with the branches.

Furyk reveled in it.

Birdsong hinted the first intimation of dawn, luring Tordan from his slumber. Despite his aches and pains, he chose not to open his eyes immediately—not until he heard someone approaching.

It was the same woman who'd brought him water the evening before. The sun was just above the horizon and he could see her more clearly now. Aside from the ragged cut of her hair, Tordan found her comely in an exotic sort of way. She didn't have the refined beauty of Rikissa, but the noble Aesir women used colors and ointments to enhance their appearance. This savage woman had no such aids he could see. She had a wide mouth, prominent cheekbones, and large hazel eyes that prompted him to stare.

She sat next to Tordan and began feeding him small bites of some strange food he couldn't identify. It tasted of fatty meat and fruit. Despite its unusual texture, it was good—though in his present state of hunger, almost anything would have been.

He continued to stare at her as she fed him, but he saw his scrutiny made her uncomfortable. She wouldn't look into his eyes. Her expression grew stern and impatient. She wanted him to chew faster. This was obviously not a task she enjoyed. When he tried to speak she shoved another lump of food into his mouth. When he'd finished it all, she gave him some water and stood to leave.

"*Pilamaya*," he said, looking up at her.

She walked off without acknowledging him. He watched her go. When she was nearly out of his line of sight she stopped and began talking with someone. When they finished, the fellow she'd spoken with walked towards him. Tordan recognized him immediately, though he was much cleaner looking than when he'd first seen him.

He was dressed from head to toe in fresh clothes, made from the same animal skins everyone in the village seemed to wear, and there were three feathers in his hair. They were large—not from any bird Tordan had ever seen—and painted with red and yellow stripes. Around his neck, on a rawhide cord, hung a giant claw. Tordan could only guess at the monstrous size of the beast it must have been taken from. At his side, in a leather sheath, he wore the dagger he'd taken when they both escaped from prison.

"Santee, I glad to see you escaped the jormun. It's good to see a familiar face, even though no one seems to know your name."

"My true name is not Santee, Tordan of the *wasichu*."

"That explains the blank looks. What is your true name, friend?"

"We are friends?"

"I helped you escaped, saved your life, brought you home. Yes, I believe we are friends. We are *kola*—if that's the right word."

The skrael folded his arms noncommittally across his chest and grunted. Tordan wasn't certain if that was a yes or a no.

A boy of 11 or 12 years ran up to them, stopped and stared at Tordan. He was certain it was the same boy he'd seen before his capture—the one he'd tried to speak to.

"Hello again. My name is Tordan," he said, wishing he could gesture. "What's your name?"

The boy looked up at the skrael for a translation and got it.

"This my son, Falling... what you call night sky lights?"

"You mean a star?"

"Yes. My son Falling Star."

"That's a proud name. I'm happy to meet you, Falling Star." To the father he asked, "How do you say Falling Star in your language?"

"*Wichahpi Kasna.*"

Tordan repeated it looking at the boy. "*Wichahpi Kasna.*"

The boy asked his father a question. The only thing Tordan understood was *wasichu*, which he knew referred to him and his people. The father's reply was also a mystery, though Tordan caught the word *iyaya*, which he recalled the woman had used when she sent the dog scurrying away. Indeed, the boy ran off, though looking like he preferred to stay.

"It's good to have a son. I'm glad you're back with your family."

He nodded. "*Washtay.*"

"So, friend, *kola*, how about untying me so I can get up and stretch a bit?"

"*Kola* is not only friend. It is more. It means partner in everything, a sharing of respect. I think you are not *kola*."

"Maybe not, not yet. Not while I'm tied to this stake like an animal. But I want to be your friend, your *kola*."

He nodded as if he understood and turned to go.

Tordan could see gaining his freedom wasn't going to be that easy. But he had to continue the attempt to make a connection.

"Wait. You haven't told me your name. Your true name."

The skrael turned around and walked back to him, a severe look on his face.

"I am known as Red Sky, he whose thoughts are strong medicine, brother to *tatanka* the great provider, defender of the Sicangu, husband of Snow Deer. That is my true name."

At that, he turned and walked away.

"That's quite a name," called out Tordan. "Mind if I just call you Red Sky?"

The skrael did not respond.

29

*Though there has been no public discussion of the matter,
I have observed that the reliance on bipedal emotions for
sensory stimulation is becoming progressively more an
addiction than casual pastime. The result has been a
disruption of normal societal activities, a degradation of
communal interaction, and an intensification of
negativity among the essences of which I have had
individual contact.*

—Osst Personal Journal

Kristina enjoyed brushing her mistress' hair. She had such beautiful long golden hair. In truth, she found most of the work she did for Rikissa enjoyable. It was certainly a better fate than working in the factories of Oseberg. She did wonder why her uncle Tordan hadn't come to see her. Surely he would soon. She was afraid to ask to see him. She was still learning everything, and it wouldn't be right yet to ask such a favor of her mistress.

Her only regret was she missed her family. Not being able to speak with Tordan made it worse. She was dreadfully lonely, especially at night, after she retired to the servants quarters. None of the other servants were very friendly with her. She gathered it was because she came from the outside and was immediately given an envied position with Rikissa, forcing one of their number into another job. That girl, who was much older, shot malicious glances at her whenever she could.

It was true Rikissa was a good mistress, and that there was as much play as work. The only thing that seemed to trouble her was her upcoming wedding. Kristina had heard enough to know Rikissa was being forced into the marriage by her parents. The fate of being forced to marry a man not of her choosing was one of the reasons she'd left Oseberg and come to Trondheim. She didn't understand why the Aesir, especially a family as wealthy as House Magnusson, would resort to such a thing. It wasn't as if her mistress wasn't beautiful. Rikissa was pretty enough to attract any man. Kristina only wished she were as attractive. She hoped someday she would be.

She counted the strokes as she brushed Rikissa's hair. She'd been told one hundred was proper, after Rikissa had asked her if she could count. That question had stung her. Of course she could count. Did her mistress think all Vanir were ignorant?

A knock sounded at the door. Kristina was surprised when it opened without an invitation to enter. When she saw who it was, she understood. It was Lady Estrid, Rikissa's mother.

Kristina had only seen her briefly, at a distance, but she'd heard whispers from the other servants of her cruelty. Rikissa herself had bemoaned her mother's stern disposition.

"Daughter, I wanted you to know the plans for your wedding are proceeding on schedule." Lady Magnusson noticed her then, and looked her over as one might a pet. "What's this? A new handmaiden? What's your name, girl?"

Kristina was almost too terrified to speak. She managed to squeak out her name.

"Kristina."

Lady Magnusson turned to her daughter and said, as though Kristina no longer existed, "Such a beautiful name for such a plain little thing."

Somewhere inside her, Kristina realized she'd been insulted. But she didn't care. She was just happy she was no longer being noticed. She backed against the wall and knelt there, trying to make herself as small as possible.

"What is it you wanted to tell me, Mother?"

"The blessed event will, of course, be held on Frigga's Day, a fortnight from now. The heilag of the Valkyrie High Council, Lady Gudhild Ingstad, has agreed to conduct the ceremony. Isn't that wonderful news?" Her mother continued, not waiting for Rikissa to respond. "I've overseen the work on your bridal crown. It's beautiful. It's much more magnificent than the simple one I wore."

Looking at her lavish clothes and the jewelry she wore, Kristina found it hard to believe Lady Magnusson ever wore anything "simple."

"I've decided Gudrik will carry the sword you will give to your husband. We can't have Furyk's scowl casting a pall over the festivities, can we? I'm also picking out the ring you'll give him. Nothing elaborate, but not inexpensive. He is the chairman's son after all.

"Let's see. What else? There's the wedding feast. Tell me, Daughter, is there anything special you would like served?"

Rikissa was surprised her mother would ask for her opinion, but wasn't anxious to give one.

"You decide, Mother. I'm certain whatever you choose will be just delightful."

"Alright, alright. There's so much to do. I should be back to it. I must speak with your father about the decorations for the Ve, and I guess I should coordinate the feast with Beatrix. Alright, my Daughter, I'm off."

Just like that, Lady Magnusson dashed off as brusquely as she'd entered. Rikissa shook her head. Then she saw Kristina.

"What are you doing there, cowering in the corner? Come, finish my hair."

Kristina rose, still holding onto the brush. Rikissa smiled at her and said, "I have a better idea. Let me brush your hair. Then we'll put some powder and rouge on you—just for fun. You'll be the prettiest handmaiden in all Trondheim when we're finished."

That made Kristina smile.

Burgrave Andersson wasn't happy when Truvor told him he'd been visiting the Lakhota village on his own. But after he explained how he'd been accepted and was in no danger, the burgrave calmed somewhat and agreed to let him continue.

It wasn't that he worried about Truvor's safety, it was that he didn't want to lose his doctor.

Storman Ragnarsson, on the other hand, was delighted to hear he'd "infiltrated the savage settlement." He interrogated Truvor about his visits, and encouraged him to continue gathering intelligence and learning the Lakhota language. Truvor answered his questions, but felt guilty doing so. Yet he knew if he didn't, Walks Apart's clan would become a target of the storman's troops. He didn't mention to either of them that the people had begun to refer to him as Wichasa Wakan Okinihan or sometimes just Hecelaya Okinihan—"Great One." Not only would it have been an embarrassing admission, but he didn't want Ragnarsson to try and use his influence with the Lakhota more than he had already.

Truvor visited the village regularly, though he found little illness anymore. He did set a broken leg once, after one of the men fell from his horse. Most of the younger men, the warriors, did not approach him, or show any inclination to be friendly. However, they did show him the same deference they showed Howling Dog. Truvor guessed it was bad medicine to interfere with a "holy" man.

135

He conducted all his language classes in the village now, and though attendance never matched that first time, more villagers were taking an active part. For many, it was simply a matter of curiosity. They all wanted to see the strange *wasichu* who had healed the sick, and he was sure many wanted to see the man some were calling Wichasa Wakan Okinihan. However, each class got a little smaller as the novelty of his visits waned, though Walks Apart and her son were always there. She'd begun to assist him, and helped Lame Bear with translations for the newer students.

Truvor found himself drawn to her in way he couldn't quite explain. It wasn't only her exotic nature, though he admitted to himself that was part of it. He admired her independent spirit and rebellious nature—her inner strength. Lame Bear told him many men had tried to court her, but she'd rejected them all. That shouldn't have pleased him, but it did.

30

Let no one see what is in your heart or in your purse.
—Book of Runes

"**A** wall of secrecy has been raised around the production of Trellestar's new weapon. We don't know any more than we did three weeks ago."
"Which is what?" asked Oleg.

"We know they've developed a new handheld firearm, but we know nothing of its specifications," said his executive manager with obvious frustration. "Our spies have seen individual parts being manufactured, but the final product has only been seen behind the closed doors of upper management."

"Hmm," mumbled Oleg, rising from his desk. "That it unusual. Why would they take such precautions? Even if someone were able to get their hands on the design specs, it would take them weeks to set up production."

"Maybe Magnusson's growing paranoid in his old age," offered the manager.

"Maybe," said Oleg, though he didn't believe the answer was that simple. "Offer a reward to our spies, for the first one to bring us a fabricated model, or at least the complete specifications."

"Yes, sir."

"How goes our green oil development?"

"I'm afraid it's proceeding very slowly, sir. The costs incurred to set up the plant, the raw materials—"

"What raw materials? I thought all we needed was algae and sea water?"

"It's not quite that simple, sir. Aside from the actual construction of the closed loop systems necessary to protect the algae from the harshness of our climate, it must be fed with several nutrients—nitrogen, phosphorus, potassium, silica, iron—it's an expensive process. And in order to produce enough fuel to make the initial investment pay off, a much larger system must be built than one we used to conduct our initial research."

"Alright, alright. I'll have to approach some potential investors personally. I've still got some favors I can call in. Are there any new developments on the Serkland front?"

"No, sir. Nothing. But I'm afraid I must report more turmoil in our Oseberg factories. We've had to break several strike attempts. Fortunately the activists are still small in number. We've had to resort to violence, and we've arrested some of the B'serker leaders."

"Good, good. If we give them no one to follow, the movement will grow lackluster." The thought of the Vanir rabble rousers somehow led to thoughts of Glyfe. "How is my son?'

"All reports are good, sir."

"I want to visit him. Arrange it."

The manager hesitated.

"Are you sure that's wise, sir? If—"

"I said arrange it."

"Yes, sir. Right away."

Oleg knew that keeping the secret of his son was crucial to his position within the corporatocracy, but that didn't completely eliminate his feelings as a father. He would visit the boy, and damn the consequences.

A kick to the ribs woke Tordan the next morning. He glared up at two savages standing over him. They had the same painted feathers in their hair as Red Sky, and as had the riders who'd captured him. Was that the mark of a warrior? He noticed one wore two painted feathers, while the other had only a single. Did that signify rank?

One of skrael said something directed at him, but he didn't understand. The other fellow knelt and began untying him. Both men were armed only with knives, but they weren't drawn. The ropes loosened around his chest and wrists and he flexed his arms as best he could until the skrael grabbed his arms again and tied his wrists in front of him this time. The other man looped a second rope around his neck and pulled it tight like a leash on a dog. When they finished they cut the rope around his ankles and pulled on the leash, forcing him to stand.

Tordan was certain, despite his depleted condition, he could've taken the opportunity to escape. With his hands in front of him and his legs free, he could've easily incapacitated his guards, grabbed one of their knives, and taken off. How far he'd get was another matter. For all purposes he'd be wandering, lost, a stranger in a strange land. Besides, that's not why he was here. His mission was to ingratiate himself with these people, learn about them, discover if they had a cure for the blight. Not only for Jarl Magnusson and his own return to the grace of Trondheim, but for Jorvik's wife, Marta. Maybe the skrael had something that could save her from the ravages of the disease.

138

His guard tugged on the leash and he followed. They walked through the encampment and Tordan kept his eyes and ears open. What he must do now was learn. In particular he must learn as much of their language as he could. Only by being able to communicate would he eventually be able to discover their secrets.

It occurred to him Red Sky was well aware of his skills. He'd witnessed the escape from House Magnusson's prison. Red Sky knew he could overcome these men and run for it if he wanted. It's likely this was a test as much as anything.

His observations confirmed "encampment" was, indeed, the right word. He saw no permanent buildings, only dozens of the same tent-like structures. All of them had designs of some sort painted on them. Almost without exception, the colors used were red, yellow, black, and white. Often these colors joined to form a circle. The circle was apparently a powerful symbol.

He saw no fields, no sign of cultivation, so he presumed the skrael were nomadic, primarily hunters and gatherers, taking what they could from the land and moving on—moving with the seasons or to follow the game they hunted.

The only weapons he saw were spears, bows, stone axes and knives. He knew they had something made from leather straps and round stones they threw, because that was what had brought him down. They also had shields, though they were small and made only of animal hides. Each one was painted, often with the same circle symbol. He didn't think they'd be much protection in battle though. Everything he saw confirmed his earlier observations that they had no weapons of steel or metal objects of any kind, other than the dagger Red Sky had taken in Trondheim. He surmised the skrael would be at a great disadvantage in any armed conflict with his own people.

The women were all dressed alike, as were the men. There was little variation—some colored stones or seashells here, fur or feathers there—but the material of their clothing was the same. They wore scraped and leathered animal skins, though he couldn't tell what kind or how many different animals. Their shirts, robes, breeches, vests, dresses, were all leather or buckskin. That meant they had no cloth manufacturing either. He saw no chairs and guessed there was no furniture of any kind, even inside the tents. There wasn't room. Everyone sat on the ground, either on hides or fur blankets or just in the dirt. The men sat cross-legged in a fashion he knew would be difficult for most of his own people. The women sat with their legs folded off to the sides.

They passed a group of boys playing a game with a large ball of some kind, throwing it, kicking it. Red Sky's son was one the players. Tordan raised his tied hands and attempted to wave at the boy.

"Falling Star," he called. "Hello."

The boys paid the prisoner no attention.

Tordan tried again. *"Wichahpi!"* he called out even louder, hoping he'd pronounced it right. *"Wichahpi Kasna!"*

The boys stopped this time, some looking at Tordan, others at Red Sky's son. Falling Star stared back at him, but didn't react. His leash-holder pulled so hard Tordan almost fell. The boys laughed and continued their game.

They'd almost reached the other end of the village when they came to a small cage. It was fashioned from wooden branches, thorn bushes, and rope, and looked like something that might have held chickens or goats. His guards opened the cage door, forced him down, and pushed him inside. One of them said something and they both chuckled in a strange, savage sort of way as they tied the door shut. Tordan glared defiantly at them, pulling the leash from around his neck. They ignored him and walked away.

It was obvious this cage could not hold him if he wished to break out. In addition, several horses were tethered nearby. Was it to humiliate him? Did they put him in an animal cage to say that's what he was to them? Was it another test by Red Sky? If he expected Tordan to try and escape, he was going to be disappointed.

She knew nothing she or anyone else could do would stop the wedding now. She was being watched too closely. Her movements were limited to the manor. She couldn't create a scandal, she couldn't even run away. Not that she would. Where would she go?

Since she couldn't do anything to stop the impending marriage, at least she wanted to complain about it. So naturally she decided to see Gudrik. She'd always been closer to him than Furyk. He was always understanding, sympathetic—traits Furyk was unfamiliar with. He would simply tell her to shut up and do what she was told. At least Gudrik would console her, and that's what she needed now.

Rikissa thought she'd slip into Gudrik's bed chamber using the servant's door in the back, like she always did as a child. It was a game she'd played with her brother. They'd see who could sneak up on the other.

It occurred to her she could try and fabricate an incestuous affair with her brother. That might be enough to get the wedding called off. She sighed. No one would ever believe it—not with Gudrik. His sexual proclivities were well-known within the manor, and probably outside it as well. Her parents certainly knew, and while they would never outwardly condone such activity, they tolerated it. At least behind closed doors.

She opened the servant's door and heard voices. She moved quietly, but only far enough to see Gudrik, naked, tied to his bed. She recognized Inguar, Gudrik's best "friend." He was naked too.

She didn't want to see anymore, and quietly backed out of the chamber.

Unable to speak with Gudrik, she felt even more alone. That made her think of Tordan.

Where was he? What was he doing? Had he forgotten her? Was he in the arms of another? Was he still alive?

31

*I want to know if you can live with failure and still
stand on the edge of a lake and shout to the full moon,
"Yes!"*

—Wisdom of Fire In His Eyes

R ed Sky had been home only a matter of days before the *wakincuzas* were
called to meet and hear of his ordeal among the *wasichu*. The Sicangu
council included the wisest, most courageous, most generous men of the
clan. Men who had the ability to both think and speak their minds clearly.
Many, but not all, were among the clan's elders.

Broken Horn, *iyotan wicasa* of the Sicangu, directed the council, but the clan
was ruled by consensus. Peer pressure and ridicule kept social order, while
justice was meted out by general agreement.

When the council had gathered in his lodge, Broken Horn tossed a handful
of cedar and sage into the fire to purify the conclave and signify its
commencement. The flickering flames played havoc with the shadows of the
council members against the *thipi*.

"I had a dream," said Broken Horn. "A powerful dream of the *wasichu* and
their monsters. They killed our people and ravaged our land.

"You know me. You know I am not a man given to fanciful speculation and
reactionary opinions. But this dream was bad medicine. I fear for the Sicangu. I
fear for the Lakhota, for the Oglala, for the Sahnish, for all the people. Our
brother Red Sky, whom we all know and respect for his deeds and his wisdom,
was captured by the *wasichu* and held for many days. I ask him to tell us what
he has learned."

Red Sky did not move from his position in the circle of men. He hesitated,
collecting his thoughts and choosing his words carefully.

"Before I begin, I must beg the council's forgiveness for my grievous error in
judgment. I was wrong about the *wasichu*. They cannot be trusted. It was my
lack of wisdom that led to the deaths of my clansmen and my own
imprisonment. I am humbled before you."

"No one among us is without fault," said Broken Horn. "We have all made
mistakes. The wisdom of Red Sky is still respected. Tell us, Brother, tell us what

you know of our enemy."

"Broken Horn is both generous and wise," Red Sky said, then paused. "It is true the *wasichu* are our enemy. Why they wish to make war upon us, I cannot say. They are a sickly people, and I think the sickness makes them crazy. They are devious as well, and they are evil. For reasons I do not understand, some even kill their own children while they're still in the womb." The council murmured as one in disbelief. "It is true their weapons are powerful. You know of their firesticks, the *mazakhan* that spit death like the rattlesnake. But I have seen even larger weapons, whose cacophony makes the firesticks sound like a child's laugh. They have many wondrous things, but they are only men—not monsters, not gods. It is true many of their number are skilled warriors, but they can be slain."

"What of this *wasichu* who is our prisoner?" asked Kicking Bull. "Is he a warrior?"

"Yes. I believe he is a warrior of great skill. He was also being held prisoner by the *wasichu*. His transgression was a family matter, involving a *wicasa's* daughter. Yet this *wasichu* helped me to escape and return to my family. He is *wasichu*, but I do not believe he is evil...or crazy. He is... different."

"Do you trust this *wasichu* warrior?" asked Broken Horn.

Red Sky paused, considering this. "I do not trust him completely, yet I admire him. I respect him. I recommend to the council that we keep him alive. At the very least we can continue to learn more about our enemy. At best we may gain a powerful ally."

"We all bear much esteem for the wisdom of Red Sky," said Kicking Bull. "But he does not know what the *wasichu* have done in his absence. They have left the plain scattered with the carcasses of the *tatanka*, taking only bits and pieces and leaving the rest to rot. The black smoke from their fires chokes the air, and they foul the land as they spread like ants across a dead rabbit. You speak the truth that they are sickly. They carry the sickness with them. A plague has fallen on the Oglala, and many have already died.

"More and more of the *wasichu* come from the sea, and their village grows daily. Already they build their walls on the lands of the Lakhota. Soon they will encroach upon the plain of the Sicangu. Red Sky is not the only one of the people they have taken. Many more have been captured, while others have been slaughtered with no more concern than one would show a mad dog. I say to you all, we will know no peace until every *wasichu* is dead, beginning with this prisoner."

143

The council took a moment to consider this. Deep in thought, Broken Horn ran his fingers across his brow.

"Kicking Bull speaks the truth. The *wasichu* are like locust upon the land. They have no respect for Mother Earth or Father Sky. They take, but they do not give. Yet there is reason in the words of Red Sky. This prisoner may be useful. For now, he lives, in the custody of Red Sky. That is all I have to say."

The meeting of the Board of Directors had transformed from an orderly proceeding to a raucous clamor of voices in a matter of seconds. The labor rights movement of the Vanir had become a volatile issue that spewed opinions. For the moment, Vikar said nothing, but he was in the minority. He imagined the giant statues of Wotan and Thor looking down at the unruly assembly with disdain.

Chairman Tryguasson was having a difficult time being heard above the tumult to restore order.

"Order!" he called out. "Silence!" He stamped his staff against the dais floor several times until the room quieted. "We must have order. Just because the Vanir rabble has become a mob, doesn't mean we should sink to their level."

The chairman's censure was enough to put everyone back in their seats.

"Now," said the chairman, "if we can act like civilized businessmen, I will entertain ideas for dealing with this so-called 'labor movement'. The chair recognizes Jarl Atterdag of Vikenex."

"It has been suggested we use our military troops to keep the laborers in line. My first impulse was to agree with this strategy. However, it seems the harsher we deal with the Vanir, the larger the rebel movement becomes. My sources say the number of actual B'serkers has doubled in a matter of weeks."

"Jarl Gripsholm of Trondtel, may it please the board. I would say a handful doubled is still only two handfuls. However, Jarl Atterdag is correct. If we take the wrong measures, we will only multiply our problems. I say, as I've said before, we need spies to seek out the leaders of the movement. Jail them, dispose of them, and the sheep will be content to graze again."

"Jarl Magnusson of Trellestar," said Vikar, standing. "Though it flies in the face of precedent, I must agree with Jarl Gripsholm." A murmur of laughter greeted this. "Cut off the head and the body will die."

"It seems a worthy suggestion," said Chairman Tryguasson. "Identify the individual leaders of this movement, each house in their own industrial units, and deal with them accordingly. In the meantime, I decree we should take no overt steps against any mass work stoppages or slowdowns that might inflame the situation. Does anyone wish to defy my decree by calling for a vote?"

Vikar looked round. There was some discussion between the jarls and their aides, but no one objected.

"Is there any other business before I call for a close to this meeting?"

"Jarl Volsung of Sveabordcorp, if it please the board. I am declaring, before the board, a patent for a flying machine."

The announcement created another buzz throughout the assembly. One of Volsung's thanes stood and held up a rough blueprint of the machine, along with an artist's rendition of what the final product would look like. It had three layers of fixed wings crossing in front of where its pilot would sit, and another, smaller wing in the rear, like the tailfin of a fish. It had two wheels in front and one aft, and a propeller larger than the model used in a thunderboat. The artist had painted it red with black trim. It reminded Vikar of a bird of prey

"As you can see, this machine looks and works nothing like the airships for which Roskildcorp owns the patent. Its aerodynamic abilities stem from its triple-winged structure. It's fueled by jor oil and uses an engine similar to that of a motorcar. We believe the engine to be of sufficiently different design, just as Trellestar's thunderboats are slightly different, as not to encroach upon any existing motorcar patent. That, of course, is a decision for the patent board."

Vikar was intrigued. He stood and asked, "Have you actually flown one of these machines, Jarl Volsung?"

"We call them aeroplanes," replied Volsung. "We have flown scale models and made many preliminary tests, but we wanted to secure the patent for our design before testing the full size models. Now that our patent has been publicly declared, we will begin testing immediately."

Vikar heard the whispers around him. No one thought the craft would actually fly. He wasn't so sure. Volsung may be a fat fool in some regards, but he'd never go public like this until he was reasonably certain of the product's potential. It may take some time to perfect, but Vikar guessed this "aeroplane" would be the transportation of the future.

32

*You do not really know your friends from your
enemies until the ice breaks.*

—Ancient Aesir Proverb

Jorvik struggled up the stoop to his front door, nearly dragging his right leg. Each time he winced in pain he recalled the blow to his knee by the filthy strike-breaker. Worse than the pain was the knowledge the man was Vanir, paid by his Aesir masters to turn against his own. With all they had to struggle against, it never occurred to him they might have to fight their own people. He shouldn't have been so foolish not to realize some men would do anything for a silver coin.

He'd barely made it home. His knee had swollen to twice its normal size, several fingers were broken, and a crust of dried blood traced the cut on his forehead. He opened the door, managed to shut it behind him, then collapsed.

He must have woken Marta, because she hurried in wearing her nightclothes. He'd no idea what time it was, except that it was late.

"Jorvik! What's happened?"

"They sent in strike-breakers. They tried to grab whoever they thought was leading the strike, but I got away. I don't know how many men they took."

"Look at you—your head is bleeding."

"My head's okay. It's my knee that's bad. I need ice."

Marta left him long enough to fill a bag with ice. He pulled himself into a sitting position there on the floor. She placed the bag on his knee as gently as she could. He winced at the touch.

"Oh, Jorvik. Why do you do this? What good will it do?"

He looked up at her and saw the tears. But there was nothing for it—nothing he could do or say to stem the tide.

"The good will come someday, Wife. The good is for Canute...and Kristina."

"But what good will it be if their father is dead? They need you to be there for them when I'm gone."

"What they need is justice. And if it takes my life, or ten thousand lives, my children shall have it."

He woke with uncertainty. He recognized his cage, but how many days had he been here? Five? Six? More? How many days since he'd left Trondheim? Tordan thought about his brother, and wondered how Jorvik and Marta were doing. He wondered how Jorvik reacted when they came for Kristina. He was certain his brother would realize it was for the best, once he cooled down. But now he wasn't there to watch over her. He believed Rikissa would keep her promise to take care of his niece, though she would be busy with her upcoming nuptials. He wondered if the man chosen for her was a good one. A high-born Aesir no doubt.

Tordan tried to battle the tedium of his captivity by studying the skrael villagers, and learn what he could of their language. But learning was difficult without a teacher to translate. So each day, twice a day, when the woman who brought him food and water came, he tried to get her to speak, to teach him more. He'd learned water was *mini* and a dried meat that tasted like beef was *papa*. The fatty mixture with berries was *wasna*. He'd learned other words as well, and was trying to form phrases, though the resulting utterances were often met by puzzled looks. One thing he hadn't learned was the woman's name, though he was certain she understood his was Tordan.

She arrived late morning, as she always did, with water and food of some kind. Today's fare was meat wrapped in a kind of bread. As he ate what she passed him through the cage bars, he pointed at the meat and said, "*Papa.*"

She shook her head. "*Talo,*" she said. "*Talo.*"

He realized it tasted different and mimicked her pronunciation.

"*Talo,*" he said, tearing off a piece of coarse bread and holding it up to her.

She responded right away. "*Aguyapi.*"

"*Aguyapi,*" he replied.

To keep her engaged, he pointed at a nearby fire where some women were cooking.

"Fire," he said. "Hot." He pretended to touch something hot and act as if burned. He wiggled his fingers as much like flames as he could and repeated, "Fire." He held out his bound hands to her, wanting a reply.

She understood immediately. "*Peta.*"

"*Peta,*" he repeated. "*Peta...*fire." He blew into his hands, making enough noise so she could hear, then waved his hands slowly across the air. "Wind."

She hesitated, then said, "*Thate.*"

"*Thate...*wind."

She'd never shown any fear around him, but she was definitely curious. She seemed intrigued that he wanted to learn her language, but never tarried outside his cage.

Tordan continued to ask questions, but once he was done eating she stood to leave.

"*Washtay,*" he said, touching his lips, then his belly, "*washtay. Pilamaya.*"

"*Toh,*" she replied before hurrying away.

He'd heard that word before in response to "*Pilamaya,*" so he guessed it must mean "You're welcome."

She hadn't been gone long when the same raggedy dog he'd seen his first day in the village slunk towards him. Not long after he'd been moved to this cage the dog had found him and was often nearby. He knew by the way the villagers shouted at the animal and were always chasing it off that they were kindred spirits. Both were outcasts. As usual, the dog came looking for scraps. Tordan brushed what he saw, which wasn't much, just outside the cage. The dog hungrily lapped it up, getting as much dirt as actual food.

Somewhere in the village someone was playing a woodwind. He couldn't see the musician, but the sound carried to his prison. The tune was new to him, but the instrument sounded exactly like the one his skaldoran mentor played.

Sheimdal had been born a Vanir and was taken as a boy by the Aesir as Tordan was. When Tordan first met him, he was already an aging warrior, but one who always had time for a song or a poem. Sheimdal had taught him everything about being a skaldor, but had also taught him to enjoy life. When his old teacher died, Tordan did just that. He must have raised his cup to Sheimdal a hundred times, and drank so much he had to be carried back to the barracks by his brothers.

The music he heard now was melodic and graceful, but he couldn't help but think how Sheimdal would have added lyrics to the tune and sung with gusto, even though his voice reminded others of a dying ox.

The old man had always treated Tordan as a son. The sense of pride he had in his young skaldor was palpable. Tordan wondered what Sheimdal would think of him now.

33

Boldly do men talk from a distance.
—Words of Chairman Wulfstan

Outside the tavern the wind howled the warning of an oncoming storm. But the clamor inside masked the approaching onslaught with gruff shouts and drunken songs. Furyk found the singing irksome, but, as it was coming from a table full of skaldors, he opted to keep his mouth shut. In here it didn't matter if he were the son of a jarl. It didn't matter who you were. One wrong word and you could find a blade in your gut.

The *Blind Crow* wasn't the kind place he usually frequented. However, Hrolf had suggested they meet here, so he'd agreed.

A rousing burst of laughter erupted and he glared at the tableful of skaldors. Low-born scum all, yet Furyk sensed an air of superiority about them. He despised them. They had their uses, but they were dogs that shouldn't be let off their chains except when needed.

"So, master Furyk," said Hrolf, trying to draw his attention from the skaldors. "What is it you wished to talk with me about?"

Furyk looked into the housecarle's eyes, plumbing the depths of his trustworthiness.

"The time is nigh."

"Time for what?"

"Time for my brother Gudrik to die."

Hrolf took a drink of his skyr and used his forearm to wipe the foam from his lips.

"To kill the son of a jarl is not a small thing," said Hrolf, looking squarely at Furyk.

"No," agreed Furyk, "it's not. But, my dear Hrolf, you'll be adequately rewarded—now and even more later, when I am jarl."

Hrolf nodded and took another drink.

"I want you to wait until after my sister's wedding. But then—as soon as you can arrange it." More laughter distracted Furyk momentarily before he turned back to Hrolf. "I can count on you?"

"I'll do my duty, master Furyk."

"...B'serker sabotage ruined my new furnishings even before they could be delivered. We must do something about these Vanir outlaws."

Estrid shook her head. She couldn't believe Lady Volsung was talking about her furniture problems at a meeting of the Valkyrie High Council.

"Please, Sister," responded Lady Ingstad, heilag of the high council, "let's allow our men to deal with the problem of the B'serkers. That's not the concern of this council."

"Of course, Sister Gudhild, I was just saying—"

"We have more urgent matters to discuss," spoke up Lady Atterdag.

Volsung looked annoyed that she'd been interrupted.

"There are rumors," continued Atterdag, "that a certain jarl has hidden away a defective child."

That got everyone's attention, including Estrid's.

"What rumors?" asked Gudhild.

"More than rumors, I should say. I've been passed information from a reliable source."

"How is this possible?" asked Estrid. "Every jarl's wife is here. We would know if any defective child was born."

"There is one jarl who has no wife," said Atterdag.

Estrid realized immediately she was speaking of Jarl Gripsholm, Vikar's long-time adversary. His wife had died in childbirth years ago, and he hadn't remarried. The child had died too—supposedly.

"You're speaking of Jarl Gripsholm, I assume," said Gudhild. "I recall Lady Gripsholm died unexpectedly, in her own home giving birth. So, too, did the child."

"But the child didn't die," said Atterdag. "It was hidden away by Jarl Gripsholm because of some defect that would have required its elimination."

"This is a serious charge, Sister Atterdag. Do you have any proof?"

"Not at this time, Heilag. Neither do I yet know where the child's being kept. I understand it doesn't reside within the Gripsholm manor. However, I'll continue my investigation into the matter."

"Yes, do. Let us all be aware of any information concerning such a breach of convention."

"We'll never breed the blight out of the upper classes if we allow such a thing," said Lady Tryguasson.

Beatrix Tryguasson seldom spoke up, but Estrid deduced her reaction had everything to do with the fact the rumors about the chairman's affliction were true.

"Now, let's speak of happier matters." Gudhild turned to look at Estrid and smiled. "The wedding of Sister Magnusson's daughter Rikissa approaches. I will conduct the ceremony, but I would like to have all the high mistresses on the dais with me. Excluding sisters Estrid and Beatrix of course. So be certain you all prepare."

"It's going to be lovely, I'm sure," said Lady Eriksson. "I can't wait."

"I can't wait until this council meeting is over," said Volsung. "There's a certain red-headed geldr I can't wait to get my hands on."

Several of the women laughed. Estrid, however, thought the comment was in bad taste, even though she too was looking forward to the Dance of Freyja when the meeting ended.

Gudhild cleared her throat. It was her sign for silence. When she had everyone's attention, she said, "Before we adjourn to more pleasureful matters, I remind you all of the courses of action regarding educational issues and the colonization of Serkland we previously agreed upon. You will each continue to use your influence, where you can, to sway those matters to toward their proper courses."

Gudhild was ancient, the oldest of the Aesir as far as Estrid knew. She was using that hoary face of hers now, gazing soberly at each of the high mistresses. They nodded in return.

Estrid's own influence with her husband was minimal these days, but that didn't mean she couldn't guide him along the proper path when needed. It only meant going about it in a more surreptitious manner.

"Is there any other business?" asked Gudhild. No one spoke. "Then, by the glory of Freyja, I adjourn this meeting of the Valkyrie High Council."

"By the glory of Freyja," answered the high mistresses in unison.

34

*The first symptoms were behavioral. Our physical
selves, kept in perpetual hibernation, suffered no ill
effects. It was the discorporeal essences that absorbed
the emotions, and eventually began to decline in
ways both subtle and horrific.*
—A Societal History/Proem

One day, under Red Sky's direction, Tordan was untied and put to work. He joined several older boys and girls, including Red Sky's own son, on a long walk from the village, to a site where they collected wood. Some of it was taken right from the ground, other pieces were cut and trimmed with a stone axe. Tordan was twice the size of any of the young workers, and given twice as much wood to carry. They hauled the wood to another location, nearer the village, but still not within sight.

He noticed the emaciated dog from the village was following them, though at a distance. He pointed the animal out to Red Sky.

"Why does everyone chase that dog away?"

"Dog belonged to *wichaha wakan*, a holy man who died," replied Red Sky. "Now the people believe it is possessed by Ikto, the trickster. No one wants such an animal. No one even wants to eat it."

"I'm sure it appreciates that."

When they'd reached their destination, the youngsters began building something—two things actually. Red Sky barked occasional commands, or suggestions, but they seemed to know what they were doing. Tordan had no idea, so there wasn't much he could help with. But Red Sky told him which pieces to grab, and where to hold them, while the others used leather strips and rope to hold their constructions together.

One of these structures was obviously a *thipi*—a word he'd learned. It was smaller than the ones in the village, and only the framework, without the animal hides to cover it. The other was a platform, built high enough off the ground that Tordan could walk under it.

When the work was nearly complete, Red Sky sent Falling Star running back to the village. In short order, Falling Star returned, leading a large group of natives. Everyone was dressed in what was obviously their finest attire, sporting many feathers and bead-worked items of clothing. Some of their faces were painted black. No one spoke, and Tordan sensed it was a solemn occasion. He saw the reason why. Four men carried a body on their shoulders. This was a funeral.

The men carried the body, which was wrapped in hides, to the platform. Others carried a fur blanket, some weapons, and other items. Tordan guessed they belonged to the dead man. The possessions were placed below the scaffold, while the four men laid the body gently atop the platform. Everyone then gathered around the skeletal *thipi*, where they began smoking from a single pipe they passed among themselves.

Sensing his curiosity, Red Sky stepped next to Tordan and said, "This is *Nagi Gluhapi*—the freeing of the soul."

Though they were standing apart from the mourners, Tordan whispered, "Why are they smoking?"

"Smoke carries prayers to Great Spirit, creator of all things, Wakan Tanka. They pray Great Spirit will accept Dancing Bear's soul. This world," Red Sky, arm outstretched, swept his hand across the horizon, "only one of many worlds on a spirit's journey."

"Will they burn the body?"

Red Sky looked at him as if he were daft. "I saw burning of a *wasichu* body. That is not our way. Dancing Bear will lie there until he is no more. His body will go back to land where he came from—land he lived on. The land, the birds, the beasts will all gain from his death. It is sacred circle of life. He was good man—brave warrior. His soul will be taken by the winds of Tahte to Wakan Tanka, who will surely accept him."

The ceremony, as Tordan thought of it, was conducted without haste, with few words being spoken. He spotted one odd fellow off to the side, away from the mourners. His clothing was strange, with haphazard streaks of color and an off-kilter cut. He was dancing, but in an odd way. When he stopped, he walked backwards. It was a performance of some kind, though everyone assembled ignored him. It seemed he mocked the ceremony. Tordan expected someone to chastise the fellow.

Tordan pointed him out with a questioning look.

"He is *heyoka*, crazy dancer. He is sacred. He invokes spirits with his foolishness."

At one point, for no reason Tordan could ascertain, everyone stood and began the trek back to the village. Everyone but one woman. Like some of the others, her face was painted black. Her hair had been cut short, without care, and blood was smeared up and down her arms where there were fresh lacerations.

"The dead man's wife?"

"Yes," replied Red Sky. "She will stay here."

"For how long?"

"Until Wakan Tanka tells her it is time to return."

Tordan watched as the woman approached the platform, fell to her knees below it, and began to wail.

Looking at her, he remembered something. The woman who fed him had the same kind of cuts on her arms when he first saw her—the same ragged haircut.

"The woman who brings my food, what is her name?"

At first, Red Sky looked as if he wouldn't answer.

"She is known as Willow Tree In The Wind. She is my sister."

"She was in mourning too, wasn't she? Did her husband die?"

Red Sky's expression became that of an gathering squall. Tordan saw the anger in his eyes. He didn't answer right away, but when he did, his voice was under control.

"Yes. Her husband was killed by the *wasichu* when I was captured."

Tordan was struck by the realization of how this woman must see him—this woman who'd been caring for him.

"Is that why she won't look me in the eye?"

"It is not right to stare at someone's eyes—especially man woman. Not...polite."

"Still, she must hate me. Why does she bring me food?"

"She does what she is told to do," said Red Sky without looking at him. "Come. We must go. There will be feasting, and your cage awaits."

"I thought you didn't put people in cages. That's what you told me back in Trondheim."

"I did not say we could not learn from the *wasichu*."

35

A tree is known by its fruit.
—Ancient Aesir Proverb

"The housecarle Hrolf is here with a report for you, sir."

"Send him in, Captain," responded Vikar without looking up from the balance sheets he was studying.

"Is there anything new I need to know in relation to this assignment, sir?"

"No, Captain. It's a personal matter. Now show him in. I'm very busy."

"Yes, sir."

Griffenfeld executed a crisp about-face and exited the room. Vikar interpreted the stiffness of his departure to mean the captain was agitated he wasn't privy to the all details of the assignment. That was good. No one should know everything a jarl did.

"Sir."

Hrolf stood at attention before Vikar's desk.

"Relax, Hrolf. Tell me, what's my son up to now."

"As I suspected he would, sir, he's finally given me the go-ahead to assassinate your eldest son."

"He has, has he?" Vikar wasn't surprised. He was certain this day would come, yet it saddened him just the same. It was a smart move on Furyk's part. In a way he was proud of his youngest son's plotting. But Gudrik was his first-born, and despite his many failings, Vikar had feelings for the boy. What worried him more, was what Furyk might do once he was next in line to inherit House Magnusson.

"Tell me, Hrolf. Are there any other plots afoot? Does my son Furyk have other plans?"

"No, sir. None he's shared with me. He does talk of one day supplanting you as jarl. But I'm certain he means in the natural course of events."

"I'm certain," replied Vikar, not bothering to disguise the sarcasm in his voice.

After a long silence in which Vikar considered a spectrum of possible ramifications, Hrolf asked, "How should I proceed, sir?"

Vikar turned away from the housecarle and looked out his window.

"I'll not interfere in sibling matters."

Vikar realized with that utterance he'd likely sealed the death of his eldest son. The thought troubled him...for a moment. Who knew what might transpire? Maybe Gudrik would surprise him. If he were wise enough, strong enough to take his place as jarl someday, he might just survive.

"You may go now, Hrolf. But keep me apprised. I want regular reports."

"Yes, sir."

Once Hrolf was gone, Vikar fought the urge to recall the housecarle—to change his mind and give the fellow new orders. But no. It must play out as it would. It was the natural course of events.

The sun was setting across the distant plain when Willow Tree In The Wind next came to feed him. The sky was aglow with an assortment of reds and oranges and yellows, while the crown of the sapphire moon was beginning to peek over the horizon.

He'd been thinking about Rikissa, and how his foray into her bed had led him to this place. He wondered how she was, and whether she were married yet. Had she grown to love her husband...or at least accept him? His affair with her seemed such a distant memory now—a reminiscence that dissipated as he glimpsed Willow approaching.

His wrists and ankles were no longer tied. His captors were no longer worried about him escaping his cage, which was more about humiliation than imprisonment. He wasn't a man to them, just another beast.

He looked closely at his caretaker's face. No sign of hate ignited her eyes when she looked at him. He expected to see it, but all he saw was the same quiet dignity he'd noticed when he'd first laid eyes upon her—the same inner strength.

She had a look of anticipation as she fed him. She'd come to expect him to ask questions about their language. Instead, he hit his fist against his chest.

"Tordan," he said, and repeated, "Tordan." He pointed at her. "Willow," he said. "*Chansasa.*"

It was how Red Sky said she was known in her language. But by the look on her face, he thought he'd said it wrong. She frowned and, for the first time, looked uncomfortable. He tried again.

"*Apawi Hanble...*Tordan." He motioned, hoping she would get the idea and say his name. He mouthed his name slowly again, but was met with a blank look.

She set the rest of his food inside the cage, along with a gourd full of water and stood.

"Tor-dan, *toksa akhe*," she said.

He knew she was saying "goodbye," or some equivalent. He responded, " *Apawi Hanble, toksa akhe.*"

When she'd gone, the scrawny gray dog slunk over and Tordan fed him what was left of his dinner, all the while thinking of Willow.

"You're a hungry little thing aren't you? I guess I'm going to have to give you a name as well," he said, throwing the last bit of meat to the dog. "I know. I'll name you Skoll after the wolf that chases the sun across the sky, trying to eat it. How do you like that?"

Tordan reached through the bars of his cage and stretched far enough to touch the dog's side. It was the first time the animal had let him touch it. He felt its boney ribs.

"No wonder you're hungry, Skoll. Maybe someday you'll catch that sun and eat it. Then will come Ragnarok, and that will be the end of us all."

36

A woman's heart sees more than ten men's eyes.
                    —Ancient Aesir Proverb

The inner hall of the Ve had taken on a much different look. Temporary porticos had been erected—one where the bride would make her entrance, the other where the wedding couple would stand with the Valkyrie heilag. The arches were adorned with, and connected by, strands of silver chains and garlands of white and yellow flowers. Beneath the arches a carpet of green and gold forged a path to the matrimonial dais. Other parts of the great auditorium had also been decorated, and Vikar couldn't help but feel the festive embellishments were out of place in this seat of the corporatocracy. Only the giant figures of Wotan and Thor remained pure. They would look down on the wedding with impassive silence.

Though the Ve seemed somehow tainted to him, Vikar knew no other location would have been appropriate for the wedding of his daughter. He'd attended the weddings of other jarl's offspring in this assembly hall, and would have had no less for his own. Just as it was to have the chief high mistress of the Valkyrie performing the ceremony. It was a matter of stature.

It seemed all other jarls, from both major and minor houses, were present. Their attendance was as much a matter of politics as it was graciousness. No small amount of business would be conducted here, both before and after the ceremony itself.

Vikar searched the crowd, looking for his wife. Instead he saw Captain Griffenfeld, dressed in his finery, approaching him.

"A blessed day to you, sir."

"And to you, Captain. You have the look of a man with sour tidings."

"Yes, sir. Your executive manager has asked me to convey to you a revelation that has come to his attention."

"Out with, man. The ceremony is nigh."

"The Trondtel Corporation has discovered a vast deposit of iron ore within its territory. Sitric believes the find is likely large enough to affect the price of your own ore."

Troubling news, but nothing he couldn't deal with.

"That's the nature of supply and demand, dear Captain. Anything else?"

"No, sir."

"Has there been any report from Tordan, or word on his whereabouts?"

"No, sir. I'd say it's unlikely he still lives."

"No doubt. Still, it was a gambit well worth the cost. I've already initiated other operations in anticipation of the skaldor's demise. I expect results soon. Enjoy the wedding, Captain. We'll speak at length tomorrow."

"Yes, sir."

Griffenfeld offered a quick bow of his head before retreating into the celebratory throng.

Before Vikar had a chance to continue the search for his wife, Chairman Tryguasson and his wife approached.

"A glorious day, is it not, Jarl Magnusson?"

"It certainly is, Lady Tryguasson."

"I'm so looking forward to the wedding feast." She giggled like a little girl. "I understand Lady Magnusson has procured more delicious foodstuffs from Serkland. I can't wait to try them."

Vikar thought it an odd thing to say on the wedding day of her son, but replied, "I'm sure they won't disappoint, milady."

"Have you heard about Trondtel's discovery?" asked Chairman Tryguasson.

"Yes, I have," replied Vikar. "Look. Here comes Gripsholm now. No doubt he wants to gloat."

Indeed, Oleg Gripsholm had smile as big as the room itself as he approached them.

"Chairman, Lady Tryguasson, Jarl Magnusson, I greet you on this wonderful occasion and wish the best for both your families."

"Thank you, Jarl Gripsholm," replied Lady Tryguasson. "We're so glad you could attend."

"I would sooner cut off my right arm than miss this occasion, milady. Vikar," he said with unexpected familiarity, "I must congratulate you on such an astute match for your daughter. Well done, sir." He turned to the chairman and his wife. "Felicitations on this match to you both as well. Your son is marrying one of the most beautiful young girls in all of Trondheim."

"I understand congratulations are also in order for you, Oleg," said Vikar, countering with his own use of the familiar.

"Oh?"

"Yes, word has spread that Trondtel has discovered a major mineral deposit.

That has to be good news for you."

"Yes, yes. Quite true. I'm afraid Trellestar's near monopoly on iron ore *is* in jeopardy. But that's business. Today is a day to celebrate a blissful and, hopefully, fruitful union."

"That it is. In fact, I see my wife and must make certain all is in order. If you'll excuse me."

Both men nodded and Lady Tryguasson said, "Of course, of course. Let me know if I can do anything to help."

Estrid was moving through the crowd of wedding guests like a bee buzzing from blossom to blossom. It was the social occasion of the year—at least as far as she was concerned—and she was making the most of it. Vikar noticed, as usual, her cleavage preceded her. But he still thought of it as the finest in the land. He caught up with her and pulled her aside, ignoring the fragrant but disconcerting scent she was wearing.

"Where's Rikissa? We don't want her to miss her own wedding."

Estrid frowned. "Don't you know what a bride does on her wedding day?"

Vikar didn't.

"She's conducted to the sauna by a contingent of Valkyries, who instruct her in the duties of a wife."

"I believe she already had her instruction from that skaldor."

"Hush, husband," said Estrid harshly, looking around to make certain no one overheard. "She's also prepared for the ceremony itself. Then she's sequestered until the wedding begins so she can pray to Freyja her marriage will be fruitful, and that she will bear many children."

"So you know where she is?"

"Of course I do. Now take your position. I see Lady Ingstad preparing to begin."

Vikar looked to the dais. The Valkyrie heilag stood there, holding the diminutive, ceremonial replica of Thor's hammer she would use to officiate the nuptials. Using both hands, she raised the hammer above her head and waited for silence. Rikissa's husband-to-be stood on the dais next to the old Valkyrie, wearing his family's ancestral sword. Vikar took his place on the other side, below the dais, while Halfdan Tryguasson stood opposite him. Standing solemnly behind the heilag were other high mistresses of the Valkyrie.

Recognition quickly spread through the gathering. Everyone took their places, standing on either side of the aisle. When everyone had settled and quiet reigned, Lady Ingstad lowered arms and placed them across her chest, holding the hammer over her heart.

Stridently she proclaimed, "This assembly will now receive Rikissa Estrid Vikarsdottir, who will henceforth be known as Rikissa Estrid Halfdansson."

The announcement of the bride's new name was the cue for a quartet of musicians. A soft, upbeat tune of woodwinds and gittern reverberated through the vast chamber as Rikissa entered under the first portico. Behind her walked Gudrik, his arms outstretched, carrying an elaborate sword.

Rikissa was resplendent in a gown of white and silver. A crown of flowers matching the garlands of the portico adorned her hair, which hung loosely about her shoulders. She held her hands to her bosom and in them she grasped a falcon's feather, symbolic of the goddess Freyja's power over love and fertility.

It had never occurred to him before, but seeing Rikissa now, he was certain old Oleg Gripsholm had shortchanged his daughter. She was *the* most beautiful girl in Trondheim. In that moment he forgot about business, about potential mergers, about profit. Instead he pictured what Rikissa had looked like as little girl. The thought made him smile.

She'd imagined her wedding day since she was a little girl. Now it was everything she'd imagined, and less. Her dress was beautiful, flowers were everywhere, there was music, and the smiling faces of the noblest houses of Trondheim greeted her. But the groom wasn't of her choosing. He seemed a good fellow, but she couldn't think of him without thinking of Tordan. Not that she ever imagined marrying Tordan. She wasn't that childish. But she thought of him now. Pictured him waiting for her on the dais.

No, no she mustn't. Edvard was to be her husband. She would be happy with him. She saw him awaiting her with a smile so proud you'd think he'd stalked and captured her himself, instead of letting his father arrange the match and pay for her devotion. Yet that was the way of it, and she was determined to make the best of it.

Rikissa spotted her mother near the front of the gathering. She was with Furyk. She laughed inwardly. Not that it was out of place for her brother to stand beside her mother, but because of an odd thought that occurred to her. Furyk probably wished he could marry their mother — at least that was the joke she and Gudrik often shared.

As she approached the dais, the solemnity of Lady Ingstad banished such absurdities from her thoughts. She looked to her father, then to Edvard, who

161

stepped down, took her hand, and held it as she stepped onto the dais. Gudrik sheathed the sword he was carrying, and stood next to his father.

The Valkyrie high mistress took the garland from her head and replaced it with a bridal crown of crystal stones set in a silver band, draped with scarlet and forest-green cords, and laced with flowers.

"Who accepts the mundr on behalf of this bride?"

"I do," said her father, recognizing his cue.

Edvard's father advanced toward hers and handed him a bag of silver coins. Rikissa knew it was only a symbol for the bridal price they'd already negotiated. Symbolic or not, it made her feel even more like a prized cow that had been bought and paid for.

"Before these witnesses," declared Tryguasson, "I pay the mundr."

After the chairman stepped back, Lady Ingstad said, "The groom will now give to his bride, the sword of his ancestors, which she will keep safe, and one day give to his first-born son."

Edvard held out the sword with both hands, and Rikissa accepted it the same way, passing it over to Gudrik to hold for her. He sheathed it an empty scabbard on his left side, then pulled the sword he'd carried from his right.

"In exchange, the bride will now give to her groom the sword she has procured for him."

Rikissa took the sword from Gudrik. It was a magnificent blade. Its hilt was encrusted with gems that glistened as sharply as its cutting edge. She handed it to Edvard, who offered a slight bow, then sheathed it in place of his own.

"The ancestral sword signifies the traditions of the family Tryguasson, and the continuation of its bloodline. The sword given to the groom by the bride symbolizes the transfer of her father's power of guardianship and protection over her, to her husband."

The Valkyrie passed to Rikissa a silver goblet filled with the traditional honey mead. This was her part, and she prayed she'd remember it correctly.

"Ale I bring thee, thou oak-of-battle," she recited, passing the cup to Edvard. "With strength blended and brightest honor, 'tis mixed with magic and mighty songs, with goodly spells and wish-speeding runes."

"A toast to Wotan," said Edvard, holding the goblet for all to see. "May all his creations be as glorious as the one that stands before me."

Edvard drank from the cup and handed it back to Rikissa.

She took it, saying, "I drink to Freyja, may she bless this marriage with boundless love and many children."

Rikissa drank from the cup and gave it back to Lady Ingstad, who set it aside. She then raised her ceremonial hammer and lightly tapped both bride and groom.

Applause erupted from the gathering, signaling an end to the ceremony. Rikissa was married.

37

Ask yourself and listen carefully to the answer.
—The Wisdom of Fire In His Eyes

Many nights had passed since he'd escaped from the *wasichu*, yet most were still troubled by dreams of imprisonment. He was always helpless in his dreams, whether bound by the *wasichu* chains or mired in a river of mud. He reached out to his people, to his family, but couldn't help them. Often he watched as his wife or son or daughter were tortured or slain outright. Sometimes the white wolf was there at his side, growling at his enemies, and sometimes he was not. In all the dreams, Red Sky could do nothing but watch with dread. He could only wrestle with his own inadequacies and wake with a start, covered in sweat.

Snow Deer would try to soothe him when he emerged from such horrific visions, but her words were of little help. She understood this, and most of the time she simply held him and wiped the sweat from his brow.

His people considered him an intelligent man. When they had a problem, they would come to him, and often he could give them an answer. Yet when he considered the science of the *wasichu*, the things he'd seen, he felt as ignorant as a newborn. There were things he knew that no *wasichu* would ever learn, but did they matter? Would they save his people—his family?

After one particularly fitful night, Red Sky decided to visit the *wichasa wakan* so he may interpret his dreams. Fire In His Eyes had been a Sicangu holy man since before Red Sky was born. He was very old. So old Red Sky thought the fire in the shaman's eyes was barely a spark these days. Still, he was a wise man who knew the ways of the Great Spirit, the portents of bad medicine and good.

Fire In His Eyes listened as Red Sky told of his dreams. The old shaman fingered his medicine bundle and nodded silently. When Red Sky had finished he waited for the elder man to consider his words.

"I have seen that, in any great undertaking, it is not enough for a man to depend simply upon himself."

Red Sky considered the wisdom of the holy man's words, but wasn't certain how they applied to him. "I do not understand."

"You carry a burden of guilt, of shame, that haunts your dreams. But the burden you carry belongs to the clan. You cannot shoulder it alone. The weight is too great for any one man. Do not weaken yourself with regret. Be strong for the clan, for your family, for the people. Relinquish the burden. Let the people be your rock, as you are theirs."

"It is a difficult thing you ask."

"I do not ask, I only observe. Ask yourself and listen carefully to the answer."

"If I have the strength to do this thing, will the dreams go away?"

Fire In His Eyes shrugged. It was a curiously birdlike movement.

"You will always dream. Dreams are powerful medicine. Master yours and you will be stronger."

Red Sky grunted as he considered the holy man's words. Of course he was right. His guilt would not help the Sicangu. Dwelling on the past would only make him weak. He must look to the future.

"Go now. Purify your spirit with sage smoke and eat from grandfather bear. His strength will be your strength."

He was let out of his cage periodically, either to walk around and stretch his legs or for menial chores like carrying firewood. Though he didn't have his sword, he found an appropriate tree branch and practiced his skaldoran routines whenever they let him out. Children would gather to watch, and from what he heard them saying, they thought he was engaging in some sort of bizarre ritual dance. He also used his opportunities outside the cage to learn more. He tried to converse with the women who usually supervised his work, but only some of them were willing. The children were alternately frightened and fascinated with him. Part of it was likely his size. He was taller and broader than any of the natives, so he must have seemed a giant to the smaller children.

His imprisonment affected him more at night, reinforcing his isolation. He would lay there and listen to the sounds of the horses neighing, the wind rustling across the prairie, and the distant howls of an animal that sounded like a dog. He couldn't avoid hearing noises of lovemaking coming from nearby *thipis*, and thought of how unabashed these people were about so many things. They seemed such a straight-forward, honest folk.

When he got the chance, he would query Red Sky and Willow about their language. They were spending more time with him, and his proficiency swelled with each day. He would even do his best to strike up conversations with others in the village when he could. They often laughed him, or his pronunciations, but most would at least reply.

He would ask not only about their language, but about their customs. Red Sky was hesitant to discuss some things, but Willow would take her time and explain as best she could.

He learned that not only did these people eat the meat of the *tatanka*, but that they used almost every part of the beast for something. Tools, clothing, medicine, religious tokens, blankets and tents, cooking utensils and bowstrings, even the ball the children played with was the animal's hair wrapped in its hide. They made glue out of its horns and hooves, and, at times, used the beast's waste as fuel for their fires.

Unlike the Aesir, or even the Vanir, these people were a true community. They shared everything, made decisions as a group, and if a man was killed in battle, the leader of his *ozuye*, his detachment, lost face. Tordan knew from his own experience in the Corporate Wars that soldiers were usually only so much fodder for their leaders. Willow told him when Red Sky was captured and her husband and others killed, her brother had been the leader. She spoke of the guilt he felt even now. Despite this, and because of his escape from the *wasichu*, she said he was still a much-respected man, maybe the wisest of all the Sicangu.

He watched one day as Red Sky interacted with his horse. It was a strange sight. He stroked the beast's flanks, combed its mane with his fingers, patted its rump, and even talked to it. The only thing in Tordan's experience he could relate it to, was being with a woman. Red Sky even played with the horse. It nudged him, knocked him back harder, then chased him. When the animal stopped, Red Sky turned about and chased the horse. Tordan had never witnessed such a relationship between man and beast. The Aesir had nothing like it—not even with their household pets. And the Vanir...well few Vanir owned any animals not destined for the butcher.

During his talks with Red Sky, Tordan learned a Sicangu boy passes into manhood through three trials. His own son, Falling Star, had already undertaken his vision quest—a journey he takes alone to gain his spirit guide and his name. He was returning from his quest the day he came across Tordan. But the name "Falling Star" would only be his first name. His deeds in life would add to his name, and many old men had very long names.

To complete his passage into manhood, he must join in the next great *tatanka* hunt and kill one of the beasts. He must also take part in his first battle. Tordan was surprised by this. They seemed such a peaceful people, so we wondered about the contradiction. Even a skaldor in-training would not be required to partake in combat so young. Red Sky would not explain exactly what this combat would be, or who he would fight against.

When he'd asked, Red Sky had told him how me might say something to Willow. Something he'd wanted to say since learning she was a widow. So he couldn't wait until she showed up that night with his dinner. When she finally did, his courage wavered and he wasn't so sure he should broach the subject.

"*Htaowastecak*," he greeted her, trying to say "Good evening."

"*Htaowastecak Ah*," she corrected him.

As she handed his dinner to him through the bars, he stared at her. For the first time, he thought of her not as some alien creature, a savage woman of the skrael, but just a woman. With this realization came the thought of how beautiful she truly was.

"*Nihingna, chuwimapuskice*," he blurted out, hoping he'd remembered it correctly. It was how Red Sky had told him to say he was sorry about her husband.

She looked into his eyes for the first time, if only briefly. He hoped she found sincerity there. He certainly saw the sadness in hers. She nodded, as if acknowledging his condolences, but stood and turned to go.

"Wait," he said. "Are you leaving already? *Ni Ehpey A*? I thought we could speak some more."

"Tordan, *toksa akhe*."

She wasn't angry, but she said goodbye and walked away. Tordan felt he must have spoken out of turn, yet Red Sky didn't seem to think anything was wrong with what he wanted to say. Maybe it was just sadness that overcame her. But he'd expressed his sorrow to her for her loss, and he didn't regret it.

38

I n the dim lamplight Jorvik searched the faces around him. They were
serious men, trusted men. Men who would give their lives for the
movement. Except for Gunnar, each had families, children they wanted to
see grow up in a different world—a better world. Unlike the others, Olav did
not work in a factory or on the docks. He was the owner of a small shop that
sold produce and other goods, and he had his own grievances with the Aesir.
His tax burden being one of them.

The group was small, kept so purposely. Aesir spies were everywhere these
days. There was nothing they wouldn't do to break the back of the labor
movement. It was important for the members of each Modi cell to be able to
trust each other with their lives. They *were* trusting each other, just by being
here.

"We should begin," said Agnar.

"Harald isn't here."

"Harald was taken by management security," said Agnar. "There's been no
word from him since."

"What if he talks? What if he names us?"

"He won't talk," replied Jorvik. "I know Harald. He'll die first."

"It's likely he will," said Agnar. "We all will if we're not careful. Last night,
the dock workers tried to strike, and security went right after the leaders. That's
how they got Harald. We've got to be more cautious. Those who are organizing
must blend in."

Agnar had become the leader of their cell. They hadn't taken a vote, or
named him leader in any formal way, but he was trusted by all, and respected
for his insight. He'd developed links to other cells, and that was crucial to the
organization of the larger movement.

"We need to develop a signal system," offered Jorvik.

"What do you mean, Brother?"

"If we can communicate through signs, hand gestures, it'll be harder for security to pick out our leaders. We already use such a system of signals on the factory floor when the machinery is too loud. We just need to expand it by anticipating what we'll need to communicate during a work stoppage."

"That's great idea, Jorvik," said Agnar. "Why don't you take the lead and develop a sign language we can use."

"Me?"

"It was your idea."

"Alright."

"Sign language is not going to get us higher pay or medical care," complained Gunnar. "We need action—a show of force."

Agnar took a deep breath and let it out.

"Our brother Gunnar has always been a proponent of more violence, and I'm afraid I must now agree with him. I believe it's time we ratchet-up our revolt. Let our Aesir masters know how serious we are. But there's no need to throw away lives in useless frontal assaults. Not yet. What we need to do is throw a wrench into the machinery. Set fire to the factories. Destroy the very tools we work with, so no one *can* work."

Jorvik always knew it would come to this. It was really the only solution. The only thing that would get the full attention of the Aesir. When the expense of dealing with the Modi exceeded that of negotiating, they might reconsider.

"Gunnar, I want you to present several plans for sabotage."

Gunnar slammed his fist against the crate he sat on. "It will be done."

"Remember this though, we want to sabotage machinery, we don't want to kill if we don't have to. Your plans must keep this in mind."

Jorvik knew Gunnar didn't care for such restraint, but the man nodded reluctantly.

"We must be careful," said Agnar. "If our efforts result in the accidental death of our fellow Vanir, we might turn potential allies into adversaries. It's a fine line we walk."

A fine line traced with jagged glass and molten metal thought Jorvik.

Truvor ran the test again—and then ran it a third time. He didn't doubt his methods, only the results. The tests all revealed his own blight was in remission. It hadn't vanished completely, but there was no doubt in his mind the malignant cells were in retreat. In his studies he'd read such a thing was very rare, but possible. Still, he'd never actually seen evidence of such, or even spoken with another physician who had.

He wasn't entirely certain whether he should be elated or wary. It was possible this was a temporary condition, and that the blight could begin to proliferate with a vengeance at any time. With that in mind, he tempered any jubilation he might have felt, deciding instead to run additional tests on other members of the Hestvoll colony who'd previously tested positive for the blight. He wanted to know if something in their immediate environment was affecting them all, or whether this unexpected turn was unique to him.

He had no idea what might have caused the remission. In the past he'd tried several concoctions of his own devise, but none of them had any effect on the blight. There was no known cure, and he'd given up trying to find one. Nothing had changed over the last several weeks that could have affected him...except that he'd been spending more time with the Lakhota.

The order had come early in the morning. His father demanded his presence...at Gudrik's quarters. As soon as the command was relayed to him, he knew the reason for it. Hrolf had done his work. Now it was a matter of playing ignorant—no, not ignorant—innocent.

When Furyk arrived, both his father and Captain Griffenfeld were there. A glance into the bed chamber told him all he needed to know. Gudrik was tied to his bed, naked, and obviously dead.

"What's happened, Father?" asked Furyk, sounding as distressed as he could manage.

"Your brother's been killed—murdered in his own bed," responded Vikar.

"How?"

"He was strangled," said Griffenfeld.

"Strangled? How horrible."

Furyk felt the stare of his father. Those cold blue-green eyes seared his flesh like ice daggers. His deceit was for naught. His father knew.

"It seems the Law of Odal now judges you fit to be my heir, Furyk. I pray to Wotan you're up to the task."

Furyk cleared his throat. "I am, Father. I'll make you proud."

"Yes, I'm sure." Vikar looked from Furyk to Captain Griffenfeld and back, adding, "Of course, there will be an investigation into Gudrik's murder."

"Of course," replied Furyk. "The scoundrel who did this must be punished. Do you think it was one of his lovers?"

"I make no such supposition," said Vikar as if the entire matter disgusted him. "I leave the investigation in the capable hands of Captain Griffenfeld."

Furyk looked at the captain. The slightest hint of a smile formed at the corners of his mouth.

He'd never had a particularly good relationship with the captain of the guard. The man thought too much of his station. He didn't know his place in the order of things. There would be a new guard captain when he was jarl. Hrolf would make a good one...if he survived the investigation.

"Now I must go tell your mother," said Vikar. "The sorrow of her mourning will cast a pall over House Magnusson."

How little his father knew his mother if he truly thought so. Her tears over Gudrik wouldn't fill a thimble. No more so than if it were Jarl Magnusson's own body lying there lifeless. Such a vision, thought Furyk, was much more foreseeable now.

39

Complete understanding of the subject species is not possible without understanding its history — its evolution.

— Osst Personal Journal

He spoke the native language so much, and his own so little, that as the weeks passed, he began thinking in their language. Tordan was still learning, but it became second nature for him to carry on extended conversations with anyone who would speak with him. This morning, from inside his cage, he was speaking with Falling Star. Earlier he'd seen Red Sky and most of the village's men ride off together, so he asked where they were going.

"They go to raid our enemies, the Sahnish," explained Falling Star. "They will take many horses."

Tordan saw the boy was upset about something.

"What is wrong? Are you worried your father will be hurt?"

He shook his head.

"My father is a great warrior, but he would not let me ride with him. He says I must go on the great hunt first, and kill the *tatanka*. Only then may I make war with the other men."

"Why are the Sahnish your enemy?"

The boy shrugged and shook his head.

"They have always been — I think."

"I know you wish to become a man, Falling Star, but you should not be in such a hurry to make war. Killing another man is sometimes necessary, but it is not something that is..." Tordan searched his knowledge of the skrael language for the right word. "...enjoyable."

"I thought you were a warrior."

"I am. I have made war. I have killed men, but I never enjoyed it."

The boy thought this over as if it were something he'd never contemplated.

"I do not think I would enjoy killing either, but I will do it when it is necessary."

Tordan reached through the sticks of his cage and scratched Skoll's head.

The dog had begun sleeping next to the cage, and would follow Tordan wherever he went. The natives had seen this and stopped chasing the dog away. Red Sky said it was a good match, and that if Tordan ever became too hungry, he could eat the dog.

Tordan would have laughed at this, except he knew that, while village's dogs played with the children and were highly valued as sentries, puppies were considered a delicacy. He hadn't actually seen any being cooked, so he wasn't certain how common a practice it was. He did know Skoll had little meat on his bones, and wasn't a likely candidate for anyone's stew pot.

He considered it only a random coincidence that, as he thought about this, Willow showed up with his morning meal.

"Good morning."

"Is it a good morning?"

He'd learned contrariness was in her nature, but she was more perturbed than usual.

"What is wrong?" he asked.

"Nothing."

He could see it wasn't nothing.

"Why are you upset?"

As she often did, she stared at him as if she wouldn't answer. But she couldn't hold back.

"The men have gone off to make war, leaving the women to do all the work—as usual," she said, pushing his food through the cage.

"That is the way of it," spoke up Falling Star.

She frowned at her nephew and he decided to say no more. She said something else Tordan had trouble translating, but her mocking tone was evident. It was something about the inherently brutal nature of men, and their need for conflict.

Tordan decided to change the subject.

"The food you bring me tastes good. There is a flavor in it unlike anything in my land."

She turned to go.

"Are you leaving already?"

"I have work to do. Woman's work," she added sarcastically

Tordan watched her go, and found himself staring at her behind—her *unze*. It had been a long time since he'd held a woman in his arms. Rikissa had likely forgotten about him now, or least no longer thought of him. He hoped she was

173

happy with her husband. No doubt she would join her mother and make a fine Valkyrie.

"I must go too," said Falling Star. "I also have work that must be done."

"Can I help?"

"I do not know. I will..."

Skoll jumped to his feet and began barking. Tordan looked towards the outskirts of the village, in the direction Skoll was barking, where a dense thicket rose up the hill from the rolling prairie. He didn't see anything, but other dogs in the village began barking as well. Then the first horse appeared out of the brush.

"Sahnish!" cried Falling Star.

More horses sauntered into view. They were painted, as were their riders, in a variety of colors. As soon as they realized they'd been seen, the warriors spurred their mounts into a gallop, and began shouting their war cries.

"Go!" he told the boy. "Alert the village!"

Falling Star ran off as Tordan kicked open his cage, splintering the door. He grabbed his mock sword and ran straight at the invaders. A quick estimate told him there were twenty-some warriors, all on horseback.

He wasn't used to doing battle with foes on horseback. Neither the Aesir nor the Vanir were horsemen. But he hoped to buy some time by making the warriors deal with him first. However, most rode around him and into the village. Then two came at him. He swung his wooden staff over his head, and with two quick swipes unhorsed them both. One lay unconscious, the other recovered quickly and came at him with an axe. The blade was black, chipped from obsidian, and sharp as glass. It whistled over Tordan's head as he ducked and side-stepped the intended blow. Before the man could recover, Tordan crushed his skull.

He retrieved the first man's bow, but found it smaller than the ones he was used to. It felt awkward in his hands, so he tossed it aside and found a fallen spear. He lifted it, momentarily testing its heft, took two quick steps, and threw it. It struck one of the Sahnish full in the back, toppling him from his horse.

Running into the midst of the melee he thought of Willow. He knew where Red Sky's lodge was, where she and Red Sky's family made their camp, so he sprinted in that direction. Some of invaders had jumped from their horses. He brained one that got in his way and kept moving. He saw Willow and another woman grappling with one of the Sahnish. The warrior knocked Willow to the ground and was about to plunge his knife into the other woman. Tordan threw

174

his staff like a spear. It wasn't weighted properly, but he had a feel for it. It slammed against the assailant hard enough he dropped the knife. He turned as Tordan reached him and screeched a battle cry, lunging at Tordan with his bare hands. Tordan caught the man in mid-air and tossed him over his shoulder into a fire pit. The move was skill, honed by years of skaldoran training. The landing place of his victim was pure luck.

Tordan herded the two women back into the nearby *thipi* and looked around. Falling Star was grouped with many of the village's older men and even the *heyoka*. They all had bows and were taking aim on the Sahnish warriors, who'd begun to fall back. Their retreat was swift, and they departed with fewer horses than they came with. Falling Star and the others whooped loudly in triumphant.

Hearing this, Willow, the other woman, and a younger girl emerged from the *thipi*. Despite their victory, there were several dead and wounded. The older men ran through the village, making certain their downed enemies were dead, while the women looked to the wounded. Falling Star ran towards them smiling proudly.

"The Sahnish have run off like dogs," he said excitedly. "It is a great victory."

To Tordan it was but a skirmish, but he let the boy have his moment.

Willow put her hand on his shoulder and he turned. "You are hurt," she said.

Only then did he notice the cut across the back of his arm. He didn't even know when it had happened.

"I will see to it," she said.

The other woman, still holding onto the young girl, looked to Tordan, nodded, and said, "Thank you."

"My mother and sister," said Falling Star.

Tordan bowed at the introduction and gave way to Willow's ministrations.

When the men returned to the village, there was a great clamor of questions and answers and retelling of events. The excitement was twofold, as the men arrived with a dozen new horses they'd taken in their raid. It had been a good day for the Sicangu.

Tordan hadn't gone back to his cage. He stayed by the fire near Red Sky's lodge, enjoying the food and a special berry juice Willow brought him. Among those carrying on animated conversations were Red Sky and his son. Falling Star was doing most of the talking. When he'd finished, Red Sky put his hands on the boy's shoulder and said something. Tordan saw the pride beaming from

Falling Star's face.

Red Sky was also greeted by his wife and daughter. When their reunion was complete, Red Sky strode purposely to his *thipi*, only glancing at Tordan. When he emerged he was carrying Tordan's sword, still in its scabbard. Tordan stood as he approached. Willow walked away, leaving the men to speak alone.

"You are no longer a prisoner," said Red Sky holding out the sword. "You are free to go."

Tordan took the sword and belted it on, feeling whole once again.

The thought of returning to the familiar halls and taverns of Trondheim was more than appealing. He longed for his old life. But what would he be returning to? He thought of the mission Jarl Magnusson had sent him on, and how he couldn't return unless he completed it.

"You may go," continued Red Sky, "or you may stay and join the Sicangu. If you stay, I will take you as my *hunka*, and you will be a member of my family. But there will be tests, trials you must undergo before you can become one of the Ikche Wichasa. I do not doubt your ability to complete these trials, should you have the desire. You have protected my family and my people. You are my brother whether you choose to stay or to go."

"I have nothing to go back to," he replied. "I am an outlaw from my own house now. I would like to stay and join the Sicangu."

"Good." Red Sky held out his hand, and when Tordan reciprocated the skrael grabbed his forearm firmly. "The world is changing," he said clasping Tordan's arm, "and there is much we can learn from each other."

40

*When a man does a thing, there are three ways he may
do it. The bad way, the good way, and the better way.
I always seek the better way.*
    —**The Wisdom of Fire In His Eyes**

Truvor spent the day with the Lakhota, getting samples from the two sources where they got their drinking water. He wanted to get the samples back to his laboratory to find out if they showed any unusual properties that might account for the natives' good health and apparent longevity. His further conversations with Lame Bear confirmed the fellow believed he was more than a hundred years old, though Truvor wasn't totally convinced.

There was also the mystery of his own blight's remission to account for. The disease continued to retreat at a rapid rate, and now only minute traces remained.

The spread of the blight in his system had been minimal to begin with—nothing like what affected Burgrave Andersson. But the ebb of the disease was still nothing short of miraculous. The possibility he was close to discovering a cure sent shivers through him. He tried not to think about it, to concentrate solely on the science, but it was impossible. The impact of such a discovery would send shockwaves through the halls of Trondheim.

He admonished himself. Such speculation was foolish, not to mention premature. At this juncture he'd no clue what was causing the remission. He knew everyone's resistance and susceptibility to the disease differed. It could simply be his own resistance had been triggered, and was fighting back. It was rare, but not unheard of. There could be nothing in the water or anywhere else that was affecting it. But he had to be sure.

He was on his way back to Hestvoll now, anxious to begin his tests. As usual, he had an escort. It was modest one, just Lame Bear and a trio of very young warriors the old man had enlisted. Truvor knew enough of their language to hear the young men grumbling about having to walk instead of ride. But Truvor didn't particularly like or trust horses, and he certainly wouldn't get up on one. It wasn't that long of a walk, and he liked the exercise.

From almost the beginning, Lame Bear had insisted they indulge Wichasa Wakan Okinihan.

It was a pleasant day, though the wind whipped up occasionally, forcing them to shield their eyes from the dust. The sun was high overhead by the time Truvor started back, though it wasn't particularly hot. Atop a hill at the horizon he spotted a majestic elk. He imagined the creature was watching them tramp through the valley below. Suddenly the elk bolted and ran for the cover of trees. Truvor was wondering what had scared it, when he saw a cluster of horsemen race over the hilltop and down into the valley towards them. His escort reacted immediately, drawing arrows to their bows and bracing for the assault.

Their assailants were obviously of another clan, though Truvor wouldn't never have known it by looking at them. Their faces were painted for war, but he'd seen the Lakhota paint themselves as well. He just never knew what they were up to when they rode off.

He was aware the various clans were often at odds, and that raids, if not all-out war, were somewhat common. Which clan these men belong to, and what had sparked their animosity he had no idea, and no time to contemplate.

The howls and shrieks they issued as they charged down the hill sent shudders of terror through him. His bowels felt as if they were going to let loose. He looked for cover, but saw none.

There were at least ten men on horseback, but they came at them too quickly for him to count. The Lakhota men let fly their arrows, and two of the attackers fell from their horses. The rest were upon them before any more shots could be fired. Truvor tried to run. He heard the pounding of hooves behind him, but was too scared to look back. Something fell on him and he hit the ground with such a thud he momentarily blacked out. As he collapsed he was certain his life was over.

He was brought back to consciousness by the popping of firearms. His first thought was it didn't make sense. The natives had no such weapons. He opened his eyes and saw maybe a half dozen members of the enemy clan withdrawing with great speed. Several more shots sounded and one of the riders fell from his horse.

Truvor sat up. Lame Bear lay next to him, a severe gash on his forehead, but he was moving. The three young warriors all appeared to be dead. When he heard the roaring approach of an engine behind him, Truvor turned and threw up his arms defensively.

The first thing he saw through the glaring sunlight was Storman Ragnarsson getting out of his motorcar. Behind him, several dozen troops were taking up positions around their armored vehicles, though they'd ceased firing. Ragnarsson stood over Truvor and made a noise as if he were stifling a laugh.

"Still want to protect these savages, Doctor?"

Truvor didn't bother to reply. He immediately checked the young men who'd been guarding him. They were all dead, so he tended to Lame Bear's laceration, ripping a sleeve from his own shirt to bind it and quell the bleeding.

"It seems, given enough time, these skraelings may do our job for us," preened Ragnarsson, knocking the dust from his breeches and straightening his chain mail. "They make war with each other as often as not. We're fortunate they're too ignorant to unite. Our intelligence reports say they'd outnumber us ten to one if they did. But I'm certain the savage mind doesn't comprehend such strategic designs."

"Storman, I need to get this man back to the compound so I can stitch him up."

"Why, Doctor?"

"*Why*? Because...because his entire clan has welcomed me and furthered important research I'm conducting." As he spoke, Truvor's voice rose in volume and anger. "Because these other men died protecting me. Because he's a friend."

"A *friend*, Doctor?" Ragnarsson's tone was light with sarcasm, but his expression was as dark as a storm cloud. "Surely you jest."

"I do not. Will you take us to the compound, or should we start back on our own?"

It was apparent from his frown Ragnarsson didn't care to be spoken to in that tone. However, he seemed to consider his options, and called to one of his men.

"Take the doctor and his *patient* back to Hestvoll."

Truvor helped Lame Bear to stand.

"Doctor, I'll want a full report of this 'important research' of yours, so I may consider whether or not your *friends* will remain protected."

The commander's words sent a chill through Truvor. He regretted he'd taken such a tone with the storman, but there was nothing he could do about it now. He'd have to reveal his theories about the blight and hope he soon discovered something more substantial than a theory.

When Jorvik returned home from the factory, his wife wasn't there to greet him.

"Marta?"

It was Canute who emerged, with a worried look on his nine-year-old face.

"Father, Mother isn't well. She's been in bed most of the day. I'm afraid she's very sick."

She *was* very sick, but they hadn't told their young son yet about the blight. Now Jorvik would have to.

"Sit down, Canute," said Jorvik, pulling up a chair himself. "There's something you must know. Your mother has the blight. It means there will be many days when she is not feeling well. She will need you to help her more and more. *I* will need you to help her."

Canute nodded. "Is she going to die?"

Jorvik wavered, not sure what to say, or how to say it. The words were a jumble in his throat. They caught there, like fish in a net.

"Everyone dies, Canute. It's up to us to help your mother live as long as possible. Do you understand?"

Canute nodded, but didn't seem reassured.

Jorvik stood, rubbed the boy's head, then went to see his wife.

"Jorvik." It seemed all she had the energy to say when he entered the room.

He sat on the bed next to her and took her hand.

"Is it bad today?"

She nodded, squeezing his hand.

"Some days I hardly notice it. But today... It's so hard to move. I feel so tired and my body aches."

Jorvik didn't know what to say. He couldn't tell her it was going to be alright, because they both knew it wouldn't. He felt a well of tears pooling in his eyes, fed by his helplessness.

"I heard you...talking to Canute," she said.

"It's time he knew," replied Jorvik. "There's no hiding it now."

"He's such a little boy though."

"He'll be alright. It's you, my love, we must take care of. Canute can help. I'll have him help me make you some food right now."

"I'm not hungry."

"You must eat, my wife. You're getting as thin as a ghost. Let us fix you something. It'll make Canute feel better if he can do something for you."

"Alright. I'll try."

Jorvik patted her hand and stood. He looked down at her and wanted to cry.

But he couldn't let himself. He couldn't let her see that. He had to be strong—
for her, for Canute. It was all he could do.

41

"You may go where you wish, but you cannot escape yourself."

—Book of Runes

Estrid ignored the laughter and buzz of gossip as the women moved through the hall of runes into the high council chamber and took their seats. She other things on her mind. Like the death of her son Gudrik. Even though she'd encouraged Furyk's ambitions, even pushed him, she was still shadowed by regret. How could she not? Gudrik was her flesh and blood. He came from her. She rationalized that Gudrik was weak. His appetites would never have let him become a strong jarl. She needed strength. Furyk had that strength, but he need guidance. That's all she done, was given him proper guidance.

"Blessed be to Freyja," said Lady Ingstad, the chief high mistress, raising her voice to begin the meeting of the Valkyrie High Council. "We all know why we've called this special meeting, so let's get on with it. First we'll hear from Sister Atterdag. What, exactly, have your people learned, Margrete?"

"We know for certain Jarl Gripsholm visited a family in Gotland, a Vanir farming community outside of Oseberg," said Lady Atterdag. "His stay was short. His driver stayed outside, and when he left he was alone. Neighbors were questioned, quietly, as to raise no suspicions. They say the family in residence brought home an infant some years ago. None remembered exactly when, but estimates do coincide with the death of Lady Gripsholm. Neighbors were told a relative died, leaving the child in their care. Glyfe is the boy's name, and they say he is 'not right,' though exactly why he's described so, they did not elaborate."

The boy's name struck a chord in Estrid, though she couldn't say why.

"I see," said Lady Ingstad, mulling over what she'd heard. "And what exactly to you make of this information?"

"It's obvious, isn't it?" asked Lady Atterdag of the council in general. "When Lady Gripsholm died in childbirth, her infant son did not die as we were told. He was spirited away so this council would not learn of his existence. The boy must be defective in some way. Why else would Jarl Gripsholm hide him?"

182

"What did you say the boy's name was?" asked Estrid.

"Glyfe."

Estrid knew that name from somewhere. She motioned for one of the lesser Valkyrie standing by as attendants.

"Retrieve the familial records for me."

The young woman hurried out, and the discussion continued.

"You're leaping to a conclusion that has no basis in the facts you've assembled, Sister Margrete," said Lady Eriksson. "What proof is there this boy, defective or not, is Jarl Gripsholm's issue?"

"Why else would he be surreptitiously visiting such an obscure village? Can you think of another reason?" No one at the table had a response. Lady Atterdag continued. "Neighbors have also said the family in question have prospered strangely more than others. I would submit Jarl Gripsholm is supplementing their income for services rendered."

"Very interesting indeed," said Lady Volsung. "Your reasoning is sound, and I might even agree, but we've no substantial evidence."

The immense tome that contained the lineages of every high-born Aesir family was laid before Estrid, and she began paging through it, looking for something specific.

"I must second Lady Volsung's notion," said the chief high mistress, "that while the premise is sound, the proof is threadbare. We need more information before we can proceed with any action."

"Maybe not."

"You've found something, Sister Estrid?"

Estrid slid the book in front of Lady Ingstad.

"I thought the name Glyfe was familiar, and it was. You can all see, according to our familial records, it was the name of Jarl Gripsholm's grandfather."

Estrid perceived this last bit of evidence, circumstantial as it was, as enough to convince most in the room. Lady Atterdag smiled as though it proved her point.

Lady Ingstad lifted her face from the book and said, "Well this does support the premise. I would still like more evidence, but let's assume, for the moment, what Sister Atterdag has proposed is correct. What shall we do about it?"

Beatrix Tryguasson, the chairman's wife, spoke up for the first time.

"I can tell you this. If such information were to become public, it would disrupt the balance of power within the board of directors. Jarl Gripsholm would lose face and Trondtel Corporation would suffer a tremendous blow."

"That's most certainly true," agreed the chief high mistress. "The question we must ask ourselves, is it in the best interests of Trondheim, the best interests of the this council, that the current balance of power be disturbed? This is not a slight matter. While we can't condone such actions, especially by a corporate jarl, neither can we ignore the ramifications of such a revelation."

"We all know of the contentious rivalry between the Trondtel and Trellestar corporations," said Lady Volsung. "Because this revelation would most definitely favor Trellestar's position, I must suggest Sister Magnusson recuse herself from any vote on the matter."

Estrid knew she couldn't disagree. She nodded in acquiescence to the motion.

"Because of the gravity of this matter," said Lady Ingstad, "I propose we take time to consider all the possible consequences, and postpone any vote until our next meeting. Are we agreed on this?"

The assent was unanimous.

"Sister Magnusson," said the chief high mistress, "though this information is potentially a boon to House Magnusson, I'm know you will honor the vow of secrecy this council is pledged to keep."

"Of course," responded Estrid.

"Then, by the glory of Freyja, I adjourn this meeting of the Valkyrie High Council."

"By the glory of Freyja," repeated everyone.

Estrid stood, wondering whether or not she would honor her vows. What was best for Trondheim—what was best for the Valkyrie High Council—wasn't necessarily best for her. She'd have to give the matter deep thought. Certainly there was a way to use this information to her benefit. How that would be was not immediately clear to her. Yes, it would require some thought.

42

*At first it was simply a novelty—an accidental
revelation that the intense emotions of the subject
species could not only be sensed, but could result
in sensations. Too late it was ascertained these
sensations were both addictive and deleterious.
In the latter stages of the addiction, we abandoned
our own pursuits and begun to live vicariously
through the bipeds.*
                            —A Societal History/Proem

H is days among the Sicangu became weeks, and those weeks passed into
nothingness. For these native peoples had no real concepts of time.
Time was unimportant, and they did not mark its passing. When he
asked Red Sky what year he was born, he responded, "The year Black Coyote
was killed." There were no clocks, no dates on a calendar, only events.

They knew the seasons, as well as the comings and goings of the moon. Each
passing of the blue sphere had a name. This was the time of Strawberry
Moon—late spring or early summer by Tordan's reckoning.

He spent most of his days both learning and teaching. The latter much easier
than the former. The most difficult thing by far, was learning the horse. He'd
ridden a horse before, though not often, and not well. He'd always felt more
comfortable on the deck of ship than on the back of an animal. He quickly
learned neither Aesir nor Vanir knew anything about true horsemanship.

"Man and horse must be one," Red Sky told him, interlacing his fingers to
demonstrate. "In battle, in the great hunt, the way a man tugs a horse's mane or
tightens his thighs around the beast can say many things. It is important for a
man to trust his horse...and for the horse to trust the man."

Red Sky's horse was a beautiful sorrel—a reddish brown color with
splotches of creamy tan. He called it Fetawachi, which Tordan learned meant
"Fire Dancer." It was named so not only because it was, according to Red Sky,
one of the fastest horses the Sicangu had ever seen, but also because it had a
particular aversion to fire, and would dance skittishly away from even the
smallest cook fire.

"The horse is of the plain," said Red Sky. "His spirit *is* the plain."

Tordan wasn't much for the spiritual, and sometimes Red Sky had a tendency to meander into the metaphysical. Tordan was more concerned with practical matters, and nothing was more practical, more a part of their lives than their horses.

You could say the skrael were born in the saddle, except they used no saddles. They bonded with their mounts, riding as if the beasts were simply extensions of their own bodies. They could hang from a horse in full gallop and retrieve a lost weapon from the ground. They could charge at you and suddenly turn the animal at angle that defied belief.

They tried to teach Tordan, but he was *wakhanheza*—like a child. Controlling the power of the beast was something he struggled with, but not as much as communication. The Sicangu could convey their wishes to the animals with word or touch—soothing them, directing them. His horse didn't seem to understand him, no matter which language he used.

Still, he didn't give up. When he fell from the horse he got right back up, and gained grudging respect for his determination, despite the laughs he elicited.

In return, Tordan taught them methods of hand-to-hand fighting they'd never imagined. He showed them throws and sweeps and kicks and holds that often confounded them. He instructed them on how to use an opponent's own weight against him, and how to disarm a man that came at you with a knife.

At first they were skeptical this *wasichu* could teach them anything. But once a half dozen of their best warriors had the wind knocked out of them, or lay disarmed in the dust, they paid closer attention. Using his vast knowledge of swordsmanship, he taught them about lines of attack, how they could use their spears to counter, feint, parry and riposte. They called his sword *mila hanska*—the long knife.

He'd become friends with Red Sky's son, and let the boy train him in the use of their bows. Archery had never been one of his refined skills, but it didn't take him long to learn the basics. Still, his education had a ways to go. He'd need to be able to shoot accurately from horseback if he were to hunt the *tatanka*. Just like Falling Star, he'd have to kill one of the beasts eventually, if he was to be considered a full member of the clan. For that he wished he'd brought a firearm with him, though he wasn't sure a single shot would fell a *tatanka*, any more than a single arrow would unless, as Red Sky put it, it was guided by Wakan Tanka to the beast's heart.

The great hunt, and the killing of a *tatanka*, was the only step left before

Falling Star became a man in the eyes of his clan. He enthusiastically explained to Tordan it had been decided his defense of the village against the Sahnish constituted his experience in battle, so he had only one deed left to accomplish to gain his manhood.

He still seemed more boy than man to Tordan, especially when he ran off to play ball with the other children. When Tordan questioned him about this, he said, very seriously, "To catch the ball is to be free of ignorance." He smiled and added, "I want to play while I can. Once I become a man, there will be no more playing."

He was no longer kept in his cage. He slept in the *thipi* with the rest of Red Sky's family. Willow, no longer having a man of her own, slept there as well. Whenever he could, whenever she wasn't overly busy with her work, Tordan tried to engage her in conversation. Sometimes she would speak politely with him, but other times, especially when others were around, she would act annoyed and try to ignore him. She would never seek out his company, but he did notice she would watch him furtively when she didn't think he was looking. He asked Red Sky about this.

"She is in mourning. It is not proper for her to be seen with you."

"Because I am *wasichu*?"

"Because you are a man."

It was a matter of morality. Tordan understood. His own people had such rules, not that he'd ever paid much attention to them.

"How long will she be in mourning?"

Red Sky shrugged as if the question were unimportant or had no meaning. Then a rare smile formed on his face.

"You will have to be satisfied with the company of your dog."

Tordan chuckled. "My dog?"

"The people have seen you feed the dead shaman's dog. Some still think the dog is evil, but they know he belongs to Sungmani Ska now."

Tordan recognized only one of the words. "Who is *Sungmani Ska?*"

"It is what the people are calling you. They see the symbol you wear." Tordan knew he was referring to the Trellestar corporate signet on his vest. "They also say when you fought the Sahnish, you were like a wolf among dogs. So they have come to call you the White Wolf."

Though he found it complimentary, Tordan wasn't sure he liked having a new name. He was Tordan Thordsson. But, after considering it, he figured they could have called him something much worse. He'd been called worse, no doubt by both Aesir and Vanir, behind his back.

"What is the name you call the dog?" asked Red Sky.

"Skoll."

"What does it mean?"

"You're going to think I'm joking, but Skoll is the name of a great wolf. It is a story my people tell—a legend. Skoll has chased the sun across the sky for an eternity, trying to eat it. If he catches the sun and eats it, that will be the beginning of Ragnarok, the end of all things—the end of the world."

Red Sky grunted, as Tordan was accustomed to him doing when he was thinking.

After a moment of contemplation Red Sky said, "I think it is not a good name for a dog."

It was Tordan's turn to shrug.

43

That which is desired by many is owned by few.
—Ancient Aesir Proverb

"So, you're now the heir to House Magnusson and all its holdings," said Estrid, watching her son's expression out of the corner of her eye as she brushed her hair. "How does it feel?"

"It feels...*right*, Mother. It feels as if it were meant to be." Furyk made a fist. "Everything I've wanted is within my grasp now."

"Yes, yes, but a man's reach should exceed his grasp," she said, purposely needling his newfound confidence. "A real man would do whatever was necessary to achieve his goals...to take his rightful place."

Furyk was stung by her words.

"Gudrik is no longer in my way, Mother. Isn't that what you...?" He caught himself, knowing it wasn't something he should say out loud, even here, in his mother's chambers. "What are saying, Mother?"

"Why nothing, just a mother's counsel. You're the only son I have now. I want you to be successful. Be a dear and brush my hair for me."

Furyk frowned, but took the brush and began stroking her hair.

Estrid looked into the mirror at her son.

"Did you know your father seeks a cure for the blight in Serkland?" She knew by his expression that Vikar hadn't shared this with him. "If he finds the cure, it'll not only be a financial boon to Trellestar, it'll mean his death is no longer imminent...at least from the blight. He could well live another 20 or 30 years."

"Thirty years?"

The thought confounded him, as she knew it would.

"Be careful!" she barked. "You're pulling my hair."

"Sorry, Mother."

Estrid stood and took the brush from him.

"Let me show you. Turn round and face the mirror."

Furyk did as he was told. Estrid removed his burnished headband and began brushing his long blond hair, following each stroke of the brush with the flat of her hand, feeling the pliable downy softness of his mane.

189

"Who knows, maybe there *is* no cure for the blight," she said, trying to soothe him before stirring the pot again. "Whether there is or isn't, you'll be jarl someday. Isn't that what's important? It doesn't matter how many years it takes, does it? After all, there's not anything you can do about it, is there?"

She watched his face in the mirror. Her words had their intended effect. She saw he was thinking about what he *could* do. She knew he didn't have the patience to wait for years, and the sooner he realized it, the better for both of them.

"There," she said, putting the brush down and placing the circlet back on his head. "Now give your mother a hug and run along. I've things to do, and I'm certain you do as well."

She pulled him close to her, feeling his strong young body in her arms. If only his mind were as strong, she thought. Maybe she shouldn't depend on Furyk. Waiting for him to act might be a mistake. Maybe destiny needed a push.

"Give me a kiss."

He kissed her cheek and left her alone.

Estrid sat back in front of her mirror and took up her brush. She was thinking of Furyk, but for some reason her thoughts turned to Gudrik. Poor Gudrik was born out of time and out of place. He was never meant for this world. Yet he'd come out of her womb, just like...

As the thought entered her head, she saw it again within her mirror. The pallid, ghostlike image of a hairless head and two accusing eyes. Estrid stifled a scream. It was him. She was certain. But it had been decades. Why now? Why was he haunting her now?

"What do you...?"

Before she could finish, the image vanished as if it were never there. She'd seen it. She was certain she'd seen it. She'd even felt its presence on her skin. It was no dream, no matter how hard she wished it were.

"Small hands," said Walks Apart, taking hold of his right hand. "You small hands."

Truvor wasn't sure why she'd taken his hand, and wasn't entirely comfortable with the sensation that ran up his arm.

"Really? I never noticed. I guess they are rather small."

Instead of letting go, she placed both her hands around his and looked at him.

"You, uh, should say it this way. You *have* small hands."

"You *have* small hands," she repeated.

"Yes, that's it."

She released his hand and he felt both relieved and ridiculous. He was a doctor. Such contact shouldn't bother him. However, he'd had little experience with women. His life had always been about study, about his work. He regarded his indeterminate feelings about Walks Apart as a silly infatuation. But that didn't mitigate them.

"You have green eyes," she said, looking into them.

"Yes, that's correct."

She ran her fingers gently over his forehead and down around his eye. "What these? What name?"

"What do you mean? Oh, the ridges? We call those wrinkles."

"Wrink-kles?"

"Yes."

"Wrinkles are for old men. You are young man."

"Yes. I'm told I frown when I'm thinking, and I guess I think too much. So you could say thinking gives me wrinkles."

She laughed. He didn't remember hearing her laugh before. He liked the sound of it.

They continued their walk in pleasant silence, with no particular urgency, even though Truvor knew his security detachment was likely getting impatient. After he was compelled to reveal to Storman Ragnarsson his blight's remission and his theory on why it might have happened, the military commander had insisted he use a motorcar with an armed escort for his trips to the village. Despite his militaristic outlook, Ragnarsson understood what the discovery of a cure could mean. He even insisted Truvor cease his language lessons and concentrate his efforts on finding such a cure.

Truvor ignored him, and went right on with the lessons. Nevertheless, he understood what the storman meant when he said "time is short." The skirmishes his troops had been involved in would soon turn to all-out war. Truvor dreaded the thought, but there was nothing he could do about it. When it happened, he was certain he'd no longer be welcomed by the Lakhota. And he knew Ragnarsson would not spare them much longer.

Unfortunately, the native drinking water provided no clues to his remission, that was now complete. He could find no trace of the blight in his body. Any joy he might have felt regarding this was tempered by the fact he had no idea why it had happened.

His next step was to gather various foodstuffs that were a regular part of the native diet. He'd collected samples of everything he'd been eating during his visits, everything the people had been giving him in thanks for his medical services. The answer had to be in the food. If it wasn't...then he wasn't sure where to look next.

"I have to go, Walks Apart. I have work that needs my attention."

"I understand."

"I may not be able to return for a while."

"I wait. *Wakta*."

Truvor wanted to tell her not to wait. He wanted to tell her he may not be able to return. He wanted to tell her that her people should go, hide, be safe. But he didn't.

His eyes were already weary of paperwork when Sitric entered, carrying the formal letter of reprimand from the Althing court.

"What does it say?" asked Vikar, leaning back in his chair and rubbing his eyes.

"It doesn't mention you personally, but it does find Trellestar guilty of corporate assassination. There's the usual language of chastisement, as well as a small fine. Nothing we didn't expect."

Vikar sat up.

"Good, good. What else do we have on the agenda for this afternoon?"

"The thane of manufacturing is waiting outside. You wanted to see him."

"Yes. Send him in."

"Good day, Jarl Magnusson," greeted the executive.

"It is if you have agreeable news for me. How goes production on the new revolver?"

"Excellent, sir. Everything is on schedule. Production has proceeded smoothly. There has only been one minor complication."

"Oh, what is that?"

"An industrial spy was discovered trying to smuggle one of the weapons out of the factory." Seeing the look on Vikar's face, the executive rushed to finish what he was saying. "He was killed trying to escape, and all firearms are currently accounted for. But..."

"But what? Speak up, man."

"I fear there are other spies we have not discovered. Or that there are those among our workers who may be susceptible to bribes."

Vikar stood, locked his hands behind his back and paced the room.

"No doubt you're right, though this is not completely unexpected. We have to assume the competition at least knows of the existence of our new weapon." Vikar stopped pacing and made a decision. "I want the patents for both the firearm and the ammunition filed immediately, but discreetly. Then I want production increased, using as much of our workforce as needed. I want the arms stockpiled. Do you understand?"

"Yes, Jarl Magnusson."

"Then get to it."

The thane offered a curt bow and left.

"I've the jor oil reports you requested," said Sitric. "Production is down, and prices are beginning to rise."

"We can't have that—not now," declared Vikar. "Rising oil prices will only encourage investors to take a chance on Trondtel's green oil venture. I want the size of our jormun fishing fleet increased immediately. We need to keep prices steady for the time being. If we can increase the available supply, we might even be able to drive prices down."

"I'll see to it immediately. Anything else, sir?" asked Sitric.

"Yes. Tell Captain Griffenfeld I want the housecarles to begin training with the new revolvers. Secretly of course. And I want you to oversee the filing of the patents. We can't afford any mistakes. I want it handled as quietly as possible."

"Yes, sir."

When he was gone, Vikar returned to his chair. As steadfast as he appeared to others, he was still unsure of his plan. He wore his uneasiness like an ill-fitting cloak. Debate raged within him. It was a risky gambit, but one, if successful, which would have an immense payoff. Yet it wasn't a course to be taken lightly. It would change the face of Trondheim and shake the very foundation of the corporatocracy.

44

*We do not inherit the land from our ancestors, we
borrow it from our children.*

—Sicangu Adage

The first time he joined Red Sky's family for dinner inside their lodge seemed a special occasion for them. Tordan could tell everyone was wearing their best, and he felt out of place in his own clothes, which had become ragged in several places. He was glad, though, Falling Star had taken him to a river where he got to bathe that morning.

Red Sky, his two children, Willow, and Red Sky's wife, Snow Deer, all sat on animal hides laid across the dirt floor of their lodge. Tordan joined them and sat as Red Sky and Falling Star did, though he found sitting cross-legged difficult with his long limbs.

"I want to thank you for letting me join you for this meal," Tordan said, comfortable in their language now.

"Sungmani Ska is always welcome," answered Snow Deer.

Tordan still wasn't used to the idea of his Sicangu name.

"I appreciate the people have given me a name, but I would wish Red Sky and his family would call me by the name given me by my father."

"Tordan," said Red Sky, motioning to Snow Deer to repeat.

"Tor-dan," she said. "Tor-dan."

"Tordan," repeated Willow and the two children.

"Thank you."

At that, Falling Star said something to his sister so quickly Tordan didn't catch it. As he did, he reached for the food laid out before them. An brusque admonishment from Red Sky stopped him.

"Please excuse my son," said Red Sky. "His father was gone too long, and he seems to have forgotten men eat first, before women and children, and he is not a man yet." Still looking at Tordan, but glancing at Falling Star, Red Sky continued. "Among the Ikche Wichasa, beating children or even speaking too harshly to them is frowned upon, though occasions may call for it. However, children are expected to sit quietly, listen and learn from their elders."

Tordan stifled a chuckle.

"In my land there is a saying that children should be seen but not heard."

Red Sky grunted. "It is a good saying." He motioned towards the food. "Please, eat."

They were all waiting for him, so Tordan picked up his *tatanka* horn spoon and dipped it into his bowl of soup. Each person had his own soup, but the rest of the meal was in various communal bowls. Red Sky stuck his fingers in one bowl and took from it some dried meat. Once the men had begun, the rest of the family started in. Tordan was relieved they didn't have to wait until the men were done, so he didn't feel the need to rush through his meal.

"This is very good," he said. "It is a sweet soup. What is it?"

"*Wojapi*," answered Willow. "It is a berry soup."

"Did you make it?"

She nodded.

"It is very good."

He saw she appreciated the compliment, and noticed Snow Deer smiled. Red Sky only grunted.

"Is it good to speak while we eat?"

"It is good," replied Red Sky.

"I know what Falling Star must do to become a man," said Tordan between bites of some kind of vegetable mush. "But I do not know what a young girl, like your daughter Two Rivers, must do to become a woman."

Red Sky gestured to Willow to explain.

"When the first signs of womanhood appear," she said, "the girl must undergo the *ishnata awicalowan*. She will be left alone in a *thipi* four days, then purified in the *inikagapi* before she can come home."

"After the *inikagapi* there will be a big party," spoke up Falling Star, then quickly hushed when his father stared at him.

"I think..." Red Sky looked at his wife, "...the *ishnata awicalowan* will come soon for Two Rivers."

Snow Deer nodded. Two Rivers looked embarrassed.

The meal was sumptuous—certainly the best he'd had since arriving in this foreign land. They'd obviously gone to great lengths to make it so. Among the foods he recognized were corn, squash, potatoes, and some kind of fowl that tasted almost like chicken.

"I have not seen any...farms." Tordan had to use his own language for the word *farms*. "Where do you grow your food?"

"Farms? I do not know this word," said Red Sky. "We do not grow food, the food grows and we find it. Unci Makha grows all things."

Tordan translated the name as Mother Earth. If they did not farm, the fruits and vegetables they eat must grow wild. What a plentiful land this was, making it an even more enticing target for the corporations of Trondheim.

"If you cultivated the ground and planted your own seeds, you could have much more food."

Again Tordan had to use words for which he knew no translation. Red Sky looked confounded.

"Unci Makha gives us plenty. Why would we want more?"

Tordan had to think a moment to come up with a reply.

"If you had more, you could trade with other clans, with the *wasichu*."

Red Sky grunted his disapproval at this idea.

"Where the herds go, we go," he used his hands as he spoke. "When Frost Moon comes, we journey south. We are *iglag un*. We do not stay in one place. How can we plant seeds and grow our food?"

It confirmed Tordan's supposition they were nomadic. However, since he'd arrived, the clan had shown no inclination to move. Of course such a life would make farming impossible.

"I understand," he said.

"Is it not the same with your people?" asked Willow.

"No, my people build great homes of stone and live there forever."

"It is true," added Red Sky. "Some are so high as to touch the sky."

"Truly?" asked Two Rivers, her eyes full of wonderment.

"Not quite all the way to the sky," said Tordan, chuckling. "However, legend says we came from the sky. One tale says a thousand years ago—many many lifetimes—my people sailed off the edge of another world in a great ship and traveled through the stars until they came to this world. It is called the Volkerwandering. But it was so long ago, the truth of it is not known. It is a story that lives only because it is passed from father to son."

"The Ikche Wichasa have a similar tale. Long ago we were carried to this world across the *wanagi tacanku*...the ghost trail through the stars," Red Sky waved his hand over his head as if it were the sky, "by one of the great thunderbirds, Wakinyan. It is said this world is only one of many on the spiritual journey of the Ikche Wichasa. When it is time, we will be carried to *yutokanl*, another world. For now, Wakinyan sleeps on *hanhepi wi thosan*...the blue moon."

Tordan found it interesting these people had a similar myth, but it only reinforced his own skepticism of such legends. It did make him wonder though.

"How long ago did this happen?"

Red Sky turned his palms up, signifying the question had no answer. "Long ago. Long before I was born."

"How old are you, Red Sky? How many Frost Moons have you seen?"

Red Sky looked uncertain. As to whether he wasn't sure how to answer or was unsure of his age, Tordan didn't know. Red Sky held up his hands, showing all ten fingers. He made a fist, flashed his fingers again, and repeated. Tordan didn't get an accurate count, but then Red Sky himself seemed unsure. But the number was greater than 70. Yet he looked no older than Tordan.

"I have seen many Frost Moons. How many...?" His expression said it was a question for which he was uncertain of the answer.

"Do you and Snow Deer have other children?"

"Yes, but they are children no longer. They have their own children."

"You have grandchildren?"

He held up nine fingers. "Only nine grandchildren," he said as if it weren't very many.

It seemed what Jarl Magnusson had told him about the skrael being long-lived was true. But was it actually something in their food, something in their environment? Or was it just the natural state of their race?

"Do your people get sick?"

"Yes, there are times of bad medicine when some are sick."

"Do they die from sickness?

Red Sky looked at Snow Deer for confirmation.

"It has happened, though the *pejuta wichasa* can usually cure them. Why do you ask?"

"Among my people there is a sickness we call the *blight*. Many have this sickness. Many die from it. It can last many years—many Frost Moons—but it cannot be cured."

"I heard your people speak of this *blight*, but I know of nothing like it among the Ikche Wichasa. Forgive me for saying so, but I think the *wasichu* are a sickly people."

"No forgiveness necessary, my friend. You are right."

Tordan thought again of his brother's wife, and of the others he'd known through the years who'd died of the blight. What if these people did have a cure? Shouldn't he find it and take it back? What if it also increased their life spans? What would this cure be? Something in their food?

He'd wondered about a certain taste, a seasoning of some sort he'd noticed before. It was in both the soup and the mash he'd eaten, and in other things he'd tasted before. Was it, or something like it, a healing herb?

"There is a flavor to your food, something I taste often. Is there something you use to cook your food and make it taste so good?"

Snow Deer said something to Willow, who responded, "*Pazuta*? We use the leaves and the flowers of the *pazuta* for flavor in many of our foods."

"It is a good flavor," said Tordan. "Some time you will have to show me this *pazuta* plant."

Shafts of filtered sunlight made their way through his windows, but Oleg Gripsholm's awareness was darkened by deep thoughts. So lost was he in his musings he didn't hear his executive manager enter. It wasn't until the man cleared his throat to announce his presence that he turned in his chair and looked up.

"What is it?"

"Sorry to disturb you, sir, but this envelope was left for you at the sentry gate by an unknown messenger." He handed it to Oleg. "Normally I'd open it myself to see if it was anything of importance, but as you see, under your name it's marked *personal*. And it's been secured with the seal of the Valkyrie."

Oleg turned the envelope over. There, indeed, was the Valkyrie seal. He couldn't imagine who among those witches would be sending him anything. Let alone something so mysterious.

"That'll be all," he said dismissively.

The manager nodded and left him alone.

Oleg used his dagger to cut through the seal and pulled a single sheet of paper from the envelope. He read it, then read it again.

To the Noble Jarl Oleg Gripsholm:

I know about your son. If you don't want his existence to become common knowledge within the halls of the Ve, you will contract the assassination of Jarl Vikar Magnusson of Trellestar Corporation. This contract must be carried out within a fortnight, or all Trondheim will know.

The letter was not signed—not that he'd expect the extortionist to sign her name. If indeed it was one of the Valkyrie who'd sent it, and not someone else who'd acquired the seal.

As the threat sunk in, Oleg struggled to control his rage. To be manipulated thusly by anyone—especially some unknown conspirator—infuriated him. He certainly had no love for Vikar Magnusson, and had even considered the feasibility of his assassination as a matter of course, but this...this wasn't the time or the reason.

Yet he saw no way around it. To make public his secret would end any hope of attaining the chairmanship. He had no choice.

"You asked to see me, Doctor?"

Vikar motioned for his personal guard to wait outside as he entered the research laboratory.

"Yes, Jarl Magnusson." Dr. Thorgrim hastened to greet him. "Thank you for coming so quickly."

"I hope this means you've found something significant."

"Yes, yes, at least we think we might have."

Vikar scowled. "You *think*? Do you have any idea how much this research is costing me? I expect results, Doctor, not thoughts."

"Of course, of course," responded Thorgrim, flustered. "We have a theory that may lead to a cure for the blight."

"A theory?"

Thorgrim rushed to continue. "A theory based both on research and the vast accumulation of all of our medical knowledge, sir. But to prove the theory, to develop the cure, we need to secure the embryonic stem cells of some skraeling females."

"Why?"

"Stem cells serve as a biological repair system. When such a cell divides, biochemical signals change the new cells into blood cells, brain cells, muscles cells, whatever kind of cell is needed. Controlling the biochemical signal is the key, and we believe we've found the way to govern that key."

Vikar was intrigued, but didn't fully understand.

"You said you need embryonic stem cells—why those?"

"We need cells that are no more than several days old, as they haven't begun to specialize yet. If we can issue the proper signal before that time, we can engineer whatever kind cell we need to repair cellular damage."

Vikar mulled this over a moment.

"Why not simply inject the embryonic cells directly into the patient?"

Thorgrim shook his head. "We've tried that without much success. Direct insertion can often lead to blight-ridden tumors where none existed before."

199

"Alright. It sounds promising, Doctor. But why do you need cells from skraelings? Why not get them from our own women, or from the Vanir?"

"Well," Thorgrim hesitated, "we're still not sure why the skraelings are apparently immune to the blight, but if it *is* genetic, the immunity might be passed on to potential patients through the stem cells. So might their longevity. The probability isn't high, but even the possibility makes it something we want to examine. Besides, I doubt the Valkyrie High Council would permit us to begin culling stem cells from our own women."

Vikar knew that was true. He couldn't imagine trying to convince his own wife of that, let alone the entire Valkyrie High Council.

"I understand, Jarl Magnusson, there will be costs associated with gathering the female skraelings, but the potential benefits, the potential profits should our theories be proved out, would be enormous."

"Yes, they would," agreed Vikar. "I'll give the order for more female prisoners."

Dr. Thorgrim brightened. "Wonderful, sir. We'll continue our work and prepare for the subjects."

"Anything else, Doctor? I've got a corporation to run."

"It's important we receive our subjects in pristine condition, sir, if you know what I mean. As I said, we need newly-formed embryonic cells, so the women must be fertilized here in the lab. There can be no sexual molestation of the prisoners, sir."

Vikar grunted. "I'll give the order, Doctor."

45

*We give thanks to our mother, the land, that sustains
us. We give thanks to the rivers and streams that
supply us with water. We give thanks to the animals
that feed us. We give thanks to all the herbs that
furnish medicines and cure our diseases. We give
thanks to the sun that looks upon us with a
beneficent eye. We give thanks to the moon and stars
that give their light when the sun is gone. Lastly, we
give thanks to Wakan Tanka, in Whom is embodied
all goodness, and Who directs all things for the good
of His children.*

—Sicangu Prayer

Tordan was astounded. Red Sky's senses were as sharp as any animal's, and he used them all. As they tracked a large elk through the woods, Red Sky spoke to him in hushed tones, teaching him as they went. First he spotted something on the ground—a sign of the elk's passing. Tordan couldn't see it even after Red Sky pointed it out. Minutes later, he detected the animal's scent.

"Tahte is with us today. If the wind blew in the other direction, the elk would smell us and the hunt would be over."

Tordan knew Tahte was the name of their wind god. Like the Aesir, these people had many gods. And like the Aesir, they didn't spend much time praying to them, but recognized their place in the universe.

"Listen," whispered Red Sky.

Tordan listened, but didn't hear anything. He started to say something, but Red Sky motioned for silence. So he kept listening. Finally he heard the faintest rustle of leaves, then the crack of a twig. Red Sky continued to advance, moving more swiftly now. He drew an arrow from his quiver. Tordan kept looking ahead, but he saw no target.

This hunt wasn't just a teaching exercise. Red Sky had explained, since the day of his arrival, the herds of *tatanka* had moved on, even though it was early in the season for such a migration. The last big hunt had been on that day. He'd witnessed part of it before he'd been captured.

Some in the village blamed Tordan for the *tatanka's* departure. Red Sky, fortunately, did not subscribe to that theory. He believed—he hoped—the *tatanka* would return. In the meantime, meat was becoming scarce, so the men ventured out daily, hunting for other sources of food.

Seconds after Tordan finally spotted the elk through the brush, it seemed to detect their presence. It stopped warily, trying to gauge the danger. Seconds later, Red Sky let loose his arrow. It flew true, piercing the animal's heart and killing it instantly. They jogged to the kill.

Tordan watched as Red Sky knelt over the elk and waved his hand over it.

"Forgive me, brother elk. I bless your spirit and thank you for the nourishment you will provide my family. Your body will become part of the people, but your spirit will live on. May Hin-Han guide it through Winagi Wichothi."

Red Sky saw Tordan looking at him quizzically.

"Respect and thanks must be shown to all things. Animals have spirits and can speak, even if you cannot hear them. Even rocks, wind, and water have their own identity. Man is bonded to the land, as are all things. Because of this, he must show respect for the water he drinks, the air he breathes, the food he eats—all things are..." Red Sky interlaced his fingers.

Tordan nodded. The idea was alien to the way of thinking he'd grown up with, but it made sense. All things were connected in the cycle of life. But he couldn't imagine Vikar Magnusson asking a goose for forgiveness before he tore off a drumstick.

Each of them grabbed a pair of legs and they headed back to where they'd left their horses.

It had been a long ride to this hunting ground. During the journey, Tordan had marveled at the breadth of the plains and the immensity of the canyons he saw. There was so much land here, so much more than even the surroundings of Trondheim, that were so mountainous as to be useless for either livestock or agriculture. But here...the thought worried him. He knew the Aesir would want this land for their own. The corporatocracy would see the profit in it, and then nothing would stop them. Surely not disorganized bands of "savages."

His worries proved to be an omen. As they rode across the plain, Red Sky spotted a thin wisp of smoke coming from the massive canyon stretched out below them. They turned toward the ridge, and when they got close enough, proceeded on foot.

They kept low to the ground, peering over the crest of the canyon. Below was a *wasichu* encampment. Looking down, Tordan realized it was the first time he'd thought of his own people using the native word for them.

It was a small troop of soldiers, maybe 50 or 60 men, a half dozen Heimdalls, a couple of scout cars. A survey expedition surmised Tordan. He looked at Red Sky and saw the fierce glint in his eyes. The man rarely varied his stoic expression, but Tordan had learned he could tell much about the mood of his companion from his eyes. Right now those eyes were lit like Thor's thunderbolts.

"As a married woman, there are things you must learn about men, and how they can be controlled," said her mother as they rode to the great tower that housed the Hall of the Valkyries.

It was a short drive from House Magnusson, but Rikissa was uneasy. She wasn't looking forward to her initiation ceremony. She had no idea what the initiation consisted of—her mother wouldn't say—but she'd heard tales. She had no desire to join the Valkyries, but her mother insisted, saying all high-born young women were inducted once they were married.

"Some things you'll learn on your own, in time. Others you'll glean from your Valkyrie sisters. The most important of which, is how you'll need to *guide* your husband's decisions. I'm sure you already know there is a power a woman holds over a man. You need to nourish this power, hone your skills of manipulation."

She been told her handmaiden needed to accompany her, so Kristina was sitting up front with the driver, behind the glass shield that had been raised for privacy. It was Kristina's first time in a motorcar and she was excited. Rikissa wished she had as much enthusiasm for the excursion.

"You represent the houses of both your father and your husband today, so it's important you comport yourself well, so as not to embarrass them...or me."

"Yes, Mother."

"Another thing...oh, we're here already."

It was a long walk from the entrance, up the spiral stone staircase of the tower. Her mother was unusually quiet—possibly saving her breath for the climb. Kristina was taking it all in, and wouldn't speak anyway. Likely having heard stories from the other servants, she was afraid of Lady Magnusson.

So Rikissa was left to her own thoughts. For no apparent reason, she began thinking of her wedding night. The bridal mead had transformed the night into a honeyed moon of sorts, but her husband proved awkward in the marriage bed. She liked Edvard—had even begun to care about him, but his love-making only left her pining for Tordan. She'd still heard nothing about where her skaldor might be. Because she'd had no word from him in such a long time, she guessed he must be dead.

"I'm getting too old to be climbing these stairs," said Estrid, between gasps. Rikissa was shocked at the admission.

They reached the outer room of the Valkyrie's aerie, where several women worked at their looms, weaving and sewing, looking for all the world like domestics. Rikissa had been here before, looking for her mother, running errands for her. But she'd never been where she was going now, into the inner sanctum, where the Valkyrie High Council met, where the rumored orgies were held.

They were led through a long but narrow hall, on the walls of which were carved hundreds of ancient runes. What they said, Rikissa could only guess. The hall led into a circular meeting room, where three other young women stood, dressed as simply as Rikissa, in white robes, their hair undone, hanging loosely. The Valkyrie sisterhood sat in the elevated seats around them, chatting as they waited for the ceremony to begin.

Her mother directed her, and she took her place with the other acolytes. Each had brought a handmaiden, who stood a few paces behind them, so Rikissa told Kristina to do likewise. When Lady Gudhild Ingstad, the old heilag of the Valkyrie High Council, walked in, those in the gallery silenced. Like the young women, she too had freed her hair, to hang about her shoulders.

She looked over the initiates and said, "Kneel."

The four young women knelt, but their handmaidens remained standing as they'd been told.

"The call to join the Valkyrie sisterhood is not only an honor, it's a duty. The duty of those chosen to work side-by-side with their sisters to maintain tradition, to shepherd and advise the purveyors of power, to staunchly guard the purity of the Aesir race, and to serve it in whatever capacity is necessary. Do you swear so?"

Rikissa and the other three women answered, "Aye."

"Someday, one or all of you may be seated on the Valkyrie High Council, making decisions that affect all the Aesir. Should that day come, be certain you are worthy." She paused, looked at each of the initiates with a stern eye, then said, "Disrobe."

Rikissa had been prepared for this, but still hesitated. Not for long, as the young women on each side of her complied immediately. She dropped her robe and tried to forget she was standing there naked, the women in the gallery staring at her. She heard the whispers of the older Valkyrie, but couldn't make out what they were saying.

"Now, by the power vested in me through the grace of Freyja, goddess of love, beauty, fertility, and sensuality, I welcome you to the sisterhood of the Valkyrie. Follow me."

Lady Ingstad turned and walked out of the room. Each of the new sisters followed her, and the Valkyries in the gallery started down to join them.

As her naked mistress was led out of the room, Kristina and the other handmaidens collected the
robes as they'd been instructed. They waited for the others to pass, then followed at a respectful distance.

Rikissa and the other unclothed women were led into a sauna room. The old Valkyrie heilag and several other women disrobed and joined them inside. Meanwhile, those who'd chosen not to enter the sauna, including the Lady Magnusson, looked as if they were preparing for a party. They directed servants who brought trays of food and drink, as well as a number of men who wore nothing but white loincloths. Most, but not all of the men had red hair, but not short as was the custom of most men in Oseberg. The locks of these men were long and flowing—even longer than was the style of most Aesir men.

The Valkyrie were very familiar with these men, in the way they spoke with them, the way they touched them. The men, who were all young, reacted much as servants would.

Elsewhere, on the terrace outside the main room, close to the sauna, Kristina saw a mound of snow. She knew there was no snow on the ground in either Trondheim or Oseberg this time of year, so it must have been hauled here from the mountains at great cost. Everything about the room, the furnishings, the food, spoke of extravagance. She'd heard stories as a young girl, but until she actually came to Trondheim, she'd had no concept of the luxury in which the Aesir lived.

The door to sauna swung open and out ran a flock of naked women, including Rikissa. They ran for the terrace and each of them bounded into the pile of snow, screaming like little girls as they did. The old heilag did not join them. As soon as she walked out, her ancient flesh sagging in ways Kristina had never seen, her own servant brought her robe.

After their brief roll in the snow, the women ran back inside and dressed. Kristina helped Rikissa with her robe.

"Let the Dance of Freyja begin!" the heilag proclaimed loudly.

The announcement was greeted by squeals of joy and loud laughter. It was the start of a party, the likes of which Kristina had certainly never witnessed. Neither had her mistress, by the expression on her face. They watched as most of the assembled Valkyrie let loose their own bundled hair, and many of them began disrobing, either in-part or entirely. Soon most were wearing very little but jewelry, abandoning all decorum and any sense of shame they may have had.

However, the bare skin wasn't the most shocking thing she saw. The women began touching the men even more, stroking them and handling them in ways Kristina had never seen or imagined.

The men, in turn, responded, and soon there were pockets of such lustful behavior that Kristina tried to avert her eyes. Yet curiosity kept her peeking. She'd certainly heard her parents grappling in the dark—what her mother called lovemaking—but she'd never seen the act. Yes, she'd seen animals coupling, but never people. It was strangely disturbing, but also exciting.

Her own mistress seemed more uncomfortable than anything. Rikissa showed no desire to participate in the orgy before them. She stood watching until it she could stand it no more.

"Come, Kristina, we're leaving," said Rikissa.

Kristina followed her mistress out of hall, stealing a last glance at the debauchery behind her.

46

*Often is there regret for saying too much. Seldom
regret for saying too little.*

—Book of Runes

Truvor was certain. All his tests were encouraging, the results always the
same, yet he was afraid to let himself believe it was true. He'd discovered
a cure for the blight. Not just a preventative, but an actual cure.

After extensive testing of the native foods and the development of various
serums he tested on infected animals, he was convinced he'd discovered what it
was that kept the natives blight-free, and possibly led to their longevity.

It was a herb, an aromatic plant, with some chemical properties similar to
garlic, but that grew above ground. It was a small, innocuous looking weed
with tiny purple flowers. The Lakhota used it as seasoning in almost
everything they cooked. They also chewed the uncooked leaves of the plant to
relieve such simple ailments as toothaches and indigestion. Walks Apart said
the herb was called *pazuta*.

Though they used the flowers in some dishes, Truvor's tests showed it was
the leaves that held the curative secrets of the plant. He'd already begun
testing, using a purer concentrated form on some of Hestvoll's inhabitants
who'd tested positive for the blight. Now he was ready to begin the regimen
with Burgrave Andersson.

"What is it, Doctor. I'm very busy."

Truvor knew the burgrave was never really busy. He just didn't like his
routine interrupted.

"I have extraordinary news, Burgrave. I'm certain I've discovered a cure for
the blight."

"What?" The burgrave's eyebrows rose at least an inch, but his eyes
expressed doubt. "How certain?"

"Well I've just begun testing it on humans, but I've had 100 percent success
with the animals in my lab."

"I suppose you want to test it on me now. Doctor, I've lost count of the
number of concoctions you've given me, none of which have impeded the
advance of my blight even a little. I don't appreciate being turned into your lab

rat."

"You don't understand, Guttorm," Truvor replied. "I haven't told you this, because I wanted to learn the reason why before I got your hopes up...but my own blight is in complete remission."

"Complete what?"

"It's gone, Guttorm. There is no trace of the blight in my body anymore."

It took a moment for the idea to sink in. Burgrave Andersson let his bulk settle into his chair. Truvor could see by his expression that several thoughts were racing through his head.

"That's...that's incredible news, Doctor. If take this medicine, how soon can we expect it to work?"

"In this new, concentrated form, I'd expect to see some change after as few as seven or eight daily doses."

"Give it to me."

Truvor handed it over and the burgrave sniffed it.

"Pungent, isn't it? I hope it tastes better than it smells."

He swallowed it quickly, then took a drink from the glass of wine on his desk.

"If this works, you know what it'll mean?"

Truvor nodded.

"You should prepare a report. I'll see it goes to Chairman Tryguasson himself. Don't make any promises about how well this cure works. Let's wait and see. Simply explain your preliminary research and early results—enough to get his attention. Do you understand?"

"Certainly, Burgrave."

"Tell me, Doctor, where did you...by Wotan's good eye, how did discover this cure?"

"Purely by accident. I made the serum from an herb that's part of the natives' diet. My own remission began because I was eating with them so often."

"So your relationship with the savages paid dividends after all?"

"Yes, it did. Do you think, if this serum holds true, the chairman will call a halt to the aggression towards the natives?"

The burgrave took another sip of wine as though the taste of the medicine still lingered in his mouth.

"Just the opposite, Doctor. I'm certain once the corporatocracy learns of this, nothing will stop them from expanding their reach on this continent. Our little colony of Hestvoll will become a very large, very important hub of commerce in short order. And you and I will see our prestige rise along with our accounts."

As the burgrave's thoughts soared with visions of avarice, Truvor's heart sank like a stone in a poisoned well. Would his discovery lead to the extinction of these people he'd come to know and respect? Or would that happen regardless? Was genocide to be their fate no matter what he did? Or was there something he could do to prevent it?

The *wasichu* preyed on his mind. The future of his people was fraught with danger and volatility. Worries consumed him, so he looked for an outlet — an escape. He'd been pondering an idea he'd had for some time, so on this morning he searched for and found just the right gourd. It was large enough and had a protuberance that would serve as a handle. He took out his *wasichu* knife and got to work. He sliced off a top portion to get to its hollow inside, then began whittling holes through its bottom half.

When he was done he sought out Snow Deer. Two Rivers told him she'd gone to the stream to wash clothes, so headed in that direction. Passing through the outlying parts of the village he spotted Tordan, Falling Sky, and some of the other young men. The *wasichu* warrior was teaching them combat techniques Red Sky found peculiar, but those gathered appeared eager to learn.

Tordan was still a mystery to him. He seemed a good man, a brave warrior, possibly even a friend. But his motives were obscured by shadow and doubt. When the time came to make war on the *wasichu* — and Red Sky knew that time was coming, as much as he dreaded it — which side would Tordan choose?

He spotted his wife draping a blanket over a prickly bush. It was the blanket he'd gotten in trade from the *wasichu* during his first contact with them, before they'd turned belligerent. He wanted to burn it, and anything to do with the invaders, but he remembered the delight on his wife's face when he brought it to her. She'd marveled at its colored patterns and its weave. Now he wanted to give her something else.

She saw him coming and responded with a look that said "what are you doing out here?"

Red Sky handed her his invention.

"For you."

She took it, turned it this way and that, puzzling over exactly what it was.

"When you finishing boiling meat or acorns or..." he held up his hands to signify other choices, "you can pour everything into this. The hot water will run through the holes and out the bottom. The food will remain."

The simple genius of the implement dawned on her and she smiled.

"This is wonderful. How did you think of it?"

Red Sky held out his empty hands.

"What do you call it?"

"I think I will call it *ohlohloka*."

"You are truly the wisest of men, my husband."

"You did not think so before we were married."

"I did, but I did not say so. It would have been unseemly for me to speak so."

She put her arms around him and he responded in-kind.

"When I was taken prisoner, I thought I would never see you again. The thought tore at my heart like the claws of a bear."

She looked into his eyes.

"I, too, cried on the inside for many days and nights—especially the nights. I longed to hold you, and thought I never would again."

"Had I not returned, you would have had to take another husband."

Snow Deer's eyes rolled at the thought.

"Who would you have chosen? Maybe Spotted Crow?"

Snow Deer grimaced.

"He is as old as the mountains."

"What about Plenty Wolf? He is young."

"Young, yes, but as ugly as the night is long."

"What about—"

She silenced him, putting her hand to his lips.

"Let us not talk about others. Not when you and I are here. Listen."

He listened. He heard the stream flowing past them, and the *cow-cow-cow-cow* call of the *siyaka*. The bird song and the trickling of the water reminded him of the first time they lay down together. It was in place just like this—a day just like this.

"Do you remember?" she asked.

"I remember."

She pressed her supple lips against his and he took her in his arms. They kissed and fell gently into the high grass of the meadow, all the while listening to the water, to the birds, to the wind.

"Gunnar is right. The time to act is now." Jorvik pressed home his point, leaving no doubt where he stood. "We must meet violence with violence."

Marta was sicker than ever. He didn't know how much longer she would live. Thinking about her illness made him angry—angrier than he'd ever been. He was determined to focus that anger on his Aesir masters. Somehow they were to blame, not only for the blight, but for all his woes. There must be retribution.

"I can no longer argue the point," said Agnar with a sigh. "All our efforts thus far have failed. Explain your plan, Gunnar."

"We must send a message to our masters. And it must be a message that's strident but clear as dawn. I propose we sabotage four separate factories at once, so there's no doubt the Modi must be reckoned with."

Agnar nodded, and the others seemed to agree, so Gunnar continued.

"Fire is the surest weapon. Agnar can use his contacts with brothers who are familiar with each location to spread jor oil in the spots that'll do the most damage. We'll ignite the fires simultaneously in the dead of night, long after the workers have gone home. With four different blazes it'll be impossible to contain them all. There will be indecision and chaos."

"There is one thing to consider," said Agnar. "Once the factories have burned, hundreds of Vanir will no longer have work. They and their families will soon be hungry."

"If hunger is the price of freedom, then I'll gladly pay it," said Jorvik. "If we stand together as a people, if we share, we can survive."

"I can help a little," said Olav, the shopkeeper. "I've some food stored. I have some money put away. But it won't last long. We must be certain everyone conserves."

"Thank you, Brother, but even with your help it won't be enough," said Agnar. "We can't just wait, and hope the Aesir will suddenly be filled with human kindness. We must follow-up the fires with a general strike. Closing four factories will hurt the Aesir, will get their attention. But stopping all commerce is the only way our demands will be heard. Each of us must spread the word, talk to those we know, and even those we don't. We must risk everything on this one opportunity. The morning after the fires we want no one to show up for work. It'll be a day of calm and quiet after a night of flaming rebellion. The silence will speak for us if we can convince everyone to hold the line, and refuse to work. We must spread the word, and tell those we tell to tell others."

"Your day of a silent strike is good idea," said Jorvik. "But the next day we should tell everyone to gather at Fisherman's Square, to demonstrate to the

Aesir our solidarity with a show of numbers. The fires, the strike, and then a demonstration of thousands."

"I agree," said Gunnar. "It's a plan with merit. But we'll need more time to organize it all, and to spread the word. It'll be dangerous. It's likely the Aesir spies among us will learn of the strike. And there are always Vanir opportunists who will talk for the right amount of silver."

"We'll tell no one outside our Modi brothers about the fires," said Agnar. "But word of the strike and the demonstration must be spread, regardless of the danger. This is an all or nothing gambit, brothers. Now, Gunnar, what are your plans for specific targets?"

It was all or nothing thought Jorvik, and he was ready for it, even if it meant his life. He was doing this for Canute, so he would have a better life, even if it meant it would be a life without parents. Tordan would take care of him, he was certain. He must find a way to contact his brother, to prepare him.

Vikar's mind was racing with possibilities as his motorcar left the shipyards. With the ongoing production of the new revolver firearms, he now had a military advantage. He'd have to move fast if he were to make use of that advantage. However, the time wasn't right. There were so many plotted moves yet to make. He had to be certain. Once engaged, there would be no going back. It would either bring success—riches and power beyond anything in the history of Trondheim—or utter failure.

His deliberations were so consuming, he didn't notice when the motorcar stopped.

"What is it?"

"A wain has broke down in the middle of the road, sir," said Captain Griffenfeld, from his seat next to Vikar. "I'll get out and see—get down!"

Vikar was only able to see a brief image of someone running towards the motorcar before the captain shoved him to the floor. Two gunshots sounded almost simultaneously and shattered glass rained down on him. Griffenfeld crawled over Vikar, kicking him in the process, and squirmed out the door. Vikar looked up. The captain was grappling with one of the assassins. A second assailant stabbed the housecarle who'd bounded out of the front of the motorcar. The driver got out and opened the other door, trying to move Vikar to safety. Before he could move, he saw Griffenfeld pull out his newly manufactured revolver and fire several times.

By the time Vikar and the driver made their way around, the captain was bent over his own man, the revolver still in his hand. The two assassins lay dead, their haken pistols next to them.

"He's dead," said Griffenfeld, taking his hand from the man's neck. "The blade plunged straight into his heart."

"That was quick thinking, Captain, and even quicker action. You're to be commended."

"By Wotan's eye, we were lucky they missed their target," said Griffenfeld. "Luckier yet I held on to this new revolver. I never expected such a brazen attack. I'll need to increase your personal security. Who do you think they worked for?"

"They could be from any number of houses," said Vikar.

"I recognize this one," said the driver. "He works for Trondtel...or at least he used to."

"Oleg Gripsholm." Vikar said the name with contempt. "I didn't think he was this desperate."

"It's possible this man was hired by someone else," suggested the captain.

"Possible, yes, but I think not. Let's be on our way, Captain."

"Yes, sir."

47

*Don't throw away the old bucket until you're sure
the new one holds water.*

—Ancient Aesir Proverb

Estrid hastened through the manor as if her heels were on fire. She moved as quickly as she could without actually running—which would have been unseemly. The news had reached her, but she had to see for herself. "Out of my way!"

A group of house servants scurried to avoid her as she rounded a corner and approached Vikar's wing. She glanced into his bed chamber, but he wasn't there. She hastened on to his office. He was alone. Apparently unharmed.

"Husband, my husband, I came as soon as I heard."

Vikar looked up from the papers he was studying. Seeing his wife out of breath, he smiled in amusement.

"Are you alright, my husband? I was told you were the victim of an assassination attempt."

"Calm yourself, woman. I'm fine. Thanks to the swift actions of Captain Griffenfeld, the assassins failed."

"It's absolutely deplorable."

"That it was attempted, or that it failed?" asked Vikar wryly.

Estrid feigned puzzlement. "Whatever do you mean? Surely you don't suggest I would prefer it succeeded? Why would I want you dead?"

"Your show of concern is heartwarming, my dear wife. I applaud you for it. But don't think me a blind fool. I've eyes and ears everywhere in the manor. I'm aware of your aspirations for Furyk, and that he answers to his mother's every whim."

She hadn't noticed the cat before, but Prince Dax suddenly launched himself to the top of her husband's desk. Vikar stroked the animal affectionately, all but ignoring her.

"I too have aspirations for our son, though they're not as hasty as yours would seem to be. How fares our daughter? I assume by now she's been inducted into the sisterhood."

Estrid was flummoxed by Vikar's candor, but thankful he changed the subject.

"Yes, she has."

"I'm sure you're pleased with that." Vikar pulled out his chair to sit. "Now, if there's nothing further, I've work to do."

"No, nothing," responded Estrid, still regaining her poise. "I'll leave you to your work."

Estrid started to leave, but stopped at the entryway.

"Regardless of what you may think, Husband, I am indeed pleased the assassins failed in their attempt."

She *was* pleased. Despite her previous machinations, she'd decided it was too soon. She was glad the attempt had failed. She wasn't prepared for Vikar Magnusson to be whisked away to Valholl...or more likely into the cold dark mists of Niflhel. Not yet. She wasn't ready—Furyk wasn't ready.

Estrid's walk back to her own apartments was much slower, calmer. But her mind was still racing. Her husband's claim to have eyes and ears everywhere worried her. That he knew of her hold on Furyk wasn't surprising, but how much did he actually know about what passed between them? Whatever he knew, it was certain he was unworried. She smiled at this. He should be worried. Yes he should.

The village *heyoka* was performing, if you could call it that. Walking backwards, sometimes almost dancing, and speaking incomprehensible words. He'd gathered a small crowd, of mostly women and children, who were laughing at his antics. Dressed in garish garb, he would alternately smile and frown and stick out his tongue.

Tordan found the *heyoka* only mildly amusing, but then he didn't really understand the sacred place this clown held in their eyes. Neither the Aesir nor the Vanir had anything like him.

His performance came to an abrupt end when a commotion elsewhere in the village stirred a buzz of excited talk. Tordan meandered over to see what was going on.

The people were calling out "*Wankatuya! Wankatuya!*" and pointing at the sky. He looked up. Quite a distance away, in a foreboding sky dotted by dark clouds, floated an Aesir airship. He found Red Sky, who was talking with some of the other men as they gazed upward.

"A strange cloud," said one of the men.

"I'm afraid not," said Tordan. "It's an airship." He used his own word for "airship," and the others looked at him questioningly. *"Wasichu mapiya wahte,"* he amended, describing it as a sky boat.

"What are they doing?" asked Red Sky.

"Scouting most likely. Watching the people or studying the terrain. They could be working with a detachment of troops."

"Do you mean there are *wasichu* warriors there?"

"Possibly."

"Let us see."

There was a chorus of agreement. The men ran to their horses and Tordan joined them, mounting the horse Red Sky had given him to learn how to ride. He still wasn't anywhere near as good a rider as the others, but at least he'd learned to hold on without a saddle.

Still, as they raced off toward the dark airship, he was far behind. By the time his steed had reached full gallop, the other men and their horses had disappeared over the hills that stood between the village and a lower plain. Tordan knew he wouldn't catch them until they stopped.

Up and down the rolling hills he rode, using the airship as his marker, until finally he caught sight of the others. They were below, at the edge of a vast grassland that spread out through the enormous valley. The airship was even more distant than before, and, at first, he thought Red Sky and the others had given up, realizing they'd never catch it. But something else had brought them to a standstill. Scores of objects scattered across the plain.

It wasn't until Tordan caught up them that he saw what it was. The otherwise verdant valley was littered with *tatanka* carcasses. Some had been carved up, apparently for their meat and horns, others lay dead but untouched. Apparently the herd had returned, or another was migrating this way.

No doubt who'd caused this carnage. Vehicle tracks were everywhere. The *wasichu* had slaughtered dozens of the beasts, taking little of their kill with them. There had been no need here—no hunger to placate. Only reckless sport.

Red Sky looked at him. His eyes said it all. They were both angry and sad. Before Red Sky turned his face away, Tordan thought he saw tears.

Red Sky called the men back to their horses and they headed for their village, slowly and more subdued than they'd left it. Tordan let them go.

Why they didn't harvest what was left on the plain, he didn't know. He knew they'd been hoping to find a herd of *tatanka*, and that they were in need of meat. Maybe the dead animals were no longer fresh enough, or maybe they considered them tainted by the *wasichu*. Whatever it was, Tordan was feeling too much shame to join them on their ride back.

Furyk's head hurt. All this technical information was too much for him. He didn't understand why he needed to know it. Was it really important to running a corporation, or was his father only testing him? Even, now, as Vikar explained the process of refining iron ore, his mind wandered. He'd much rather be in the hills with his hunting falcon, or visiting his favorite brothel down by the wharf.

"...to produce the purest iron, we must burn away the impurities in a blast furnace and add limestone. Using the iron to form the strongest steel requires carbon and...are you listening to me, Furyk?"

"Um, ah, yes, Father."

"No you're not. I can see it in your eyes. You have that far-away look."

"Really, Father, it's all...very interesting. But what does it have to do with running a corporation?"

Vikar slammed his fist onto his desk. "Are you that ignorant, boy?"

He had Furyk's full attention now. His father hadn't called him "boy" in quite some time. It made him feel as if he *were* just a boy again. He didn't like the feeling.

"You must know every aspect of the business to be able to make sound decisions," fumed Vikar. "If you don't know the difference between a stock certificate and a proxy appointment, you'll never be able to manage Trellestar."

"Don't you have...you know, thanes for that sort of thing?"

An exasperated sigh escaped Vikar's lips as he dropped his head to his chest. When he raised his head again, Furyk saw the look of disappointment in his eyes. He was surprised how much the expression pained him.

"If the time ever comes that you're running Trellestar, you'll have to make dozens of decisions every day. If you leave it to others, you'll lose control of the very thing you crave to possess. And don't think your mother will be able to help you. She knows nothing of running a business. She hasn't told you that, has she?"

The intimation was his father knew something of the conversations Furyk had with his mother. But that wasn't possible, was it?

"I'm trying to learn," said Furyk, realizing his words escaped with a whine.

"Try harder. By Wotan's good eye, you'll have to try much harder if you want to be jarl someday."

Furyk believed his father took pleasure in belittling him. He didn't like to be belittled. He didn't like it at all. He was about to say so, when someone came up behind him. It was Sitric, his father's executive manager.

"Sir, the chairman is on his way to see you."

"That's fine, Sitric. Go now," Vikar said to Furyk. "I'm going to find you a tutor, to teach you the ways of the corporatocracy. Wotan knows I don't have the patience to do it. You'd better put your mind to it, boy."

Furyk said nothing. He turned and walked out of his father's office, past Sitric. He was certain the little man had a smirk on his face.

How dare his father call him "boy" in the presence of the hired help? It was infuriating. But he wouldn't be able to demean his son much longer. Knowing how iron ore was made into steel or not, it wouldn't be long before the day when Furyk would be jarl, and the great Vikar Magnusson would only be a memory.

Chairman Tryguasson lurched into his office out of breath and sat without ceremony. His face was paler than usual and his eyes rheumy. The gaunt chairman had never appeared so old. He saw how Vikar was looking at him.

"It's the blight, Cousin. It's starting to take its toll. It won't be long before the Valkyrie take me away to Valholl."

Vikar poured a cup of wine and handed it to the chairman.

"I worry my son won't be able to manage Roskildcorp when I'm gone," he said, wheezing like a fractured musical instrument. "Edvard's not strong enough, not ruthless enough. You'll help him, won't you, Cousin? Guide him?"

"Of course I will. But we must make certain you live long enough to teach the boy yourself."

"And how will that be accomplished? Is there a cure for the blight you're keeping a secret?"

"Not yet, but we're very close."

The chairman perked up. "Yes?"

"My researchers tell me they're about to make a major breakthrough. They need just one thing to finalize it."

"Well, what is it, man?"

"They need several savage females of child bearing age. They're going to impregnate them, then harvest their embryonic stem cells."

"Why?"

"They believe the cells can be engineered to fight the blight, and maybe even pass on the longevity of the skraelings. As the commander of our military forces in Serkland, you'd have to give the order, Chairman."

"How many of these females would they need?"

"I'm sure a dozen or so would be an adequate inventory, but the more the better."

Chairman Tryguasson stood. "I'll give the order at once. There's no time to waste."

"One more thing. Your officers must be certain to order there be no rapine. The women must not be defiled. After their arrival in Trondheim they'll be impregnated with skrael semen to insure maximum effect."

The chairman nodded, turned to leave, then looked back at Vikar.

"The truth, Cousin. What are the prospects this experiment will actually result in a cure?"

"I'm no scientist, but those working on this are among Trellestar's brightest minds. They seem convinced it will work."

The chairman nodded. "I'll see to it your specimens are delivered as soon as possible."

48

Even he who walks slowly gets there.
—Sicangu Adage

Tordan was weary with boredom. Hunting was the main occupation of the men in the village, but he was not a skilled hunter. At times he accompanied the other men, but he felt like he was more hindrance than help. He spent some time teaching his skaldoran fighting techniques to a few of the younger men, but he had no real duties to keep him occupied.

He tried to lend a hand where he could. However, the women wouldn't let him assist with most of their labors, which they told him in no uncertain terms was women's work. He *was* allowed to gather wood. Of course, that was really child's work.

On this afternoon he went foraging with Willow, to whom he'd expressed his feelings of uselessness on many occasions. She let him carry an extra basket.

Skoll trotted along behind them. He'd taken to following Tordan wherever he went around the village, and most of the people had come to accept him as the dog of Sungmani Ska, though a few still shooed him away. Other dogs did not follow their masters around, so it was still an unusual sight. Tordan had taught Skoll a few simple commands, and, despite his age, he was a quick learner.

Tordan had developed a certain rapport with Willow, though it wasn't anything like the associations he'd had with women in Trondheim. The rules here were different, the traditions and conventions more strictly adhered to. He'd certainly developed an attraction to her, but wasn't entirely sure how to proceed. So he kept his desires to himself. Partly because she revealed no overt signs of interest in him. She was friendly enough, but he saw nothing else. The fact she allowed him to accompany her to pick berries and herbs should have told him something—the least of which being she was no longer in mourning. However, it didn't occur to him anything had changed.

She was quiet for the most part. It was usually up to Tordan to begin the conversation.

"I have not seen Two Rivers since yesterday," he remarked as they walked. "Has she gone somewhere?"

He realized it was a dumb question as soon as he voiced it. A young girl would never go anywhere, stay anywhere, except with her parents.

"She has begun the *ishnata awicalowan*. Soon she will be a woman."

"So, she stays alone in a *thipi* for four days?"

"Yes, in a special *thipi* built by her father. Her grandmother or others will instruct her in the ways of being a woman, and she will pray she is worthy. Then she will be purified in the *inikagapi*."

"What is that?"

"It is the *tatanka* ceremony, conducted in a sweat lodge. *Inikagapi* has another meaning. It means maker of life. A woman is a maker of life."

"I understand."

They walked in silence for a while before Willow stopped in a lush meadow and knelt down. She began uprooting small green plants with tiny purple flowers and putting them in her basket.

"What is this?"

"It is the *pazuta*."

"You use this *pazuta* in everything you cook?"

"Not everything—most things."

He picked one of the plants and sniffed it. It had a peculiar odor. He wondered again if this could be the magic cure that kept the people of Serkland healthy and gave them long lives. Was it the leaves or the flowers? He had no way of knowing if either had any effect. Maybe these people were just inherently healthy. But if this was the cure, he could return to Trondheim, his mission fulfilled. What then? What if he returned and discovered it wasn't a cure?

He contemplated this as he continued to help her pick the *pazuta*, which was plentiful in this meadow.

As if reading his mind, she asked, "Will you stay with the Sicangu, or will you return to your own people someday?"

It was a question he'd been pondering for some time himself, and hadn't fully resolved it in his own mind. Uncertainty dogged him no matter which choice he made, but then, that was the nature of life. Undoubtedly he'd become enamored with these "savages"—a term he'd long ago realized was a misnomer. For the most part, these people led serene lives. They were spiritual and civilized in their own way. He found the sheer candor of their nature soothing. It was so contrary to the courtly intrigue and regimented life of a housecarle he was used to. Yet staying here was, in some ways, a betrayal. Not so much to House Magnusson, but to his skaldoran brothers...and to his family. Could he make that choice?

Willow glanced at him as she continued picking her herbs, waiting for his reply.

"It is not an easy decision to leave one's people. But I think I would like to stay with the Sicangu. I would like to stay with you, Willow."

She smiled and blushed at the same time, but went right on harvesting her *pazuta*.

Kristina was still packing her mistress' belongings when a knock sounded at the chamber door. Both now lived in House Tryguasson, which meant Kristina was doing her best to ingratiate herself with an entirely new household staff. But she'd returned to House Magnusson today, to finish packing.

She opened the door to find one of the housecarles standing there.

"Lady Rikissa isn't here," she said to the housecarle.

"I'm not here for your mistress. There's a woman and a boy from Oseberg here to see you."

From Oseberg? It must be her mother and brother Canute thought Kristina. She was surprised they'd come to visit, but happy they'd found her before she'd left House Magnusson for good.

"They're waiting at the rear entrance to the kitchen," said the housecarle.

"Thank you," she said, hurrying past the man and nearly breaking into a run down the corridor.

As soon as she found them she threw herself into her mother's arms.

"Oh, Mother, it's so good to see you."

She wrapped her arms around her mother and instantly knew something was wrong. The older woman nearly collapsed from the strain of their contact. Kristina held her up and looked at her. It was plain she was ill—very ill.

"What's wrong, Mother?"

"I've come about your father."

"No, what's wrong with *you*? You're not well."

Kristina guided her mother to a ledge where she could sit, and Canute followed, trying to help as well.

"I have the blight, daughter."

Her mother didn't know she'd overheard her parents, and already knew about the blight. But it had gotten worse since she'd left—much worse. Her mother shouldn't be traveling.

"I'm so sorry, Mother, but you shouldn't have come here. You should be at home, in bed. I should go home with you, and take care of you."

"No, no, that's not why I'm here. Canute is taking good care of me."

Canute tried to smile, but Kristina saw he was worried for his mother as well.

"Why are you here?"

Her mother started to answer, but coughed instead.

"It's your father. He's been arrested and brought here to Trondheim. No one will tell us why he's been taken, or exactly where. I'm not even certain he's still alive." Her mother looked at Canute, and Kristina saw she immediately regretted saying such a thing in front of him. "I was hoping you or your uncle Tordan might be able to find out what's happened to him. I asked to see Tordan, but was told he wasn't here. They wouldn't tell me where to find him, so I asked for you."

Her father arrested? Her mother ill? A wave of shame struck her. Here she was, enjoying her new life in Trondheim, while her family struggled. Kristina was so choked by guilt she couldn't speak.

"I know Uncle Tordan will help," said Canute. "He's a skaldor. He can save Father."

"Yes, he can, Canute," she said finding her voice. "I'll find our uncle, and we'll find Father. But you both must go home. Canute, you must take care of Mother until Father comes home. Now wait here. I'm going to get you some food for the journey."

Kristina hurried back into the kitchen, resolute now that she would find Uncle Tordan no matter what she had to do. Her mistress would help her—she was sure.

49

*I observed a group of females gathered for a primitive
birthing process. It proved to be a messy, noisy affair
in which the newborn was plucked directly from the
maternal body. Due to the proximity of my observations,
the emotional emanations were much stronger than
normal, though not wholly unpleasant—until the
birth mother began to wail. At that moment the wave
of emanations overwhelmed both my understanding
and ability to endure. The psychic sensations were as
unfamiliar as the creatures themselves. I absorbed
them with an odd combination of pleasure and pain.
It required a singular effort to engage my departure.*
—Osst Field Notes/010277939

The men sat to the right—the women to the left. Two Rivers sat in the place of honor, surrounded by a good portion of the village. She was trying to repress a big grin, but having little success. It was the first time Tordan had seen her without her hair in braids—the way all the young girls wore their hair.

Everyone was dressed in their finest, even if it wasn't much. Like most of the women, Willow's hair had been freshly adorned with feathers and shells. She was smiling more than Tordan had ever seen her, and was prettier because of it.

Tordan didn't have any fine clothes to wear. Those he had needed mending, which Willow helped him with, promising to make him new ones. But he cleaned up, and even borrowed Red Sky's Aesir dagger to scrape the hair from his face. He'd hadn't been clean-shaven since he was a lad, and it felt as strange as anything he'd undergone since his arrival in the village. However, he felt it helped him to fit in better with the other men of the clan.

As a respected leader of the Sicangu, a *wicasa*, the rite of womanhood for Red Sky's daughter was an important event. The old shaman, Fire In His Eyes, conducted the ceremonial aspects of the *ishnata awicalowan*, and everyone, even the children, were respectfully quiet.

After a sort of hop-step-and-a-jump dance, Fire In His Eyes waved some feathers in the air over Two Rivers, placed a *tatanka* skull next to her, and intoned something Tordan couldn't fully translate. Something about the Great Spirit, the *tatanka*, a girl arriving as a woman, and the giving of a gift.

"Wakan Tanka unsimala yo. Wicincala tatanka ouncage wak'u kte lo. Tokata winunhcala ihunni kte wacin yelo. Tatanka ouncage wak'u kte lo."

This was followed by much whooping and drum banging by those gathered, signaling the beginning of the party. There was singing, eating, dancing, and even body painting, though Tordan refrained from the latter. There were games for both children and adults, and throughout the festivities Two Rivers was presented with many gifts. Tordan had learned giving was much more important than receiving to these people. A man was known by the gifts he'd given—another aspect he admired.

Red Sky's daughter received clothing, animal skins, various trinkets, and even a couple of horses, that Willow explained to him would make her more attractive to potential suitors. Not long after the *ishnata awicalowan* a girl's father was expected to find her a husband—usually one much older, a warrior who had proven himself.

Tordan didn't have anything to give, so he used Red Sky's dagger to carve a flute for Two Rivers. He'd never made such a thing before, but he'd watched his skaldoran master craft one once. Even so, Red Sky gave him a few tips as he carved it. It wasn't much of a gift, but Two Rivers accepted it graciously.

He wasn't much of a dancer either, but he tried to join in. Apparently, the men and women danced separately, which he found odd. But he managed to catch Willow's eye as he danced. His movements were so awkward it was all she could do not to laugh. She stifled one or two giggles, but the rest of the women weren't so polite. Tordan was sure he could give the *heyoka* a run for his money...that's if the Sicangu used money.

Tordan noticed Red Sky, Broken Horn, and some of the other leaders took their leave of the party for some time, but he didn't pay much attention. He was too busy trying his best to win the attentions of Willow. He was singing her an old drinking song her knew, much to her delight and the laughter of her friends, when Red Sky reappeared. Tordan watched him say something to Snow Deer, then acknowledge his daughter with a pat on the head. He spoke to several others, but it wasn't long before he approached Tordan and Willow.

At first he gave them both a look Tordan translated as *What's going on here?* Then he said, "Tomorrow morning we go."

"Go where?" asked Tordan.

"*Iglag un*. Everyone goes. We move the village."

"But Frost Moon is still long away," said Willow.

Tordan didn't know if she were frightened or just perturbed, but she was definitely surprised by the news.

"Is it because of my people—the *wasichu*?"

The change in Red Sky's expression was slight, but Tordan noticed the grim nature of it.

"It is not because of the *wasichu* we move, but because the coming of the *wasichu* has chased away the *tatanka*. We must follow the herds."

The news was making its way through the gathering, and the mood was noticeably subdued. Many made their final good luck, good life wishes to Two Rivers and left the party. Tordan thought he should say something to the guest of honor as well, but when he turned to ask Willow what would be appropriate, she too was gone.

"A number of rabble rousers have been taken into custody, sir. It's possible they're among the B'serkers who are behind the labor unrest."

"Have them questioned. Even if they're not B'serkers themselves, they should be able to give us names of those who are. See to it that...what's that noise?"

Sitric exited to see what the commotion was outside his office. A moment later he returned.

"It's your wife, sir. She insists upon seeing you."

"Let her in," said Vikar, frowning.

Estrid swept into the room looking as indignant as she could manage. As usual, her perfume proceeded her.

"How dare your lackeys try to prevent me from seeing you."

"They had their orders, Wife. I wasn't to be disturbed."

"Certainly those orders don't apply to me. You'd best have a word with Sitric, and explain to—"

"What is it, Estrid?" Vikar knew if he didn't cut her short, she would go on and on. "Why did you find it necessary to interrupt my work?"

She didn't respond right away. Instead she closed the double doors to his office and sat.

"The Valkyrie High Council has learned something very interesting, Husband. Something I'm not supposed to share with you."

226

Vikar's interest was piqued. "But you're going to share it with me anyway, aren't you?"

"No one must know I told you this, Vikar. It would mean my expulsion from the Valkyrie."

"Yes, yes, I understand. Now what is it?"

"Oleg Gripsholm is keeping a defective child in secret—his child."

"I thought his child died at birth, along with his wife."

"So did everyone. He kept it that way. But the child lived, even though his wife died, and he's hidden the boy away with a Vanir family."

"That's very interesting." Vikar considered the information, and the possible ramifications should it become common knowledge. It could be useful, at the proper time.

"You don't seem very aroused by this news—news I risked everything to bring you," said Estrid, dissatisfied with his response.

"No, no, on the contrary. I fully appreciate the information, and the risk you're taking. I'm only contemplating how I might best use it."

Estrid made a noise that meant she wasn't entirely placated.

"There's something else."

"Oh?"

She hesitated, and Vikar knew she wasn't certain she wanted to reveal what was on the tip of her tongue. Yet he knew her well enough to know she would.

"I've seen our son—I've been seeing him."

"Furyk?"

"No, our first son."

It took Vikar a moment to realize to whom she was referring. When he did, he glowered at her. He didn't like to be reminded of his own deficiencies. The memory of his malformed first-born was a secret he tried to hide even from himself.

"What do you mean you've seen him?"

"I've seen him. His ghost has visited me."

"That's foolish talk. There's no such things as ghosts. This thing you've learned about Gripsholm merely put it in your head, and you dreamt it."

"No, no, I tell you I saw him—more than once—before I knew of Gripsholm's child."

"You're daft, woman. Forget these visions you say you've had. No good can come from such talk. Go now. Leave me to my work."

Estrid stood. "I'm not crazy. I *have* seen him. I don't know what he wants, or why he visits me, but he does."

She left him, but even after she was gone, Vikar couldn't free his mind of what she'd said. It had been so long ago, he'd forgotten it. Why she'd dredged up that particularly sullied bit of the past now, he didn't know. Certainly she was scheming in one way or another...or she was going mad. Either way, he wouldn't let it interfere with his plans.

50

We will be known forever by the tracks we leave.
—Lakhota Saying

Tordan marveled at the efficiency with which the Sicangu made ready for their journey. Preparations for the move were remarkably well-organized and swift, like a highly disciplined military operation. Everyone had their own task and went straight at it. They had no wains, instead they used what they called a *hupawaheyunpi*. It was a type of litter made with two poles and a *tatanka* hide, loaded with a family's possessions and hauled behind a horse. Smaller versions were hauled by some dogs. By mid-morning, the entire village was packed and ready to go. Except, Tordan noticed, for one very old couple.

He'd never met them, but he seen them around the camp. They were an ancient-looking pair, man and wife, and he wondered how elderly they must be to look so old among these long-lived people. They did not appear to be preparing to depart as was everyone else. He queried Red Sky.

"They will stay here," he said.

"Stay here alone? They will die."

"It is their time."

"That's not right," said Tordan indignantly. "You do not just leave old people to die."

Red Sky sighed.

"It is their decision. They have decided they are too old to make the journey with the clan."

"Even if it is their choice, how can you let them? How can you not help them?"

"We respect their decision. To do otherwise would be *echa*, a sign of disrespect."

"It's not right," said Tordan.

"It is our way."

Tordan was still disturbed by the idea as the villagers, on foot and on horseback, began their migration. The old couple stood in front of their *thipi*, waving goodbye, and no one seemed to shed a tear or have any misgivings over leaving them, though many in the village stopped to say farewell.

Though he couldn't reconcile this aspect of Sicangu life, he censured himself as unfit to judge. He was a stranger, a *wasichu*, a member of a clan with its own sordid laws and traditions.

Rikissa returned to her new quarters in House Tryguasson after breakfasting with her husband and his parents. She halted outside her door. A strange sound came from inside her chamber. It sounded like sobbing.

She opened the door and found her handmaiden on the floor, crying.

"What's wrong, Kristina? What's happened?" she asked, helping Kristina to her feet. "Has someone harmed you?"

"No, no, it's not me. It's my father. He's been arrested and brought here to Trondheim," she said, trying to wipe the tears from her face. "My mother came to tell me. No one will say why he's been taken, or where. I must talk to Uncle Tordan. He'll help—I know he will. Please, milady, please tell me where I can find him."

Rikissa sympathized with the girl, but there had been no word from Tordan since he'd fled to Serkland. In all likelihood, he was dead. But she didn't want to add to Kristina's misery by telling her that.

"Tordan is no longer in Trondheim. He's gone on some kind of skaldoran mission. I don't know where he is."

"Oh no," sobbed Kristina, beginning to cry once more.

"Don't worry. I'll help you find your father."

"You will?"

"Of course. Being the daughter-in-law of the chairman gives me some influence." Even as she said it, she hoped it was true.

"Oh, milady, thank you—thank you."

"You can thank me when we've found him. Now, let's clean up that face of yours. We can't have my handmaiden looking like a ragamuffin."

Estrid dashed down the corridor, the picture of a mad woman, her garments flying behind her. Servants scurried out of the way. Housecarles looked for danger, thinking someone was chasing her. Even Prince Dax retreated before her.

Estrid ignored them all. Nothing was chasing her except her own fear. She'd seen the spirit again—the ghost of her dead child. She even imagined it tried to speak to her.

She ran until she was out of breath—until she reached Furyk's quarters. The door was bolted.

"Furyk!" she called out, banging her fist against the door.

The door opened to Furyk's scowl. He looked freshly woken.

"What is it, Mother?"

Estrid brushed past him without a word, and he shut the door behind her.

"We must be rid of your father. You can tarry no longer. It must be done."

"What are you talking about, Mother? You're acting very strange. What's wrong? What's happened?"

Estrid realized she *was* behaving oddly. I mustn't tell him of the ghost she thought. He'll never believe me. I must compose myself.

She took a deep breath, trying to relax. Furyk went to his wash basin, threw water on his face and grabbed a towel.

"Now what is it, Mother? What's happened?"

More poised now, Estrid said quietly, "You must eliminate your father—soon."

"Why? The blight will take him. He's too well-guarded, too clever. We can wait."

Now her own lie, the lie she told Furyk about Vikar being infected with the blight, was coming back to bite her. There was no waiting. Either she and Furyk were going to usurp control of Trellestar now, or they never would. But she had to convince him.

"Your father believes he's found a cure for the blight among the savages."

Furyk looked at her with a frown of disbelief.

"Why do you think he negotiated the chairman's medical research division as his bridal price? Why do you think he communicates with his lead researcher so often? He told me the savages have some kind of cure. That they don't suffer from the blight, and that they live extraordinarily long lives. It's only a matter of time before he discovers how to replicate the cure for himself."

Furyk's demeanor changed. She saw the worry in his face as he contemplated what it could mean. She hastened to fan the dim spark of his thoughts.

"How long are you willing to wait to become jarl? Are you willing to wait ten years? Twenty? What if your father finds the key to longevity and lives to be 100? How patient are you willing to be, my son?"

He'd turned his back on her, still thinking. Estrid came up behind him, placed one hand on his shoulder and stroked his hair with the other. She felt the aggravation roiling through him.

"We can do it, my son. You can take your rightful place."

Furyk pulled away from her and turned around. "Yes, but we must be cautious. This thing must be carefully planned. Father is no fool. He knows I was behind Gudrik's death. He knows what I covet. It won't be easy."

"Nothing worthwhile is ever easy, my son. But you're right. We must be prudent. We must take every precaution. We'll have only one chance."

Kristina waited quietly as Rikissa persuaded her husband to help. It wasn't easy. He had qualms about freeing a "B'serker" from prison, but Rikissa told him the charges were false, and that he was innocent man. Kristina knew her mistress had no idea whether Jorvik Thordsson was guilty or not. She was only saying what she needed to get her husband's help.

Kristina didn't know if her father had broken the law or not, but, based on whispered conversations she'd heard over the years, she suspected he had. He hated the Aesir, and she imagined he was capable of committing any crime against them.

Edvard looked at Kristina. She sat huddled in a corner of the room. He must have took pity on her, because he told Rikissa, "Alright. I'll see if I can free him."

Kristina's heart leapt with joy. She wanted to run and hug Edvard, to thank him. However, she knew that wouldn't be proper, so she restrained herself, following Edvard and Rikissa out the door when her mistress motioned for her to come.

She was told to wait outside the entrance to the prison while Edvard and Rikissa entered. Kristina had no idea if they would be successful, but she was bolstered by the looks of encouragement Rikissa gave her on the way there. Still, she waited with trepidation. The longer she waited, the more she worried. It seemed to take forever, though, in reality, it wasn't long at all before Edvard and Rikissa emerged with her father.

Kristina ran to him. He was covered with bruises and cuts. One eye was swollen shut and he limped as he walked. He looked so battered she was afraid to touch him, but gave him a gentle hug anyway.

"Father, what happened to you?"

"Don't worry," Jorvik told her, "I'm alright." He turned to Edvard. "I suppose

I must thank you for my release."

"No need. I didn't do it for you," replied Edvard. "It was a favor for my bride."

Jorvik turned to Rikissa. "Then I thank you, milady."

"The Lady Rikissa is my mistress, Father."

"Then I thank you doubly, for watching over my daughter."

Kristina saw the effort it was taking for her father to show deference to the Aesir he hated so much. She knew how he felt, but his face was so beat-up she was certain Edvard and Rikissa couldn't tell. Edvard's aversion for him was obvious.

"I told the captain of the guard you worked for me, and had been mistakenly arrested," said Edvard. "I don't know what crimes you were arrested for, and I don't want to know. But you should leave immediately for Oseberg, in case other questions are asked that I can't answer."

"What about my fellows still in prison?"

Edvard snorted in disbelief. "It was fortunate I was able to secure your release. I can do nothing for any others."

"Father, you must do as he says. You must go home. Mother is very ill."

Jorvik looked at her. His eyes revealed his pain, but he said nothing.

"Mother needs you," said Kristina.

Jorvik nodded.

"Come," said Rikissa, "we will escort you to the railway."

51

I have come to fear for the future of our race.
Reproductive rates have experienced severe declines.
The desire, the obligation to reenter the corporeal form
in order to mate has been sublimated by the craving of
bipedal emotions that cannot be absorbed once the
process of merging the discorporeal essence with the
corporeal body has occurred. That the coalescence is
both painful and tedious has proved a greater
discouragement than at any time since discorporation
first began. Though I have witnessed this decline, and
documented it, I can do nothing myself, as I have
advanced past the age of either breeding or coalescing.
—Osst Personal Journal

Their trek took four days.

Tordan wondered if the new site for their village was chosen because of its location near a source of water and good hunting grounds, or simply because four was a special—even sacred—number among these people. He did not ask.

They traversed barren plateaus, crossed grassy plains, and rode under great natural stone arches Tordan was certain would collapse upon them. Always to their right, in distance, he saw dark swollen mountains—to the left bleak desert. The land astounded him with its diversity, impressed him with its ruggedness, and often left him speechless with its beauty.

Skoll trotted faithfully alongside his horse the entire way. Though the dog had filled out since Tordan had begun feeding him, he worried the animal wasn't strong enough for such an expedition. But Skoll kept up, as did every dog, child, and pregnant woman. Some walking, some riding, most doing both at stretches.

At journey's end they began reconstructing their village at the edge of a forest. Tordan wasn't sure the site was strategically sound, and he mentioned it to Red Sky.

"Wouldn't it be better, safer, for the village to be deeper in the forest where it could be concealed?"

"Possibly, but the forest is the home of the Hunkpapa. We do not want to encroach upon their land."

"Are they friendly?"

"Yes, but we've had little contact with them."

Several riders raced into the encampment, stirring up a great cloud of dust as they came to a halt. They were all yelling and whooping about something. Tordan caught the word *tatanka*, and as quick as they could, many other men mounted up and they all galloped off. Tordan moved swiftly to keep up with them, but once again he trailed behind.

He followed them as best he could across a ridge that narrowed and unfolded into an easy decline of undulating hills. Fortunately, he never lost sight of them, and it wasn't long before the men pulled their mounts to a halt, skirting the edge of a vast plain just beneath the hills. When he caught up he saw what the others were looking at. Roaming the plain below them, were hundreds of the shaggy beasts. No, not hundreds—thought Tordan, revising his estimation—thousands.

The looks of pure joy on the faces of his comrades were a delight to Tordan. This is what they'd journeyed for, what many had prayed for. The *tatanka* were the lifeblood of the people, and here were plenty. The Sicangu would thrive in the coming days. At least, thought Tordan, until the *wasichu* encroached even further into their territory.

When Jorvik limped through the door, Canute came running. He ignored the pain as his son grabbed him around the waist.

"Father! Father, I was afraid I'd never see you again."

"What's that? Why would you think that?"

"You were arrested, taken to Trondheim," said the boy. "You always told me prisoners of Trondheim never return."

"I'm fortunate. Kvasir was watching over me."

Canute looked up to him with solemn eyes—too solemn for a boy of his short years.

"Mother is very sick. I've tried to help, but I can't make her well again."

"I know you've tried, Canute. But sometimes even the gods are helpless. Can you find some food for your father?"

Canute nodded.

"You prepare something for us while I look in on your mother."

He found Marta in bed, awake, but looking as if she needed sleep.

"Oh, Jorvik. You're home."

Jorvik bent down next to the bed and took her hand. "Yes, I'm home."

"Then Tordan managed to free you?"

"No, it wasn't Tordan. I never saw him. It was Kristina's mistress, the Lady Rikissa and her husband, Edvard Halfdansson."

"The chairman's son?"

Jorvik nodded.

Marta reached out and touched his injured face. "What have they done to you, my love?"

"It's nothing. I'll be fine. But you—how are you?"

She hesitated, as if not wanting to speak of it.

"The blight takes its toll. Most days it's difficult to leave my bed, but I manage." She grabbed the bed covers to throw them aside. "I should get up now and prepare your supper."

Jorvik put his arm on hers to hold her. "You rest. Canute is making supper."

She didn't argue. It was apparent to Jorvik she didn't have the strength to object.

"He's a good boy," she said.

"Yes, he is."

Marta stared at him for along moment, then asked, "Will you return to the Modi?"

Jorvik had asked himself that same question during the journey home, but had found no answer.

"I'm not going anywhere," he replied. "I'm going to stay by your side."

Marta smiled, closed her eyes, and fell asleep so quickly Jorvik worried death had taken her. But he could still hear her breathing, and feel the warmth of her skin. For how much longer, he didn't know. His anger had long since subsided, and all he felt now was helpless.

It was apparent some of the younger children were unsettled by the relocation of the village. Though most paid no attention, Tordan noticed it, and so did the *heyoka*. He gathered together many of the children around his fire and began telling stories.

Tordan sat outside the circle of children, remaining unnoticed in the dark, but listening to the tales.

When the *heyoka* finished one story, a little boy spoke up.

236

"Tell us the story of Unktehi and the Wakinyan Oyate," eagerly suggested the boy.

The *heyoka's* expression grew serious, as if he were contemplating the danger of relaying such a tale, then waved his hands so suddenly some of the children flinched.

"I will tell you of Unktehi the water monster who would have destroyed the old world if not for the Wakinyan Oyate—the thunder beings. Unktehi was angry because the people did not worship him. So he made it rain for many days, until the rivers and lakes overflowed and the plains became marshes. The thunder beings came to protect the people, they fought with Unktehi and all his little water demons. The ground trembled from their battle, lightning crackled through the sky, and it rained even more."

The timbre of the *heyoka's* voice rose and fell with irregular cadence. The children were entranced by his flamboyant gestures and facial contortions, that didn't always match the story, but were intriguing just the same.

"Unktehi was winning the battle on the ground, so the thunder beings took to the air and used their lightning to start a great fire. The fire grew hotter and boiled Unktehi until the monster was only steam that rose up into the sky and vanished."

The *heyoka* turned away as if finished, but whipped around unexpectedly. His gaze trailed across his audience and he said softly, "The monster was defeated, but when it rains, you never know if Unktehi will return."

"What do the thunder beings look like?" asked the littlest of girls.

"They are giant birds," offered an older boy.

"That is both true and false," said the *heyoka*. "It is true the thunder beings are also called thunderbirds. But no man has ever seen the Wakinyan Oyate. Only in visions can a holy man or a *heyoka* see the them."

"Have you seen a thunderbird in your visions?" asked the boy.

The *heyoka* shook his head *no*, but said "Yes, I have," as was his contrary way.

"What do they look like?" asked another child.

"A thunder being has no form. Its body billows and transforms like a cloud. It has no head, but it has eyes. It has no body, but it has wings. It has no legs, but it has claws. It has no mouth, but it has a beak."

The *heyoka* looked around as if to see if anyone dare doubt him.

"It is the charge of the thunder beings to protect the people and purify the land. They love that which is clean and pure and truthful. They scorn what is dirty and impure. It was because the land of the old world was threatened by impurities that Wakinyan, the greatest of the thunder beings, carried the people across the ghost path, through the stars, to this world."

"Is it true Wakinyan sleeps on the moon?" asked the older boy.

Again the *heyoka* shook his head *no*, but said, "Yes. The great thunderbird sleeps on the moon, awaiting the day he will be needed again."

"When is that?" asked another child.

The *heyoka* turned and began walking away. But as he reached the rim of the firelight he turned back and said, "No one knows."

The *heyoka* walked off, leaving the children to chatter among themselves, some agreeing with what he'd said, others offering differing accounts told them by their parents or grandparents.

Tordan left them as well. He walked away, looking towards the night sky. The moon was there, phased to only a sliver, but as blue as the sky would become by morning. He considered the *heyoka's* tale of the great thunderbird, and wondered what kind of mayhem would be enough to call it forth.

52

A male is born, but a man is made.
—Sicangu Adage

Before they could hunt the *tatanka*, they had to be purified, much as Two Rivers had to be purified before becoming a woman. The Sicangu were big on purification, thought Tordan. They were a very spiritual people, though their ritual ceremonies differed from the Aesir only on the surface. Both had their traditions—their superstitions.

He, Red Sky, and Falling Star would join other men in the *inipi* to purify themselves before the big hunt. It was a singular moment for Falling Star. The instant he brought down one of the beasts, he would be a man in the eyes of the people. Already Tordan saw the pride in his eyes as he joined the other men. As the son of Red Sky, much was expected of him, and he knew it. Tordan knew, from his observations, Red Sky was highly regarded by his people. He saw it in the way the other men addressed him, queried him on various matters, and by the deference with which the women treated Snow Deer. He was a true *wicasa* of his people.

They all wore nothing but loincloths, which left Tordan self-conscious. It wasn't the lack of clothing, but the fact his so-very-white skin stood out among the Sicangu. A few of the men teased him about his paleness, and made a point to refer to him as Sungmani Ska—White Wolf. He took it in stride, smiling with them as they walked barefoot to reach the *inipi*, which was the name of the purification ceremony as well as the structure it would take place in. It was built some distance from the village, near the small river that ran out of the forest. Unlike their *thipis*, it was round and fully covered with hides. It was built so low to the ground they had to crawl to enter.

A pit had been dug in its center, and lined with stones. A fire was blazing in the pit and it was already very hot inside. The men sat cross-legged around it as the old shaman began, what seemed to Tordan, a one-sided conversation, dousing the stones with water as he spoke.

Fire In His Eyes was speaking to the spirits, and though Tordan understood little of what he was mumbling, he presumed he was asking them for a successful hunt. He wondered what their reply was.

The steam rose up and billowed throughout the tented structure. The heat became even more stifling. It was not unlike the saunas Tordan had often used with his fellow skaldors. That had always been about relaxation. There were no spiritual aspects to it.

Once the *inipi* was filled with steam, the shaman tossed a handful of sage and cedar shavings into the fire, mumbled something else Tordan didn't understand, and sat with the others.

Red Sky had explained much of the ceremony to him beforehand. He said some of the men would experience visions. If a vision was sufficiently foreboding, with portents of evil or danger, they would decline to join the hunt. If so, no one thought less of them. In doing so, they were looking out for the clan, not just themselves. Tordan fervently wished he would have no such vision. He was anxious to bring down one of the beasts himself.

It was the first *inipi* Red Sky had undergone since his capture by the *wasichu*, and he felt much in need of purification. The *wasichu* had left a scourge upon his spirit, and he longed to be cleansed. That it was the first such rite for his son added an extra measure of gratification.

Immersed in the searing steam, sweat oozing from his pores, he clutched the bear claw hanging from his neck and let himself be consumed by the moment. He prayed silently for the welfare of his people, for the fortunes of them all in the coming hunt, and especially for his son. He prayed to Wakan Tanka that Falling Star would be triumphant in this, his final quest for manhood. As he prayed, a vision came to him. He saw Falling Star pulling an arrow from a slain *tatanka*. But the vision quickly vanished, replaced by one of battle—a battle between his people and the *wasichu*. He saw many of his people die, though none of the dead had faces. As quickly as it had come to him, the vision dissipated. Now he saw something else. Something he didn't understand. It was a ghostlike apparition. A floating essence, like a disembodied head, but not a head. It was a snowy white creature with a limbless, rounded body and a short tail. It had eyes but no mouth, yet it spoke to him. Its words, if that's what they were, were incomprehensible. Yet its emotions were bright and clear. Despair, regret, fear, confusion, sorrow—Red Sky felt each one as a physical sensation emanating through his body. The ethereal entity began dissolving, changing. Slowly it took on a new form, a new color, an azure glow. It became the moon, yet it still had the creature's eyes.

The sound of many voices severed Red Sky reluctantly from his vision. The others were leaving the sweat lodge. He saw Tordan follow Falling Star outside. He shook himself and sweat spewed from his face. Everyone had exited, except Fire In His Eyes. He stared at Red Sky, but said nothing. Had the old shaman shared his vision?

Red Sky made his way outside and stood in the cooling air. He looked up. The sun was beginning to fall in the sky, painting the distant hills ochre and orange. The moon was nowhere to be seen. As was customary, the other men were leaping into the river. Red Sky spotted his son splashing about and ran to join him.

Furyk, sipped his skyr, wishing he had a decent glass of wine instead. His companion, however, seemed content, and that was all that mattered for the moment.

Furyk had suggested they meet once again in the *Blind Crow*—not because he took any pleasure from the foul stench of the place, or the louts that populated it—but because he knew it was unlikely any high-born Aesir would see them together here.

Hrolf took another drink, then treated himself to an unrestrained belch, that Furyk noted attracted not the least bit of attention amidst the drunken revelry of the establishment.

The place was so noisy, Furyk couldn't whisper and still be heard. Nonetheless, he kept his voice low as he spoke.

"With my brother gone, it's now only a matter of time before I succeed my father as jarl."

"Aye," agreed Hrolf, "that's the truth of it now."

He searched the housecarle's expression for any sign the man had a grasp of what he intended.

"If only that time could be hastened," said Furyk, "I'd sooner be able to reward those who've been loyal to me."

"True," responded Hrolf offhandedly, "but even Wotan cannot sever a length of time."

"It's not time I seek to sever."

Furyk stole a furtive glance at Hrolf, but the man revealed nothing by his expression. If he understood what Furyk was alluding to, he gave no sign.

"Let's have another tankard," said Hrolf.

Furyk had hardly touched the one he had, but signaled for the barmaid. He resigned himself to allowing more time to make his intentions clear to the housecarle, without, of course, actually stating them. He wasn't the fool his father thought he was.

53

*It has been officially established, by the council, that
the subject species is having a negative effect upon
our populace. Some now want to return them to their
own world, but the skills needed to engage the great
ship no longer exist among us. Indeed, it is not known
if the ship would still function. Others want to
exterminate the bipeds, though most agree that
would be as immoral as the experiment that brought
them here. A suggestion to the council that the
creatures have a say in their fate proved to be unpopular.*
—A Societal History/The Great Debates

Though unquantified by the Sicangu, time still passed. The sun rose and set. The days grew by hours, rising robustly in the morning, lingering in the afternoon, and vanishing with the sunset. At some point in their passing, a millisecond that came and went unnoticed, he was no longer just Tordan the skaldor. He became more...and less. He became one of the people.

Without even realizing it, Tordan had made a decision. He'd decided not to return to his life as a housecarle of House Magnusson. He was resolved to stay with the Sicangu, no matter what the future might hold. He'd even adopted the Sicangu outlook of time. The future was today. Today he would join his new brothers in his first great *tatanka* hunt. He would kill one of the beasts and be fully accepted as a man among them, as would Falling Star.

Not that he didn't approach the hunt with trepidation. Unlike Red Sky's son, he hadn't been preparing for this moment all his life. It didn't matter he was more than twice the age of the boy, Falling Star was still a much better horseman. Tordan was skilled enough with their bows to trust his aim, but in hunting the *tatanka* he'd have to shoot while on horseback at full gallop, releasing the reins and guiding his mount with only his knees. He'd practiced this without great success and decided he'd be better off using one of their lances. It was like a spear, but longer, and you didn't throw it so much as thrust it into your target. Of course he'd used spears as a skaldor, but the balance of the Sicangu spears, without metal tips, was different. He declined using a throwing spear as well.

With a lance he'd have to ride in close enough to pierce the animal's tough hide, but not too close. The key was to let go at just the right moment. If you released too soon, you'd miss your target—too late and you could get pulled off your horse. He'd been instructed by Red Sky to aim just behind the beast's left shoulder, where its heart was located. Tordan wasn't totally confident about using the lance either, but he was determined to slay one of the creatures even if he had to dismount and use Thor's Razor.

After he finished preparing Fetawachi for the hunt with food and prayer, Red Sky let Snow Deer paint his horse. She was known as a superior artist among the Sicangu. When she'd finished with his mount, she painted his own face. As she did, his thoughts were of his son, who, today with the blessing of the Great Spirit, would become a man. Though he was confident in the skills possessed by Falling Star, he was still a boy in many ways. It was not unusual for someone to be hurt during their first hunt. Even seasoned warriors had been seriously injured beneath the thundering hooves of the *tatanka*. It was natural for him to worry about Falling Star, but he didn't let the concern overwhelm him.

When Snow Deer had finished, he sought out his son. He had asked Fire In His Eyes to paint Falling Star's face before the hunt to provide an extra measure of good fortune. The shaman had painted two crimson stripes across his forehead for protection, and a yellow star on his cheek, symbolizing his name. Red Sky grunted his approval.

Fire In His Eyes said a prayer over Falling Star and left them. Red Sky rested his hand on his son's shoulder and looked into his eyes. He saw pride and confidence. It was good.

"Becoming a man means many things," he said. "It is not only about the hunt. It is not only about making war. A true man takes care of his people and his family in many ways. Often it is necessary to make sacrifices in this cause. Someday you will have a wife and children of your own. You will cherish them, provide for them, protect them as do all the people."

Falling Star nodded.

"It is also good to be proud, for humility is the act of a stupid man. A man speaks of his exploits, but doesn't lie or exaggerate."

"I understand," replied Falling Star. "I will always do my best to make you proud, Father."

His son's words flowed through his ears but caught in his throat. It was an emotional reaction he was not expecting. It took him a moment before he could speak without faltering.

"When you were born, you cried and the world rejoiced. Live your life so that when you die, the world cries and you rejoice."

"I will try, Father."

Dawn's ever-reaching fingers stretched across the plain as they approached slowly, quietly, from upwind, so as not to spook the herd. The hunters and their mounts were all painted. Red Sky's horse had circles around its eyes, with flames fanning back off the circles, befitting its name. Red Sky's own facial embellishment was quite elaborate. Somehow it made him look even more stoic than usual.

Tordan had even let Willow paint his face, though he found the procedure awkward and uncomfortable. She'd chosen to paint only one side of his face with streaks of white. He guessed she was saying something about the duality of his spirit, but he didn't question her about it.

Willow and most of the other women trailed the hunters by some distance with the horse-drawn litters they would use to haul the skins and meat of the animals back to the village.

Tordan had just said a quick prayer to Thor that he wouldn't be returning to the village on one of those litters, when the howl sounded and the hunters urged their horses into full gallop. No longer worried about deception, the men shouted and howled and whooped as they closed in on the herd. Tordan was too busy managing his steed to join in the chorus, but he admired their gusto. As usual, he trailed the others, but kept as close as he could to Falling Star and Red Sky.

The sounds startled the *tatanka*, which broke into a run as a single mass. Tordan heard the ground shake more than felt it. The closer he got to the herd, the more terrifying that sound was. They were huge and deceptively fast for their size. Their hooves kicked up dust that billowed all around him, stinging him, nearly blinding him. It filled his nose with a coarse smell, and his mouth with a taste that made him want to retch. One hand on the reins, one on his lance, he wished only that he not be unhorsed. The thought of actually killing one of the beasts became secondary.

Through the windblown grime he watched with amazement the prowess of Red Sky as he brought down a huge bull with his first arrow. Then another and another. Soon Red Sky vanished into the chaos and dust of the stampede, but Tordan saw Falling Star sink three arrows into one of the animals—the third one finally sending the creature into a tumble Tordan barely avoided.

He could no longer just observe. It was his turn.

He guided his horse toward the closest *tatanka* and lowered his lance. He gripped it tightly, while at the same time reminding himself he'd have to let go at the proper moment. He was within two arm lengths now, and the brute's headlong charge didn't falter. With the lance wedged into the crook of his arm, he aimed it back of the animal's left shoulder and thrust it forward with all his might. He felt it go in, but released his hold a fraction of second late. The *tatanka's* front legs buckled and the inertia ripped Tordan from his horse. He landed on his side, rolled and came up quickly. Fortunately he was on the periphery of the herd, but scores of the beasts were still coming at him. He dove behind the *tatanka* he'd slain—hoping it was indeed dead—and used its body as a shield. He held his breath as the remainder of the herd avoided their fallen brethren.

When the last of them passed, Tordan stood and looked around. Dozens of dead animals draped the plain, but there was no sign of his horse. The other hunters had turned off the herd and were circling back. Red Sky rode up to him, stared, looked around in a sort of mock search, and looked back at him. Fetawachi added a derisive whinny of its own.

"Where is your horse, Sungmani Ska?"

"Very funny," said Tordan, dusting himself off. "Hey, I got one, didn't I?"

Tordan saw his lance had broken. He pulled the jagged piece from the *tatanka*.

"Yes, you got one," responded Red Sky, dismounting. He walked to the dead animal, pulled his Aesir knife out, and cut into the beast. He removed a hunk of the creature's innards, an organ of some kind, and held it out to Tordan. "Eat."

Tordan took hold of it. It was still warm. "Eat this?"

"Yes. Eat."

Tordan's face wrinkled with displeasure, but he took a bite. It had a rich, exotic flavor that wasn't bad. Still, he wished he had a tankard of strong skyr to wash it down.

"It's good," he said, exaggerating only slightly.

Red Sky folded his arms across his chest and grunted. "I never liked it much myself."

54

The Great Spirit pours life into death and death into life without spilling a drop.

—Sicangu Adage

There was no question now. The tests were conclusive. Every member of the colony he'd given his concentrated form of *pazuta* to was showing signs of remission. A few, like himself, no longer had any signs of the blight. Burgrave Andersson, who'd likely had less than a year to live before he started treatments, was also in remission.

Now that Truvor was positive his formula worked, the question was—what should he do next? He'd purposely been vague with his last report, after the burgrave's prediction that news of a cure could lead to the extinction of the native population. Already the Lakhota were suffering from their contact with Truvor and his people. The *pazuta* was not a cure-all. They had no immunity to diseases common in Trondheim, and many had fallen ill. That was bad enough. But, if the what he heard was true, Storman Ragnarsson would soon have more men, more military armament, and would begin to expand Roskildcorp's Serkland territories. He couldn't be a part of that.

Nothing he might do would prevent the inevitable devastation, but neither would he stand by and do nothing.

He considered falsifying his report, saying he'd developed a cure without mentioning the native herb. However, that lie wouldn't likely stop the military incursion. Besides, it was his duty as a doctor to do what he could to stop the spread of the blight afflicting his own people. He couldn't deny a cure needed by thousands, no matter what the consequences.

After much deliberation, he came to a decision. He needed to see Burgrave Andersson.

Much to her boredom, Edvard was going on and on about his research. She didn't understand half of what he was saying, so she paid little attention. Her husband was a masterful talker, but the more he got carried away with a subject, the more Rikissa tended to think of Tordan.

Tordan might sing a song or recite a poem, but he didn't talk much. He was a man of action. He was fun. Unlike Tordan, Edvard wasn't very passionate. He was ardent enough about his studies and his theories, but in the bedchamber passion was lacking.

Rikissa began to think it was because she wasn't attractive enough. Yet she'd caught the eye of a skaldor, who had risked everything to be with her. The ambiguity of it gave her a headache. She blamed her parents. They'd forced this match on her. She'd been used, like any other asset of Trellestar. A commodity with which her mother and father had strengthened their political alliances. She hated them.

"If that's indeed what happened, then—"

A knock on their chamber door interrupted Edvard's prattle. She hurried to open the door, looking for any diversion. She recognized the man there as the chairman's executive manager. His look of despair was palpable.

"I've come with distressing news," he said, addressing Edvard. "Your father has succumbed to the blight. The shade of Jarl Halfdan Tryguasson has passed on to Valholl."

Rikissa looked to her husband. He looked dumbfounded. He knew his father had been ill, but apparently hadn't prepared himself for the inevitable outcome. For the first time since she'd known him, he was speechless.

Despite her ambivalence towards him, Rikissa couldn't help but share his sorrow. She felt something for him—enough to go to him and take his hand.

"Your father was a great man," she said, trying to console him.

"That he was, milady," agreed the manager.

Edvard still said nothing. After a long moment of silence, the executive manager cleared his throat and spoke again.

"Young master, you are now Jarl of House Tryguasson, soon to be known as House Halfdansson, chief executive officer of Roskildcorp, chairman pro tem of the board of directors. What are your orders, sir?"

Rikissa looked up at Edvard's face. It was white, white as death. He still didn't speak. He looked as if he couldn't.

"Don't dally, Doctor. Tell me the results of your tests."

Burgrave Andersson didn't bother to get up from his desk, though his expression revealed the urgency of his concern.

"Good news, Guttorm. Your blight is in remission. If it proceeds as it has in others, you could be completely free of it in a matter of weeks."

As if invigorated by the news, the burgrave slapped his meaty hands to his desk and pushed his bulk up from his chair.

"That *is* good news, Doctor. Well done!" He walked around and wrapped both his hands around Truvor's much smaller one, and shook it enthusiastically. His breath reeked of wine. "How can I ever repay you? To think, not long ago, I was resigned to hear the call of the Valkyrie. Now..."

"It's not only you, Burgrave. I've had success with each test subject."

"And your own blight? Has it returned?"

"I'm completely free of the disease," said Truvor. "There's no sign of it."

"Wonderful. You know what this means, don't you, Doctor? It means we can both get out of this backwoods colony. In fact, I believe we should take your cure to Trondheim in person—together. Glasses will be raised in our names, that's for certain."

"I'm afraid you'll have to endure the glory by yourself, Guttorm. I can't go with you."

"What? What do you mean?"

"I'm going to stay here. In fact, I'm going to leave Hestvoll to do what I can to help the Lakhota. They're suffering from a number of diseases they've contracted from us. It's because of them we've found the cure to our blight, so there is a debt to be paid."

Guttorm snorted. "Nonsense, Doctor. They're savages. Whether they die from disease or from Ragnarsson's bullets matters not." The burgrave moved back behind his desk. "You can't leave now. This is much too magnificent a moment in the history of the Aesir. I'm sure there will be further tests. They'll want you to take part. By the eye of Wotan, I'm certain you'll direct any such tests."

"I've a small quantity of the herb, as well as some of my concentrated formula to send to Trondheim, along with all of my findings and test results. I'm hoping the formula can be synthesized without the herb itself. It'll take some time, but a synthetic is the most practical long-term solution. They won't need me for that. I must do what my conscience tells me, and it tells me I'm needed by the Lakhota."

"Doctor," said the burgrave, his voice chilled with authority now, "you know as well as I do, that in several weeks time there will be no Lakhota. The horse men will soon be extinct. There is nothing you can do to prevent it. You can't help them."

"Even so, Burgrave, I must try."

"I'm sorry, Doctor, but I forbid it. I'm ordering you to remain on the compound. You're no longer allowed to leave for any reason. Do you understand?"

Truvor stared into the burgrave's eyes. What he saw there was unfamiliar—a deadly earnestness he didn't recognize. He'd seen it before in men like Storman Ragnarsson, but not in Guttorm.

"I understand why you've given such an order," said Truvor. "I hope you understand why I must do what I must. Good day, Burgrave Andersson."

Truvor turned from the burgrave's desk and walked out. Behind him he heard, "I'm warning you, Doctor. I'll not condone disobedience. Mark me!"

Truvor expected the burgrave's reaction, but not his vehemence. It didn't matter though. His plans were already in motion. Lame Bear was waiting.

55

Not every bipedal emotion is dangerous — or, at least,
some are much more dangerous than others. Of course,
the more violent, the more conflicted the emotion, the
greater the stimuli, the more potent the psychoactivity.
— Osst Field Notes/010286119

Tordan noticed many of the same folk who'd gathered for Two Rivers' *ishnata awicalowan* were in attendance for the naming ceremony of Falling Star. Of course he'd already been named by his father, but now that he'd completed the three trials of manhood, he would officially be given the name by the clan.

Everyone sat around a crackling fire and watched as the clan shaman conducted Falling Star into the circle. Another man kept up the steady but slow beat of a drum. *Dum*...one, two, three, four, five...*dum*.

Fire In His Eyes held up a piece of tree bark. "On this are written the names that have, until now, belonged to the son of Red Sky. In the name of the council and all the people, I commit them to the fire." He threw the bark into the flames. "Those names are now smoke, and are known no more."

The shaman pulled a ceremonial pipe from his shirt, filled the bowl, lit it, and handed it to Falling Star. He inhaled and exhaled.

"The son of Red Sky endured the vision quest, whereupon he saw a star fall from the sky. When the Sahnish attacked the people, he sounded the first warning and help to fight off the invaders as a warrior should. In the great hunt he slew the mighty *tatanka* to feed his people.

"By these deeds his has proved himself a man, a warrior of the Sicangu. By his deeds may he always be known. I proclaim his name to be Falling Star." Fire In His Eyes took the pipe from Falling Star, held it up with outstretched arms and said, "Falling Star." Everyone assembled repeated the name. He turned and faced a new direction and said the name aloud once more. This time Tordan joined in. The shaman repeated the name four times, once for each direction, and when everyone had repeated it for the final time, the drum stopped, followed by much whooping and yelling and shouts of congratulations. Tordan had grown to like the exuberant nature of the Sicangu — the way they howled and whooped when they fought, when they hunted, when they partied. It was their way of throwing their emotions to the wind, baring their naked souls for everyone to see.

Afterwards was the feasting, the dancing and singing, and more drumming. Tordan congratulated Falling Star, told him it was a good name, and taught him the forearm greeting of the Skaldoran Brotherhood. It wasn't really proper for anyone outside the brotherhood to use the greeting, but Tordan had become very fond of Falling Star. He was like a little brother.

As was the custom, the men and women sat separately during the feast, but Tordan kept exchanging glances with Willow. When he saw her walk off, he followed.

"Where are you going?" he asked when he caught up with her.

"Nowhere. Just out into the night to look at the moon."

"Were you hoping I would follow?"

She blushed and turned away.

"I'm only joking," he said. "Don't go."

She turned back, but kept her head down.

"It was a good ceremony—the naming of Falling Star. Did you have such a ceremony?"

"Yes, though it is different for a girl."

"How did you get your name—Willow Tree In The Wind?"

She glanced at the moon in recollection. It was bright, almost full, and the reflected light set her face aglow. Yet it seemed to him a skeptical moon that shone down upon them with a cynical light. Why he felt that—at that moment—he didn't know.

"I was a flighty girl. I used to run off and hide behind my favorite tree all the time. A willow tree. I thought it was beautiful. I knew it symbolized wisdom, so I thought it would make me wise. It was not a very wise hiding place though, as my mother always knew where to find me."

"So that's how you got your name?"

"Yes."

Tordan reached out and took her hand. For a moment she let him before pulling away.

"The willow is also known as the moon tree," she said as if to distract him.

"Why is that?"

"I do not know. But I know we use it for many things. The bark of the willow is for pain, and the juice of the bark is used for tanning hides."

Tordan decided she looked uncomfortable.

"I'll go now and leave you to the moon. Good night."

He turned and took two steps before she stopped him.

"Do not go."

He looked at her and she looked back, staring into his eyes for a moment before she looked down again.

"How were you named?" she asked.

"My people name a baby as soon as it is born. We have two names, one that is ours and one that comes from our father. My name is Tordan Thordsson. My father's name was Thord. My children would take the name Tordansson."

"You have no children?"

"No, not that I know of."

She looked at him like that was a strange thing to say.

"I have never had a wife," he added.

"Why not?"

"Well, I—"

"There you are." It was Red Sky and he was frowning. He looked at Willow. "You should go now. Snow Deer is looking for you."

Willow glanced at Tordan, but hurried off without saying anything.

"You must do something soon," he said to Tordan when she'd gone.

"What do you mean? Do what?"

"You and my sister. The people are beginning to talk. It is not right."

"I don't want to upset the people, or you my friend. What is it I should do?"

"If she is your *winchinchala*, you should marry her."

It wasn't the response Tordan was expecting, and his face must have revealed his surprise because Red Sky displayed a rare smile.

"Come. It is not time to talk of such matters. Kicking Bull has returned from a raid on a *wasichu* outpost. He brings many things."

He followed Red Sky back to the village where there was much excitement over Kicking Bull's plunder. He'd taken an entire wain and its contents. The women were already claiming blankets and cooking utensils, and two were alternately looking into and fighting over a mirror. They'd also brought back some horses, but they weren't the large work horses he seen in Trondheim. They must have been horses the *wasichu* troops had taken from another clan. There were bags of grain and dried meat, and beneath it all was a box of firearms. Red Sky picked one up and looked it over. It was a long barrel rifle.

Kicking Bull rode up on them, jerking his horse to a dust swirling stop.

253

"The *wasichu* did not fight well. Many of them ran like women."

Tordan looked at the scalps hanging from Kicking Bull's belt. He'd heard of the practice of taking trophies from their enemies, and even seen some — though none so fresh. Most of these were red-haired. Likely they were Vanir conscripts transporting supplies, not highly-trained housecarles or skaldors.

Tordan pointed at the scalps. "They were not the best of the *wasichu* warriors. Real warriors wouldn't have run, no matter how fierce the enemy."

Kicking Bear laughed with disdain and goaded his horse away at a gallop. He rode off to join another group of approaching riders, who escorted an additional captured wain. Much to Tordan's surprise, he saw that hitched to it was a field cannon. Red Sky tossed the rifle to Tordan and walked over to inspect the cannon. He ran his hand down the barrel and looked into the muzzle.

"You will show us how to use the *wasichu* weapons," said Red Sky.

Tordan wasn't certain if it was a question or a command, but he nodded. "I will, if that is what my friend wants."

The measured beats of the kettledrum were spaced far enough apart to let Vikar to begin formulating a plan before another resonant boom would deflect his thinking and remind him why the major and minor houses had gathered on the wharf. Not that he'd forgotten. He simply had more important matters on his mind.

The funeral of a chairman was the both the grandest and most solemn occasion of its kind. Everyone of any significance was there. Most to pay homage, some to silently disparage, others to scheme. For Vikar it was a little of each.

He stood at the forefront of those assembled, along with Estrid and Furyk. Next to them was Lady Tryguasson, Rikissa, and her husband, the new Jarl of Roskildcorp, Edvard Halfdansson. The marriage of Rikissa linking their two families had been a masterstroke, largely carried out, he admitted to himself, by his wife. It had become a key element of his strategy, and was about to pay a dividend.

As the procession of white-robed Valkyries passed slowly by, bearing the pallet upon which rested the body of Halfdan Tryguasson, Vikar planned his next move. He was worried he didn't have quite the backing needed to become the next chairman—not without prolonged negotiations and many unacceptable compromises. In fact, at this point, it was more likely his chief rival Oleg Gripsholm could secure the votes needed for the chairmanship. That was a gamble he wasn't willing to wager on.

The whiff of a sea breeze returned his attention to the funeral.

The Valkyrie honor guard made its way down the pier leading to the longboat that would carry the former chairman to Valholl. He was dressed in his finest, as were those who'd gathered in respectful silence to see him off. Vikar glanced to his left where nine Vanir B'serkers had been hanged as a tribute to Jarl Tryguasson and a gift to Wotan.

It was a deadly game he was about to play. One misstep could cost him not only the chairmanship, but possibly his life. Vikar knew he needed to move slowly, but every fiber in him strained to push forward. That he was destined to be chairman he'd known for many years. He'd waited, he'd maneuvered, he'd prepared, he'd even made distasteful concessions. Now—now that he was so close, patience was a commodity he was growing short of.

The Valkyrie lowered the pallet onto the longboat and reformed their two columns for the slow walk back up the pier as the plodding beat of the drum continued. The dock workers untied the boat's moorings and, using their poles, pushed it out and away. Its sail, emblazoned with the Roskildcorp sea snake logo, was at once caught by the wind. The airstream turned the craft a few degrees starboard and sent it towards the mouth of the harbor.

The skaldor who'd secured the honor walked to the end of the pier, bow and torch in hand. He set the torch into its place in the piling, drew an arrow, nocked it, and placed its head into the fire. He pulled back, aimed, and let loose. The flame drew an arch across the skyline before landing truly in the prepared tinder of the longboat.

Vikar watched as the flames spread. Soon the former chairman would be nothing but memory and ash. Vikar decided, at that moment, he would use the information Estrid had brought him. The revelation that Gripsholm had spared a defective child and hidden him away with the Vanir would be enough to cost him at least a few precious votes. Unaligned houses such as Volsung of Sveabordcorp and Eriksson of Vineland Enterprises were among those such a disclosure was likely to sway. Others would certainly follow.

Once the longboat's sail was engulfed by fire, the entire craft became an inferno. Its progress slowed, but it continued to drift on course out of the harbor. It would burn down to the waterline, and, with Njord's blessing, be carried out to sea. If it washed ashore, a thunderboat would quietly be assigned to tow it out. Some facades must be maintained.

56

*Certain things catch your eye, but pursue only those
that capture your heart.*

—Lakhota Saying

"You pull back the bolt, drop in the cartridge, then push the bolt home—
like this."

Tordan had been teaching the Sicangu how to use the captured
rifles most of the morning. So far he was only demonstrating how to load and
eject. They all wanted to fire the weapons, but they had a limited amount of
ammunition, so he made them wait. After teaching them to use the sights on
their firearms, he let each man squeeze off a round or two, if nothing else, so
they'd become accustomed to the noise.

There was much celebratory whooping and hollering when a target was hit.
But the frequency of such strikes was too rare for Tordan's liking. It might take
more ammunition than they had for each man to become proficient.

After the day's instruction ended, Tordan gathered the weapons. Most of the
men left to hunt, while he collected his half-made gittern and set off to be alone.
He was carving the instrument out parts of cedar and fir trees. Willow had
showed him how they made glue from the hooves of the *tatanka*, but he hadn't
yet assembled all his parts. Unlike the four-string instrument he'd owned in
Trondheim, he was planning a five-string gittern. At this point, though, he
wasn't certain any of it was going to come together. He was learning as he
went—never having actually created anything like it before.

While he was working, Red Sky joined him. He didn't say anything at first.
He just sat and watched as Tordan worked.

"What will it do—this thing you make?"

"It will make music, if I do it right."

Red Sky nodded as if music were a good thing. He watched quietly a while
longer before speaking.

"Our warriors are anxious to use the *wasichu* weapons, even on their hunts."

"I understand," said Tordan. "But they must understand bullets can't be re-
used like arrows. Unless we have many more, I think they should be saved
for...for when they are needed most. But that isn't for me to say. That is for Red

Sky and the other *wicasa* of the Sicangu to decide."

"Young men are impatient, but you are right, my friend. Tell me though, when do you think we will need these weapons?"

Tordan didn't look up from the piece of wood he was carving, and he didn't respond right away. When he did, his voice was flat, unemotional.

"You will need them when the *wasichu* come. They *will* come, my friend. It's only a matter of time. They'll come for your land, for your *tatanka*, for anything they think they need."

"You are certain of this?"

Tordan looked up.

"Kicking Bull has told us of the trail of iron the *wasichu* are building. They are tracks for a railway. It's how great numbers of *wasichu* travel. So, yes, they will come...and soon. I think Red Sky knows this to be true as well. Only he doesn't want believe it."

Red Sky nodded, but didn't reply. He continued to watch Tordan work.

"When I was in the *wasichu* prison, I many dreams—bad dreams," said Red Sky. "I...I still have them at times. Sometimes in the dreams, a white wolf is at my side, trying to protect me."

Tordan looked at him quizzically. "You think I'm the white wolf you dream of?"

"I do not know. We did not know of each other when I first dreamed the dream. But I think there is a reason you are here, with the Sicangu. What that is, only Wakan Tanka knows for certain."

"I think I might know the reason I'm here," said Tordan. "There is something I want, but I don't know how to ask for it."

"Tell me," said Red Sky. "Tell me what it is you want."

Tordan set aside the piece of wood he was working on.

"I want to make Willow my wife. But I don't know how. I don't even know if it is permitted, because I am *wasichu*."

"Does my sister want to be your wife?" asked Red Sky.

"I, uh...I don't know for certain. I think she might. I haven't asked her because I didn't know if such a thing could be."

"It is true. Such a thing has never happened. But the Sicangu have accepted Tordan as one of them, as Sungmani Ska. I think such a marriage would be accepted as well. However, it is not for anyone else to say. It is only for me to say. Since my sister lost her husband, it falls to me to decide such things."

"And what *do* you say?"

Red Sky thought a moment—a long moment for Tordan, who was afraid he would reject the idea of his sister marrying a *wasichu*, friend or not.

"I say, to strengthen Tordan's place in the Sicangu, he should become my *wichoun*. You might say in your language 'brother in blood.' If you were to undergo the ceremony, no one would question your right to marry my sister."

"We have something similar in my land. It's a bond between of brotherhood between two men called the *fostbrooir*."

"Ours is a simple ceremony, but an earnest matter."

"I would be proud to call Red Sky *brother*. And what would my brother think of such a marriage?"

"I think you would make a fine husband. Now, let us talk of your bride's price. She is a good worker you know."

Vikar was reading the production reports on his new revolvers when Edvard Halfdansson was admitted to his office. Likely the young fellow was befuddled by his new position as Jarl of Roskildcorp, and wanted Vikar's advice. Vikar would need Roskildcorp's support, so he greeted Edvard as an equal.

"Come in, Cousin, come in. Sit. What can I do for you? How goes the running of Roskildcorp?"

As if he'd been on his feet all day, Edvard accepted his invitation to sit.

"It's exhausting," replied Edvard. "I never realized how much work my father did. It's all so very complicated."

Vikar smiled. "It'll become easier as times goes on. Once you learn everything, I'm certain things will proceed like clockwork. I'm always here should you need advice."

"Yes, I know. I appreciate that Jarl Magnusson."

"Call me Vikar—you're a jarl now yourself—no need for titles in private."

"That could be difficult. I've always thought of you as Jarl Magnusson. I'll try to remember, though it seems there's so much to remember now that my father is gone."

"What is it I can help you with today?" Vikar gestured at the folder Edvard was carrying. "Do you have some ledgers you need me to interpret?"

"No, no, nothing like that." Edvard handed him the folder. "I brought this for you. It's a report from the doctor at Hestvoll that was sent to my father. Since my father transferred our medical research division to Trellestar, I concluded this should go to you."

"Of course—thank you," said Vikar, scanning the documents. "Anything of importance?"

"Yes, there well could be. Apparently, this Dr. Truvor Svein believes he might have discovered a cure for the blight in some native plant. He's sent what I would call a rather threadbare report, along with some samples of the plant. You'll find them in the pouch. He suggests our scientists try to synthesize it."

Vikar did his best to rein in his exhilaration. His own expedition of scientists had returned from Serkland empty-handed. They'd found nothing that would explain the abundant health of the savages.

"You're right. This could be important, assuming there's any validity to it. I'll have my best men look it over."

Vikar casually laid the reports aside and said, "This Dr. Svein should be transferred back to Trondheim with more samples and more extensive notes, don't you think, Cousin?"

"I would agree," said Edvard, "except, according to the burgrave in charge of Hestvoll, the doctor has vanished."

"What?" Vikar fumed, finding it difficult to control himself.

"Apparently Dr. Svein had quite a bit of contact with the natives, and Burgrave Andersson believes he's been captured or killed."

"If he still lives, he must be found and returned to Trondheim," said Vikar as if giving a command. Not wanting to be overbearing, he softened his tone. "Don't you agree, Cousin?"

"Certainly. This could be a huge advance for medical science." Edvard stood and looked blankly out Vikar's window. "Unfortunately it comes too late for my father."

"Yes, that is unfortunate."

"I'm certain you're busy, Jarl...Vikar, so I'll leave you now. "

Edvard made for the door, but Vikar stopped him.

"This Dr. Svein, you'll have a search conducted for him?"

"Yes, of course," replied Edvard absentmindedly. "I'll give the order to the storman posted there."

"Good, good," said Vikar. "And I'll let you know if there's anything substantive in these reports."

Edvard only nodded as he left.

Alone, Vikar studied the reports more carefully. It seemed this Dr. Svein had already conducted some preliminary tests that were very promising. But this plant, this native herb he spoke of, he didn't even name it. Fortunately, he'd been smart enough to send samples. If Vikar's people could create a synthetic version, and it worked, it would change everything, and Trellestar would emerge as the most powerful, most lucrative corporation in Trondheim. Then the chairmanship would be his—without the need to use force.

During the many days he lived with the Lakhota, Truvor continued to conduct language classes, not only teaching his own, but learning theirs. Despite growing animosity towards the *wasichu*, they'd accepted him. Everyone was friendly. Everyone except Howling Dog. The shaman had still never spoken to him. Yet he watched him almost constantly. He even watched his language classes from a distance. Whether he was learning along with the rest, Truvor couldn't say.

Truvor learned the Lakhota had very little medical knowledge, likely because they had so little illness—until the *wasichu* had come. They knew how to set broken bones and use salves to heal cuts, but not much more. For illness they used the *pazuta* plant and some other herbs, but Truvor didn't know if the *pazuta's* curative powers extended to other illnesses.

Truvor was training Walks Apart to be his nurse. She assisted him when he cared for someone in the village. Though there had been very few cases of pig's bane in the Lakhota village once he'd gotten it under control, one day Lame Bear took him to a neighboring clan where the disease's spread was rampant. He'd exhausted his supply of vaccine by then, and had no way of making more, so he tried something else. He used blood transfusions from the Lakhota who'd been given the vaccine, and had, he hoped, developed their own immunity. To his knowledge, this had never been tried. But it seemed to work, though there were still outbreaks.

While the Lakhota were willing to donate their blood, the members of the Oglala clan were frightened of the transfusions. It took quite an oratory by Lame Bear to convince some of them to give it a try. Still, many refused.

Truvor was also down to an emergency supply of his medications, so he did his best to teach the Oglala to keep the sick hydrated, and keep them cool if their heads became hot. Wishing he could do more, but satisfied he'd done all he could, he and the other Lakhota departed.

Before they reached their village, a rider came to them with news that their *wicasa*, Grey Cloud, had fallen ill. They hurried home and found Howling Dog with Grey Cloud and his family. The shaman made no attempt to prevent

Truvor from going to the man. He stepped aside and observed.

The Lakhota, Truvor had been told, were the largest of the clans populating Serkland. Grey Cloud was their *wicasa*—their leader. Truvor knew if he could restore the old man to health, word would spread, and more would be willing to accept that his medicine was good. So he decided to use of some his emergency stores of medication. There was no guarantee, but he believed Grey Cloud would be fine in a few days.

57

You must live your life from beginning to end.
No one else can do it for you.
　　　　　　—Wisdom of Fire In His Eyes

He kissed her and she kissed him back—eagerly. They lay in the tall grass, invisible to anyone who might wander by. Not that Tordan was worried about being discovered. Though their behavior was inappropriate by strict Sicangu standards, the people tended to look the other way when it came to romance. Besides, Skoll had followed them from the village and lay nearby. Tordan knew he'd alert them if anyone were to approach.

Just then he wasn't thinking about whether they'd be seen. He was too caught up in Willow's embrace, the smell of her skin, the touch of her lips against his. Despite his enthrallment in the moment, he wondered if he should let their passion consume them and lead to its logical conclusion. Before he could decide, Willow took his hand and placed it between her legs. It appeared there was no decision to make. They'd come a long way since he'd first met her—when she wouldn't even look him in the eye.

She was a woman who'd been without a man for some time. He knew she wouldn't hold back. Even so, Tordan considered showing some restraint. He wanted to wait—at least until he'd asked her. But in their current state of arousal, he knew it would be difficult.

Then Skoll began barking.

It was just a few yips, but enough that Tordan lifted himself to see above the tall grass and Willow fretted to hurriedly straighten her clothing.

Tordan saw no one approaching from any direction. He looked at Skoll and realized by the dog's reaction that it had seen a rabbit or some other creature it wanted to run after. Either the old dog was too loyal to leave Tordan, or too lazy to actually give chase.

Tordan took the disruption as a sign from Freyja. He sat up, letting his passion cool. Willow saw his change in attitude and sat up as well, though she looked puzzled.

He began formulating in his mind how he would ask the question, but before he could get it out, she spoke.

"You've never told me anything about your family. Have you brothers and sisters?"

"I have one brother, but no sisters. My brother, Jorvik, is married and has two children, a boy and a girl. They are my only family."

"What of your father and mother?" she asked, picking a piece of grass from his tunic.

"They're both dead."

"My father and mother are with the great spirit as well. They were killed in a raid by the Sahnish when I was still young."

"This feud, this *khiuse* the Sicangu have with the Sahnish, it must be very old."

"Yes. I cannot remember a time when there was peace between our clans."

"There needs to be peace—peace between all the clans," said Tordan. "Soon the *wasichu* army will come, and all the peoples will need to unite as one against them."

Willow made a noise of disbelief. "I don't think the Sicangu will ever have peace with the Sahnish."

Tordan heard the loathing in her voice each time she said *Sahnish*. He sensed it went deeper than the death of her parents. If both the Sicangu and the Sahnish felt the same, an alliance would be difficult. And there were many other clans who likely had feuds of their own.

"I lost my parents when I was young as well," he said, changing the subject.

"How did they die?"

"They didn't die—at least not when I was young. I was taken from them as a boy to be trained as a skaldor. They died many years later, but I never saw them again."

"You were taken from them? Were you taken in a raid?"

"No, no. It's difficult to explain. I was taken by the Aesir, a powerful clan—more powerful than my clan—the Vanir. The Aesir take much from the Vanir, but give little in return."

"Then it *was* a raid," she said.

"Well...yes, I guess you could call it that."

"Will there ever be peace between Aesir and Vanir?" she asked.

"Not if my brother has anything to say about it."

"Then why do you believe the Sicangu will ever have peace with Sahnish?"

She had him there. Tordan had no answer for her, but he replied, "Because they must. They must join forces or they will vanish from the land like the snow in spring."

"The *wasichu* are so powerful?"

"Yes. They are."

Willow looked at him with the gravest of expressions.

"When they come, will Tordan fight with the *wasichu*? Or will he fight against them?"

Tordan took hold of her and replied, "Sungmani Ska will stand with the Sicangu."

He kissed her and she kissed him back with the fervor of a woman afraid she'd never kiss her man again. They embraced and fell into the grass—their passion unleashed once more.

With great effort, Tordan pulled his lips from hers and said, "You are sweet medicine, Willow Tree In The Wind. I wish to make you my wife. Will you marry me, Chansasa?"

The delight on her face was obvious as she stifled a giggle. Yet she answered with more aplomb.

"Yes, I will marry Sungmani Ska. But first you must ask my brother."

"I already have. Red Sky has given his permission."

She smiled, playfully pushed him over, and pounced on him. They had no more need of words.

The time for subtlety had passed. Furyk's patience had reached the end of its very frayed rope. He was ready to be jarl. He wanted it now, and was no longer willing to tiptoe towards his objective. He'd been greasing his housecarle Hrolf with skyr and women for weeks now. The man had already successfully removed his older brother Gudrik. Now it was his father's time.

Hrolf had never been on an airship, so Furyk arranged for a flight aboard Trellestar's own *Sleipnir*. As they looked down over the towers and rooftops of Trondheim, he saw Hrolf was impressed by their gods-eye view. He wanted the housecarle to see, to feel the grandeur of what could be theirs.

In truth, Furyk knew once his father was in the arms of the Valkyrie, Hrolf would be more a liability than an asset. How could he trust such an assassin? He would have to be dealt with. But that was a concern for another day.

"It's a magnificent view. I feel like I'm riding Wotan's eight-legged steed," said Hrolf. "It never struck me so on the ground, seeing them floating by. But these airships are indeed marvels of science."

"The future holds many marvels for us, Hrolf. Nothing will be beyond our grasp once my father sits in Valholl...or Niflhel, if the gods decree."

Furyk studied the man, but he displayed no reaction. He looked around to be certain no one could overhear.

"It's time, Hrolf. It's time for you to earn your place in my corporation. It's time for my father to die."

Hrolf didn't reply for several moments. Furyk's ire rose with each silent second.

"Are you certain this is the course of action you want to pursue, master Furyk?"

"Am I *certain*? Of course I'm certain, man. This is the culmination of everything I've planned—everything I've dreamed of. It's why I've promised to make you a storman. A storman doesn't hesitate when called to battle. Do you waver at such a task?"

"No. I only want to be certain you realize how fraught with danger such a path can be."

"We all live with danger, dear Hrolf. But only the bold prosper from it."

58

*Though I have attempted to restrain myself, and
limit my sojourns to the homeworld, I too have
fallen victim to the compulsions of the bipedal
effusions. Each emotion radiates with its own effect,
its own flavor. The absorption of these emanations
can be, at times, rapturous.*

—Osst Personal Journal

Sitting in the sweat lodge with the other men, naked but for a loincloth, eyes closed, Tordan was reminded of the saunas he enjoyed as a skaldor. Those memories led to others, carrying him even farther back to his days as youngster in Oseberg. He could never have imagined as a boy where life would take him. How strange he should end up here, in a foreign land, learning new customs from people oddly different than his own. Yet that had been his life since the day he was taken from his parents. Trondheim had been a strange place at first. A strange place full of new ways, different people. He'd undergone years of training, he'd fought and killed in the Corporate Wars, and then he'd met Rikissa. Now, because he'd listened to the lust of his manhood instead of the wisdom of his mind, he was here. Stranger than it all, *here* was where he wanted to be.

Someone nudged him. It was Red Sky. The men were filing out of the makeshift lodge, so Tordan followed his friend.

Once outside, the men ran for the river. They plunged in, yelling and whooping as they did. Tordan followed them. The water was like ice— shocking yet invigorating.

The men had gone to the sweat lodge on the outskirts of the village to purify themselves for battle. Red Sky had said it was time for Tordan join the Sicangu in body as well as spirit. To do that, he must partake in a raid against the Sahnish.

Tordan saw nothing pure about warfare, but he was committed to the Sicangu. Their clan was now his clan. Their ways his ways.

They returned to the village where the women were painting their horses with protective symbols and signs of past glories. Willow came to him, and without a word, began painting Tordan's face.

"Are you ready, my friend?"

Tordan turned to see Red Sky, wearing a trio of eagle feathers and painted with Snow Deer's usual skill. He looked as fierce as Tordan had ever seen him.

Tordan gestured at the hide shield slung over his arm.

"That shield doesn't look sturdy enough to stop an arrow," said Tordan.

Red Sky lifted the shield, which was painted with several circles in various colors, all surrounding a red sun.

"It is not the *wahachanka* itself that protects me, but the symbols painted upon it that guide and defend my spirit."

Willow pulled his head back so she could finish her face-painting.

"Will your designs protect me from harm?" he asked jovially.

"Your skills as a warrior will protect you," she replied. "I only make you pretty."

Willow smiled, but Tordan knew she did so only to hide her concern.

She put her paints away and he buckled Thor's Razor in place.

"Now I'm ready," he said.

Red Sky put something in his hand. They were *wowasake* leaves. Tordan had tried them before. They were a stimulant of some kind.

"Do not chew them until we are close enough to smell the Sahnish."

Falling Star rode up on his horse. He was painted as were the others, but too skinny to be very fierce-looking. Though he'd already attained manhood, this would be his first raid. Tordan thought him too young for such a thing, but it wasn't his place to say. All he could do was ride close to the boy, and do what he could to protect him, because he knew Red Sky would not.

Red Sky was the *blota hunka* of this raid. He was accountable for all the warriors, and if any of them died, he would take responsibility. It would be wrong of him to watch out only for his son, no matter his feelings.

They did not carry the guns they'd taken from *wasichu*. The object of a raid was not to kill, but to take as many horses as they could without killing. That did not mean no one would die. It was likely some would—both Sicangu and Sahnish. But it wasn't the objective. It was considered more impressive to steal a man's horse or knock him to the ground than kill him.

"*Akayake!*" called out Red Sky, leaping onto Fetawachi.

Tordan pulled himself up onto his horse and took a moment to offer a smile to Willow before he rode off with the others.

"So what are you telling me, Doctor?"

"I'm afraid, sir, the plant samples were dead by the time we received them, and our tests have been unable to produce any chemicals that affect the blight or anything else for that matter. We're going to need fresh samples—living plants, for us to be able to determine whether or not there's any substance to the claims of this Dr. Svein."

Curse that miserable doctor, thought Vikar. He should have been bright enough to send living plants, unless he was looking to use his discovery as leverage. That's what Vikar would have done. But now the worthless fellow had disappeared into the bowels of Serkland—likely into the stomachs of the local savages.

"Doctor, I want you to assemble a small team of qualified men. I'm going to send them to our Serkland colony, and have them find samples of the plant themselves."

"But, sir, surely you don't suggest we risk—"

"I don't suggest, Doctor, I'm giving you an order. See to it. They'll depart on the next outbound ship."

Vikar was going to use every resource he had to find out if this cure were genuine. He'd need to speak with Edvard as well—make certain the boy would assist in anyway needed. The board vote was coming up too. Vikar expected his support, but he didn't take anything for granted.

It was a successful raid, in that they returned with a dozen Sahnish horses, and no one died. At least none of the Sicangu died—Tordan wasn't certain about the Sahnish. He'd used the flat of his blade when one of the Sahnish has taken aim at Falling Star, but doubted he'd even drawn blood.

Of their own, Two Bears had taken an arrow in the back, but he would live. There were other minor wounds—Tordan had scraped his leg against a tree, but that was due to his own lack of horsemanship. He *had* taken three of the Sahnish ponies himself.

Red Sky rode up next to him.

"Three horses. Luck was with you today."

"A skaldor makes his own luck," replied Tordan, and then laughed.

"Yes, three fine horses. That is a good price for your bride."

Red Sky held out his hand, and, at first, Tordan didn't know why. Then he realized, and handed Red Sky the rope that held the captured horses.

Red Sky let escape a rare smile and laughed as he urged Fetawachi ahead, pulling the Sahnish ponies behind him.

There was much celebrating on their return to the village, and a large feast awaited them. But they'd hadn't yet sat to eat when the ground began shaking. Horses cried out and dogs yipped and howled. So violent was the tremor, and so long lasting, that several *thipis* collapsed.

When the shaking stopped, Tordan looked at Red Sky. Both had felt such quakes before, but Tordan couldn't remember one so powerful.

"Wakan Tanka must be angry," said Red Sky.

"About what?"

Red Sky held out his hands as if to say "who knows."

It was the opening Tordan had been waiting for. He'd been wanting to broach the subject, but didn't want to offend.

"I don't say I know what Wakan Tanka thinks, my friend," said Tordan, "but maybe He is angry because of the raid—because the Sicangu and the Sahnish continue to fight with each other when a stronger enemy looms."

"What do you mean?"

"I think raiding the Sahnish is foolish. I think any clan that fights another is foolish, when what they need is to unite against the *wasichu*. If they don't, the *wasichu* armies with their field cannons and their airships, will make an end to the people."

Red Sky looked at him as if he'd blasphemed, but Tordan saw his mind at work.

"I say this only because I care about the Sicangu. I say this because I *am* Sicangu," said Tordan. "I will say or do whatever I need to, to protect them."

Red Sky said nothing, but there was silent agreement on his face. He walked away without speaking.

59

He who surrenders in business, surrenders in life.
—Words of Chairman Wulfstan

Vikar sat in the Trellestar section of the Ve, doing his best not to let his nervousness show. Normally cool and calm no matter the situation, he realized the vote taken today would bend his fortunes one way or the other. Right now, the scale was leaning towards the opposition.

Sitric and his assistants were making the rounds. Vikar pretended not to notice them, but he did. He watched as they went from house to house in the Ve gallery, trying to gleam any bit of information he could from their reactions. Finally, Sitric made his way back to Vikar's side.

"A few houses still refuse to commit one way or the other," said Sitric. "But it appears Trondtel has the votes to elect Gripsholm as chairman."

Vikar didn't react—at least not visibly. Inside he was angry—angry so many houses would vote against him. But at least now he knew what he must do.

"What would you have me do, sir?" asked Sitric.

"Nothing. Sit and be quiet."

As was tradition, representatives of Roskildcorp still occupied the chairman's dais. Until a new chairman was elected, Halfdan's son Edvard would serve as chairman pro tem. However, by the end of the day, Roskildcorp would vacate, and another house would preside from the dais. Yet there was more at stake than the limited control of the corporatocracy that the chairman would hold. Ultimate authority over the Serkland colony of Hestvoll would also belong to the new chairman, and Vikar couldn't let that fall into the hands of Oleg Gripsholm. Not now, not when he was so close to finding a cure for the blight.

Vikar knew he had Edvard's support for the vote, but, unfortunately, the young jarl didn't have his father's sway with other voters.

The boisterous hum that created a din within the great hall grew quiet as Edvard stepped onto the dais. He hesitated, started to speak, then realized he hadn't been nearly loud enough. Vikar saw how uneasy he was. The assembly settled some more, waiting for the chairman pro tem to begin again.

"I, Edvard Halfdansson, Chairman Pro Tem of the Board of Trondheim and all it holdings, call this meeting of the Board of Directors to order. Is there any challenge to my authority to do so?" Silence greeted him, and Vikar saw the relief on his face. "Having heard no objections, I authorize a commencement of the proceedings."

Quickly, the head of House Gothfrithsson stood.

"Jarl Gothfrithsson of Ruslagen Group, if it please the board."

Ruslagen was a strong ally of Trondtel, so Vikar knew what was coming.

"With your permission, Chairman Pro Tem, I propose a vote on the chairmanship, and nominate Jarl Gripsholm of Trondtel."

Gothfrithsson sat, looking too smug for Vikar's liking.

"Do I hear an assent to Jarl Gothfrithsson's proposal?" Edvard asked the assembly.

A jarl from one of the minor houses stood and offered the needed assent to place Oleg Gripsholm's name on the ballot. That was followed in quick succession by the nomination and assent of Vikar by his own allies.

"Are there any other nominations?" Edvard's question was greeted by silence. "Then I call for—"

"A point of contention, Chairman." Vikar stood, looking at the dais.

"The chair recognizes Jarl Magnusson of Trellestar," said Edvard. "What do you contend?"

"Before the vote is taken, I feel it's my duty to share pertinent information that has only recently come into my possession."

Multiple cries of dissent resonated through the Ve, but Edvard pounded the chairman's staff against the dais for order. Vikar looked in the direction of House Gripsholm, but saw no awareness on the face of his rival of what was to come.

"Is this information germane to the vote, Jarl Magnusson?"

"Indeed it is, Chairman."

"Then proceed."

"It has come to the attention of House Magnusson, that there has been a breach of propriety by House Gripsholm."

More angry murmurs filtered through the Ve as Vikar continued.

"Years ago, when Lady Gripsholm died in childbirth, it was believed her child died as well. We have learned the child is alive, and being cared for in secret by a family of Vanir. Why has Jarl Gripsholm hidden this child?" Vikar glanced at Gripsholm and saw the wretched look on his face. "The answer is obvious. The child is defective, and should not have been allowed to subsist. Its very existence is a threat to the purity of the Aesir."

Incensed threats and accusations of dishonor filled the hall. But there were supportive shouts for Vikar as well, and calls for the censure of House Gripsholm. Many others sat in stunned silence. Vikar knew those were the key votes. The ones no longer certain which way they would turn.

Edvard pounded his staff again for order, but calm was slow in coming. A pair of his aides whispered in his ear, and he waited patiently for quiet before he spoke. Gripsholm's aides were doing likewise, but he was ignoring them. The Jarl of Trondtel sat stone-faced, with no hint of the defeat he knew was imminent.

"I won't ask if you have any proof to support your accusation, Jarl Magnusson, though I'll assume you possess such. Nor will I ask Jarl Gripsholm to either confirm or deny such claims. While you may have found such information to be relevant to the vote, I believe it's a matter that must be taken up with the Valkyrie High Council, and not something that falls within the purview of this board.

"If there are no further contentions, I call for the vote. Houses wishing to support Jarl Gripsholm as chairman of the board of directors, light your staves."

Vikar counted the flames that lit the hall. Inwardly he smiled.

"The count has been made. Extinguish your staves." Edvard waited until all had complied. "Now, houses wishing to support Jarl Magnusson as chairman of the board of directors, light your staves."

One of Edvard's aides lit the staff of House Halfdansson as the others counted and conferred with the chairman pro tem.

"The count has been made. Extinguish your staves." He waited again before continuing. "The count is 13 for House Gripsholm, 19 for House Magnusson. By the vote of this assembly, witnessed by the gods, Jarl Vikar Magnusson is elected chairman of the board of directors."

More dissatisfied murmurs sounded, though not nearly as vociferous as before.

"There being no further business, I, Edvard Halfdansson, Chairman Pro Tem of the Board of Trondheim and all it holdings, now call this meeting of the Board of Directors to a close. Is there a challenge?"

Hearing no challenge, Edvard rapped his staff three times against the dais.

272

60

*What is in the stars is on the earth, and what is on
the earth is in the stars.*

—Lakhota Saying

Snow Deer and Willow chased Tordan away. They, along with Two Rivers, were putting the finishes touches on the *thipi* they were building. The *thipi* that would belong to Tordan and Willow once they were married.

He offered to help, but they said it was women's work, and that a man did not see his new lodge until the day of his wedding. So Tordan went looking for Red Sky. The sun had set by the time he found his friend. Red Sky was sitting by a small fire on the outskirts of the village, looking upward.

"Do you see something?" asked Tordan, sitting next to him.

"Just the stars. I am curious about them."

"My people are great seafarers who use the stars to guide them, but I know little of the art. What are you curious about?"

"I know the stars are not always in the same place. Do you see those five there? The ones shaped like an arrow?" He drew his finger across the sky until Tordan nodded. "The arrow used to be in the southern sky. Tonight it is in eastern sky. But if the stars are moving, why is the arrow shape always there? Why does it not divide into five separate stars?"

Tordan shrugged. "I have no idea."

"I wonder," mused Red Sky, "is it the stars that are moving, like the sun and the moon...or is it the world? It does not feel like the world is moving."

Tordan looked up. He saw hundreds of tiny specks of light, but they meant nothing to him.

"I've really never noticed."

"We are taught the stars are the breath of Wakan Tanka. There are many stories of the stars, passed down from father to son, but the old tales don't match what I see in the night sky. There are stories about Mato Tipila and Winchincala Sakowin, but those star formations are no longer there."

Tordan knew mato tipila meant bear's *thipi*, and Winchincala Sakowin was the seven little girls, but he didn't know what Red Sky meant about them not being there any longer.

"As children, we were told stories about the stars too," said Tordan. "One tale speaks of how, as the gods battled, they kicked their great fire and sent sparks and embers into the night sky. We learned the gods live on the moon in their wondrous city of Asgard, and that they travel across a bridge of rainbows to Midgard."

"Midgard?"

"It's what we call this world."

Red Sky stirred his fire and with a stick and watched as a few stray sparks wafted into the air.

"Our peoples tell different tales and our gods have different names. I wonder what the truth of it is?"

"Likely we'll never know...until we die," replied Tordan. "A day that can wait for many years as far as I'm concerned. Thor forgive me, but I don't really care for gods much."

Red Sky grunted. Whether in agreement or to ward off any ill fortune, Tordan couldn't be sure.

They sat in silence for a long minute, staring into the fire. The breeze shifted and the smoke swirled left, then right. Tordan found himself enjoying the moment—the aroma of the burning wood, the elemental grace of the flames, the raw simplicity of tacit comradeship.

"You know," said Tordan, "compared with the wealth of Trondheim, your people have so little, and yet, you have everything."

"We have what we need," said Red Sky. He stood and tossed the stick he was holding into the fire.

"Are you prepared to become my brother?"

"Sure. Right now?" Tordan stood, brushing himself off. "Do we need to gather everyone and—owww!"

Red Sky had pulled out his knife—the steel dagger he'd taken from the *wasichu*—and sliced Tordan's forearm. Quickly he cut his own as well.

"This is not a thing for others. This is between you and I. Hold up your arm."

Tordan complied. Red Sky pressed his arm against Tordan's. Their wounds mingled.

"We bleed together now, Sungmani Ska. We are brothers, now and forever."

"We are brothers," repeated Tordan. "Now and forever."

His executive manager stood there, patiently waiting to find out why he'd been summoned, but Oleg Gripsholm wasn't ready to speak. The truth was, he wasn't ready to put voice to what he'd already decided he must do. Saying it aloud would make it real—a reality he never thought would come to pass.

Generations of blood and silver invested by his family, all his years of hard work, the sacrifices he endured to make Trondtel one of the largest, most powerful corporations in Trondheim—all for naught now. All because of a single decision. A foolish, sentimental decision he'd made upon his wife's death.

He told himself he'd had enough of the corporate world—the risky investments, the devious plotting and wrangling. But it wasn't true. The truth was he'd enjoyed every day. Now those days had come to an end.

"I want you to consolidate my personal holdings. I'm going to retire."

"Sir? You...you can't retire. What about Trondtel?"

"Trondtel will survive," said Oleg cheerlessly. "I'm going to name my nephew—what's his name? Oh, yes, Lodbrok. I'm going to name Thane Lodbrok Gripsholm as the new Jarl of Trondtel."

"Lodbrok?" said the manager as if he couldn't believe his ears. "He's hardly qualified to be jarl."

"Then I trust you'll nursemaid him through the transition and teach him what he needs to know," replied Oleg gruffly.

His manager nodded.

"I also want you to tell the Vanir family I'm coming to get my son."

61

*I was standing on the highest mountain of them all,
and round about beneath me was the whole hoop of
the world. And while I stood there I saw more than I
can tell, and I understood more than I saw; for I was
seeing in a sacred manner, the shapes of things in the
spirit, and the shape of all shapes as they must live
together like one being.*
—Wisdom of Fire In His Eyes

Falling Star and some of the other young men had found something. They rode into the village flush with excitement, telling anyone who would listen about their discovery. No one paid much attention until Red Sky and Tordan heard what they described. It sounded familiar.

Falling Star and two other young men led them back to the site of their discovery. In the face of a cliff was a cave entrance that hadn't been there before. Tordan surmised the crevice must have opened during the last quake.

They journeyed inside, but not far before they found what had excited the young men. In the darkness of the cave the thing glowed. It was a soft white glow—not bright enough to light the entire cavern, but enough to make it stand out.

There was no doubt is was a structure of some kind. As soon as he saw it, Tordan exchanged looks with Red Sky. Except for the damage done to it by a partial cave-in, it was a smaller version of what they'd found on the island.

Everything about it was rounded. The smooth white rock-like material it was constructed from wasn't rock, but Tordan still wasn't sure what it was. Amidst the rubble were courtyards, cracked archways, and hundreds of hive-like chambers. He also noticed, here and there, the same kind of runes carved into the structure. Tordan was convinced it was a language of sorts.

"What is this place?" Falling Star wondered aloud.

Red Sky shook his head as if he had no reply.

"No beast made this," said Falling Star. "Tordan, is this the work of the *wasichu?*"

"No, it's definitely not. I think whoever built this, whatever race of creatures lived here, is long dead."

"They are dead, but their ghosts are still here," said Red Sky. "Let us leave this place. The dead are not our concern."

On the way back to village, as they slowed to rest their horses, Red Sky rode up beside Tordan.

"It is strange that twice now we have seen that which neither of us has ever seen before. And each time we were together."

"It's strange, but I don't think it means anything," replied Tordan.

"Everything means something," said Red Sky. "Though this mystery is beyond me. Are you certain this is not an ancient *wasichu* thing? Something before your time."

"I'm certain. You saw for yourself. Whatever it was, it was not built for men." Red Sky grunted in agreement.

They rode on until Red Sky's horse began to whinny and stomp.

"Fetawachi is troubled," said Red Sky.

He whispered something to his horse Tordan couldn't hear. The skaldor was always amused his friend spoke with his horse as if the beast could understand him, and vice versa.

Falling Star, who was leading the group, called out, gesturing at the sky.

Tordan looked up. It was an airship.

It was likely soaring too high to notice them, and wouldn't care about a handful of riders regardless. But judging by its course, it was likely it had passed over the Sicangu village. No doubt marking its location.

Red Sky looked at Tordan, his eyes asking the unspoken question.

"They're mapping the terrain, charting where the various clans are located. The Sicangu need to move into the forest, or find caves where they can stay hidden. Otherwise, when the *wasichu* come, they will know where to find us. The women and children will be in the open, vulnerable to attack."

"Your words are wise, and I know you care about the safety of the Sicangu, but we are a people of the plains. Hiding among the trees or living in caves is not our way. But I see the danger. We will move the village again, and we will move it each time the *wasichu* find us."

"What's this report, Captain?" Vikar only glanced at it before tossing the paper aside. "Why do I care about this?"

"Sir, it seems Roskildcorp's missing doctor has resurfaced," said Captain Griffenfeld. "I know you previously expressed an interest in this Dr. Svein."

"Dr. Svein—yes, yes, most definitely. I thought he was dead. What do you mean he's *resurfaced*?"

Vikar's eyes flashed from the captain to his executive manager and back again, looking for an explanation.

"The report is from Storman Ragnarsson, commander of the corporate forces in Serkland," said Griffenfeld. "He says there are several accounts of an Aesir doctor living among the savages, curing their illnesses, apparently making a name for himself among the horse men. Ragnarsson seems certain the man is Dr. Truvor Svein, who disappeared from Hestvoll several weeks ago."

"Did you know about this, Sitric?"

"Yes, sir. That's why I had Captain Griffenfeld bring it directly to you."

"By the eye of Wotan, I want this man found!" Vikar slammed a fist onto his desk.

"Sitric and Griffenfeld were both taken aback. Vikar Magnusson seldom let his emotions loose. Normally he was a cool and calm as glacier.

"I want you to send a detachment of troops, along with some of your best skaldors to bring this doctor back to me."

"Yes, sir."

"And, Captain, I want you to pick out a replacement for yourself."

"Sir?" Captain Griffenfeld didn't bother to disguise his astonishment.

"As chairman of the board, and commander of the Federated Corporate Army, I'm promoting you to storman. I want you, personally, to lead this mission, using whatever assets you believe are necessary. I want this Dr. Svein."

"Yes, sir."

"Sitric, I want to expand the number of troops we have at our disposal. Do we have enough capital?"

"Not for any major buildup, sir."

Vikar frowned and began pacing behind his desk.

"If we're going to take control of Serkland and all its mineral and agricultural wealth, we're going to need a much larger army. And, gentlemen, we *are* going to expand our holdings in Serkland. Even if it means exterminating every last horse man on the continent." Vikar stopped his pacing. "Sitric, I want you to augment the rate of conscription among the Vanir. We need more troops and more arms, even if it means selling some of Trellestar's lesser holdings. I want each thane to make cuts within his own branch. There's always fat that can be trimmed. Look into it and make your recommendations to me."

"Sir, are you sure it's wise to increase conscriptions at this time—with all the unrest among the Vanir?"

"They'll do their duty if we have to go house to house and make it clear they serve or their families suffer. Any man without verifiable employment and a steady work record will be drafted. Any man convicted or even accused of a crime will be inducted—and that includes those B'serkers. We'll give them something to fight."

Vikar took a deep breath and looked at the two men.

"Well? You both have your orders. Get to it."

Vikar knew the other corporations weren't going to like it if he began depleting their labor force, but he would tell them it was a temporary measure necessary for the security of the Serkland colony. That would appease them for a while. Soon—very soon—there would be nothing they could do to interfere with his plans.

62

*It doesn't interest me how old you are. I want to know
if you will risk looking like a fool for love, for your
dreams, for the adventure of being alive.*

—Sicangu Adage

R ed Sky was in high spirits on the day his sister was to marry his brother
Tordan. Her first marriage had been brief, and there had been no
children. He knew this saddened her, and hoped her union with Tordan
would produce many fine nieces and nephews.

The wedding feast began midday and would last until sunset. Red Sky had
escorted his brother to the feast, then stepped aside as the other men took him
roughly, but good-naturedly, and forced him to sit in the circle, and cajoled him
into eating all that was offered. Willow Tree was there, but sitting with the
women on the other side of the circle. She was dressed in her marital garments,
with feathers and sea shells affixed in her hair.

"She looks very happy," said Snow Deer.

Red Sky grunted.

"I remember the day we were married," she said.

Red Sky responded, "You can remember so long ago?"

He smiled, but she wacked him across the head with the flat of her hand just
the same.

At one point during the feast, four drummers crafted a beat and the young
women sitting with Willow Tree coaxed her up. The women, including Two
Rivers, began dancing around the circle of feasters, and kept at it until they
tired.

There was much laughter and many joyful smiles as the feasting continued.
Stories were told—often about other weddings—and many jokes of a bawdy
nature were passed from group to group.

Red Sky was not only happy for his sister, but for all the people. They
needed to laugh, to smile, as often as they could. If Tordan was right about the
coming of the *wasichu*, there would be few enough times to laugh in the days
ahead.

Midway through the festivities, Tordan stood. Red Sky knew what was
coming. He'd told his brother what he planned was unusual, that a man did not

280

give his bride-to-be a gift directly, but that he saw no harm in it.

Tordan held up his hands for quiet, and soon all eyes were on him. He was holding onto the musical thing he'd made—what he called his *gittern*. Two Rivers joined him. She had the woodwind Tordan had carved for her.

"I want to thank you, my friends, for gathering today for my wedding. I also want to thank you for welcoming me into the clan of the Sicangu. I've composed a song for my bride that Two Rivers and I would now like to play."

Willow Tree looked both pleased and embarrassed. Her friends seemed impressed a man would do such a thing for her.

Two Rivers began the song, her woodwind light, melodic, like a meandering stream, or the wind gently brushing the leaves of a maple tree. It was quite beautiful. Snow Deer elbowed her husband and they exchanged proud smiles.

Tordan soon joined in, plucking the strings of his gittern in a rhythmic pattern that somehow blended with the melodic notes of the woodwind.

Red Sky saw the people were intrigued. They'd never seen or heard such an instrument—such music as this.

While the woodwind continued to carry the lead, one of the drummers spontaneously joined in with a soft beat, and Tordan began singing.

Red Sky wasn't certain Tordan's rough voice was a good companion for the lilting music, but it was not unpleasant. However, Tordan wasn't always easy to understand when he spoke the Sicangu language, and, as it turned out, he was even less so when he sang. Still, Red Sky thought he could make out most of the words.

> *Oh sweet medicine*
> *Proud Willow of the plains*
> *She's sweet medicine*
> *Who mourns but does not weep*
> *Oh sweet medicine*
> *Willow of my dreams*
> *Great Spirit make me worthy*
> *Of this sweet vision*
> *The winds of life*
> *Blow in four directions*
> *Willow do not bend*
> *But blow to me*

Two Rivers ceased playing and only the sounds of the gittern lingered. Red Sky saw others from village drawn to the wedding party by the unusual sound.

281

Both Tordan and Two Rivers began singing.

Sweet Medicine
Sweet Medicine
Sweet Medicine

Their singing faded and the music stopped.

Much whooping and hollering greeted the song's end. The feasters had enjoyed it. His sister still looked somewhat embarrassed, but there was also great pride in her face.

The feasting continued until the sun began to set. That's when Fire In His Eyes arrived, arrayed in feathers and bones, his body nearly covered in paint of all colors. Four of the tallest Sicangu warriors were with him. Red Sky guessed he'd selected them, because Tordan was so tall.

"The time of the joining has come," he announced.

The warriors lifted a large *tatanka* hide over their heads, each holding one corner. In their free hands, they held spears. Pushed by their friends, Willow Tree and Tordan stepped under the hide. Red Sky and his family, along with many others, lined up behind them. Even Tordan's dog, Skoll, followed.

Fire In His Eyes led the procession through the village loudly proclaiming the marriage as he went. Those who hadn't taken part in the feasting called out their congratulations as the wedding party passed.

When the procession reached the outskirts of the village, the women took Willow Tree and hurried her away. That was Red Sky's cue. He led Tordan alone to the his new lodge.

"You must build a fire inside your home and await the coming of your wife."

"Am I...are we...married now?"

Red Sky laughed. "Yes, you are married. Do you feel different?"

"I'm not sure. No, I can't say that I do."

"You will." Red Sky clapped him on the back, smiling. "You will."

Red Sky left him alone, but didn't go far. He wanted to be sure his brother had no trouble building the fire. He didn't. He'd just got it going when a small group of women approached the lodge, singing and carrying torches. Six of the women held onto a *tatanka* hide that Red Sky knew contained his sister. When they reached the entrance to the *thipi,* they threw back the flap and deposited Willow Tree unceremoniously inside her new home, at the feet of her husband. Giggling, they hurried off, and then began singing.

Red Sky turned to go as well. He was confident his brother Tordan would know what to do next.

63

*I am convinced our initial apathy regarding the
subject species has been our ultimate undoing.*
—Osst Personal Journal

"**B**lessed be to Freyja," said the chief high mistress, looking sterner than
usual. "I've called this special session of the high council due to an
accusation made against one of our own. Sister Ericksson, as the
accusing party, you have the floor."

Estrid knew why they'd been called to meet. She knew, but she wasn't
worried.

Lady Ericksson stood, cleared her throat, and began.

"You're all familiar with the recent events surrounding the vote by the board
of directors to elect a new chairman. Before the vote, Jarl Magnusson of
Trellestar revealed to the board the existence of the defective child fathered by
Jarl Gripsholm. The revelation influenced several votes among the board,
giving the chairmanship to the Jarl of Trellestar. I accuse Sister Magnusson of
violating the policy of this board and her oath of silence, passing information to
her husband that this council had sealed, and disrupting the balance of power
with the corporatocracy."

Finished, Lady Ericksson sat.

Lady Ingstad looked pain, but she continued.

"Sister Magnusson, do you have a response to this accusation?"

"I do," said Estrid.

"Then you have the floor."

Estrid stood, looking calm and composed.

"It's true the board of directors has elected my husband as chairman of the
board. It's also true he revealed the existence of Jarl Gripsholm's illicit child to
board, though I can't say for certain whether that had any effect on the outcome
of the vote. However, I deny violating my oath—an oath I take very seriously. I
did *not* reveal the existence of this child to my husband. He has his own sources
of information, and used them to the best advantage of his corporation, as
would any jarl."

Estrid relinquished the floor by returning to her chair.

Lady Ericksson looked outraged. Skepticism colored the faces of other council members.

"Sister Ericksson," said the chief high mistress, "do you have any evidence of this alleged violation? Are there any witnesses?"

Lady Ericksson stood, flustered now.

"Of course there are no witnesses. I have no proof to show this council, Chief High Mistress, but I think we can all surmise how Jarl Magnusson came into possession of the information. I call for a vote of censure against Sister Estrid Magnusson."

Lady Ericksson resumed her seat as many of the council members exchanged looks.

"Does anyone on this council have anything of substance to add?" queried Lady Ingstad. "Is there any evidence to support this accusation?"

Silence was the only response to her questions. The chief high mistress contemplated this for several seconds, but Estrid never wavered. Her demeanor remained above reproach.

"I'll not call for a vote of censure, as we have nothing but supposition to sustain this accusation. Sister Ericksson, as chief high mistress of this council, I must reprimand you for making such a serious accusation without corroborating evidence. Guesswork and supposition, logical or not, are not the foundations for leveling charges against sister members."

Lady Ericksson looked aghast that she'd been reprimanded. Estrid stifled a smile.

"Does anyone have anything they'd like to add to today's proceedings?"

Lady Ingstad surveyed the faces at the table. No one, it seemed, had any desire to speak.

"Then, by the glory of Freyja, I adjourn this meeting of the Valkyrie High Council."

"By the glory of Freyja," answered the high mistresses in unison.

The outcome of the meeting was predictable. Estrid knew that. So did most of the women. Yet Lady Ericksson had chosen to make the accusation anyway. Was it her sense of duty? Estrid wasn't sure. The woman had done so at the risk of making an enemy of the chairman's wife. Not a very clever move on her part. Fortunately for her, Estrid was the forgiving kind. She wouldn't hold it against Lady Ericksson...unless the need arose.

All eyes were on Tordan. Broken Horn, Red Sky, Kicking Bull, Fire In His

Eyes, all the *wakincuzas* of the Sicangu clan had assembled inside the lodge of
Broken Horn, the clan's *iyotan wicasa*. They were the leaders, the ones who
decide. They'd asked Sungmani Ska to join their council meeting, to tell them
about the *wasichu*.

No one looked at Tordan as if he were the enemy—as if he were *wasichu*. To
them, he was Sicangu now. They would listen to his counsel, and accept it as
truth. Despite their acceptance, guilt clawed at the pit of Tordan's stomach. He
felt guilty because he *was wasichu*. He also felt a tinge of guilt that he plotted
against his brothers, the skaldors, whom he knew would lead any invasion. But
he'd already made his choice. He wouldn't turn back now.

"The *wasichu* are not like the Sicangu or the other peoples. They crave to own
the land and the minerals that dwell within the land. They use these minerals
to make their cities, their motorcars, their weapons, their wealth. To the
Sicangu, a wealthy man is one who owns many horses. The *wasichu* wealthy
own many different things. To them, the accumulation of wealth is the ultimate
hunt—the end justifying any means."

The men who'd gathered around him shook their heads and grunted at the
oddness of such thought. Fire In His Eyes made a gesture Tordan took as the
warding of evil.

"The *wasichu* have weapons—many weapons."

"We have *wasichu* weapons too," said Kicking Bull, referring to the paltry
few they'd captured.

"Yes, my friend Kicking Bull, we do. And we will take more. But the *wasichu*
have many many more of these weapons than we will ever have. They have
more weapons than there are stars in the sky. They have all kinds of weapons,
weapons you never imagined, new weapons they are creating every day. They
have armored motorcars, airships, explosives..." Tordan didn't go on. He'd
made his point. The bleak expressions around him were evidence of that.

"Is Sungmani Ska certain the *wasichu* will come?" asked Broken Horn.

Tordan nodded.

"They will come, most certainly. I'm sure, even now, they prepare their
invasion."

"Let them come," said Kicking Bull. "We will fight them."

"We *will* fight them," agreed Red Sky. "But we must be wise. Sungmani Ska
is a warrior who has fought many battles. What is your counsel, Brother?"

Tordan thought of the battles he'd fought. There were not that many, and
they were long ago. But he'd fought in the Corporate Wars when he was

285

young—memories he cared not to recall. The truth was, he was a highly trained warrior who wasn't very warlike. He preferred sonnets to swords, the arms of a woman to the clutch of chain mail.

"I think it best the Sicangu fight as they have always fought, as warriors of the horse."

His suggestion was greeted by nods and grunts of agreement.

"But that does not mean fighting the *wasichu* army head-on. A frontal assault would be foolish, like the dance of the *heyoka*. We should harry the *wasichu* forces as they move across the land. Hit them quickly and ride away, as we raid the Sahnish. We should fight them as one hunts a deer. Stealth and surprise should be our weapons. The forests, the mountains, the rivers should be our allies."

Tordan knew by the reactions of those gathered in the lodge, that his words had the desired effect. His point was made. Nodding heads signaled agreement.

"This is my advice. I am not *wakincuza*. I cannot say what you will do. That is for you to decide. But whatever your decision, I will stand with you against the *wasichu*."

"Sungmani Ska speaks wisely, and we listen," said Broken Horn. "If we are to defeat the *wasichu*, if we are to survive, we will need his wisdom. I say Sungmani Ska should be a member of the council. Does anyone object to this?"

It was apparent everyone agreed this was wise.

"Then it is so. Sungmani Ska is *wakincuza*." Broken Horn turned to look at Tordan. "What is your counsel? What needs to be done to prepare for the coming of the *wasichu*?"

Tordan wasn't certain how his next recommendation would be received, but he knew it was vital.

"The Sicangu cannot fight the *wasichu* alone. The Lakhota cannot fight the *wasichu* alone. The *wasichu* know there are many clans. They will rely on this to formulate their strategy. They know victory will come much easier if they war with only one clan at a time. If they face a divided foe, they will conquer. We must not allow that to happen. We must convince all the clans to join together." Tordan saw the looks of doubt creep into their faces. "The Sicangu must fight side-by-side with the Lakhota, with the Sihasapa, with the Oglala, with the Hidatsa, and, yes, even with the Sahnish."

At the mention of the Sahnish, there were many rumbles of dissent. The idea of fighting alongside their sworn enemies made their stomachs churn and their blood boil. It was obvious to Tordan such an alliance would be hard to forge. But he knew it must be.

Broken Horn raised his hand for silence.

"Though we may not want to hear of such a thing, our brother's words ring with wisdom. All the peoples face a common enemy. Old grudges must be put aside. The Lakhota must bury the knife they have used against the Minneconjou, and the Sicangu must break the lance that separates them from the Sahnish. It will not be an easy thing, but I see it is a necessary one."

"I agree," said Red Sky, wanting to quickly add his voice before anyone considered objecting. "It will soon be time for the Naca Om. We will go, and we will convince the other clans of the need to end old feuds and begin a new alliance."

Tordan recalled Red Sky had spoken of the Naca Om. It was part council meeting, part social gathering, part judicial arbitration to try and resolve territorial disputes—held once each year on neutral ground. Representatives of all the clans would attend. Though there was always much bickering among the various leaders, no fighting amongst the clans was allowed. To do so created a great loss of respect for one's clan.

If there were ever to be a united front against the invasion, the Naca Om was the place it would happen.

287

64

What breaks in a moment may take years to mend.
—Ancient Aesir Proverb

Rikissa peered down into the courtyard from her vantage point. Below her terrace was the usual sights and sounds, the mundane bustle of servants going to and fro, finishing their late afternoon chores. She couldn't imagine they enjoyed their life. She was certain they must hate their lives, as she did hers—though for dissimilar reasons.

The odd thing was, she couldn't picture exactly what kind of life she'd rather have. She certainly didn't wish to be a servant, nor a minion of Oseberg—not from what she'd heard of the life of the Vanir. She did yearn for a little adventure, some excitement that didn't leave each day as dreary as the next.

The truth was, she still wished she were with Tordan, despite the fact he'd gone away without her. Though she hadn't forgiven him for that, she knew it wasn't totally his fault. Her father would likely have had his head, had he not escaped. But why hadn't he come for her? She would have gone with him— gone anywhere. Even to that savage land of Serkland.

Now he was likely dead, and she was left to rot in this perfumed prison.

"Milady."

Rikissa turned from her window. A housecarle was standing by her open door.

"You have a visitor. The Lady Magnusson asks to be admitted."

What did her mother want? She had half a notion to deny her entry, but boredom and curiosity prevailed.

"Admit her," she told the housecarle.

She knew it was a mistake as soon as she said it. What could she possibly have to say to her mother? The overbearing crone never bore anything but bad news.

"Darling Daughter," said Estrid, sweeping into the room like a bird of prey. "How is life in House Tryguasson—I mean House Halfdansson?"

As usual, her mother was wearing a dress so extravagant it was more fit for a formal gathering than a casual visit, while, at the same time, revealing an abundance of cleavage more apropos of a brothel.

"What do you want, Mother?" she said with more bitterness than she intended.

"Can't a mother visit her daughter? Must I want something?"

"You usually do."

"Such anger in your tone. Have I done something to offend you?"

"Offend me? Mother, everything about you offends me. Have you forgotten you forced marriage upon me? That you conspired to kill my unborn child?"

"Surely you're not still upset over that?" Estrid waved the back of her hand as if it were ancient history. "You know as well as I do it was necessary. What would you have done, unwed, with a bawling Vanir brat? You know your father wouldn't have allowed you to remain in House Magnusson. Where would you have gone? What would you have done? I understand your lover has long since disappeared."

"He escaped, Mother. Escaped because Father imprisoned him, and was going to execute him."

Estrid had made her way to Rikissa's closet, and was running her fingers over some of her newer clothes.

"That's not the way I heard it, Child. I heard the man had many lovers, and left you for them."

"You're such a liar, Mother. You've always framed the truth with whatever fiction suited you. I know what happened to Tordan. Captain Griffenfeld told me."

Acting as if she hadn't heard a word her daughter said, Estrid stepped to the window and gazed into the distance.

"You know, you're not the only woman to ever lose a child."

"That makes it alright?"

"I lost a child. He would have been your eldest brother. He was...he wasn't right. He couldn't be allowed to survive and pollute the Aesir bloodlines."

Rikissa had never heard of this. Her mother had given birth to a defective child?

"I didn't shy from the task—from what needed to be done. I didn't relegate it to another. The child was my failing, so I took it upon myself."

"You killed your own child?"

Estrid turned and looked at her. Rikissa was drawn to her mother's emerald eyes. There was something about them. Something not quite right.

"Yes, I took the life of my own child. Now, all these years later, he haunts me. His ghost appears before me, rebuking me with his silence."

Her mother's attention wavered and, for a moment, she seemed not to know where she was.

"Rikissa? What am I...?"

Estrid looked around the room, then hurried to the door.

"I must see Beatrix—Beatrix Tryguasson. She's here isn't she?"

Before Rikissa could reply, her mother darted out the door and was gone.

It took her a moment, realization coming to Rikissa slowly. But when it did, she was certain. Her mother had gone mad.

Before she could fully enjoy the satisfaction of such an concept, she was overcome with dread. Never had she been so fearful of becoming her mother, than she was just then.

65

*A man who has a great vision must follow it as the
eagle seeks the deepest blue of the sky.*
—Wisdom of Fire In His Eyes

It took Tordan a moment to shake off the slumber when Willow tried to
rouse him.

"Husband...husband."

She was insistent, and her insistence made him realize something must be
wrong. He sat up quickly.

"What is it?"

"My brother is here. He needs to speak with you."

"Alright."

Tordan crawled out of the *thipi* and found Red Sky pacing. His distress was
apparent.

"What's wrong, Brother?"

"It is Falling Star."

"Is he still sick?"

"He is worse. I fear the sickness might take him."

Falling Star and a handful of others in the village had been stricken by a
mysterious ailment only days ago. It was mysterious because the Sicangu were
rarely ill.

"Fire In His Eyes says he has seen nothing like it. None of his medicines have
worked," said Red Sky. "We have been told of a great shaman among the
Lakhota who has been curing the sick. We are going to take those who have
fallen ill to this shaman. I want you to go as well."

"Certainly, if you want me, I will go."

"This great shaman is said to be *wasichu*."

"*Wasichu*?"

"Yes," replied Red Sky. "He has been living among the Lakhota, but I do not
know how well he speaks the language. So we may need you to speak with
him."

"Of course. I'll get ready. We should use the wain we captured from *wasichu*
to carry the sick."

"A good idea, Brother."

"Better use the horses we took with it. They'll be better trained to pull it. I'll drive."

"I will see to it. Tell your wife. We could be gone several days."

It was normally little more than a half day's ride south to the Lakhota village, though it took longer because the wain full of sick could only travel so fast over some ground. The trek offered Tordan another glimpse of the beauty and variety that was Serkland, with its great yawning plains, its ancient glacier-carved canyons, and its tranquil meadows. Once, in the distance, he saw a herd of wild horses running up the side of a mountain. But he didn't enjoy the vistas as much as he might have. The vermillion decline of the sun cast doleful shadows in their path, and Tordan's worried thoughts kept returning to Falling Sky and the others who were ill. He wondered if there truly was a qualified physician living with the Lakhota, or just some charlatan. It even occurred to him he could be another spy planted by the Aesir.

Tordan learned from Red Sky the Sicangu had been on friendly terms with the Lakhota for as long as he could remember. It was from the Lakhota they first learned about the *wasichu*, and attempted to trade with them. What they called the great *wasichu* encampment was closer to the Lakhota than any other clan. Strangely, though, they hadn't been attacked as had other clans. Tordan guessed it might be because the Lakhota were the largest of the clans, and the *wasichu* weren't prepared for such a conflict yet. Red Sky said the Lakhota believed their great shaman had used his magic to protect them from the invaders. That could mean his spy theory was correct.

When they finally arrived, they discovered the *wasichu* shaman already had a large tent full of patients—a three-sided affair the Lakhota had specially constructed for him. He was a slight man with unusually short hair. He looked exhausted as he went from patient to patient, checking pulses and temperatures. He was so preoccupied, he hadn't even noticed their arrival.

Red Sky gestured at those inside the tent. "That man is Oglala. So is that one. Those over there are Hunkpapa. I think that woman is Wahpeton."

So it wasn't only the Lakhota. It seemed word had spread about the great *wasichu* shaman, and all those who'd fallen ill were being brought to him.

Tordan saw several of the patients were receiving blood transfusions from other, healthier-looking people. He'd seen doctors use the same setup during the Corporate Wars, but they were usually dealing with massive wounds and amputations.

Red Sky spoke with one of the women assisting the doctor. She, in turn, let the doctor know more patients had arrived. The doctor told her something, but didn't look up. Instead he left the big tent.

The woman returned to Red Sky.

"*Hecelaya Okinihan* must rest and eat now. Lay those who are sick over there, and he will see to them soon."

She spoke the same language as the Sicangu, but Tordan heard different inflections in certain words. He wondered how long the doctor had been here, and whether he communicated in the Lakhota language, or if the woman who assisted him had learned his.

"I'm going to speak with him," Tordan told Red Sky.

Truvor was so tired, once he sat inside his *thipi* he didn't know if he could get up again. He was even too tired to eat. Maybe he'd just take a little nap before returning to his patients.

Fortunately, the transfusions were working. Those who'd been given the pig's bane vaccine had developed an immunity their blood passed on. That, combined with the fact the natives of this land were already the healthiest people he'd even seen, had led to a nearly one hundred percent recovery rate. He attributed their good health, at least in part, to their consumption of the *pazuta*, which also, he theorized, extended their lifespans. Though he still had no proof of that.

Everything was working fine. If he could just get some rest now, he'd go back and—

"So you're the *Great One*."

Truvor opened his eyes, startled to hear the language of his homeland. The man who stood before him was obviously not a native, though his bronzed skin and some of his clothing gave him the look of one.

Truvor sat up quickly, defensively scooting back.

"Who are you? What are you doing here?"

"Easy, Doctor. I'm not the enemy. I'm here with the Sicangu. I live with them."

"How? I mean how did you...?"

"It's a long story."

"I'm listening," replied Truvor, not bothering to disguise the suspicion in his voice.

293

"My name is Tordan Thordsson, a skaldor born of the Vanir."

A skaldor? They were the trained warriors of the Aesir. Warrior-poets if you believed in that kind of thing. He'd heard of Vanir being trained as skaldors, but the only contact he'd ever had with any was during the Corporate Wars, when he'd treated many of them. *What would a skaldor be doing here? Was he spy for Storman Ragnarsson?*

"And *your* name, sir?" said the fellow as if he'd been waiting for a reply.

"Truvor Svein—Dr. Truvor Svein."

"Good to meet you, Dr. Svein. I understand you've made quite a reputation for yourself here. How did you come to be treating these people?"

"No, no. First you tell me what a skaldor is doing dressed like that, here with these people. What are you, a spy?"

The fellow laughed. "Yes, I guess I am. At least I was supposed to be. I was retained by House Magnusson. Jarl Magnusson seemed convinced these Serklanders had some magic potion that would cure the blight. He sent me here to find out what it was."

Truvor's suspicions were confirmed. This man was simply the forefront of the invasion to come.

"So, did you find this *potion*?"

"I didn't really look. I discovered the Sicangu to be a virtuous and honorable people—noble without the fixed nobility of some wealthy house. I made friends among them...I even took a wife."

Truvor was struck by the sincerity of the fellow. He'd left his world behind even more than Truvor had.

"How long—how long have you lived with them?"

The skaldor shrugged. "Since Thunderstorm Moon I think."

He'd lived with his clan longer than Truvor had been with the Lakhota.

"And you, Doctor. What's your story? Are you also a spy?"

"I am not," he replied indignantly. "I was employed by Roskildcorp and assigned to the colony they've established on Serkland. Hestvoll it's called."

"I've heard of it."

"I began teaching some of the natives our language, and learned many had been infected by pig's bane."

"So that's what it is."

"Yes. It was passed to them from us, from blankets or other things we've traded with them, or maybe even from direct contact. Pigs were among the livestock we imported to the colony. The problem is, they've never had any contact with the bane, so they have no built-up immunity. It can be deadly to them in just a short time."

"So you began treating them?"

"Yes, and like you I've come to respect them, care about them. I fear for them. I know the storman in charge of Hestvoll's military forces has orders to expand their holdings."

"I expected they would," said the skaldor. "I've been trying to help the Sicangu prepare."

"It's frightening," said Truvor, desperation oozing from his words. "They think of these people as savages at best—animals at worst. I could no longer, in good conscious, continue to take orders from the corporation. So I ran off to do what I could for the Lakhota. Now all the clans are sending their sick to me."

"That's why we've come. We've got several people who are very sick, including a boy who's a good friend of mine. Will you come look after them, Doctor?"

"Certainly," said Truvor wearily.

The skaldor turned to leave, but Truvor grabbed his arm.

"There's one other thing I worry about."

"What's that?"

"The *magic potion* you talked of. It's not magic, and it's not a potion, but it does exist. It's a plant that makes up a regular part of the native diet."

"*Pazuta*?"

Truvor was stunned. "Yes. How did you know?"

"I didn't really," said the skaldor. "It was just a hunch. I know it's in almost everything they eat."

"Yes, yes. It took me weeks to stumble on it, and more time developing a serum I tested on members of the colony who were stricken with the blight."

"And...?"

"It worked. The *pazuta* serum actually cured them. Erased all signs of the blight from their cells. I myself was stricken. Now I'm perfectly healthy."

The skaldor's face grew dark.

"Do they know about the serum? Does Roskildcorp know about the *pazuta*?"

Truvor swallowed, then nodded. "They have some of my notes," he said, the guilt a hammer striking at his insides. "They know I developed a serum that works. They have some dead *pazuta* plants, but those won't do them any good. I doubt they'll be able to develop their own serum without some live plants."

"Then they'll be coming for sure," said the skaldor. "They'll be coming and they won't stop until they have the cure, and until they rape this land of every last thing they can profit from."

66

There is no deceit in death.
—Ancient Aesir Proverb

Vikar walked with a purpose. His strides were long and steady. Though some small part of him argued against this course, he would not be swayed—even by his own inner voice. Furyk had made his choice, and he'd chosen wrongly.

When he came to Furyk's door, he did not bother to knock.

"Wait here," he told the fellow who trailed him, "until I call for you."

Vikar pushed the door open. Furyk was pulling on his boots.

"That won't be necessary," he stated matter-of-factly.

"What? Father? What are you doing, bursting in here? What's wrong?"

Furyk looked startled, angry, and worried, all at the same time.

"I had such high hopes for you, Furyk. I thought you were sturdy enough, that you had the right amount of guile and ruthlessness. But it turns out you were overly ambitious."

Furyk stood. "What are you talking about? I was about to go dine with—"

"You're not going anywhere. I know about your plotting, about how you've taken it upon yourself to interfere with my plans on several occasions, how you've defied my orders. I know about your fratricide."

Furyk stood his ground, but his face took on the expression of the mischievous child who'd been caught drinking honey mead.

"Yet all that I could have forgiven—even admired. What I cannot forgive are your plans of patricide."

"What are you talking about, Father. I have no such plans. I would never—"

"Hrolf," called Vikar loudly enough for him to hear.

At the sound of his name, the housecarle appeared in the doorway, and all the denials died in Furyk's throat. He glared at Hrolf.

"You betrayer," snarled Furyk. "Have this man arrested, Father. He killed Gudrik."

"I know all about it," responded Vikar. "I've been aware of your plotting from the beginning. Hrolf is a loyal housecarle. One who will be rewarded accordingly. It's you who've betrayed me."

Furyk glanced to his left, looking for a way to run. But there was no escape and he knew it. He made a sound deep in his throat, almost like the guttural of a trapped dog.

"I did it to ease your pain, Father. I didn't want to see you waste away from the blight."

"The blight? I've no such illness, you fool. You think I believe your attempt to usurp me was undertaken as a mission of mercy?"

Vikar laughed.

"You don't have the blight?" Furyk looked perplexed. "But she told me..."

"Who told you?"

Furyk had only one card left to play, so he played it.

"Your wife told me. She said it was better you didn't linger through the pain and suffering of the blight."

It was Vikar's turn to be caught off guard. But he wasn't shocked by the revelation his wife had lied.

"That's right," said Furyk. "It wasn't only me, Father. Your own wife, my mother, has plotted against you as well. It was she who prodded me to kill Gudrik, to kill you and take my rightful place as jarl. It was her from the very beginning."

Vikar wavered, processing what he heard. He didn't doubt what Furyk was saying. There was no surprise in his words. The confirmation of Vikar's own suspicions caused him to reflect for a moment.

He approached his son, and Furyk took a single, defensive step back. Vikar laid his hand upon Furyk's shoulder. He stared into his close-set green eyes, looking for what he wasn't sure. Furyk scowled, but didn't move.

"Be a man, Furyk. Don't blame your ambition on others. I can respect your desires—even your enterprise. But be a man. Admit your aspirations. Announce your claim for all the world to hear."

"Alright, Father. I admit it. I wanted your house, your corporation, your wealth and power. I wanted to be jarl, and I didn't want to wait until I was as old as you. I plotted, I schemed, I ordered the death of my own brother. I did it all, and I'd do it again."

"Yes, yes," said Vikar stridently. He clapped hand roughly on Furyk's shoulder with each *yes*. "Now you're a man. Now you sound like my son."

Vikar looked into Furyk's eyes once more, turned and walked away. As he did, he gave the slightest nod of his head to Hrolf. With that nod came the realization he'd lost another piece of his own immortality.

He didn't see the dagger the housecarle pulled. He didn't observe his son's reaction as his would-be fellow conspirator came at him. Nor did he witness the blade being thrust into Furyk's heart. But, as he walked away, Vikar heard the escape of Furyk's breath as the lethal blow was delivered. There was no other sound—no cry of pain. It was as it should be.

67

He who strives to control fate shall never find peace.
— The Wisdom of Fire In His Eyes
*He who seeks to acquire a mastery of providence shall
never find prosperity.*
— Words of Chairman Wulfstan

They spoke in his language, because they all spoke it better than he spoke theirs. And everything they said was true. Even before they opened their mouths, Truvor knew the truth of it. But what they wanted from him—it was absurd.

"It's the only solution, Doctor. It's the only way to save these people," said Tordan.

"Listen," added Walks Apart. "He speaks wisely. I do not want war, but if war comes, I want to protect my people, my son."

Lame Bear nodded and Red Sky said, "War *will* come. The drums of the *wasichu* already begin to beat."

Truvor knew the man spoke metaphorically. The corporate army wouldn't signal their attack with drums. They'll swoop in with an overwhelming force, destroying village after village.

"The Naca Om has been set," said Red Sky. "It will be held seven days from now on the plain of Makha. Peoples from all the clans will be there."

"It has to be then, Doctor," urged Tordan. "It can't wait. You must use your influence to unite the clans against the coming invasion."

"I can't do that. They're not going to listen to me. Most of them don't even know me. I'm just another *wasichu* invader. Look at me. I don't even look like a warrior. I'm weak. They'll never listen to me."

"They will listen, Dr. Svein," said Lame Bear. "You are Wichasa Wakan Okinihan. They will listen to you. It is your destiny."

Truvor shook his head. He was no great holy man. He was no great anything. He looked into Walks Apart's eyes and saw the pleading there. She wanted him to help her people, and he wanted to. But this?

"I'm a doctor, not a warrior, not a storman. How can I give orders to kill? I've taken an oath to heal people."

Tordan snorted derisively.

Truvor turned to him and said defiantly, "Skaldors aren't the only ones with honor."

"Sorry, Doctor. I meant no disrespect."

"Yes you did," responded Truvor passively. He was quiet for a moment, still contemplating what they were asking him to do. Still weighing the alternatives. "You're asking me to turn against my own."

"Haven't you already?" asked Tordan. "Haven't you disavowed your allegiance to Roskildcorp? Aren't you as much a traitor in their eyes as I am? But I don't think of myself as a traitor—not to my people, the Vanir, not to the decent among the Aesir. There are good and bad people everywhere, among every race. This is your chance to stand up for the good."

"Tordan speaks truth," said Red Sky. "Listen to your heart. It will tell you so."

The man was right. Truvor knew it. He knew what the right thing was, but he didn't know if he could do it. He didn't know if he had the courage.

Truvor turned and walked away from all of them. Tordan tried to call him back.

"Doctor—"

"Let him go," said Walks Apart. "He will do what he needs."

What he needed was to think, to listen to his own voice without interruption. But would that make his choice any easier? He doubted it as much as he doubted himself.

When word came to her, she couldn't believe her ears. She berated the messenger, called him a liar and chased him out of her chamber, swinging her hairbrush at him. Yet she knew it was the truth. She felt it in her heart. It was too much for a mother to bear.

First Gudrik, now Furyk. Both her sons were dead. First one had killed the other, then... The messenger didn't say how Furyk had died, but Estrid was certain she knew. His plot, *their* plot, had been discovered. Vikar had either ordered his own son's death, or done the deed himself. Either way, no matter how many details he knew, he likely blamed her. Was she next? Did it matter now that Furyk was dead?

She threw herself on her bed face first and let the tears run their course.

After a while she turned over and stared at the ceiling. Maybe all was not lost. Maybe Vikar knew nothing but Furyk's bumbling treachery. There was always Rikissa and her husband Edvard. He was a jarl now. He had resources.

But what would people say about Furyk? What would her sister Valkyries think? Both her sons killed under her own roof. Would they say it was a tragedy? A comedy of justice? Would they laugh behind her back?

Where had she left her robe? Was she supposed to visit Beatrix Tryguasson today, or was that tomorrow? She must speak with the house baker about his breakfast pastries. They were much too dry.

Her mind raced with a flurry of half-considered notions. She couldn't finish a single thought, nor separate it from the next. Nothing was clear. Everything was a clutter, until she saw it.

Her ghost had returned.

Why not? Was this not the most opportune time for it to haunt her?

It appeared slowly, out of nothingness, and floated there above her bed. She could still see the ceiling through the apparition, yet it had color—the color of milk. The color of a newborn's skin.

But it wasn't an infant. She sensed that—she saw that. It had all the aspects of a disembodied head, but it wasn't a head. It had a short tail and eyes, but no arms, no legs. It spoke to her, though it had no mouth.

She didn't hear words. She didn't hear anything in her ears. But she felt it— felt its passion, its anguish, its regret, its dread, its desire to communicate, to be understood.

"Why do you haunt me?" cried Estrid. "Why? What do you want?"

It didn't respond. Instead it began transforming. It took on a new color, its eyes vanished, its tail receded. Estrid was no longer looking at a ghost. Now she saw the moon. The sight of it there, hovering above her, was more astonishing than the specter that haunted her. Suddenly, a pair of eyes opened on the surface of the moon and stared at her.

Estrid screamed and the moon vanished.

68

Where the wolf's ears are, the wolf's teeth are near.
                                    —**Book of Runes**
*They are not dead who live in the hearts they leave
behind.*

                                    —**Lakhota Saying**

I t was a hard rain. Lightning ruptured the sky and its thunderous
accompaniment unsettled the horses. The wind howled through crevices in
Truvor's *thipi* like a beast unbound.

The storm lasted for hours, foreshadowing muddy environs for days to
come. Truvor listened to the rain for a long time before he managed to fall
asleep. He had much to think about, and had still reached no decision by the
time he let slumber take him.

He dreamed, strangely enough, about Burgrave Andersson. He was more
rotund than ever in the dream, and he was chiding Truvor about his affection
for the skraelings. Truvor had wanted to talk back, to disagree, but he couldn't.
The burgrave never stopped talking, and Truvor felt nothing but frustration at
his inability to speak. Suddenly the burgrave was gone, and Walks Apart was
there. Still he couldn't speak. He wanted to tell her something, but he couldn't.
She just smiled. He reached for her, then—

Violent hands grabbed him and forced him onto his stomach. It took several
moments for Truvor to realize he wasn't dreaming anymore. His hands were
tied behind him, and he was yanked to his feet.

When a streak of lightning lit the gloom in his *thipi* he saw he was
surrounded by bearded soldiers. At least four of them. Before he could utter a
word, one of the men gagged him.

"Let's go," ordered another.

Two men grabbed him from each side and didn't wait for him to come
along. They hauled him along, his bare feet dragging behind him.

Outside his *thipi*, there was fighting. A few of the Lakhota had awoken and
seen the intruders. Truvor caught a glimpse of Walks Apart running towards
him before he was pulled away and could see or hear nothing but the storm. A
short distance from the edge of the village, another flash of light revealed three

303

or four armored motorcars, and a couple of scout cars. Truvor realized the fury of the storm must have obscured the rumble of the approaching vehicles, enabling the soldiers to drive near the Lakhota village without being heard.

It hadn't even occurred to him yet, why they'd come for him. It all happened too fast. He was thrown roughly into one of the vehicles and felt it take off. Then he had plenty of time to think, and to worry about those who'd tried to come to his rescue.

Tordan and Red Sky were woken by Lame Bear. He was drenched, but his face carried more alarm than just the worries of a storm.

"They've taken Wichasa Wakan Okinihan."

Tordan knew he was talking about Dr. Svein.

"What do you mean? Who has taken him?"

"The *wasichu*. Come."

Tordan and Red Sky followed him out of the *thipi* and found many of the people had been roused. One of the Lakhota warriors dragged in a corpse and dropped it in front of them. The man was wearing the livery of the corporate army.

"Gather your warriors," said Red Sky. "We will track them."

"In this storm?" questioned Tordan.

Red Sky only looked at him with the hint of a smile.

It didn't take long for Red Sky to find their tracks. Even with the rain washing away most of their trail, there was plenty to follow. Once he pointed it out, even Tordan could see. The soldiers had come in a number of vehicles.

Normally, depending upon the terrain, it would be difficult for men on horseback to catch up with even the slower Heimdalls—given their top speed was fairly equal, and the fact horses would eventually tire. However, the muddy ground would slow the heavy vehicles, and maybe even halt their progress if they got stuck in the mire.

They had more than 50 warriors moving at full gallop, and Tordan did his best to keep up. His horsemanship had improved greatly, but he still was no better than a child when compared to these men of the plain. Fortunately, they slowed now and then to be certain of the trail they were following. That gave him time to catch up.

Tordan knew they had to catch the detachment before it reached the main settlement, where, no doubt, fortifications had been built. But he had no idea how far away the colony was, or, for that matter, how much of a headstart the troops had.

His concern proved for naught. In less than an hour, they came upon the invaders. One of the Heimdalls had indeed become stuck in the mud. Instead of abandoning it, they'd stopped and several of the soldiers were trying to push it through the muck. Apparently, in their conceit, they'd not considered the possibility the savages would come after them.

The contingent of Lakhota warriors cried out and swooped down upon the soldiers, who were outnumbered as well as surprised. Many died in the first charge as arrows and spears flew. One of the scout cars attempted to flee and several of the warriors gave chase. Tordan dismounted as soon as he reached the fray, and drew Thor's Razor.

He didn't have to wait long. A burly figure came at him, battleaxe drawn back above his head for a massive blow. His foe was faster than he anticipated, and he almost lost his grip on his sword as he parried and sidestepped the cut. He countered, but found the man ready with his shield. His blow glanced away, but Tordan thrust his shoulder into the shield and knocked the big fellow to the ground. He wheeled, ready to thrust the killing blow into his downed enemy, but stayed his hand.

The rain had ceased. Night had begun to give way to daybreak, but there was enough light for him to see the man's face.

"Magnir!"

The man on the ground blinked twice.

"Tordan?"

Red Sky and several Lakhota were all around them now, shrieking whoops of victory.

"Do you yield?" asked Tordan, his voice hopeful.

Magnir looked at the warriors around him, bows drawn, spears at ready. He dropped his axe.

"I yield."

Tordan held out his hand. Magnir grasped the offered hand and Tordan pulled him to his feet.

Tordan heard a familiar voice and turned to see Dr. Svein. Ever the healer, he was telling the Lakhota not to kill the men they'd captured. The warriors moved in quickly and bound Magnir. They were about to haul him away when Tordan stopped them.

305

"I want to speak with him."

"What are you doing here, Tordan? Why are you with these...? I heard you escaped with one of them, but, by Wotan's good eye, I thought by now you'd be dead."

"As you can see, old friend, Wotan had other plans for me. What were your orders?"

"Why, to come in here and take the doctor back to Trondheim."

"Why?"

"By the gods, I don't know. I only know what Griffenfeld told us. That Jarl Magnusson wanted the doctor, and that we had to take him back, or we might as well not go back at all."

"Griffenfeld's with you?"

"Yonder."

Tordan followed Magnir's gesture and saw the slightly wounded captain among the captives.

"Well, old friend, I can tell you that you won't be returning to Trondheim with the doctor. So you might as well stay here with me."

Tordan smiled. Magnir looked around him, then smiled back.

"I guess I don't have much of a choice."

"You have a choice, Brother," said Tordan, invoking their Skaldor bond. "I'm giving you a choice. But I think once I explain, you'll understand why I'm here, and what I'm doing."

"Like you said, it's chancy going back to face Jarl Magnusson without the doctor, so I think I'll stay. I can't wait to hear the tale you have to tell. I imagine there's a song or two in it."

"One or two."

Tordan moved behind Magnir and cut his bonds.

Red Sky had been standing, observing but saying nothing. Tordan looked at him and said, "This is my brother skaldor. He is a great warrior, and has chosen to join us."

"If you say so, Brother. He who is your brother is mine."

Magnir looked back and forth between the two men, having no idea what was being said.

"Bring me that one," said Tordan, pointing out Griffenfeld.

Hands and legs tied, two Lakhota picked up Tordan's former captain and dumped him in the mud in front of him.

"Sorry about the rough treatment, Captain. But these people aren't very friendly when you invade their homes and kill their brethren. They're also very fond of Dr. Svein."

Griffenfeld rolled over and leaned back so he could see who was speaking to him.

"Tordan Thordsson? You're alive? What in the name of—"

"I think you'd better be quiet and just listen, Captain."

"It's not captain anymore. It's storman. Storman Griffenfeld." He threw his head back and inhaled so that his chest expanded as he said it. But lying in the mud, tied so he couldn't move, his facade of importance was almost comical.

"A storman, eh? No doubt you earned it. Look, Captain—I mean *Storman*—these people would like nothing better than to roast you over a slow fire and cut off your parts so you could watch them boiled in a stew," said Tordan, embellishing more than a bit. "But I'm not going to let them. You were always fair with me, so I'm going to let you live. I'm going to send you back to Jarl Magnusson, and you can hope he's as magnanimous as me."

"He's no longer only a jarl. He's chairman of the board now."

"By the tits of Freyja, has everyone been promoted in my absence? I guess that explains why you're working with corporate troops. Anyway, I'm going to release you and these other men, so you can return to Trondheim and tell the chairman to leave these people alone. Tell him if he withdraws from Serkland, there can be peace. If not, there will be a war so costly he might not be able to afford the price."

Griffenfeld snorted with contempt. "You think these savages can stand up to the war machine we can assemble? To the havoc we can rain down upon them?"

Tordan shrugged. "I want you to tell Magnusson that if he calls off his dogs and withdraws from Serkland, we will share with him the cure for the blight."

Griffenfeld's expression told him a lot.

"So, you had no idea why Magnusson wanted the doctor. It's because he's discovered a cure for the blight, here, among these people. That's what Magnusson wanted. No doubt to increase his fortune a hundredfold. If there's peace, all the people can share this cure—and I do mean *all* the people. Aesir and Vanir alike."

Tordan wasn't sure what Griffenfeld thought of this. It was obviously new information, and he was still making sense of it.

"I'll tell him," said Griffenfeld. "I don't know if it'll matter, but I'll tell him."

There dissent among the Lakhota was loud and unyielding when Tordan said he was going to free the prisoners. But after he explained what he was doing to Truvor and Red Sky, Truvor calmed the Lakhota warriors and said it was being done with his consent. That placated most of them, and they agreed to let the men go free after stripping them of their weapons and supplies, and setting fire to the remaining vehicles.

Neither Truvor nor Tordan's skaldor friend were capable horsemen, so Truvor rode with one of the Lakhota, while the skaldor rode behind Tordan. He hated it. It wasn't so much he disliked horses, as he feared them. But he had no choice.

The rain had ceased, and the sky was beginning to clear by the time they returned to the village. As soon as Truvor arrived, he was rushed to see to those who were wounded trying to prevent his capture. A few of the wounds were serious, but he thought they'd all survive. As he treated them, he kept looking for Walks Apart, thinking she would come to aid him. Finally, when he was almost done, he glanced up. Lame Bear was standing over him. His face was somber, but then he wasn't one to smile much.

Truvor stood, wiping his hands clean.

"What is it, Lame Bear? Are there more wounded? Where is Walks Apart?"

The old fellow didn't say a thing, but his look begged Truvor to follow. Truvor walked with him to the far side of the medical tent. He saw Walks Apart's son standing there—standing over someone. Then he knew. His heart sank as he ran. He fell to his knees over Walks Apart and checked her pulse. Even before he did he saw the dagger wound running from her belly to her chest was a fatal one. She was dead.

The last time he'd seen her, she'd been running toward him, screaming at the soldiers who were taking him. She died for him—because of him. If only he'd never left Hestvoll...if he'd listened to Burgrave Andersson and returned to Trondheim, she'd be alive. Her death was on his hands as surely as if he'd wielded the knife himself. He'd never even gotten the chance to tell her he'd come to love her. He'd been afraid to.

He had no idea how long he cried over her lifeless body. But when he looked up, Tordan, Red Sky, and Lame Bear were standing over him.

Truvor stood.

"I'll do it. I'll do what I can to unite the clans."

69

I have seen that, in any great undertaking, it is not
enough for a man to depend simply upon himself.
—The Wisdom of Fire In His Eyes

The plain of Makha was a collage of campsites. Representatives of the nine clans were beginning to gather for the Naca Om. Tordan smiled at the irony when Red Sky told him the number. Nine was the Aesir's number of good fortune.

Similarities existed between each clan, but also differences. The Hunkpapa wore the more brightly colored feathers of forest birds, and their garments were predominantly green. The Hidatsa came down from the high mountains wearing thick furs, but soon shed them. They were not proficient horsemen like the people of the plain. They'd walked all the way to the village of the Minneconjou, where they'd been given horses to ride. Tordan found the Minneconjou an especially friendly people, but the Sahnish contingent did nothing but glare at the Sicangu—who returned the fierce stares in-kind. The harshest looks were aimed at Tordan and Truvor. Many of those gathered had never seen a *wasichu*, but it was apparent they'd heard stories—and not good ones.

At first, only the *wicasas*, the shamans, the *wakincuzas* of each clan's council would arrive. The first few days would involve the settling of any disputes that might exist between the clans, any judicial or more serious matters. Later, many more people would arrive for the more festive aspects of the gathering. Falling Star had traveled with Red Sky and Tordan to see his first Naca Om, though he would not take part in the actual council meeting. Willow, Snow Deer, and Two Rivers would follow later with many other Sicangu. Magnir was told to stay at the Sicangu village. Two *wasichu* among them would be enough to explain.

Though bad blood existed between some clans, no fighting of any kind was allowed. To do so would mean a great loss of respect for the clans of those involved, and immediate expulsion from the Naca Om.

In the days preceding the great gathering, Tordan formulated tactics with Red Sky and the others. They would broach the idea of uniting the clans at the

309

very start, before any other divisive subjects were raised. Red Sky believed those in attendance would be more receptive before they can began haggling about lesser matters—before old quarrels surfaced. It was their hope that once the severity of the invading *wasichu* was made clear, no other matters would need be discussed. To explain the seriousness of what faced them, it was decided Broken Horn would speak. He was known to all, and well-respected. They would, explained Red Sky, listen to his words. However, resistance to such an idea was expected. When it came, the Lakhota *wicasa*, Grey Cloud would ask permission to let Truvor speak. Word of the doctor's work, of the coming of Wichasa Wakan Okinihan had reached many of the clans, but not all. It was Tordan's idea that when they first arrived at the Naca Om, Red Sky, Lame Bear, and even Falling Star should do their best to spread rumors that the legendary figure had arrived among them. His hope was, by the time the council was held, at least the idea of Wichasa Wakan Okinihan was in all their heads.

Tordan and Lame Bear had done their best to prepare the doctor. They coached him on what to say and how to say it. Fortunately, he already had a basic grasp of the Lakhota language, which all the clans spoke—with minor variations. However, his timidity was a problem both his instructors warned him about.

"These are great men, great warriors you will be speaking with," Lame Bear told him. "They must believe you are strong as well. They must believe you are Wichasa Wakan Okinihan. Many will doubt you. Many will doubt the wisdom of uniting the clans. You must convince them."

"I'm no orator."

"You must be, Doctor," said Tordan. "For the sake of us all."

"What if they ask outright if I'm this great sacred one of legend? What do I tell them?"

"You take up the mantle and run with it," Tordan told him. "If you don't, if we don't manage to unite the clans, then their annihilation is almost assured."

When night fell and the *wakincuzas* gathered for the beginning of the Naca Om, Tordan sat with Kicking Bull, behind Broken Horn and Red Sky, while Truvor was given the place of honor next to Grey Cloud. Tordan saw the anxiety in Truvor's face. He had little confidence the doctor could pull it off, but there was nothing more he could do.

The *iyotan wicasa* of the Hunkpapa clan, by virtue of his age, would lead the Naca Om. Tordan had no idea how old the fellow was, but he looked a

310

hundred. Which meant he was probably closer to two hundred.

When the ancient *wicasa* stood, with help from his fellow clan members, it signaled the commencement of the Naca Om. Everyone hushed and looked to him. He began with a greeting to all those in attendance, and prayed to Wakan Tanka that wisdom would prevail. Then, as had been prearranged, he gave the floor to Broken Horn and, with assistance, resumed his seat.

Broken Horn stood, but before he spoke he scanned the faces around him.

"I see before me, gathered in peaceful council, Oglala, Sihasapa, Wahpeton, Hunkpapa, Lakhota, Minneconjou, Hidatsa, Sahnish, and Sicangu. It is a good thing I see. Because together we are strong." He reached up and plucked a long gray hair from his head. "A single hair is nothing. It has no strength." He pulled each end of the hair, breaking it in two. "But many hairs, braided together are strong. A single strand of hemp breaks as easily, but a hundred strands wound tight make a rope strong enough to hold the wildest of stallions."

Broken Horn paused, visibly sighed, and looked over his audience again. Truvor might not be a great orator, but Broken Horn obviously was.

"You have all heard of the coming of the *wasichu*. Some have been unfortunate enough to feel the force of their weapons. Others have suffered from the sting of their sickness. They came to our lands with the pretense of trading, but now they take without giving. This man..." Broken Horn gestured towards Tordan. "...was once of the *wasichu*. But let there be no mistake, he is now Sicangu. He is Sungmani Ska, brother to Red Sky. He was a great warrior among the *wasichu*, and has told us of the many strange weapons they use. He has told us they will come and they will keep coming until they have taken everything and killed all the people. I believe Sungmani Ska. I believe if we do nothing, there will be no more Sicangu, no more Sahnish or Lakhota or Oglala. No more Sihasapa or Wahpeton or Hunkpapa or Minneconjou or Hidatsa. The people will vanish from the land like the morning mist, and there will be no tomorrows. I believe all this will happen...unless we join together." Broken Horn interlaced his fingers and held them up for all to see. "If we unite, we will be strong—maybe strong enough to push the *wasichu* invaders back into the sea that spewed them forth."

Broken Horn sat and immediately the respectful silence ended. Shouts of both agreement and dissent ascended from the gathering into the star-filled sky. One of the Sahnish stood.

"The Sahnish will never ride with the Sicangu. They are tricksters, disciples of Iktomi. We will not listen to them."

The Sahnish sat back down and Grey Cloud stood quickly, forcing several others to forestall their attempts to rise.

"Will you listen to Wichasa Wakan Okinihan?" Every voice but Grey Cloud's grew quiet at mention of the mythic figure. "Many of you know of the *pejuta wichasa* who has cured not only Lakhota, but Oglala, Wahpeton, Hunkpapa, Sicangu. His magic has brought many back from the edge of death."

Tordan saw Truvor cringe at the word *magic*.

"He is not *wasichu*. He is not Lakhota. He says he is here for all the people. I, Grey Cloud, would have you listen to him now."

Grey Cloud urged Truvor to stand, then seated himself. Truvor hesitated, surveying the skeptical faces before him. Silently, Tordan prayed to Thor the doctor would have the courage to say what was needed.

"I am not a man of war. I am a healer. I know much about the art of healing, but nothing about the art of war. For that you must be guided by the warriors among you. But I do know what Broken Horn says about the *wasichu* is true. Their soldiers come even now, even as we speak. They will keep coming until they've taken all of your horses, all of your women, all of your lands. They will slaughter the *tatanka*, they will cut down your forests, and they will poison your rivers."

The doctor paused. Whether for effect or to gather his thoughts, Tordan wasn't sure.

"The only way you will have a chance to defeat them, is to act as one."

A member of the Sihasapa delegation stood in obvious disrespect to Truvor.

"How do we know you are Hecelaya Okinihan? The one who was foretold of—the one who will unite the clans."

This was the moment of truth. Tordan suspected it would all turn on what was said now.

Truvor held out his open hands. A common gesture Tordan had learned meant "who knows the answer?"

"I never said I was the Great One. Others have said it—not me."

"Are you Wichasa Wakan Okinihan?" asked the Sihasapa warrior.

"I don't know," replied Truvor, looking right at the man. "Only Wakan Tanka knows for certain. I only know I speak the truth about the *wasichu*, and I will do what I can to stop them."

The Sihasapa man sat, looking satisfied with the answer, as did many others. Whether he knew it or not, it appeared to Tordan the doctor had said the right thing—not claiming to be the legendary chosen one. His humility might win the day. But many others were still dubious. Assorted shouts of disapproval were voiced. Some called him a fraud, others declared him an agent of the *wasichu*.

They needed more convincing, but instead, Truvor sat back down. At once, the fellow sitting on the other side of Grey Cloud stood. Tordan knew he was the Lakhota shaman, Howling Dog.

"Do you doubt the prophecy?" he asked the dissenters angrily. "Why does it exist, if not for us to believe? The word of Wakan Tanka tells us that one day Wichasa Wakan Okinihan will come. He will heal the sick, and he will unite all the people against a common enemy." The shaman pointed at Truvor, who looked at his defender with an astonished expression. "He has healed the sick. I have seen him with my own eyes. His powers are greater than mine. Now he seeks to unite the clans against their enemy. Will you spurn him now? Will you turn away Wichasa Wakan Okinihan and spit in the eye of Wakan Tanka?"

Still angry, Howling Dog sat. There were many murmurs, but no more shouts of dissent. When no one showed a desire to speak, the ancient Hunkpapa *wicasa* was assisted to his feet.

"We have heard much this night, and we have much to consider. We will speak again of this tomorrow. Until then, let wisdom and honor be your guide. That is all I have to say."

Instead of bursting in, Vikar pounded on the double doors to his wife's chamber. There was no response. Her maid servant told him she was inside, but he heard nothing. He opened the doors, stepped inside and closed them. No one else need hear what he had to say.

Estrid was there, looking out her window. What she saw in the dark he didn't know.

"Wife."

Still she didn't turn or acknowledge his presence.

"Estrid, what are you doing?"

"The moon has eyes," she said.

"What are you talking about?"

Vikar approached her.

"The moon has eyes. Eyes that never close. Always watching. Always there."

He took her by the arm and spun her around.

"I don't know what kind of act this is, but it's not going to work."

There was a look in her eyes he couldn't fully describe. But it wasn't the look of the woman he'd been married to for almost 30 years. As she focused on him, the strange glimmer in her eyes faded, and she sounded once again like the Estrid he knew.

"What do you want, Husband?"

"I want you to deny you plotted with Furyk to have me killed. I want to know my wife would have no part in such a conspiracy."

Estrid sighed as if he spoke of trivialities, and sauntered away from him.

"What would you have me say?"

"The truth, Woman!"

She laughed. "The truth? Whose truth? *Your* truth? Furyk's truth?"

"I want to hear *the* truth. And I want to hear it from your lips."

Estrid sat before her mirror, picked up her brush, and began grooming her hair.

"I won't deny I wanted the best for our children—all our children. But you stood by while one was killed, then you killed the other."

"Don't pretend you had nothing to do with Gudrik's death. Yes, I stood by and let my sons settle their own affairs, but I didn't stoke the fires of their ambition."

"You're quite the father, aren't you?" taunted Estrid, still brushing her hair, still staring into her mirror. "Three sons, and they're all dead."

"Three sons? What are you...?"

He realized what she was referring to. He'd never considered that thing a son.

"Yes, yes, he watches. He's here with us, always watching."

"Are you mad, Woman?"

Even as he said it, Vikar realized the truth of it. He'd seen the signs—little things—for weeks now. Whether her plotting with Furyk was cause or effect, didn't matter. Either way, her treachery still injured him—though he would never fully admit it to himself. Furyk he understood, even expected. But his own wife?

"He comes to me you know. He doesn't talk, but I hear him."

Vikar could almost forgive her ambition, her plotting, but her descent into madness would weaken his public standing. He couldn't allow that. Not now—not when he was so close to realizing his ultimate goal.

"You'll go to live with your sister in Jutland."

"Why would I do such a thing? He's here. I must stay here with him."

Vikar came up behind her and forcefully turned her from the mirror.

"I banish you from House Magnusson. Do you understand? You're to pack your things and leave at once."

"Banished?"

"Yes, banished. And you can take your ghosts with you."

Vikar turned and strode angrily out of the chamber, not bothering to close the door behind him. He hadn't gone far when he passed a couple of servants. He stopped and looked at them. Seeing his expression, they cringed.

"Lady Magnusson is leaving for an extended stay in Jutland. Pack all of her things and let me know when she's ready to depart."

"Yes, sir. Right away, sir."

Vikar continued down the corridor, still seething. He was angry with his wife, with her insanity, even with himself—though he'd be damned to Niflhel if he knew why. He turned a corner and saw Prince Dax sitting atop a cask of wine. He stopped and reached for the cat. Dax had always had a calming effect on him, and that's what he needed right now. He stroked its fur and thought of Rikissa, and how she'd played with Dax as a kitten. Was it that long ago? How old was this cat? He suddenly had an urge to visit his daughter. Was it the memories of her and Prince Dax? Or was it because she was the only family he had left?

Truvor had no idea if the council of the Naca Om had been convinced. He'd been shocked when Howling Dog, who'd never spoken to him, who eyed him with distrust since the first time he'd seen him, spoke in his defense. Though it wasn't really Truvor he was defending, but the idea of Wichasa Wakan Okinihan, and the need he must have seen to unite the clans.

Truvor was sitting with Tordan and the youngster Falling Star the next day, before the second gathering of the Naca Om, when Lame Bear, Red Sky, and Kicking Bull came to them.

"We have been talking with others, and we have been listening," said Lame Bear. "The Hidatsa will not agree to join us. They say the *wasichu* have not bothered them, and that they are safe in their mountains. However, all the other clans are ready to agree."

"Even the Sahnish?" wondered Tordan.

"Even the Sahnish," replied Red Sky.

"All but the Hidatsa have accepted the doctor as Wichasa Wakan Okinihan," said Lame Bear. "He will be *iyotan wicasa* of all the clans in their fight against the *wasichu*."

"I don't know how to fight a war," objected Truvor.

"Do not worry, Doctor," said Lame Bear. "You are the holy one. You are not expected to do battle yourself. You are the spiritual leader of the people. Tonight the *wakincuzas* will choose a *blota hunka* to lead the fight. They will select one who is strong, who is wise and brave, and who knows the *wasichu* well. From the talk I hear, I believe it will be Red Sky."

Kicking Bull grunted his approval. Red Sky showed no reaction, but his son beamed with pride. Truvor figured it was a burden as well as an honor, so no reason for the man to express himself one way or another.

"If this is true, I will need your council, Brother," said Red Sky to Tordan.

A flurry of calls sounded across the encampments. A rider was approaching at a rough gallop. He was Sicangu, barely more than boy. Red Sky made his way to the newcomer, followed by the others. The young man dismounted as soon as he saw his fellow Sicangu.

"The *wasichu* came," he said breathlessly.

"They attacked the village?" asked Red Sky.

The fellow shook his head, still catching his breath. "It must have been a small party. They crept up outside the village. When a group of women went to the river, they took them."

"What do you mean they took them?"

"They took the young women with them, killed the rest."

"How many?"

"Six taken, three dead."

"Who?"

"Two Rivers was among those taken."

Truvor didn't know who the fellow was talking about, but he knew by the reaction of Tordan and Falling Star that it was someone close to them. Red Sky remained stone-faced.

"Willow...Snow Deer?" queried the skaldor anxiously.

"They were in the village. They were not harmed."

Tordan's obvious anxiety was quelled, but only momentarily. He exchanged looks with Red Sky, who turned to the rider and asked, "How long ago?"

"They were taken yesterday morning. Looking Horse took some men to track them. They were on foot, but their tracks vanished."

"They probably came in by airship," said Tordan. "I'm sorry, Brother. There will be no tracking them now."

"Will they take her across the sea to where they took me?"

"I don't know," replied Tordan. "She will likely be held at the settlement for at least a while."

Red Sky considered this and said, "Come, we must prepare for the Naca Om." He walked off without another word, followed by the others.

Truvor grabbed Tordan's arm and stopped him.

"Who is this Two Rivers?"

Tordan tilted his head towards Red Sky.

"His daughter."

70

Sometimes war is the cost of doing business.
—Words of Chairman Wulfstan

The newly anointed storman stood at attention in his office, waiting to be recognized. Vikar made him wait. He still hadn't decided how to punish the man's failure.

"Storman Griffenfeld," he finally said, "I understand you've returned without Dr. Svein."

"Yes, sir."

"Explain your dereliction."

"We managed to capture the doctor, sir, but the storm that covered our incursion ultimately bogged down our vehicles. The horse men pursued and caught us in the open."

"Then tell me, why aren't you dead?"

"I would have been, sir. But Tordan was among the savages."

"Tordan? The skaldor we set free with the savage?"

Vikar couldn't believe the man had survived all this time.

"Yes, sir."

"Did he have any information for us? Did he say anything about a cure for the blight?"

"Yes he did, sir."

Maybe he didn't need the doctor after all.

"Well out with it, man. What did he say."

Griffenfeld hesitated before responding.

"He said if we withdraw our troops from Serkland, there can be peace. If we refuse, there will be war."

"What? That's it? What did he say about the cure?"

"There is a cure—at least that's what Tordan said. He said if we withdraw peacefully, they will share the cure with us."

"He gave you nothing? No samples—no word on what the cure was?"

"Sir, Tordan is one of them."

"One of them? What does that mean?"

"It means he's joined the horse men. He is no longer an agent for House

318

Magnusson. He's gone native, sir."

"By the fires of Niflhel, I'll see his eyes gouged out and his entrails splayed across my keep!"

Vikar was incensed. He should have never allowed the traitor to live. First he impregnates his daughter, then he flouts his orders and even turns against his own kind. Well the skaldor has sealed his fate, and that of his savage friends. If they refused to give Vikar what he wanted, he would take it.

"Sir, will you withdraw and make peace with the horse men?"

Vikar looked at Griffenfeld with loathing.

"Make peace? With those savages? There will be no peace. My hand is forced. Now there will be bloody war. Let that be the legacy of the skaldor's treachery."

"But the cure for the blight..."

"We will take the cure, and we'll exterminate any vermin that get in our way."

Vikar saw the look on Griffenfeld's face.

"Are you averse to war?"

"No, sir. It's just that..." Griffenfeld didn't finish. He straightened back to attention and said, "Shall I return to duty, sir?"

"Yes, but you can take off that uniform. A captain's garb will suit you fine. Set your affairs in order, Captain. As soon as I have the backing of the board, you'll be going back to Serkland, along with the rest of the corporate army."

"Yes, sir."

"Dismissed, Captain."

The strikes had been broken. Gunnar was dead, Olav had been arrested, and Jorvik had no idea what had happened to Agnar. With his Modi brothers gone, and Marta's illness, Jorvik had simply gone back to work, trudging forth to the factory in the morning, dragging home at night, doing what he could to make Marta comfortable.

He no longer had the strength to fight, and, apparently neither did many Vanir. Not enough had the strength to hold out against their Aesir masters. They'd given in, and, except for occasional instances of sabotage that proved some Modi still operated, the production lines ran on schedule.

Jorvik hated that he'd resigned to his life as it was. But he no longer had the resilience to act on his hatred. As the strikes had been broken, so had he. It was only when he thought of how his son faced a similar fate, did his ire rise. He could only hope Canute's time would foster a new generation of Modi. For his seemed dead.

Jorvik was distracted by such thoughts as he made his way home from work. Twilight had passed, and the rodents had begun to creep forth from vague pools of shadow to reclaim the streets. He ignored them, as he did his fellow Vanir. His head was down, his shoulders slumped with exhaustion, when two pairs of arms grabbed him. They hauled him off the street into a darkened alley and forced him to the ground, knocking the breath out of him.

He looked up, fighting the dizziness, and saw Agnar.

"Well, Brother, you seem to have survived your trip to Trondheim in good health."

"Agnar, I thought you were in prison...or dead."

"I escaped that fate, and it seems you did too," said Agnar, suspicion in his eyes as well as his voice. "Tell me how you bought your freedom. What secrets did you tell? Which brothers did you name?"

"I named no one. I said nothing," responded Jorvik angrily. "I'm only free because my daughter works for House Tryguasson. She begged her lady to have me freed."

"There is no more House Tryguasson, or didn't your Aesir friends tell you about the chairman's death?"

Jorvik struggled to his feet, pushing off the two men who tried to hold him.

"I've no Aesir friends. You know me better than that, Agnar."

"I thought I did. But now...?" said Agnar, raising his hands to express his doubt.

"What about your brother?" questioned one of the other men. Jorvik didn't know either of them. "He's Aesir."

"My brother works for House Magnusson, but he's no Aesir. And I haven't heard from him or seen him in many weeks."

"I believe you, Jorvik," said Agnar. "I believe you still hate the Aesir. I can hear it in your voice. The question is, are you still willing to do something about it?"

"Do what? The strikes failed. Most of the Modi were arrested or killed. What is there left to do?"

"Do you give up that easily? We're not done. The Modi will rise again. The only question is whether you're with us, or whether you'll be content to bow to your Aesir masters."

Jorvik returned Agnar's severe stare in-kind, and said, "I bow to no man."

71

There is more in the heart of man than money can buy.
—Book of Runes

Vikar was running late, so Sitric briefed him inside the motorcar on his way to the Ve. Much had been happening. Now he not only needed to concern himself with the day-to-day operations of Trellestar, but with the duties relegated to the chairman of the board. Despite the additional work, he couldn't wait to step atop the chairman's dais for the first time. He'd waited a lifetime for this singular moment.

"The first shipload of troops has been dispatched to Serkland, and the new wave of conscripts have begun their training. Also, Dr. Thorgrim has alerted me that the select batch of female savages has arrived, and he plans to proceed with his experiments, unless you have new orders."

"No," said Vikar. "Let him proceed. What about the vote?"

"I have several executives circulating among the representatives, trying to determine which way they'll go. I'll report to you as soon as I have the information."

"I must know as soon as possible."

"Certainly, sir," said Sitric. "That covers everything, I believe, except I wanted to caution you that our capital assets have diminished to dangerously low levels. If word gets out..."

Sitric didn't bother to finish the thought. Vikar knew exactly what would happen.

"It's a temporary situation. It'll be resolved shortly."

The motorcar pulled up to the Ve. Vikar and Sitric got out. His personal guards and several Trellestar thanes were waiting for him. The guards would follow him only as far as the entrance. The rest would assist him in managing his first board meeting as chairman.

Before he reached the entrance, a man and young boy approached him. His guards immediately stepped forward to intervene, but Vikar, seeing who it was, waved them off.

"Oleg Gripsholm. I didn't expect to see you here. I was told you retired from corporate life."

"That's true, Jarl Magnusson—no, excuse me, I apologize—I mean, Chairman Magnusson."

Vikar nodded his acceptance of the apology.

"I only came here today, to thank you," said Gripsholm.

"Thank me? Thank me for what?"

"Because of you, I've been reunited with my son, Glyfe. It's a joyous thing, I tell you."

Vikar looked down at the boy. By his size he must have been eight or nine years, but the expression on his face, the way he didn't seem to focus on anything and stood there fidgeting, was strange. The boy didn't look quite right. Yet it was obvious Gripsholm was happy.

"So I thank you, Chairman, and wish you ongoing fortune with all your pursuits."

"Ah, yes, well..." Vikar wasn't certain how to respond. "May fortune be with you as well. But I must get to the meeting."

Vikar and his staff were already moving away when Gripsholm responded, "Of course, of course. Good day to you, Chairman."

Vikar continued into the great hall disconcerted. Gripsholm's appearance perturbed him. How could a man he'd defeated on the field of commerce, who'd undergone such a reduction in status, be so happy? And with a son whose capacity was obviously diminished? It made no sense. Yet Gripsholm had a son. Vikar no longer did.

He passed through Wotan's colossal legs and made his way to the chairman's dais, below the Tree of Commerce tapestry. Once there he took a moment to look back at the statue. It must have been his own mood, because he could have sworn Wotan glowered down at him. But even the gods couldn't sour him this day.

The herald in the outer corridor proclaimed the commencement of the meeting, and warned the door to the great chamber was about to be sealed. A few stragglers made their way to their appropriate sections. With a wry smile Vikar noted the new Jarl of Trondtel—an inexperienced boy who would have been no match for him even if he didn't hold the chairmanship. Let Oleg Gripsholm be happy in his retirement. Vikar had what he wanted.

The massive door to the hall slammed shut and Vikar stood immediately, thrusting his staff against the dais floor several times for silence.

"I, Vikar Magnusson, Chairman of the Board of Trondheim and all its holdings, call this meeting of the Board of Directors to order. Is there any

322

challenge to my authority to do so?" No one spoke. "Having heard no objections, I authorize a commencement of the proceedings."

"Jarl Volsung of Sveabordcorp, if it please the board."

Vikar nodded in customary recognition and Jarl Volsung continued.

"I must officially protest the chairman's expansion of the conscription act."

A swell of assent rippled throughout the hall, and Vikar noted the more vocal corporations.

"Not only has this reduced the available labor force by a significant percentage," said Volsung, "but it's escalated the unrest among the Vanir. I warn the board, there will be rioting in the streets if we're not judicious with our authority."

"Jarl Njalsson of Bjorco, if it please the board."

His man, right on cue. Vikar nodded.

"Are you saying, Jarl Volsung, we should kowtow to the more rebellious elements of the Vanir? Are we to let the red heads rule us?"

Scattered laughter greeted this, but Vikar winced at the slur. A minority of Aesir were born with reddish hair.

"Are we not Aesir—sovereign by right of birth?" continued Njalsson. "Do the Vanir not owe us allegiance? Do they not owe us their very livelihoods?"

Vikar saw Sitric making his way up the dais.

"Shall we open our ledgers and our bank vaults, and let the Vanir run our corporations? We might as well let the skraelings."

This prompted even more laughter.

Jarl Njalsson resumed his seat as Sitric whispered in Vikar's ear, "We don't have the votes. We still need to sway three or four members."

Several jarls stood as to speak, but Vikar raised the chair's staff, signifying he had the floor. If he didn't have the votes, he'd have to change some minds by revealing the secret he'd been holding onto.

"I have important news for this board—for all of Trondheim," said Vikar, his voice resounding throughout the hall. "Trellestar has made a momentous discovery that will change our lives forever. Our medical researchers, working tirelessly, have developed a cure for the blight."

Vikar paused as the expected murmur swept through the corporate body like a rogue wave.

"Though more tests need to be conducted, it's also possible this cure may extend the average lifespan. However, one of the main components for this cure can only be found in Serkland. That is why, exercising my authority as

chairman, I've already dispatched a detachment of corporate troops to
Serkland, to obtain quantities of this ingredient. It will be necessary for us to
secure large segments of the region, and the skraelings may prove
uncooperative. So I plan to send even more troops. Thus the reason for the
temporary increase in conscriptions. I would like to have the endorsement of
this board before I commit more of our forces. I'm sure you'll agree this is a
worthwhile venture—nay, an historic one."

"Jarl Gothfrithsson of Ruslagen Group, if it please the board."
Ruslagen wasn't an ally, but Vikar nodded anyway.

"We must honor the chairman's word that such a cure exists," said
Gothrithsson in a tone that called the existence of such a cure into question.
"But even so, Chairman Magnusson suggests sending the vast majority of our
forces across the sea at a time when we face major unrest here at home. The
Vanir problem will not go away. Though we've quelled their strikes, we've
done it with the use of force. Don't be naive enough to think the problem has
simply vanished. The discord is still there, still simmering beneath the surface
calm that lies over Oseberg for the moment."

Gothrithsson sat as the former chairman's son stood.

"Edvard Halfdansson of Roskildcorp, if it please the board. Do you
understand what Chairman Magnusson is saying? He has a cure for the blight.
What could be more important? How many of you have lost family members to
this disease? How many of you suffer from it yourselves? You won't admit it
publicly—I know. But I will. My own father, the former chairman of this board,
died from the blight. How many hundreds, how many thousands can be saved
with this cure? I say we martial our forces and take whatever we need for this
cure. You would honor my father by voting in favor of this measure."

After Edvard sat, many other jarls claimed the floor, one after another—each
with a different viewpoint on the matter. Vikar gauged their sentiments,
weighed the temerity of their opinions, and decided to chance the vote.

When the last jarl who wished to speak resumed his seat, Vikar raised his
staff once more.

"I call the discussion to an end, and propose a vote. Is there a dissent?"

No one spoke against the vote. While there were many jarls who would not
support Vikar no matter what the issue, he knew they all were intrigued by the
possibility of a cure. Enough, he hoped, that some would forego their
animosity.

"Then I call for a vote. Houses opposed to securing a cure for the blight, light your staves."

Vikar phrased the question hoping those wavering would not want to go on record as opposing a cure. He counted the flames that lit the hall. It wasn't a lucky number, but Vikar never let superstition get in the way of business. Sitric confirmed the number with a whisper.

"The count has been made. Extinguish your staves." Vikar waited. "Now, houses wishing to support sending troops to Serkland to secure the cure, light your staves."

Some of the staves were slow to light, but after some hesitation, Vikar saw he had the support he needed. Not that he would have let a negative vote stop him. He was on a course with destiny, and even if he had to defy the board, he was going to see it through.

"The count has been made. Extinguish your staves." He waited for Sitric to confirm the numbers. "The count is 13 against, 19 in favor. By the vote of this assembly, and witnessed by the gods, the chair will take whatever measures are necessary to secure the territory of Serkland."

72

*The paradox of our demise as a race is that we
brought it upon ourselves — or our ancestors did,
depending upon your perspective. Either way, it was
our arrogance that fueled the flames of our impending
extinction — conceit to think we could toy with the
universe and mold it to our liking.*

— Osst Personal Journal

R ed Sky and Tordan set out for the *wasichu* village early in the morning.
They wanted to study the enemy, and, hopefully, find Two Rivers. Deep
in his heart, Red Sky feared his daughter was already gone — taken across
the sea. Even if she wasn't, he knew there was little chance they would actually
see her...or could free her.

On their way across the high plateau, they observed a large detachment of
wasichu troops moving through the valley below them. They dismounted for a
closer look. Tordan pulled out the device he'd taken from the *wasichu* that made
everything appear nearer than it was. He called it *field glasses*. After taking a
look, he shared it with Red Sky.

There must have been ten times a hundred of them — a force already larger
than the warriors of any single clan. Red Sky worried that even the combined
strength of all the clans might not be enough to stop the invaders.

"They've got something new — I've never seen before. They've mounted
small field cannons atop some of their Heimdalls — their armored cars. That'll
give them more mobility."

They continued to observe for a few minutes, and Red Sky saw a great wind
swirling through the valley, gathering dust, becoming larger, stronger as it
approached the soldiers. It howled and churned and blew straight into the
troops, who broke ranks seeking whatever shelter they could find. Several of
their vehicles choked on the dust and came to a standstill.

"It's Tahte," said Red Sky. "He impedes our enemy."

"Aye, it'll take a while to clean their intakes after that," replied Tordan. "But
it's going to take more than your wind god to make them turn back. Let's keep
moving."

The closer they got to the sea, and the *wasichu* village, the more airships they saw. Red Sky counted four of the flying boats—each shaped like the cocoon of a butterfly, each as black as a raven's wing. He wondered just how many the *wasichu* might have. The ships paid no attention to a pair of riders, sounded no alarm, so he and Tordan reached the outskirts of the settlement without incident. From there they watched and counted.

There were many more *wasichu* than when Red Sky and been taken. Soldiers were everywhere, with more disembarking from one of their large boats. He saw another vessel departing, and wondered if Two Rivers were aboard. He tried not to think about what she would face at the foul hands of the *wasichu*.

Red Sky turned to Tordan and said, "There are already many soldiers, Brother. How many more will come?"

Tordan shrugged. "I don't know. They might be able to put together a force of six or seven thousand, though most of those would be poorly-trained, half-motivated conscripts. What worries me more is their armament. Men we can stop. But armored motorcars, cannon, airships loaded with bombs—we must devise a way to overcome those."

Red Sky grunted contemptuously.

"It took only the dust and the wind of Tahte to slow them. I think they're not so strong."

"True, but we can't call up a dust storm at will—unless you have powers you haven't told me about."

It was Red Sky's turn to shrug—a gesture he'd picked up from his friend. Tordan turned back to look at the *wasichu* settlement.

"It's too bad we can't run a herd of *tatanka* down their gullets," said Tordan. "That would give them pause, eh?"

Red Sky considered it and replied, "Why not?"

Tordan looked at him to see if he was joking. He wasn't.

Rikissa had been summoned. Whether the summons was an official one from the chairman of the board or a more informal one from her father, didn't matter to her. Her first impulse was to ignore it. With everything that had happened, she was glad to no longer be a member of House Magnusson. She no longer thought of it as a bastion of family pride. Indeed, she had no family left. Just an uncaring father who'd never been more than a distant figure of authority.

Yet, when she was notified the motorcar had arrived, she felt an unexpected longing to see the manor once more. She convinced herself she wanted to see Prince Dax, cuddle him in her arms. He was family, and she missed him. She thought of taking him home with her, but realized transplanting such an old cat into a new environment would be unfair to him. Let him spend the rest of his days roaming the familiar halls of House Magnusson.

After much inner debate, she relented, made herself ready, and went down to the motorcar. Part of her was curious. Why would her father want to see her? Why now, after showing such little interest for so many years? Was he lonely? No, not the great Jarl Magnusson, now chairman of the board of Trondheim.

Upon arriving at the manor, Rikissa purposely didn't go straight to her father's office. Instead she searched out Prince Dax, finding him asleep in one of his favorite spots, near the kitchen hearth. She scooped him up and he peered lazily up at her. Soon, though, she had him stoked into full purr.

She carried him with her as she looked around the manor. Her old chamber was still as she'd left it—which surprised her. Of course there was no other use for it. House Magnusson had become a ghost manor.

She'd delayed it as long as she could. Finally, resolutely, she made her way to her father's office. She passed Sitric on the way.

"He's waiting for you, milady."

She walked into the office still carrying Dax.

"Daughter," said Vikar upon seeing her.

He rose from his seat and made his way around the desk to greet her. She thought he may have intended to hug her—which he hadn't done in many years—but when he saw Dax in her arms, he deferred.

"Sit down, sit down."

Rikissa complied, and set the cat on the floor. He rubbed against her leg a few times, then curled up under her father's desk—another of his favorite places.

"How have you been? How's life in House Halfdansson?" asked Vikar, pacing back and forth as he spoke. "Is that husband of yours treating you well?"

Rikissa was bemused. Her father had never shown much interest in her well-being—at least not to her face. Especially not when he married her off with no concern for her own feelings.

"Edvard treats me well," she replied coldly. "He treats me with more respect than anyone else ever has."

Vikar responded, either unaware or simply disregarding the slight.

"And does his respect include blessing your union with children?"

"What?" The question caught Rikissa off-guard.

"I'm asking you, Daughter, if you are with child. Certainly enough time has passed for such an event."

Rikissa still couldn't connect a reason to his query. What did he care if...?

"I'm not with child, Father. I was once. Remember?"

Vikar waved his hand dismissively. "Now you are married. Now it's time to have children."

"What do you care?"

Vikar stopped pacing and leaned towards her, resting his hands on his desk.

"I must have a grandson. A boy of my blood to carry the familial flame. Someone to preside over Trellestar when I'm gone. Of course the boy would carry the name Edvardsson, but that—"

"What if I have a girl, Father?"

"Then you'll try again."

"Again and again and again, Father?"

Vikar nodded ever so slightly and sat.

"Is that all I am to you?" asked Rikissa. "A brood mare fit only to provide you with grandsons?"

"Of course—"

"Of course it is," she said, no longer bothering to conceal her hostility. "I know the truth, Father. You've banished your wife, seen one of your sons killed, probably had a hand in the other's murder, and now you want someone to carry on your legacy?" Rikissa stood, trying to control her anger, but unable to. "What gives you reason to think I would do this for you if I could? Are you under the impression I care about your desires, Father? Do you think I owe you a debt of some kind? I would sooner kill myself than breed for you."

Rikissa took a last look into her father's eyes before she flounced out of the room. The look on his face had been one of astonishment, and she reveled in it.

329

73

*Battle tests a warrior's skill, defending his home his
heart.*

—Sicangu Adage

R ed Sky had fought many battles in his lifetime, taken part in uncounted
raids against rival clans, killed and wounded many men, but the brutal
conflict this day surpassed them all. Never had he seen anything so
bloody, so vicious. The night would echo with the cries of women lamenting
the loss of their men. He was fortunate Snow Deer's voice would not be among
them. A flying bullet had pierced his side, but it was a minor wound.

The day had begun like any other, until word came that a large contingent of
wasichu soldiers were making for the Lakhota village. Sicangu and Oglala
warriors, the two closest clans, had joined with the Lakhota in an attempt to
halt their enemy's advance. Or at least slow them enough that the Lakhota
people had time to strip their *thipis*, pack their belongings, and journey
northward.

Tordan counseled against a direct assault, advising the warriors to harry the
larger force—to strike and retreat. But there had been little time to formulate
coordinated tactics, and many of the warriors ignored his advice. The first
assault surprised the *wasichu*, yet behind their armored vehicles and chain mail,
they suffered few casualties. When the mounted warriors came around for a
second attack, the *wasichu* were ready, and many brave men fell.

Tordan said their enemy had a new kind of *mazakhan*—small firesticks that
didn't have to be reloaded, firing many times. They had little range, so Tordan
urged the warriors to stay back, use their bows, but many failed to heed his
warning, looking to grapple with the hated *wasichu*.

It was a slaughter.

Red Sky hoped he would never see the like again, but feared he would.

At least they'd been successful in slowing the advance of the *wasichu*. By the
time they made their way to the site of the Lakhota village, the people were
gone—safe for now.

As they retreated, their souls battered, their bodies bloodied, Red Sky's
thoughts turned to his missing daughter. Defeat compounded his despair, and

convinced him he'd never see Two Rivers again.

But Tordan had a plan. One to defeat the *wasichu*, another to retrieve Two Rivers—if she were still alive. Tordan believed she was. He said they wouldn't have taken her if they only wanted to kill her. Red Sky hoped he was right. He was not one given to prayer, but he prayed to Wakan Tanka that Two Rivers was unharmed. He prayed, too, Tordan's plan would lead to victory, and drive the *wasichu* from their lands before many more cries of lament were heard.

They came for him, but he hid. They were going to take him and put him in their army—take him away from Marta when she needed him the most. Jorvik wasn't going to let them. Like many of the Modi, he'd been out warning others of the ongoing conscriptions. Any man not performing a vital function was being taken. Any man with a criminal record, any man even suspected of sedition, any man without a sterling record of employment, was to be inducted. Jorvik was eligible on all accounts.

He'd worked little since Kristina had secured his release from prison. He spent much of his time caring for Marta, and scheming with his Modi brothers. He even had to steal to be certain his family was fed.

It was fortunate Canute was too young, or they would have taken him as well. As it was, the boy had been finding odd jobs to help what little he could. More than ever Jorvik was glad Kristina had gone to work in Trondheim. At least there she was safe—taken care of. And it was one less mouth for him to worry about feeding.

The conscriptions had been good for one thing. They'd spread even more discontent among the Vanir. Seeing husbands, brothers, sons, torn from their families was rousing the people to rebellion faster than neglect or mistreatment ever had. Even now he and his Modi brothers were planning an assault on the burgrave of Oseberg. When he was dead, when his enforcers lay mutilated around his corpse, the Aesir masters would know they had a fight on their hands.

It no longer mattered whether the Vanir could win such a fight. Life for so many no longer had much value. Death was more desirable than such a continued existence.

74

We learned to be patient observers like the owl.
We learned cleverness from the crow, and courage
from the jay, who will attack an adversary   ten
times its size to drive it off its territory. But above
them all ranked the chickadee, because of its
indomitable spirit.

—**The Wisdom of Fire In His Eyes**

Willow had quietly, solemnly finished painting his face when a shadow passed over him. Tordan looked up, shading his eyes, half expecting to see a giant airship. But it was only a large bird.

"The eagle flies high today, Brother." Red Sky, his face already painted for battle, walked up leading Fetawachi. "It's a good sign."

"Aye. We'll need all the luck we can get."

"I said nothing about luck," replied Red Sky. "The eagle is a portent of good fortune, not a charm to be carried into battle. He will not aid us in this fight, but his presence speaks loudly."

"Hold still!"

Tordan turned to see what Willow was complaining about. She was painting Magnir's face, and he wasn't happy about it.

"Is this necessary?" he asked Tordan.

"It is if you don't want to be mistaken for the enemy," said Tordan, buckling Thor's Razor to his side. "Besides, your face could use a little decoration."

"I'd laugh, but your wife would stick me."

Tordan saw Red Sky put his arm around Falling Sky's shoulders—an unusually affectionate gesture for a Sicangu. He said something to his son Tordan couldn't hear, but there was no mistaking the pride of his expression.

The painting of the men and their horses was the final act of preparation. They'd already undergone the purification ceremony, sharpened their knives, made their arrows, practiced with their spears, gathered their *wowasake* leaves. More importantly, Tordan had explained his strategy in detail to the *blota hunkas* of each clan. Each would have its part to play. Each had wanted to be on the forefront of the attack force. But the key to it all had taken three days of maneuvering, and it hadn't been easy. A *tatanka* herd could be a stubborn thing.

Though he expressed confidence with the clan leaders, Tordan wasn't entirely certain his plan would work. His biggest worry was that the Aesir commander wouldn't take the bait. Endeavoring to ensure he would was the riskiest part of the plan—at least for one of them.

Trailed by two armed soldiers, Truvor followed the captain into the burgrave's office. It had been a long time, but nothing appeared to have changed. Neither the room, nor the people in it. He might have wished himself elsewhere at that moment, but he was here...and he had a role to play.

"What is it, Captain?"

As soon as the question flew from Storman Ragnarsson's lips, he spotted Truvor.

"He showed up at the gate, wanting to surrender," said the captain.

"Dr. Svein, I'm surprised to see you," said Ragnarsson.

"It's good to see you've finally come to your senses, Doctor," said Burgrave Andersson.

"No doubt he's had his fill of living with the filthy savages," said Ragnarsson. "You couldn't take it anymore, could you?"

Truvor would have preferred to remain silent rather than give in to the storman's goading, but he must stick to the plan.

"I felt it was my duty to return and reveal my cure for the blight, so that all the people would have access to it," said Truvor, embellishing a lie with the truth.

"Always the humanitarian, eh, Doctor?" mocked the storman. "Your change of heart comes a bit late. I'd execute you on the spot, but the chairman wants you back in Trondheim. Apparently he's convinced this cure of yours will work. I have my doubts."

"Come, Storman," countered the burgrave, "he's cured me hasn't he?"

"According to who? According to him? Have you been examined by another doctor? Has anyone else tested you?"

Truvor saw doubt wash over Burgrave Andersson's face.

"Doctor?"

"You're cured as much as I am, Guttorm," replied Truvor. "The cure works. Whether the blight will return at some point, I can't say. More testing needs to be done. That's why I've come back. I need proper facilities."

A messenger hurried into the room and whispered something to the captain.

"A large force of savages has been spotted riding this way, sir," said the captain.

"Friends of yours, Doctor?"

"I stole away. They don't know I came here of my own accord. They may think I was kidnapped again."

"And now they've come to rescue you. How admirable," scoffed Ragnarsson.

"There needn't be any bloodshed. If I could speak with them, I could—"

"Bloodshed is why I'm here, Doctor. Surely you know that," said Ragnarsson. "Let's go to the observation tower and take a look at your would-be saviors, shall we?" To the captain he ordered, "Bring him."

At the first sign of attack, the *wasichu* had sought refuge inside their timber and stone walls and closed their gates, as Tordan had said they would. Now Red Sky, and warriors of the Sicangu, the Lakhota, and the Sihasapa carried out their assault. However, there was little they could accomplish by such a frontal attack. They set fire to their arrows and shot them over and into the walls, but the *wasichu* soldiers were able to quickly douse the flames. Until the *wasichu* came out of their stronghold, there was nothing Red Sky and his warriors could do that would distress the *wasichu* any more than a fly bothers a bear.

Still, they continued to make forays against the fortification, riding in and out too fast for the soldiers firing their *mazakhan* from atop the walls to hit anything. Above them flew one of the *wasichu* airships—a buzzard waiting for the spoils of war.

Then the cannons began firing—just as Tordan said they would.

Red Sky ordered all his warriors back, out of range. But one volley exploded close enough to decimate a group of warriors retreating from a sortie against the main gate. It appeared most of them, men and horses, were dead, but Red Sky saw one man rise weakly to his feet. Without hesitation, he urged Fetawachi into a mad dash, ignoring the continuing barrage. When his warriors saw where he was headed, a great swell of whoops and war cries rose even above the clamor of the cannon fire.

Leaning half-way off his mount, galloping at full speed, Red Sky let the unhorsed warrior grab hold of his arm and swing himself up behind Red Sky. Another, even louder roar of approval sounded from the warriors.

"A valiant if futile act—don't you think, Doctor?" asked Ragnarsson as they watched the rescue. "You could almost admire these horse men for their courage, though I doubt they know the meaning of the word."

The storman continued to watch as the feathered and painted warriors whooped and hollered, waving their bows and spears above their heads, while remaining just out of cannon range.

"Listen to them," said Ragnarsson. "Like a pack of wolves baying at the moon—animals staring at a light they see but don't understand. "It's almost as if they're challenging me to come out and face them. What do you think, Doctor?"

"Let them go," said Truvor.   "They can't do you any harm."

"You still have love for these savages, don't you? Well, I'm afraid I can't just let them go. That's not why I'm here. My orders are to exterminate any that get in my way, and to claim all of Serkland for the corporatocracy. Besides, I can't let their challenge go unanswered, or their feeble attack unpunished.

"Captain, martial our forces. Full armor, all battalions. I want them ready immediately."

The captain hurried out.

"But, Storman," said Burgrave Andersson, "I thought you were waiting for the arrival of more troops before commencing your campaign."

"This is no campaign, Burgrave, just an exercise. Eradicating this small band will be good practice for my men, as well as an abject lesson for the savages."

"Don't do it, Ragnarsson, I beg you," said Truvor. "It'll be a slaughter."

The storman didn't respond or even bother to look at him. Truvor didn't know whether to be glad or sad. Part of him really didn't want Ragnarsson to go out there. The part of him that was still a healer.

"Signalman," said the storman to the man perched atop the observation tower, "signal the airship. If the savages try and retreat, I want them followed."

Ragnarsson headed for the door as the signalman began waving his flags. But the storman stopped and turned before exiting.

"I'll bring you a souvenir, Doctor. What would you like? An ear? What about an entire head?"

He didn't hear Ragnarsson laugh as he left, but imagined him doing so. Truvor only hoped now that Tordan's plan would succeed.

"Don't worry, Doctor," said Burgrave Andersson. "I'm still grateful for your cure. I'll do what I can for you in Trondheim."

And I'll do what I can for you, thought Truvor.

The afternoon breeze was gentle off the sea. The sun hovered warm and full of bright promise in a cloudless sky, while a flock of grey geese flew overhead, unaware of the tempest about to be unfurled below.

Red Sky and his men waited patiently as the gates opened and the armored vehicles rolled out. They waited until the troops on foot followed. They waited until the canons began firing. Then Red Sky called for a withdrawal—but not at full gallop. They moved just fast enough to stay out of range of the canon, moving up the valley towards the ruddy cliffs.

The two forces, Red Sky and less than 200 warriors and thousands of *wasichu* soldiers, kept the same pace for a short time, until the *wasichu* horde halted and ceased their cannon fire. The *wasichu* leader wasn't a fool. He suspected something. But Tordan had anticipated this possibility as well.

Red Sky watched as the *wasichu* began waving their signal flags. The menacing airship above them signaled back. Red Sky didn't know what they were saying, but when the airship stopped hovering and began flying on ahead, he knew they were looking for a trap.

At that moment, dozens of Sahnish warriors broke from cover and charged into the right flank of the *wasichu*. Another group, these Minneconjou, attacked from the left. The attack was brief. The mounted warriors rushed in, fired their arrows, threw their spears, then turned and hastened to reach Red Sky's forces.

Red Sky prompted his men to provoke the enemy once more, and they did with their voices and their gestures. Tordan had said if the *wasichu* stall or lose interest, we must motivate them. It worked. Both the vehicles and the troops on foot began moving again. Coming at Red Sky as fast as they could. He waited, letting them get closer before turning his men up the valley once more. The valley that would soon become a grim canyon, despite the bright afternoon sun.

Truvor and Burgrave Andersson watched the battle from atop the observation tower using field glasses. Though, so far, it hadn't been much of a battle—more of a chase. Just as Tordan had planned.

The signalman above them watched as well. His running commentary was for the benefit of the officer in charge of the tower, who stood next to the burgrave.

"They've began the pursuit again. It doesn't look like they took many casualties with that attack. The airship is moving ahead. They've been ordered to look for any more hostiles that might be lying in wait. The airship is dropping altitude—I imagine to get a closer look at what's beyond the canyon walls. They're signaling again. They're warning about something, but it's unclear. They've—by the beard of Brage! There's fire onboard."

Truvor saw the flames on the side of the airship as well. He didn't have to be close enough to see, to know when it had dropped close enough, a group of the natives' best bowmen hidden atop the canyon ridge were ready. He didn't have to look to know what would happen when those flames reached the gas inside the airship.

Tordan turned at the sound of the explosion. It was louder than the crack of Thor's hammer—far louder than the distant sounds of artillery. The ebony airship had become a ball of crimson and amber flame—no longer flying, but falling.

Euphoric shouts and victory whoops erupted all around him, but Tordan knew it wasn't over yet. He reluctantly turned from the blazing ship to aim his field glasses at the approaching army. Just a little closer, he thought.

Come on, just a little more. He waited a little longer. *Now!*

He gave the signal.

At the mouth of the weathered canyon, Falling Star and the dozens of riders with him began driving a massive herd of *tatanka*—just as they did for the hunt. It wasn't long before thousands of the beasts were on the move, heading into the canyon where the only outlet led to the valley where the Aesir chased Red Sky and his men. But Red Sky knew what to expect. When he saw the rising dust, he would know how close the *tatanka* were.

Tordan saw Red Sky's contingent turn and ride up a narrow gorge where Magnir waited with hundreds of more warriors. They would wait until the beasts had passed, then they would follow, and deal with whatever remained of the enemy.

Like a great black cloud of pestilence the herd collided with the forefront of the Aesir army. Armored vehicles were overturned, scout cars that did not flee fast enough were tossed like toys, and the soldiers on foot, whether they tried to run or stand and shoot at the brutes, were trampled into a bloody pulp.

It was a tremendous sight, but Tordan didn't watch for long. He mounted his horse and led the warriors with him down into the valley to finish it.

75

What is life? It is the flash of a firefly in the night.
It is the breath of an elk in the wintertime. It is the
little shadow that runs across the grass and loses
itself in the sunset.

—Lakhota Saying

Truvor had spoken the truth. It was a slaughter. Only not the one Storman Ragnarsson expected.

The onslaught of the stampeding beasts had been so brutal, Truvor had to lower his glasses. It wasn't easy for him to be party to so many deaths. His conscience troubled him, but he managed his guilt with memories of Walks Apart. When he raised the field glasses to look again, he saw most of the survivors, dazed and bloodied, were surrendering.

Burgrave Andersson wasn't watching. He stood speechless—not a condition Truvor had ever known him to afflict him.

"There will soon be hundreds of native warriors at your gates, Burgrave. You have only a handful of soldiers left. Surrender, and I promise no one else need die this day. Otherwise they will burn down your walls and kill anyone who resists."

"You knew about this," said the burgrave. "You were part of this. You *wanted* Ragnarsson to go out there. You baited him. You never intended to go back to Trondheim."

"What I knew, Guttorm, is that I couldn't stand by and allow Storman Ragnarsson to commit genocide on these people. I still hope to return to Trondheim and bring my cure for the blight...someday. But it will be on my terms."

The gates opened, and Tordan saw Truvor standing there. Next to him was, he guessed, Hestvoll's burgrave. Behind them were the remaining troops, all disarmed.

"Put these men with the other prisoners and secure the settlement," he told Magnir. "Doctor, there's a wain waiting for you. You're needed to tend the wounded."

Truvor hurried past him with his medical bag, and Tordan strode up to the fat burgrave.

"Burgrave Andersson, I presume."

"Guttorm Andersson. I appear no longer to be the burgrave of this colony."

"That's right," said Tordan. "But I've some questions only a former burgrave can answer."

Andersson nodded in acquiescence.

"Where are the rest of your forces?"

"The rest? There aren't any. Oh, there are a few patrols out, but no more than that. You've just crushed Storman Ragnarsson's great army."

"When do you expect reinforcements?"

"The next ship should arrive any day."

"A short time ago, you captured a group of young native women. Where are they?"

"I'm afraid they were transported back to Trondheim in the last ship."

"How long ago?"

"It departed a week ago I believe."

Two Rivers and the others are still alive. I must tell Red Sky.

The valley floor was a fetid marinade of blood and crushed body parts. Truvor had seen the results of war before, but nothing like the befouled ground he stood on now. He avoided looking at the horrific landscape by keeping himself busy tending to the individual wounded of both sides. It was a monumental task—an impossible one. When someone approached him he was about to tell them they had to wait. He looked up and saw Red Sky standing over him, carrying a battered body.

It was Falling Star, the boy he'd cured of the bane—Red Sky's son. The paint on his face had been smudged and smeared with his own blood. His limbs were bruised and broken.

Red Sky laid him gently the ground. Truvor bent over him and checked his vital signs.

"What happened?"

"He fell from his horse among the *tatanka*," said Red Sky without a trace of emotion.

"I'm sorry, Red Sky. There's nothing I can do. He's dead."

Red Sky voiced no cry of anguish, no words of vengeful fury. He didn't react in any visible way. He bent down, took his son in his arms, and lifted him. Truvor wondered at the detachment of the man. Yet, before Red Sky turned to walk away, Truvor saw the mist in his eyes.

Vikar knew most of the jarls were perturbed to be called to an emergency meeting of the board of directors, but he'd done it specifically to express the gravity of the matter at hand. When they were seated he called the meeting to order and explained the urgency of the situation.

"As you all know, the state of affairs in Oseberg grows more dire with each passing day. Work stoppages, protests, even sabotage have diminished production to unacceptable levels. I'm sure you'll all agree something must be done, and done quickly to quell this rebellion.

"Yes, yes it *is* a rebellion. I don't use that word lightly. If we don't quash the rabble now, this insurgency will spread like the blight over our economic system. Order must be restored. Production in our factories and fisheries must be brought back on schedule.

"The upheaval has gone on too long—gone too far. To restore order, we must send troops in to enforce the law. But we can't use corporate troops, as their ranks are swollen with conscriptees. Sending Vanir against Vanir would be problematic, and likely incendiary. So I propose to send only Aesir troops to suppress this uprising. That will mean each house must contribute a number of their own housecarles to the venture."

The murmurs had been minimal until he suggested using housecarles. Now objections were shouted across the room. Vikar sat and let each jarl, in turn, have his say on the matter, while Sitric made note of who supported his proposal, and who didn't.

As they spoke, a messenger hurried to Vikar's side and whispered in his ear. The news couldn't have been better as far as Vikar was concerned. A corporate army induction center in Oseberg had been destroyed with an incendiary bomb. He would make good use of it.

When each jarl who wanted to speak had, Vikar stood and reclaimed the floor.

"The chair recognizes there is no consensus on this matter at the moment, and urges each corporate officer to consider all the ramifications involved before we take a vote. However, there has been a new act of terrorism in Oseberg I must deal with. I declare a recess to these proceedings, which shall be resumed on the morrow."

Shouts of opposition to the recess came one after another, but there was nothing they could do. The chairman was within his rights to call for a recess at any time, and Vikar knew it. He and his staff hustled out of the hall and towards his waiting motorcar.

Vikar was annoyed but not surprised. He'd hoped, but hadn't expected, the board to give its full support to his plans. It was minor setback. He'd still get what he wanted, but now he'd have to use other means of eliciting their approval. It couldn't be helped. They'd forced his hand.

Roadblocks had been set up outside the neutral grounds of the VE. The most vocal dissenters to his plan would be arrested for conspiring to aid the rebels. The charges would never hold up in an Althing court. Before such trials were ever held, the charges would be dropped and the arrested jarls released. After the vote of course.

"I've separated Aesir from Vanir, as you suggested," said Magnir. "Most of the Aesir are officers, and a majority of the Vanir were conscripted. I know a couple of the Vanir from my early days in Oseberg."

"Bring them over," said Tordan.

Magnir went to get the prisoners.

"Why did you separate them?"

"Because the Vanir have no love for the Aesir—presently company excluded, Doctor—and I have an idea they would turn against them, given the chance."

"I assume then, you have some new plan."

"I wouldn't exactly call it a plan yet, but I'm thinking on it."

Indeed Tordan had an idea, but he wasn't ready to share it.

"What do you need me to do?"

"Can you make more blight serum?"

"Yes, now that I have access to my old lab again."

"Well, Doctor, I want you to make as much serum as you can."

"What for?"

"You've heard the expression 'the carrot or the stick'?"

"Yes," replied Truvor with a puzzled look. "What does that have to do with anything?"

"The serum is the carrot. The Vanir are the stick."

"I don't understand," said Truvor.

"Like I said, I'm still thinking on it."

"Alright, I'll start making serum."

"Good," replied Tordan, looking around. "Have you seen Red Sky."

"He's gone."

"Gone where?"

"Kicking Bull told me he left to take his son's body home. He spoke to no one."

"I should have known," said Tordan. "I should have gone with him."

"He knows you have work to do here," said Truvor. "Here come your prisoners. I guess I'll get to my work so you won't have an Aesir skulking about."

Tordan ignored Truvor's jest. He was still thinking about Falling Star. He remembered the first day he saw him. How he was fascinated with his father's *wasichu* captive, and how proud he was after his first *tatanka* hunt. He'd become a man, but in Tordan's eyes he'd still been a boy.

So much pain. He didn't think he could endure the suffering Red Sky had borne. First he was captured and imprisoned, then his daughter was taken, and now his son was dead. All the while his land was being invaded, his people attacked. Still he'd held his head up, remained composed and serene—at least on the outside. He'd even accepted Tordan, a *wasichu*, as a brother. Given his place, Tordan didn't think he could do the same.

"Here they are, Brother."

Tordan turned to see Magnir with a pair of soldiers. One had been bandaged on both his head and arm. The other wore some nasty bruises.

"This is Horik, and that's Steinthor. I knew both of them when we were just pups."

Tordan studied them, trying to look as stern as he could.

"You were both conscripted into the corporate army?"

They nodded.

"Do you feel it's your duty to continue to fight for the corporatocracy?"

"I never thought it was my duty," spoke up Horik. "They forced me. They threatened my family—like they always do."

"Is that so?"

"It's true," added Steinthor. "None of us wanted to be here, fighting these...horse men. We'd rather be home, in bed with our wives."

Tordan waited, letting them think he was considering their fate. The truth was, he already knew what he was going to do.

"Do all Vanir feel the same way?"

"Most," said Horik. "Some joined up just because they like a good fight.

Some don't care about the struggle."

"What struggle?" asked Tordan.

"The struggle of the workers—the protests, the strikes."

"What strikes?"

Tordan looked at Magnir.

"You've been gone a long time, Brother," said Magnir. "There's been quite a fracas going on in Oseberg. Like he says, there've been strikes, sabotage, massive protests in the streets. Before they shipped me out, it sounded like the radicals were taking over."

"We're not radicals," objected Steinthor loudly, then lowered his voice. "We're just people tired of being stepped on. People with families who want the same rights and privileges as our Aesir overlords."

"You sound like my brother," said Tordan. "Tell me more about this fracas."

Tordan began plotting even as the two Vanir soldiers described the current situation. If this rebellion in Oseberg were disruptive enough, it meant Chairman Magnusson and the corporatocracy would be fighting wars on two fronts. Their resources would be stretched thin. They would be unable to continue shipping troops to Serkland.

It was time to take the battle to them.

76

*The most useful thing about a principle is that it can
always be sacrificed to expediency.*
—Words of Chairman Wulfstan
Don't sail out farther than you can row back.
—Book of Runes

Since the arrest of five prominent jarls the day before, Vikar had been
inundated with angry messages, both from the incarcerated jarls'
corporate offices and the jarls from other corporations. He didn't expect a
gracious atmosphere when the board meeting in the Ve resumed...and he didn't
get one.

As he strode to his dais, catcalls and outright insults followed him. He
expected it. But soon enough they would all be silent. Soon they'd realize he
was not to be crossed.

When each corporation's representatives had been seated, he gave the signal.
All around the chamber, corporate troops rushed in, blocking the entries and
exits. Each of the soldiers carried a firearm.

A great uproar sounded throughout the chamber. The rage was palpable,
the representatives even more vocal than before. It was nothing Vikar hadn't
anticipated. When several representatives attempted to walk out, they were
turned back by the soldiers.

Vikar waited until the angry clamor calmed somewhat. He stood and raised
his staff.

"I, Vikar Magnusson, Chairman of the Board of Trondheim and all it
holdings, call the resumption of this meeting of the Board of Directors to order.
Is there any challenge to my authority to do so?" Angry shouts greeted him, but
Vikar ignored them. "Having heard no objections, I authorize a commencement
of the proceedings."

Before he could even sit, one of the jarls stood to demand the floor.

"Jarl Edvard Halfdansson of Roskildcorp, if it please the board. What is the
meaning of bringing armed soldiers into the Ve? I must protest, Chairman. This
is a violation of all established protocol. I insist these men be removed at once,
before any further business is conducted."

Shouts of assent followed the motion made by Vikar's own son-in-law, making it obvious even his strongest allies were outraged by his maneuver.

Vikar stood and waited for relative silence.

"You all are aware of the increased incidences of violence, of yesterday's destruction of a military depot. Now I've learned of a direct threat by Vanir terrorists against this body. Therefore I've ordered additional security for your own well-being."

"Then why aren't they outside?" someone shouted.

Vikar glared in the direction of the question. "If there are any more outbursts, I'll have the offending party removed from this meeting."

He looked around the chamber. The muttering all but ceased.

"These security forces will remain in place until the crisis is resolved. And, I might add, lest any of you doubt their effectiveness, each of these men is armed with a new weapon for which the patents have already been filed. We call it a *revolver*, and it's capable of firing nine times before reloading. So, you see, we are safe from any Vanir incursion."

This led to more indignant murmurs.

"Jarl Eriksson of Vineland Enterprises, if it please the board. I demand to know why several jarls, the heads of their corporations, were arrested and detained after our previous meeting was called to recess."

There were more howls of agreement with the speaker, despite Vikar's threats. He waited for them to calm.

"These men were arrested on suspicion of conspiring with Vanir rebels. If enough evidence is produced, they will be tried for those crimes. If not, they will be released."

"Jarl Gothfrithsson of Ruslagen Group, if it please the board. I propose an immediate vote on the chairmanship, and nominate —"

"You're out of order, Jarl Gothfrithsson," bellowed Vikar, cutting him off. "No such vote can be called during such a security crisis. No change in leadership of this board will be allowed until all threats to the corporatocracy have been eliminated. Any further such proposals will be considered threats to our security, and open the member in question to prosecution for conspiring with terrorists."

Vikar saw the board members were flummoxed by his declaration. They had no response, because such an assertion had never come before the board.

"Jarl Volsung of Sveabordcorp, if it please the board. Chairman, am I to understand you're declaring a hostile takeover of this body?"

345

"Not at all, Jarl Volsung. The work of this board of directors will proceed unimpeded. Before the recess, we were considering the necessity of sending regiments comprised only of Aesir troops to suppress the Vanir uprising. In addition, each house would contribute a number of their own housecarles— let's say 40 per major house, 30 per minor." The number sent another wave of shocked rumbling through the chamber. "This deployment of troops is still necessary, and the chair supports it most strongly." Vikar paused to let what he was saying sink in. "I call for a vote. Houses wishing to support this proposal, light your staves."

There followed much discussion among the various jarls and their executives. Vikar gave them time. Slowly torches began blooming around the chamber, followed a by a swell of acquiescence. Even the thanes who were replacing the arrested jarls voted aye. Vikar's intimidation ruled the day. It was unanimous.

77

There is no death. Only a change of worlds.
— **Sicangu Adage**

After Hestvoll was taken, many of the warriors left to go home, even after it was explained to them the war wasn't over. Red Sky's departure was part of the problem. The other was the various clans were still not used to working together. Tordan knew they saw only that the *wasichu* on their lands had been defeated. They didn't fully grasp the long-term threat that still existed.

Tordan needed to speak with Red Sky, to convince him what they needed to do next. He left Truvor, Magnir, and Kicking Bull in command of Hestvoll, and rode all night with a few others of the Sicangu to reach their village.

Magnir was certain he could convince most of the Vanir conscriptees to join them. As part of their plan, they would make every effort to make it appear operations were normal throughout the colony. An unknown number of airships surveyed the Serkland territory, and when they returned Tordan wanted them to be unaware Hestvoll had new masters.

Though it had only been a single day since Red Sky had returned home, Tordan arrived too late for Falling Star's funeral. He wanted to see Willow, but first he must speak with Red Sky. He found Snow Deer outside her *thipi*, going about her daily tasks. He didn't know what to say to her, but he tried.

"My heart is torn and my spirit is full of emptiness," said Tordan. "I will miss the smile of Falling Star, and the sound of his laughter."

Snow Deer looked up at him and placed her hand on his cheek as if *she* were consoling him.

Not so long ago she thought she'd lost her husband. Now she'd lost a son and a daughter in a matter of weeks. Yet she carried herself as stalwartly as any warrior. He wondered if Red Sky were as strong.

She must have read his face, for she said, "He is inside. I will tell your wife you have returned. She worries."

"Thank you."

He entered the *thipi* and found Red Sky sitting cross-legged, staring blankly into a small fire. His face was still painted black from the funeral, but smudged in places. His eyes glittered like gemstones in the firelight. Whether they flickered out of anger or emptiness, Tordan couldn't tell.

He sat across from his friend and said nothing for a few long moments. He wanted to support Red Sky in his time of mourning, but he also wanted to motivate him.

"Falling Star was a good man," he finally said, breaking the silence. "He will be remembered for the man he was by the Sicangu."

Red Sky nodded, but didn't respond right away.

"My son was a man, but he was still very much a boy. He never had the chance to..."

Red Sky fell silent again.

"Boy or man, he was brave," said Tordan. "Though his life was brief, it was as bright as the star for which he was named. I will remember him for his curiosity, his enthusiasm, and his friendship."

Red Sky nodded again, but didn't speak. Tordan sat quietly with him a while longer before broaching the idea that had been pulling at him like a herd of horses.

"I have a plan to rescue Two Rivers."

It took a few long seconds for the words to register, but when Red Sky raised his head and looked at Tordan, there was new life in his eyes.

"Tell me of this plan."

Kristina knew all wasn't right with Rikissa and her husband. Her mistress had come to share her most intimate thoughts with her, and Kristina always listened dutifully.

Rikissa often complained of boredom, of being ignored, of having to compete with Edvard's academic pursuits, as if they were mistresses. She'd also been upset by her father's demand she give him a grandson. She was angry her father still thought he could command her.

Rikissa wasn't happy, despite the luxury she lived in. Kristina didn't always understand her unhappiness, but she did her best to sympathize. She knew her mistress was impulsive, and when she said they were going to the Hall of the Valkyries Kristina thought it just another impulse.

Rikissa hadn't been to the hall since the day of her initiation ceremony, so Kristina was surprised to hear they were going back there. She was more surprised when, after they arrived and wine had been served, one of the

Valkyrie declared it was time for "the Dance of Freyja," and her mistress disrobed with the others.

Kristina watched it all from the far edges of the room, along with the other handmaidens. It was a spectacle of lust and debauchery she'd never thought to envision. Right away, Rikissa selected one of the men in white loincloths and led him to a divan where she began stroking his long rusty hair, and playing with other parts of him as well—as if he were a toy.

The room was a cacophony of laughter and wantonness. More than once Kristina turned her eyes away, then looked back—both repulsed and attracted to the tableau playing out before her. Old women, young women—it didn't seem to matter—flounced around the room wearing little, if anything. The men were playthings, servants who did as they were told. Kristina saw things she never imagined—learned things she wondered if she'd ever need to know.

Despite everything she saw, Kristina was not entirely certain her mistress was enjoying herself. She knew it was Rikissa's unhappiness that had fanned the fires of impulse and led her here, but she didn't believe it was what her mistress truly desired. She admitted to herself she didn't know *what* Rikissa wanted. From Kristina's perspective, her mistress had everything she needed — everything Kristina could have wanted. But it wasn't enough.

Tordan looked into Willow's eyes and saw she knew what he was going to say before he even spoke.

"I must go away."

"Will you come back?" she asked.

"Of course I will come back," he said, gently taking hold of her arms. "I don't want to leave you, but I must help my friend. I must try to end the *wasichu* threat—the threat to my wife, to my people."

"I am afraid, once you go back to your homeland, you will want to stay."

Tordan shook his head. "No, no, this is my home now. I want to help my brother and his family, if I can, but I won't stay there. I am Sicangu now. I am yours."

Willow smiled.

"Then there is something I must tell you before you go." She hesitated and he looked at her questioningly. Before he could ask she said, "There is a child in my belly—your child."

Tordan was caught by surprise, though he didn't know why he should be. But he didn't want to remember what happened the last time he was told that, so his wit took over.

"Well, I hope it is my child," he said and laughed.

Willow did not understand his jest and frowned. Tordan figured his attempt at humor had been lost in translation, so he kissed her—an expression needing no translation.

"You have given me another reason I must go. I must do what I can to eliminate the threat to our child and all the children."

"There will always be threats, my husband. But if you will be there, I will always stand beside you to face them."

"Wise and beautiful," he replied, once again looking into her eyes. "That's why I married you, you know? That and your delicious deer stew."

This time she understood his quip and smiled.

"I have asked Broken Horn to watch out for you. Now I will have to tell him about the child."

"It is still a long time before the child will come," she said. "You will come back to me before then, if Wakan Tanka wishes it."

"*I* wish it. I will be back to see our child come into this world."

Tordan knew, even as he said it, he was making a promise he wasn't sure he could keep. His plan was fraught with danger, and there was a good chance he wouldn't survive. Willow knew that too. But neither of them was going to give it voice. He was going to depart with all the joy and optimism he could muster.

"Goodbye, my love," he said taking her into his arms and kissing her. It was sweetest kiss he'd ever tasted.

Sitric came into his office with a frown, but waited to be recognized.

"Yes, what is it?"

"Jarl Halfdansson is at the gate, demanding to see you, sir. I was going to send him away, as I have the other petitioners, but I wasn't sure—"

"Send him in."

"Right away, sir."

Vikar knew why young Edvard had come, and it wasn't to tell him a grandchild was on the way. Edvard, like the other jarls, was upset over the tactics Vikar had used during the last board meeting. He didn't care. They were going to have to get used to it. Now that he held the chairmanship, and controlled the corporate army, Vikar wasn't about to give it up. His leadership was vital to the corporatocracy, especially now.

"Chairman Magnusson," said Edvard as he was shown into the room by

Sitric, "thank you for seeing me."

"Of course—we're family," responded Vikar from his chair. "Have a seat."

"I don't come on a family matter," said Edvard, remaining standing. "I come as the CEO of Roskildcorp, and at the behest of several of my peers."

"Your peers? Your peers would stab you in the back and gut your corporation, given the chance," said Vikar with an angry scowl. He softened and added, "It's the nature of the beast."

"I won't bother to debate you on that point now," said Edvard. "I won't even dispute the wisdom of your decisions regarding Serkland and Oseberg. I've come to protest your orders authorizing the use of armed guards within the Ve. My father never would have sanctioned such a blatant disregard for convention."

"Your father was a great chairman...in his day," said Vikar. "But this is a new day, a new regime. I represent the future of the corporatocracy, not its past. Believe me, Cousin, I know what's best."

"Even if I believed that, there are many other jarls who don't. They see you as a usurper, and there is talk they will each bring their own housecarles to the next board meeting. If they do, the Ve will no longer be neutral ground, it will be a battlefield."

Edvard's concern was earnest, but Vikar smirked.

"That would be foolish of them. I've many more men at my command, and superior arms. It would be a bloody exercise in futility that would profit no one. I think they know that."

"I don't understand you," said Edvard. "I don't understand why you're doing this."

"You don't need to understand," said Vikar, standing. He walked around his desk to within an arm's reach of his son-in-law. "I promised your father before he died that I would advise you. So listen to me, Cousin. I'm going to quell the uprising in Oseberg, gain control over all the wealth of Serkland, and consolidate my chairmanship with more troops and new weapons. My advice to you is...don't get in my way."

78

*I have come to appreciate the irony that I, a social
historian, am now the last of my kind. How much
longer my essence will survive is the subject of self
speculation, since there are no others to offer an
opinion. I no longer trust my senses of reasoning or
logic, as they continue to deteriorate, as have the
essences of my fellow beings. However, I will continue
to record my observations for as long as I am able.*
—Osst Personal Journal
Courage is not fearlessness, it is acting while fearful.
—Sicangu Adage

It was an incredible thing, this *air* ship. Tordan had explained to him what
made it rise above the ground, comparing it to a bubble that rises to the top
of a lake. But a bubble would burst once if reached the surface. Likewise, he
knew such a ship could burst into flames like dry prairie grass. He'd seen it
himself.

Despite his apprehension, Red Sky climbed into the monstrosity's belly. He
had to. His daughter was being held a prisoner in the same place he once was.
He tried not to imagine the horrors Two Rivers might be facing, but his
imagination was too strong. If she were still alive, he must rescue her, even if
he had to fly on Wakinyan himself.

Because he believed his daughter was still alive, he'd left his village, left his
wife at a time he should be joining her in mourning for his son. It was still hard
for him to accept that Falling Star was dead. There was still so much of life
ahead of him that he'd had no chance to live.

As the airship ascended, Red Sky looked back over the mountains toward
the Sicangu village. It was too far away to see, but he knew in which direction it
lay. He knew Snow Deer was there, waiting for him, praying to Wakan Tanka
he would return safely, with their daughter. Yet more was at stake than their
two lives. If Tordan was right, and Red Sky believed he was, it was even more
important they stop the *wasichu* now. If not, they would cross the sea again,
invade the lands of the Ikche Wichasa, rape the forests and valleys, and kill the

people. There must be an end to it, no matter the cost.

As they rose even higher, and moved out over the open sea, Red Sky couldn't help but be struck by a sense of wonder. He fondled the medicine bundle Snow Deer had made to protect him, not so much for protection but for comfort.

To fly through the air like this, through the realm of eagles and gods... If a man could do this, what couldn't he do?

Tordan considered using a couple of thunderboats, but figured an airship would be faster, given good tailwinds, and would be less likely to run into any problems on the way. They were lucky. The winds had been favorable, and they didn't have to fly through any storms. They crossed the sea in less than two days.

Red Sky had been hesitant about boarding the dark vessel, saying flying was for birds, not men.

"We're not really flying like a bird," Tordan had said, trying to ease his concerns. "We'll be floating, like a seed carried by the wind or the smoke that rises from a fire."

Red Sky's frown said he was neither smoke nor seed, but he climbed aboard the airship's passenger compartment. The truth was, Tordan had his own trepidations. He'd never been in an airship either.

Their party consisted of himself, Red Sky, Magnir, Steinthor, Horik, and two other Vanir who were part of the airship's regular crew, and could both operate its engine and navigate. After speaking with the other Vanir, Tordan was certain he could trust them. They hated the Aesir more than his brother did.

The plan, such that it was, was for the airship to land on the outskirts of Oseberg. Hopefully somewhere it wouldn't be seen right away. Steinthor and Horik would make contact with members of the insurgency, Magnir would travel to Trondheim and try to locate Two Rivers, while Tordan and Red Sky went to see Jorvik. Tordan knew even if Jorvik wasn't a B'serker himself, he'd know where to find them.

Both Thor and Wakan Tanka must have been watching over them, because everything went according to plan. He hoped things were going as well back in Hestvoll, and that Truvor and the few trusted Vanir he'd left in command were going to be able to carry out the second part of his plan.

After they arrived, Tordan and Red Sky walked under the cover of night to Jorvik's house. He'd considered trying to disguise his friend, but decided against it. Such a disguise wouldn't hold up under close scrutiny anyway, and he wanted the Vanir to know who their allies were.

Jorvik seemed unwilling to believe his eyes when he opened the door. It was only then Tordan realized he must look somewhat different than he had the last time he'd visited his brother. Not only his lack of facial hair and sun-darkened skin, but his clothing—which was a patchwork of his old skaldor uniform and garments Willow had made him.

"Tordan?"

Jorvik stood there, staring at the pair of men who'd come to his door so late at night.

"Are you going to invite us in, Brother?"

Jorvik didn't say anything, but motioned them inside, scanning the street to see if anyone had seen them.

"What are doing here? Where have you been?"

"I know you have many questions, Brother, but I could use something to drink to wet my tongue first. Skyr, if you have it. I think water for my friend."

Jorvik looked at Red Sky, noticing him for the first time. "What...who...?"

"Sorry, I should have introduced you. This is Red Sky, he whose thoughts are strong medicine, brother to *tatanka* the great provider, defender of the Sicangu, husband of Snow Deer. But you can just call him Red Sky. Red Sky, this is my brother by birth, Jorvik."

Red Sky nodded and Jorvik nodded in return.

"I have no skyr," he said, handing both of them cups of water.

"My thanks," said Red Sky.

Jorvik looked surprised. "He speaks our language?"

"Yes," replied Tordan, "though not as well as I speak his."

Jorvik shook his head as if it were all too much for him to assimilate.

"You look tired. You've obviously come a great distance," said Jorvik. "Sit."

Tordan pulled out a chair from the kitchen table and Red Sky imitated him, though he didn't appear very comfortable on the wooden seat.

"It's been countless weeks since we've heard from you," said Jorvik, joining them at the table. "Where've you been?"

"It's a long story, but I'll try to shorten it. I was sent to Serkland on a mission for House Magnusson, but I met my friend here, learned about his people, and even took a wife."

"You have a wife?"

Tordan nodded.

"I'm no longer in the service of House Magnusson, and that's one of the reasons I'm here."

"What reasons?"

"First of all, where are Kristina and Canute? How is Marta doing?"

"Canute is asleep. Kristina is in Trondheim, working for the Lady Rikissa, as you arranged. Marta is asleep also. She is...she's not well."

"The blight has grown worse in her?"

"Much worse."

"Then I come with good news." Tordan reached into the pouch Willow had made for him, and pulled out one of the vials of serum Truvor had given him "This is a cure for the blight. This is for Marta, and I have more."

"A cure? How? I thought...there was no cure," stammered Jorvik.

"There is now. It's another tale, but an Aesir doctor discovered this herb Red Sky and his people season their food with. He used it to create the cure. He says it's been tested and it works fairly quickly. In a few weeks Marta should be fine."

Still stunned by it all, Jorvik responded, "It's...it's hard to believe—everything you're telling me. I don't know what to say."

"Say you'll wake Marta and let her have her first dose. Dr. Svein said just a small spoonful each day until it's gone. I couldn't bring much with me, but eventually we'll have enough for everyone in Oseberg who's afflicted. We'll even give it to the Aesir, if they mind themselves."

"What are you talking about? What are the *other* reasons you've come for?"

"I want you to put me in touch with the B'serkers—or whatever they call themselves."

"They call themselves the Modi, and I'm one of them," said Jorvik proudly. "What do you want with us?"

Tordan looked at Red Sky, smiled, and turned back to Jorvik. "We want to start a revolution."

It took a couple of days, but Jorvik managed to get his Modi brothers to come listen to Tordan. He thought Agnar would have an open mind, but hadn't known the others in his new cell long enough to be sure how they'd react. Additional members of the underground were present as well, but Jorvik didn't know them. They were brought to the meeting by Tordan's compatriots—Steinthor and Horik.

As Tordan spoke, Jorvik watched the faces of his fellow Modi. He saw expressions of distrust, suspicion, and disbelief. Before Tordan could even finish his initial proposal, he was interrupted.

"Why should we ally ourselves with these savages?" asked one of the men Jorvik didn't know.

"Aye," said another. "What do these horse men have to do with us?"

Tordan took a deep breath.

"The people of Serkland are much like you. If they didn't fight back, the boot of the Aesir would be as firmly on their necks as it is on yours now. But they *have* fought back. That's why this is the time to strike." Tordan banged his fist on the table as he gave voice to the words. "We've come from a great victory over the corporate army. Their forces in Serkland are either dead, imprisoned, or have joined us."

"What do you mean *joined* you?" asked Agnar.

"Many of those who survived the battle were Vanir conscripts. Like you, they have no love for the Aesir. They were torn from their families and forced to serve the corporatocracy. Now they're ready to turn against their masters, to join you in open rebellion, if you have the courage."

The Modi grumbled at Tordan's inference.

"There's something else, as well," said Jorvik. "Tell them."

"The people of Serkland have a cure for the blight—one they will share with all who join them against the forces of Trondheim."

Jorvik saw his fellow Vanir were astonished by the news. The blight was something they'd lived with all their lives, like the rising sun and the blowing wind. None of them had ever even considered the idea of a cure.

"How do we know there's such a cure, Skaldor?"

"How do we know it works?"

"He's lying."

"He's not lying," said Jorvik angrily. "I've already given the cure to my wife."

"And is her blight gone?" wondered Agnar.

"It doesn't work that fast," said Tordan. "It takes ten days or more, depending upon how far the disease has progressed." There were more grumbles, so Tordan continued quickly. "It's been tested by an Aesir doctor. A doctor who's joined us. He's cured not only himself, but others. The Aesir have already tried to take him, to steal the cure, but we stopped them.

"You know what'll happen if the corporatocracy gets the cure. They won't share it with the Vanir. It'll be for them and them alone."

Nods of agreement were shared around the table, but then Agnar stood. For

356

a moment Jorvik feared he was going to walk out of the meeting. If he did, the others would follow.

"I believe you, Skaldor," said Agnar. "At least I believe you're telling us what you believe to be the truth. But cure or no, how does your victory in Serkland help us here?"

"If you'll sit, and listen, I'll tell you of my plan," said Tordan. "Then you can decide for yourselves. If you're as determined to win your freedom as I think, you'll listen."

Agnar looked at his fellow Modi, then resumed his seat.

"The majority of the corporate army was in Serkland, so the Aesir forces are as depleted as they've ever been. There will never be a better time to strike.

"As we speak, there is a ship on its way from Serkland, carrying both Vanir soldiers who have joined us, and brothers of my friend Red Sky, who have bravely left their own land to come to ours. These are men who know nothing of seafaring, who have never been on a ship. Yet they risk their lives to come here and aid us in our fight against the Aesir. They are wise enough to know the Aesir must be stopped now, while we have the advantage."

Jorvik glanced at the horse man who'd chosen not to sit at the table. He stood a few steps behind Tordan, listening to the talk. How much he understood, Jorvik didn't know, but he seemed to take it all in. What Jorvik *did* know, what Tordan had shared with him, was that his brother couldn't be certain the ship was actually on its way, and how many fighting men would be aboard.

"In addition to this ship, I'll go to Trondheim with Steinthor and Horik, and we'll speak with other Vanir soldiers. If we can convince them to turn against their officers, we'll have a three-pronged force. That is, if the Modi, and the people of Oseberg, will rise up and join us to end the Aesir domination."

Jorvik had never been prouder of his brother than when he heard him utter those words. The very idea had been what he'd struggled for nearly his entire life, yet the concept was almost incomprehensible. To be free of the Aesir yoke? That was a dream he yearned to make a reality.

79

As my last act, I am producing a communication that will be translated into the language of the most technologically advanced bipeds, and sent to their settlement. I will explain their origins and express our regrets for having removed them from their homeworld. I feel it is the civilized thing to do.

—Osst Personal Journal

The anxiety of waiting for the ship from Serkland to arrive was a burden Tordan was unused to. Never had he been responsible for so much. His days as a carefree skaldor hadn't prepared him to be the architect of a revolution. He worried maybe he'd cut off more than he could chew.

He and the others put their time waiting for the ship to good use — organizing the Modi. But they needed more than just the hardcore radicals, if their plan were to succeed. Fortunately, the more they spoke of an all-out rebellion, the more Vanir that wanted join them. The recent escalation in conscriptions had angered the population. The families of the soldiers not only sided with the insurgents, they aided the Modi in contacting their loved ones, and helped convince the conscripted soldiers within the ranks of the corporate army to join the revolt when the time came. Though the truth was, it didn't take much convincing. Hostility against their Aesir masters was ingrained in them from childhood. All they needed to know was that there was a chance — a chance to throw off their chains.

Once their plans were set, and everything was in place, there was nothing more for Tordan to worry over. He'd done all he could, devising strategy with the Modi leaders. Their forces would strike several vulnerable points. When the army was called out, the Vanir conscriptees would mutiny, and the Aesir would face a fight both from without and within. The rebels lacked weapons, so the mutiny was key to the entire plan. Without it, Tordan doubted the Vanir would have the numbers to succeed.

The ship finally did arrive, carrying both the Vanir conscriptees who'd joined them and a large number of warriors from the various clans. Unexpectedly, Truvor was with them. When Tordan asked him why he'd come, he said the Serklanders wouldn't go without him. Many of them feared traveling across the sea, and wanted the protection of Wichasa Wakan Okinihan.

Truvor's knowledge of the cure was too valuable to risk in battle, and, as he made plain, he was no warrior. So he agreed to stay with Marta, and check on her progress. Jorvik was happy to have a doctor with her—even one who was Aesir.

When nothing remained for him to do, Tordan approached his brother.

"Just before the assault, Red Sky, Magnir and a couple of his skaldor brothers are going into Trellestar, to find Red Sky's daughter. At the same time, I'm going to make my way into House Halfdansson and find Kristina."

"I'm going with you," said Jorvik, as Tordan knew he would.

"No, Brother. I'm going alone. It'll be much easier for me to get inside and find her by myself. And I need you out here, making sure the attack is carried out on schedule and according to plan. I promise you I'll protect her, and bring her to you."

Tordan saw his brother wanted to argue, but he realized Tordan was right. He held out his hand and Tordan took it.

"Good luck to you, Brother," said Jorvik.

"Good luck to us all," replied Tordan. "May the hammer of Thor be with us this day."

Magnir had discovered several female prisoners were being held in the medical research division of the Trellestar corporate building. He assumed Two Rivers was among them. Red Sky hoped he was right.

They had a plan to enter without violence, but were ready to fight their way in should the need arise. He and Magnir were accompanied by two other skaldors. Red Sky knew this meant they were capable men, the best warriors of the *wasichu*. Magnir knew and trusted these men, so Red Sky did as well.

It was almost dawn when they reached the building. Red Sky looked up at it and saw the enormous symbol of the wolf and the moon Tordan had worn when they first met. Magnir and the other two men were wearing it now.

Red Sky remembered this place. The memory coiled up dark and tight—a snarling, enraged beast within him. It was where they'd taken him when he'd first been brought to this land—a prisoner in chains. He wore chains again now, but they weren't locked. They were part of the plan.

Magnir approached the two guards at the door. His compatriots stood shoulder to shoulder behind Red Sky, who kept his head down, staring at the ground like one beaten.

"Prisoner transfer for medical research," Magnir told the guards.

One of the guards looked them over.

"It's too early," said the guard. "There's no one in there yet."

"We'll have to wait then," said Magnir. "Those are my orders."

"They going to breed this one or neuter it?"

"Breed him? Why would they do that?" asked Magnir.

The guard shrugged. "Who knows what they're doing. All I know is they've got a bunch of skraeling girls in there."

"I don't know why they bother with this research stuff," said Magnir. "They ought to just cut their throats and be done with it."

"Aye, I'm with you there," said the guard. "Alright. Take him in."

Red Sky's hope soared as they entered. He was no expert on the *wasichu* language, but the men spoke as if the prisoners were still alive. He'd come so far, and was so close now. He wanted to run down the passageway calling his daughter's name. He knew that would be foolish, so he restrained himself and followed Magnir, his head still down.

They traversed corridors and climbed stairs, passing no one. It was still early, but soon the building would be crawling with *wasichu*. He wanted to hurry, but Magnir continued casually, revealing no outward haste. Finally Magnir stopped and tried to gain entrance to one of the many doors they'd passed. It wouldn't open, so he drew his sword. It was a long, sturdy blade, much like Tordan's weapon. He forced the blade into the narrow fissure along the door and with one motion pushed the sword to the side and snapped the door open with the *crack* of splintered wood.

Beyond the door was a large space, full of instruments Red Sky had no knowledge of. But farther back were cages. These he recognized. He slipped off his chains and ran to the enclosures. There at least a dozen young women, all wearing white garments that looked like flimsy *thipi* covers. Most were asleep, but a few had woken at the noise. Yet even those that woke were as if still half asleep. They seemed ill—not fully aware. Then he saw Two Rivers.

Red Sky pulled out his hidden knife and was about to work it into the lock that stood between him and his daughter.

"Hold there," said Magnir.

Red Sky turned to look at him with an expression that said nothing would make him wait now. He saw Magnir was holding up the keys. He knew from his own time as a *wasichu* prisoner what they were.

"Let's use these," said Magnir, hurrying over and unlocking the cage that held his daughter and two others.

Red Sky bent down where Two Rivers was laying. She was barely awake.

She looked up at him, but said nothing. She didn't appear injured, but something was wrong with her.

"Daughter, it is I, your father. Wake up."

She continued to stare up at him, but could barely keep her eyes open. He shook her.

"Wake."

She looked at him again. "Father?"

"Yes, yes. I'm here to take you home. Are you ill? Can you walk?"

Her eyes closed again.

"It looks like they're all sedated—drugged," said Magnir. "We're not going to be able to get them all out of here."

Red Sky scooped up his daughter and stood holding her. He looked around at the other women. None of them appeared able to walk. Magnir was right—they couldn't save them all. But he swore to himself he'd return and free them as soon as he could.

"The sun will be up soon," said Magnir. "The assaults will be starting. We need to get out of here."

Tordan waited outside House Halfdansson until a lone housecarle emerged, likely coming off duty and headed to his favorite tavern. It was still dark. The rebel attack would begin as soon as dawn grazed the city. He still had a couple of hours. He followed the housecarle until they reached a likely spot, and pounced on him.

He pummeled the fellow into unconsciousness and hauled him down an alley. There he took the man's tunic and vest, with its Roskildcorp signet, and tied him to a garbage bin.

Tordan was prepared to fight his way in, if his ruse didn't work, but the guards at the door didn't give him a second look. All he had to do was find Kristina. But he'd never been inside House Halfdansson, even when it had been House Tryguasson. It was a large manor, with several levels. If it was anything like House Magnusson, there could be 30 rooms or more. He'd have to find someone who could direct him.

He didn't wander long before he happened upon a chamber maid.

"I'm looking for Lady Halfdansson's servant girl, Kristina."

"I believe she's in the lady's chambers," responded the maid.

"Where's that?"

She gave him a curious look, no doubt wondering why he didn't know.

"I'm new here," he said. "But I'm supposed to fetch her for the jarl.

His answer seemed to satisfy her.

"Up those stairs, turn to your left, down the corridor past the first two doors."

"Thanks," he said, but she was already walking off, about her business.

When Tordan found Rikissa's chamber, the door was open and Kristina was inside, picking clothes off the floor. She looked sleepy, as if she'd only just woken. There was no sign of Rikissa.

Tordan stepped inside and shut the chamber door behind him. Kristina looked up.

"Uncle Tordan!"

Tordan put a finger to his lips to signal for silence, but Kristina ran to him and jumped in his arms.

"We thought you were dead," she said, starting to cry.

"I will be if you don't quiet down," he replied.

"Where have you been? What are doing here?"

"I know you're full of questions, girl, but this isn't the time. We have to get out of here."

"Leave? Why?"

"Because Tyr's about to let loose his dogs, and I promised your father I'd keep you safe."

"My father? I don't understand."

"Your father's waiting for you. Now, no more questions. Let's get going."

"Who are you? How dare you...?"

Tordan recognized the voice and turned.

"Tordan!" exclaimed Rikissa in surprise. "You've returned." She rushed into his arms, much as Kristina had done. "Oh, Tordan. I thought you were dead."

"A common misconception it appears."

"I've longed for you to return to me."

Rikissa embraced him and her lips sought his. Tordan fought the natural impulse to return her kiss, and held her at arm's length.

"I know you have many questions, but I can't answer them now. I have to get Kristina out of here."

"Why? What's wrong?"

Tordan sighed, realizing it wasn't going to be as quick and easy as he hoped.

"There's going to be an attack—an all-out rebellion. I've promised Kristina's father I would take her to safety. You should find a safe place as well. Somewhere to hide until it's over."

"I don't understand. Until *what* is over?"

"The Vanir are rising up against their Aesir masters," he said, still holding her arms. "It's going to be bloody. Do you understand that? I don't want to see you hurt."

"Let me go with you," said Rikissa. "I'm not happy here—I've never been. I want to be with you. That's all I've ever wanted."

Tordan shook his head and let go of her arms.

"I can't. You can't. You have a husband. I have a wife."

She looked as if his words had impaled her.

"A wife?"

"I'm sorry, but I have to go. Kristina."

Tordan grabbed hold of his niece's arms and they fled the chamber.

❧

80

It is my fervent hope the subject species will discover
peace of mind as its society evolves. For it is that lack
of serenity which has doomed my own race.
—Osst Personal Journal

Those who enslave others are destined, one day, to be
enslaved themselves.
—Declaration of the Modi

Rikissa was still livid by the time she reached Trellestar. Her fuming had only swelled when she discovered her father had left his manor early. She'd screamed at the motorcar driver, who'd already been surprised to be summoned so early, to take her to the corporate building. Now the object of her fury, he drove like a madman, hoping to placate her. Fortunately, they didn't have to go far.

She burst into her father's office past the two housecarles stationed outside his door. They were as surprised to see her at this time of the morning as the driver had been, but they knew who she was and made no attempt to stop her.

"There's going to be an insurrection, Father. You've got to do something," she blurted.

Vikar barely looked up from the papers he was studying, and then only to glower at her as if she were as demented as her mother.

"What are you babbling about, Daughter?"

"The Vanir are going to rebel. Tordan is back. He told me."

"What? You've had a bad dream, that's all. Now leave me. I've been working all night. You have a husband to soothe your nightmares."

"It wasn't a dream!" Rikissa practically screamed. Vikar put his papers aside, but didn't move from behind his desk. "Tordan has returned," she said much calmer. "You remember the skaldor Tordan? The one who impregnated me. He came to my chambers less than an hour ago, took my handmaiden—his niece. He said he was taking her to safety because the Vanir were about to rise in revolt. I begged him to take me with him, but he refused."

The anger in her voice was clear, even to her father, who was now listening, but didn't seem very disturbed.

"The skaldor I sent to Serkland is back in Trondheim? Interesting. In any

364

case, he's an outlaw. I'll have him arrested."

Rikissa stood very still—stunned.

"You *sent* him to Serkland?"

"Yes," replied Vikar indifferently. "He had a choice—not that he knew it. Carry out a mission for me in the Serkland territory, or face death for defiling my daughter. I'm surprised he survived."

Rikissa was no longer listening to her father. She walked slowly across the roomy office toward the terrace, where she saw the sun beginning to creep above the horizon.

"All this time I thought he left me, but you sent him away," she said softly to herself. "Now he has a wife...and I a husband."

"What are you mumbling?" asked Vikar, returning his attention to his paperwork. "What's this you said about a revolt?"

Rikissa opened the silver embossed glass portals and stood there at the entry to the terrace.

"He said there'd be blood."

"Blood? You mean this Tordan fellow said that? The Vanir are always talking rebellion. It's the way they cope with their dreary lives. I wouldn't worry." Vikar waved his hand to punctuate his lack of concern. "You should go home now. Your husband's likely wondering where you are this time of the morning."

Rikissa no longer heard her father. She walked out onto the terrace and for a moment stared at the rising sun. At the opposite end of the scarlet-draped skyline, the moon still lingered, just a sliver skirting the horizon, more indigo than blue in the dawn.

Gazing out across Trondheim, memories surfaced inexplicably. She remembered a time when she was little, being teased by her older brothers. She recalled playing with Dax when he was a kitten. She thought of her mother, but those thoughts were mostly dark. She thought of the baby that never was, then a recollection of her wedding flashed past her mind's eye, and she thought of Edvard. She remembered her time with Tordan—how joyous it was, how brief. She thought about how he was out there now—out there somewhere...with a wife. Her brooding subsided. She realized she cared enough about him that she could be happy for him.

Rikissa pulled her dress above her ankles, stepped onto a small table, and then onto the parapet. She heard her father call her name before she took another step.

"Rikissa?" Vikar turned in his chair and looked to the terrace. "Rikissa?" he called louder.

He heard a muffled noise from outside. It sounded as if something had been broken. He got up from his desk and walked to the terrace.

"Rikissa, what are you...?"

Rikissa wasn't there. He looked back into his office. He didn't see her. He fought a moment of panic, telling himself his fear was ridiculous. He ventured to the edge of the terrace and looked down. At first he saw nothing, then...

Rikissa's crumpled body lay twisted atop a pile of scattered rubbish.

His first reaction was shock, then rage. *How could she do this?* But his ire didn't last long. It was quickly replaced by something just as egocentric—grief, and the realization that now he was truly alone. He had no family. There would be no grandchildren. He would die, and House Magnusson would cease to exist.

Unless he didn't die.

His mind raced haphazardly, as he continued to stare blankly at Rikissa's lifeless body.

What if the skraelings' cure for the blight isn't just a potion for long life? What if it's an elixir of eternal life?

He knew, even as he thought of it, his reasoning was tarnished by the trauma of the moment, by the random chaos of too many ideas. That didn't stop him. His thoughts continued to run wild until he looked up. Smoke was rising from the city. Not just in one location, but in three.

Why would there be a trio of fires?

"Jarl Magnusson!"

He heard a voice, but was still trying to comprehend why there were so many fires.

"Jarl Magnusson."

Vikar turned from the terrace and saw Sitric.

"We're under attack," said Sitric, so out of breath he barely got the words out. "The Vanir have launched assaults at several key areas around the city."

The Vanir...an uprising? Rikissa had tried to warn him, but he hadn't listened.

"Call out the army," ordered Vikar. "Warn each of the jarls to fortify their manors."

"Sir, the army has already been alerted," said Sitric. "But we're getting reports that many of the postings are dealing with sedition within their ranks.

Most of the Vanir conscriptees are refusing to follow orders, and are even turning against their officers."

As they made their way out of the building, he looked down at Two Rivers in his arms. She was awake, but barely. Though he'd found her, his anger at what they'd done to her had only been magnified. What kind of men could do this? What kind of monsters?

Thinking they must be close to the place where they entered, Red Sky and his compatriots rounded a corner and came face-to-face with four *wasichu*. The four froze momentarily, caught off-guard by the intruders. Among them was a familiar face. One Red Sky would never forget.

It was the *wasichu wicasa*. The one who'd imprisoned him. The one who'd spoken to him as if he were an animal. He also was the one, who apparently had stolen his daughter.

Shaking off their surprise, two of the *wasichu* drew their weapons and charged. Without a word, Red Sky passed Two Rivers into the arms of Magnir as the other skaldors engaged the enemy. Red Sky dashed through the combatants and pulled his knife. He saw only one thing—one enemy, and he ran at him with a war cry that resounded off the walls of the corridor.

The fourth *wasichu* cowered behind his leader, but the *wicasa* himself was not a coward. He pulled out a knife as well. It was a blade with a glistening, ornate handle, but a formidable weapon all the same.

Rage that had been locked away, confined to smolder within his innermost consciousness, boiled out of Red Sky. He hurtled toward his enemy, intending to drive his knife into the man's neck. The bearded *wasichu* raised his arm defensively, enough to deflect Red Sky's knife. Both men went down in a tumble.

Each regained his footing and faced the other. The *wasichu* had a minor wound on his arm, but he didn't seem to notice. He was looking at Red Sky.

"*You,*" he said with a mix wonder and recognition. "What are you—?"

Red Sky lunged before he could finish. The *wasichu* thrust a sweeping cut at him, but he easily dodged it, and with a maneuver Tordan had taught him, used his foe's own momentum against him. Red Sky threw the *wasichu* face-first to the floor and was on him in an instant, his knife pressed to his adversary's neck. His fury was a thunderstorm inside him. Erupting emotions pent-up for so long he didn't know they existed. Images of his imprisonment, of his son's battered body, of all the dead, the hundreds of people the *wasichu* had killed, incited him. He howled, an angry, wounded bear, ready to lash out and tear the world asunder He grabbed his foe by the hair and pulled his head back to cut his throat.

Tordan had only an approximate idea where Jorvik and his cluster of insurgents would be, but he found them sooner than expected. They were right outside the Roskildcorp building. A group of them almost mistook him for the enemy, until they saw he was with a young girl. They took them straight to Jorvik.

"Kristina!"

"Father!"

They ran to each other, colliding in a hug that warmed Tordan's heart. He gave them a moment before getting his brother's attention.

"How goes it?"

"We've gotten word there are still several skirmishes going on throughout the city, but we're meeting with only minor resistance," said Jorvik. "It seems the corporatocracy's power was sturdy on paper, but only as long as the Vanir acceded to their rule. We'll win this day, Brother."

"Then what?"

Jorvik was taken aback by the question.

"What do you mean?"

"I mean, have you thought about what's next?" asked Tordan. Not waiting for an answer, he added, "I've got to find Red Sky and Magnir—make sure they made it out."

Tordan ran off, leaving Jorvik standing there with a perplexed look.

Every fiber of his being had wanted to pull the knife tightly across the *wasichu* throat, and sever the life from his enemy. He'd killed before. To kill this man would have been as simple a thing as batting away a horse fly. But realization came to him in flash of unexpected calm. It would have been too easy, too painless a death when pain is what really mattered. This man, this savage creature had treated him as an animal, brought death to his family, his people. His end would not come so quickly.

Red Sky backed away from the *wasichu*, this leader of his clan, looked at him bound in his own chains, pinioned against the wall of his own prison as Red Sky had once been, and grunted in approval.

81

We are all related.

—**Lakhota Saying**
The afternoon knows what the morning never suspected.
—**Ancient Aesir Proverb**

It all transpired much easier and quicker than Tordan ever imagined...at least until *they* arrived. That was beyond imagination.

Not that the negotiations for peace were simple, or without quarrel. The fact the Aesir suddenly found themselves with little authority to back their demands took some getting used to...for them. Their concessions would not come without difficulty, but they would come. The Vanir held the position of power now, and Truvor had the secret of the *pazuta* with which to coerce the Aesir. The doctor served as intermediary for the two sides, being Aesir himself, but with empathy for both the Vanir and the natives of Serkland. Tordan thought he was the perfect choice.

Tordan recognized some of the CEOs who took part in the talks. He knew Jarl Ingstad of Transcorp by sight and Jarl Volsung of Sveabordcorp by reputation. Son of the former chairman, Edvard Halfdansson seemed the most reasonable delegate representing the Aesir. Tordan didn't know him, but knew he was the one who'd married Rikissa. Word of her death had reached Tordan, and it saddened him. But Halfdansson didn't seem to let it affect his demeanor. Tordan didn't know whether to despise him for it, or admire him.

Oleg Gripsholm of Trondtel came out of retirement—or so Tordan was told—to take part in the talks. From what Tordan witnessed, he added a conciliatory voice to the proceedings. As for Vikar Magnusson, he was still imprisoned where Red Sky had left him. The rebels had stormed the Trellestar building and continued to control it, as they did many strategic locations within the city. No one on the Aesir side of the negotiations had asked for the release of Magnusson, so he remained in custody. Apparently he had few, if any, friends among them.

Taking the lead on the other side of the discussion were his brother Jorvik, Agnar of the Modi, and Bronur, an elder skaldor who, like Tordan and Magnir, was Vanir. Red Sky took part as well, as the people of Serkland had a stake in what was being decided.

Tordan had been invited to participate, but declined. He was no mediator. He sat with the Sicangu, and the other warriors who'd come from Serkland, translating for them what he felt was important. There was little to tell them at first.

Many of those who'd taken part in the uprising sat in a rough circle around the negotiators, right there in the plaza of Njord, close to the docks, near the sea god's fountain. The Aesir had wanted to take the talks indoors, to the Ve, but the Vanir had balked. They wanted nothing to do with Aesir tradition. Agnar argued their talks should be out in the open, not behind closed doors.

Chairs and tables for the participants were brought to the plaza, and the bickering commenced. Defeated though they were, it seemed to Tordan the Aesir were unwilling to give much to the peoples they'd grown so used to oppressing. At least until, at one point, Bronur reminded them of their rather precarious position, given Vanir insurgents held the city. Jarl Halfdansson reluctantly conceded the point, but said it was the Aesir who knew how to run the city, to organize production efficiently, and keep the wheels of commerce turning smoothly.

Agnar stood to address this point when a strange noise sounded above them. Heads bent back to look up, and hands shaded eyes from the sun.

The glare was so bright, Tordan didn't see it at first. It sounded like a great engine powered by a staccato gale. Whatever it was, it was getting closer, descending from the sky.

At first, Tordan wondered if it was the chariot of Thor, or maybe Wotan himself, come to chastise the squabbling mortals. Then he saw it. It was no chariot—at least not like any he'd envisioned. Nor was it any mode of transportation he'd ever imagined a god using. It was a machine—a great metallic monstrosity as large as a Jor-hunting ship.

It had bird-like wings, but at the end of each gigantic wing were whirling blades, like the prop of a thunderboat, but fifty times the size. The blades spun parallel to the wings as the ship descended towards an open area of the wharf. Anyone who was close ran to get out of the way.

The ship hovered for a few moments as a trio of wheels dropped from its belly, then continued down until the wheels touched ground. The great blades continued to spin, but the roar of the engine diminished, and the spinning slowed.

Those gathered in the plaza were as astounded as Tordan. Many took up their arms, even though they appeared too confounded to use them.

A door opened on the side of the ship and a stairway dropped to the ground. A smooth-faced man appeared at the opening, looked out, and proceeded down the stairs. He was followed by a woman and another man, this one with a dark beard. Their skin was white, but their hair color more resembled Red Sky's people. They were dressed strangely too, in a type of material Tordan couldn't identify. The men wore loose breeches that reached their ankles. One wore white, the other brown. Their tunics matched their breeches in color, but were embroidered with odd designs. The woman wore a short white robe, embossed with gold and green thread. It bared one shoulder and both legs above the knee, and seemed more appropriate for the sauna than traveling aboard such a ship. Tordan admired the contours of her form, her dark eyes and long dark hair. She was a beauty, wherever she came from.

Despite their strange mode of travel and foreign appearance, Tordan knew immediately these people were humans, not gods. But those around him weren't so sure. He saw it on their faces. They were apprehensive, uncertain who or what these strangers were. But at least they weren't monsters, so swords were sheathed and firearms lowered.

The strangers walked towards the gathering. A path opened to the leaders of the negotiations. The newcomers stopped once they were close enough to be heard over the fading noise of their ship's engine. The smooth-faced one raised his hands in a gesture of what looked like surrender, but Tordan knew that's not what he was doing.

"We are friends," he said with a strange accent. "We are Helikonians, children of Zeus, and we come in peace to share our wisdom and understanding."

Several of the negotiators stepped forward, edging closer to the strange visitors who'd descended from the sky. Tordan didn't join them, but he moved to where he could hear what was being said more clearly.

"Where do you come from?" asked Edvard Halfdansson, who was the first to approach the foreigners.

The stranger hesitated before answering.

"As Athena would say, that is a question with more than one answer. Our cities are on the far side of this planet. Today we have traveled a great distance from our homes in Helikonia. I am Adrastus. These are my companions, Zephira and Diodoros."

"I hope you don't mind if we save our introductions?" It was Oleg

Gripsholm who took another step forward. "First, I'd like to know what your intentions are. Why are you here?"

"We have been...watching you, studying you," said Adrastus. "We have satellites—you might think of them as eyes and ears in the sky. We have used them to learn your languages so we might communicate, to watch your...progress."

"What did you mean, the question has *more than one answer*?" asked Truvor. "Do you come from somewhere else?"

Adrastus looked to the woman at his side, Zephira, unsure of what to say. She took a step forward.

"Though we believe you are unaware of this, our origins are the same as yours," said Zephira. "Our people, like yours, were brought to this world. Our ancestors lived in the city of Helike almost three millennia ago, before they were taken by a race of beings so alien in nature, neither you nor I would recognize them as sentient creatures. But they were. They were much more advanced in the sciences and in technology than even we are now. We did not even know of their existence until we discovered a message they had left for us. Even after it was discovered, it took us decades to solve the mechanism that transmitted the message."

With her raven hair she looked like no woman of either the Vanir or the Aesir, but she reminded Tordan of Willow. He tried not to think of how much he wished he were with her now.

"You say we were also brought here?" asked Edvard.

"Yes. Their concepts of time are not easily translated, but according to the message, your forefathers were taken from their birthplace at least a thousand years after the seizure of the ancient Helikonians. Those from the other continent," he gestured toward Red Sky, "were taken many centuries later."

"We have a legend of such a journey," said Edvard. "It's called the Volkerwandering."

"The legend is true," said Adrastus, "or at least its roots likely grew from reality."

Tordan thought about the stories of the Volkerwandering he'd heard as boy, and the tale of Wakinyan, the great thunderbird, told him by Red Sky. He'd never believed the stories, but now it appeared there was some truth to them.

"Do these creatures live on this world?" questioned Bronur.

"They did at one time, long before we were brought here. However, they emigrated to the planet's moon, where they lived an existence that was primarily ethereal in nature. We do not fully comprehend it ourselves," said Adrastus.

Tordan and many others looked up at the sky. The moon, though, and had long since disappeared below the horizon.

"Are they still there—on the moon?" asked Truvor.

Adrastus shook his head and said, "No, their race is extinct. We believe the last of their kind died decades ago."

"How do you know this?" questioned Bronur. "How do you know they're not still up there?"

"Because we have been there," said Zephira.

"You've been to the moon?"

Edvard was incredulous. So was everyone else. Even after what they'd seen and heard today, the idea of traveling to the cyan sphere that was so far out of reach, left most of those gathered murmuring in disbelief. Tordan, however, had gotten to the point where he would believe almost anything. Nothing, on this day at least, seemed too fantastical.

"Yes," responded Zephira. "We found remnants of their civilization, as strange as it was, but no signs of life. Whether they had physical form at the end, or existed only as some form of energy, we cannot say. Some amongst us believe they have been in contact with the spirits of these beings, but the truth of that is still debated."

"We believe they knew they were dying," said Adrastus, "and that is why the left us the message."

"Why didn't they leave us a message?" asked Bronur, an edge of suspicion sharpening his query.

"We do not know," replied Adrastus. "Maybe they did, and you have not discovered it yet. Maybe they sent the message to we Helikonians because we have been here longer than you, or because we had the technology to contact you and share the information."

That made sense to Tordan, but what he wondered was *why*. Why would these alien creatures have gone to the trouble to bring them here?

Just as he thought it, his brother gave his question voice.

"Why?" asked Jorvik. "Why would they do this? Why bring our forefathers here?"

"In their message to us," said Adrastus, "they explained it was part of a scientific experiment conducted by their own ancestors. They expressed regret for the act of abduction, as well as the hope we might solve our conflicts and find peace and tranquility on this world. That is why we have come here today."

"What do you mean?" wondered Jorvik.

"We did not decide to come here without much debate," said Adrastus, glancing at Diodoros, the other foreigner at his side. "Many believed we should remain isolated, that we should avoid contact with cultures that were less...cultures that were so different. But it was decided the regrets of our abductors, and the knowledge of our origins on this world should be shared. We also believe in the hope for peace they espoused. The logic and necessity of peace is one of our primary tenets.

"We have witnessed your conflicts, watched how the violence spread and amplified, and we have come to offer our services as intermediaries. It is our hope a lasting accord can be reached by all factions."

Their intentions seemed honest and noble enough, thought Tordan. But he wasn't sure tossing yet another point of view into these negotiations would help matters. He hoped so. He hoped there would be peace, and that his days of fighting were over. He'd always been more of poet than a warrior anyway. Now he just wanted to spend his days making love, singing songs, and raising children.

The thought reminded him once again of Willow, and the child she carried. He must get back to her. He didn't need to be part of this haggling. His work was done. He wanted to go home.

82

Wherever you are standing is the center of the world.
—Wisdom of Fire In His Eyes

R ed Sky had seen many strange and astounding things in the *wasichu* world, but none so wondrous as the flying *wahte* that carried them home. When Red Sky's part in the talking was over, the Helikonians offered to take him and the other clan warriors home. It had been an amazing experience. The most fantastic of it being that it took less time to cross the sea than it took to his wife to prepare a meal.

Before leaving, Red Sky had secured for his people, for all the clans, the promise their lands would not be invaded, and that they would be left in peace. In turn, he agreed to let the *wasichu* keep their settlement called Hestvoll for the purposes of trading with any clan who wished to.

As for himself, he had no desire to trade, or to have any further contact with the *wasichu*. He'd seen enough of their world, and didn't care for what he'd seen. He only wanted to return to the life he knew before he'd ever heard of such strange peoples.

Whether that would be possible, he didn't know. All he knew was the rising of the sun always brought new days, and life always carried on its back new challenges.

Red Sky also agreed to one other thing. He understood the *wasichu* were afflicted with a disease his friend Truvor believed the *pazuta* herb could cure. He told the leaders of both the Aesir and Vanir clans they were free to cultivate their own herbs, and use them as they saw fit. They would be allowed to farm the lands in the areas near Hestvoll, growing whatever they wished, as long as they didn't cross certain boundaries. The Helikonians were also interested in the curative powers of the *pazuta*. They had nothing like it in their own lands.

Whether the *wasichu* would honor their pledges, he couldn't be sure. But he knew they had problems of their own to resolve. They were still arguing over matters obscure to Red Sky when he and Tordan departed.

At their request, the Helikonians landed at the Hestvoll settlement. Red Sky was grateful to be back on the ground, and to see Fetawachi in good health and waiting for him. Before he, Two Rivers, Tordan, and the other Sicangu

375

departed for their village, they spoke with Truvor, who traveled with them to harvest more *pazuta* and collect his scientific notes. Red Sky invited him to come live with the Sicangu. He thanked Red Sky for the invitation, but declined. He told them the clans no longer needed him, but that his own people did. He assured Red Sky he was not really Wichasa Wakan Okinihan, but he hoped the name would endure as a symbol of peace and unity.

Truvor said he wanted to return to his homeland, to be a part of the changes he hoped would make for a better world. What's more, he wanted to continue to work on his *pazuta* cure.

While he believed in the doctor's sincerity, Red Sky also sensed the sting of sorrow within him. Perhaps he tried to bury the pain beneath his quest for a cure. Perhaps returning to live with the people would be too strong a reminder of the Lakhota woman he cared for. Both could be true. Red Sky would not question Truvor's noble endeavor, and he understood the man's wish to return to his own people. He was anxious to return home as well. So anxious, he rode Fetawachi harder than usual in his haste. But the horse showed no fatigue.

When they reached their village, each man went his own way, to be reunited with his family. There were some who did not return, and Red Sky would mourn for them. But not today. He would not be sad this day.

He watched as Tordan spotted his wife, sprang from his horse like a mountain cat, and sprinted to her. He swooped her up his arms and kissed her, then noticed the slight swell of her belly and stroked it gingerly, as if it might vanish at his touch.

Red Sky chuckled at the sight, but his heart soared to see his sister and her husband reunited. *Washtay*, he thought, it is good.

He and Two Rivers dismounted as well, and when she saw her mother, Two Rivers ran to her. Even as Snow Deer embraced their daughter, her eyes met his. They spoke to him more than words. He was home, he was safe, and he'd brought home their daughter.

Red Sky went to her, thinking how much he had to tell her of his journey. He wondered how he would explain to her that all the peoples were brought to this place, to this world, by creatures they'd never even seen—by star people, the *mikake*. How would he explain it when even he didn't fully understand it?

He still puzzled over it. *Were* they alien creatures or the Wakinyan Oyate of legend? Was it a great flying *wahte* like the one used by the Helikonians that brought the Ikche Wichasa to this world, or was it Wakinyan, the great thunderbird?

As he was drawn into Snow Deer's arms, felt her warmth, her love, he decided it didn't matter. It was the will of Wakan Tanka that they were here to live...and live is what they would do.

ACKNOWLEDGMENTS

I'm grateful to biochemistry professors Tom Huxford and Robert Metzger of San Diego State University for their scientific insight into stem cell research. I also want to thank astrophysicists Neil deGrasse Tyson and K. E. Saavik Ford of the Hayden Planetarium, and San Diego State University professor of physics Calvin W. Johnson for sharing their knowledge about blue moons and other planetary bodies. Much gratitude to David Perez for taking my concept for the cover and making it a striking reality.
This book is dedicated, in part, to the memory of Dax, the smartest, most human cat I've ever had the privilege to know.

ABOUT THE AUTHOR

Novelist, journalist, satirist...Bruce Golden's career as a professional writer spans more than three decades and endeavors in more media than you can shake a pen at. Born, raised, and still lives in San Diego, Bruce has worked for magazines and small newspapers as an editor, art director, columnist, and freelance writer; in radio as a news editor/writer, sports anchor, film reviewer, feature reporter, and the creator of "Radio Free Comedy"; in TV as a writer/producer; as a communications director for a non-profit; and as a writer/producer of educational documentaries on public health for the state of California.

In all, Bruce published more than 200 articles and columns before deciding, at the turn of the century, to walk away from journalism and concentrate on his first love — writing speculative fiction. Since devoting himself to that end, he's seen his short stories published more than 100 times across 11 countries and 15 anthologies. Along with numerous Honorable Mention awards for his short fiction, including those from the Speculative Literature Foundation and L. Ron Hubbard's Writers of the Future contest, he won Speculative Fiction Reader's 2003 Firebrand Fiction prize, was one of the authors selected for the Top International Horror 2003 contest, won the 2006 JJM and the 2009 Whispering Spirits prizes for fiction. *Red Sky, Blue Moon* is his fourth novel.

You can read more about Bruce's books at: **http://goldentales.tripod.com/**

Made in the USA
San Bernardino, CA
21 August 2013